Computing Love

A Novel

Inspired by *A Course in Miracles*

Allan Ramsay

ISBN: 978-1503283305
ISBN: 1503283305

• • •

This is a work of fiction. Characters, corporations, institutions and organizations in this novel are either the product of the author's imagination or, if real, are used fictitiously without any intent to describe their actual conduct.

Image Credits

Klein bottle, public domain, https://goo.gl/MPZMhF

Mysterious figure, John McCrone, https://goo.gl/bRXAsG Creative Commons, Attribution-Share Alike 3.0 Unported license

Cover design: Allan Ramsay & Asif Akbar, https://goo.gl/iB8mEY

References

Various quotations used in *Computing Love* come from the 1972 *A Course in Miracles Original Edition.* Such quotations are noted using the following style:

Book-Chapter.Section:Paragraph(s), where Book is noted as T (Text), W (Workbook) or M (Manual for Teachers).

Example: ACIM OE T-11.VI:46-48 refers to Text, Chapter 11, Section VI, Paragraphs 46-48.

Dedication

An astonishing curriculum awaits discovery. It exists apart from all concepts of time, beyond any notion of space.

This story is for all those who have, who do, and yet will follow such a curriculum to the end of learning where Knowledge Is.

Contents

Part I

Curriculum

During the 1960s, hippies roamed the Haight-Ashbury district of San Francisco with free music and freer love diffusing through the nation. The Age of Aquarius held the promise of peace and love for all humanity—literally, a 20th century Renaissance. A New Age seemed ready to blossom upon the planet. One that might become a near-nirvana where people everywhere not only got along, but cooperated for their mutual benefit and loved one another, without the boundaries of neighborhoods or nations diminishing their mutual love and respect. Yet the unfortunate predilections of humanity dashed those lofty dreams as the decades ground on, leaving a wake of conflict, war, destruction, misery and the same, tired promise of eventual death for everyone on the planet.

Also during the 60's, what became a seven-year project took over an Ivy League university psychology professor's life. Amid much questioning and wondering and bewilderment, she—a non-practicing and agnostic Jew—sat as words and ideas entered her mind, seemingly from nowhere. Those words began with clear instructions: "This is a course in miracles. Please take notes."

She transcribed words from that other-worldly source for seven years and gradually realized she was transcribing a training course, or even more. In fact, its twelve hundred pages formed an extraordinary and complete *curriculum* that gave humanity new guidance designed to help people choose a better way to live amid the strife of wars and fears of war, genocide, pestilence, anger, hatred, murders, crime and poverty that had plagued mankind since cavemen began fighting over territory and food. It promised far more than any Aquarian New Age could imagine: It promised an escape from hell.

Those who eventually chose to study the curriculum were ordinary people—"seekers," sufferers who'd hit the lowest points of their lives, and yet others who chose to test the curriculum to see if it held any answers that made sense. The curriculum cautioned each of them to understand a basic concept:

"You have learning handicaps in a very literal sense. There are areas in your learning skills that are so impaired that you can progress only under constant, clear-cut direction, provided by a Teacher Who can transcend your limited resources. He becomes your Resource because by yourself, you cannot learn. The learning situation in which you placed yourself is impossible, and in this situation you clearly require a special Teacher and a special curriculum.

"You do not know the meaning of love, and that is your handicap. Do not attempt to teach yourself what you do not understand, and do not try to set up curriculum goals where yours have clearly failed. Your learning goal has been not to learn, and this cannot lead to successful learning."*

Kyle Williams came into earthly life in the closing minutes of December 31, 1999, two decades after the death of the psychology professor. Now, in 2032, working as a physicist and computer expert, that curious curriculum is about to thrust itself into his life with consequences far beyond the most preposterous dream any man or woman could imagine.

---

* ACIM OE T-11.VI:46-48

CHAPTER 1

Dreaming

Kyle Williams leaned back in his chair and frowned at the computer screen. Frustration and a sense of defeat filled him, as they had every evening lately. He had been struggling for months to complete the software he needed to build the world's first quantum super computer.

He studied a page of software code for what seemed to be the twentieth time. *Why can't I get this right?* He touched the switch that turned off the screen. *Screw it. That's enough for today.*

The small warehouse behind the office area beckoned. He'd installed a few pieces of exercise equipment in an unused corner months ago. Those machines gave him an outlet for his frustration, but he didn't think of them that way. Instead, he'd often heard the traditional wisdom about sedentary jobs: Sitting will kill you. What could be more sedentary and lethargic than sitting and hammering away at a keyboard for ten or twelve hours every day? Kyle chose to keep his belly flat, his arms muscled, his six-foot body healthy. With the premature death he'd already seen in his family, he took responsibility for his own health. With a vengeance.

He sat down on a rowing machine, strapped his sneakers into the foot pedals and dialed the resistance to mid-range. As he pulled the hand grips, the machine's counter began tallying the calories he burned as he exercised. Five minutes into the session he broke sweat, then set the machine's resistance to maximum.

A personal trainer had once emphasized the importance of a gentle stretch and warmup before working out. Tonight, and every night, Kyle ignored that advice and dove right into a strenuous workout. *My body is tough; I don't need to coddle it. Don't need to warm up.* What is a body? It's a neutral thing with no mind of its own. It's a vehicle that carries a mind, an intellect around with it. Push it. Press it. Make it perform. Keep it healthy. Yeah, take care of it, but no need to indulge it.

After twenty minutes of heavy exertion, he moved from the rowing machine to the chin-up bar. Twenty-six. Twenty-seven. Twenty-eight. Then, with arms trembling, he pulled just once more, struggling to reach the bar with his chin. *Should be able to do thirty...* He stood for a minute to catch his breath, then knocked out a hundred jumping jacks, flailing his arms and legs as fast as he could. H-I-I-T. High intensity interval training. Push everything to the max. Blow it out. His heart pounded so fast he heard his pulse inside his ears. He imagined new neurons growing in his hippocampus. From the jumping jacks, he went to pushups and knocked out forty. His CoFone, a wonder of technology that combined a powerful computer with a smartphone, sounded an alert from across the room, warning him he had exceeded his max heart rate for too long. He strode to the break room and chugged a bottle of water.

Same damn ritual every day. Write software that doesn't work, then exercise to avoid death by sitting. My whole project. My life. Everything's stalled. Dammit!

Building a quantum super computer had become his life's purpose and his obsession. Quantum computers would be able to solve massive problems that had plagued mankind for centuries. They could bring a new age of comfort and peace to the world.

But they could also do great damage. Having access to a machine that could solve nearly any problem almost instantly would give its owners incredible power over others. Governments and industry had been working to build successful quantum computers for years, making slow but certain progress. After much study, Kyle became convinced the release of such machines could plunge the world into a living nightmare, a meltdown. Worries about the irreparable damage quantum computing machines could do plagued him.

Kyle worried about damage scenarios that were financial. Except for small, routine purchases made with cash, every electronic transaction between banks, every credit card purchase, every movement of currency via the Internet required encryption to prevent theft and fraud. Quantum computers were known to be extremely effective at breaking encryption schemes, which would allow bad actors to disrupt worldwide financial networks, annihilating commerce and trade worldwide.

Equally dangerous, he worried about politicians. They had been using the Internet, social media and "big data" analytics to manage and influence elections for the last twenty years. A quantum system would give them unparalleled power. Kyle foresaw the day when parties that had the most powerful quantum system would decide elections, rather than the raucous and partisan vote of a nation's citizens.

Yet military applications posed his greatest concerns and the greatest threats to humanity. The world's fastest conventional computer for more than ten years, China's Sunway TaihuLight super computer running at 93,000 trillion calculations per second had ruled the world of computation. Then, in 2030, a faster machine, built to simulate nuclear explosions, ran more than four times faster. A quantum system could theoretically run thousands of times faster, giving weapon designers the tools needed to build bombs so deadly that a handful could obliterate an entire continent.

Two camps arose around quantum computing, polarizing people. One group, which included commercial, academic and governmental organizations, evangelized the benefits such machines would bring to humanity. Others who favored social reform and progressive solutions foretold an unending avalanche of doom that would cause global catastrophe. For Kyle, it had become critically important to launch his quantum supercomputing project *first* so he could dominate the market before others could do the damage he foresaw.

He left the break room and walked through the office turning off lights. Security lights glowed dimly and the sign pointing to the lobby shone red with the word EXIT. Kyle's small company, eZo Systems, occupied two thousand square feet in a single-story building. Its lobby faced the parking lot, which, at nine o'clock, was dark.

Get home. Get some sleep. Start again tomorrow. Kyle set the security alarm and locked the front door. He drove north from West

Palm Beach, weary after another solitary day of failure. His mind ran in circles. The demons of self-doubt crept over him again tonight, asking him the same tired questions: Are you up to this? Smart enough? You ever going to finish this project? Whatever made you think you could invent a quantum computer? No one else has been able to…

He glanced in the rear-view mirror and saw no cars behind him. Only darkness on a moonless night. His headlights pierced the black for only a couple of hundred feet. *Even if I see only a short distance ahead, I can drive like this all night. I can get to my destination no matter how far away it is. What's it going to take to get this software running? Is it like driving in the dark? Can I get it working even if I can't see the whole path?*

He drove to his tiny condo in suburban Palm Beach County, Florida. He ate a sandwich, drank a Michelob, pulled the Murphy bed down from the wall and collapsed into it, exhausted. After a few twists and turns, he fell asleep. He dreamed.

He's walking on a beach, but fear consumes him. He's gasping for breath and he knows he is about to die. Someone is going to kill him for what he did to that woman. Marci is dead. He knows, without knowing how he knows, that Marci died at his hand.

There. Marci's broken body lies in the sand. Just off to the right palms are swaying, while gulls and pelicans coast over the surf to the left.

Her body is out of place in this paradise. He stares at her twisted frame. Her long brunette hair festoons around her face with seaweed inextricably entwined. It's as if someone had braided it, like hair extensions, into her coif. Her right arm and leg are tangled into impossible positions as bones and ligaments were torn free from their sockets. Her face, though, is almost beatific. A slight smile graces her blue lips with no sign of pain, no scrunched-up lines on her forehead. No clenched jaws on her cold, hard face. Her eyes, mercifully, are closed. Transfixed in his dream, Kyle stands above her, staring, trying to understand what had happened. How it happened. And for God sakes, *why?*

From out of nowhere, someone screams at him, bellowing his name. *You! Kyle Williams!* A man runs toward him with a weapon. It's got dials and knobs on it. It's no ordinary gun. It glows an angry red. Somehow, Kyle knows it inflicts indescribable pain before it finally brings a lingering, horrific death. It shoots powerful energy bundles—strange pulsating corpuscles. They're made of soul-searing, unimaginable *fear.* They paralyze and drive a man far beyond any fear a mortal can imagine.

Kyle turns away from Marci's cold body and runs. The sun shining on the sandy beach casts miraculous orbs of brilliant color everywhere. The old high school mnemonic that abbreviates all the colors of the rainbow flashes through his mind: ROY.G.BIV—red, orange, yellow, green, blue, indigo, violet. As he runs, he discovers he can run faster by stepping on the indigo and violet colors splashing on the sand. He lurches forward and glides over the sand. He gains ground with inhuman speed, but knows there's no place to hide. He stops to face his attacker and somehow take him down.

A blast of fear rockets past his right shoulder and almost knocks him to the ground. There's no way he can survive that weapon. Kyle's legs tremble in the aftermath, becoming like Jell-O. He zigs and zags, tripping and falling as he turns and runs away from his attacker. He searches for each indigo or violet splotch. Another globby fear corpuscle shoots past, this time screaming through the summer air with insane terror. It veers above him like a bolt of lightning, then spins off into the surf. The water boils where it lands. Just a few steps more and another fear blast shrieks from the weapon. Kyle hears it wailing through the air. It hits him squarely at the base of his neck, driving him to his belly like a sack of rocks, helpless but fully conscious. In a moment, his assailant stands over him. He takes aim at Kyle's mid-section and bastes his entire body with pure, alien terror, pouring wave after wave of horror and unrelenting fear into his inert flesh.

The sun goes dark and an avalanche of blackness smashes down on Kyle's dream body. His eyes stop working. His mind watches in horror as life leaks out of him. No point in calling out to God. God's never helped with anything. Kyle's lungs, liver, his stomach, all his internal organs convulse. The attacker slathers him again. Now his feet and legs. Groin. Head. Mere agony would be a welcome relief from this horror. Kyle's heart howls in pain and explodes inside his chest. Every cell of his body shrieks. His limbs thrash involuntarily. A *grand mal* seizure escorts Kyle out of life, into the eternal sleep of death.

Then, with a spasmodic jerk, he wakes up in his bed, panting. He gulps for air and grabs his chest. The veins in his scalp pulse at each erratic heartbeat. The clammy sheets stick to his skin.

My GOD! Chills run up and down his body. The hairs on his arms stand up and goosebumps cover his flesh. He peels the soggy sheets off his naked body and lies there, trembling at his imagined death.

He crawls out of his Murphy bed and hobbles to the bathroom. His hazel eyes stare back at him from the mirror, but his eyelids stretch wide open like a raving maniac. He slaps his face. Hard. Then again. His light brown hair flies out with each jerk of his head. He covers his face with his hands. His body wants to turn and sprint to a place of safety. But where?

Who was that woman, Marci? He recalls her face, so peaceful despite her poor, broken body. How her hair, interwoven with seaweed, splays out, like an ornate frame enclosing a work of art, as she lay dead on the sand.

For God's sake, pull yourself together, man. Enough of this crap! Get real. Get normal. Do something. He looks away. *Coffee. I need coffee.*

He takes a few steps into the kitchen. There, with his back to the entrance, a man stands at the stove, stirring something in a pot. As Kyle approaches, the man turns to face him, "Good morning Kyle. How about some breakfast?"

What? He knows my name! A new flood of chills erupts and Kyle sucks in a gulp of air. The man's face won't come into focus.

Kyle steps toward the faceless man, challenging him. He shouts: "How'd you get into my condo? Who are you? What are you doing in my kitchen?"

No answer. The man just stands there, holding a long-handled wooden spoon, watching Kyle. He puts out the energy of a rather gentle guy. Kind. Friendly. Harmless. Instead of throwing this home invader out the door, Kyle asks him again in a quieter tone of voice: "Who are you?"

"I'm a friend." The man smiles and now his face comes clear. He seems at ease. "I'm here to help you understand the dream you had."

He knows about my dream? "What about my dream?"

"Dreams are hard to understand. They seem real when they're happening, don't they?"

Kyle flashed back to the final death throes of his nightmare, then to the vision of that woman lying dead on the sand. "Yes! I killed someone in that dream. A woman. Marci." Standing in the kitchen doorway, he realizes he's naked. He stares hard into the man's face. Something scary is going on.

"Who are you?" he demands again.

The man pauses, as if trying to ensure there could be no chance of misunderstanding.

"Kyle," he says, "You might not realize it and you probably won't believe it, but you're still *dreaming*, my friend. You're dreaming you had an unpleasant dream and now it's over." He paused again. "Yet, as you stare at me right now, you're unable to remember who I am."

Maybe if I rattle my brain this will all go away. This can't be real. Kyle shakes his head. He searches his mind for the man's name, which seems to be hiding in some lost memory, but comes up empty.

The man lays the spoon aside and turns the burner down to simmer. He comes closer and puts a hand on Kyle's shoulder. His hand is warm, comforting. Even loving. "You *perceive* some things, Kyle, but you don't have real *Vision* while you're dreaming. You're dreaming you're looking at me. You're dreaming you're trying to remember my name. None of that works, although you don't yet understand why."

The front door handle of the condo turns and the hinges squeak. The dead woman from the nightmare walks in, obviously alive and healthy. Kyle freezes in place, his eyes glued to Marci as she walks toward him.

She smiles. "Hello Kyle, glad to see you again."

Kyle stands transfixed, as if his feet have sprouted permanent roots. His mind's eye conjures a vision of her dead on the beach: *I killed her. She's supposed to be dead.*

She smiles at him kindly and reaches up to cradle his face in her hands. In an instant, an overpowering sensation of tranquility floods through him. All feelings of confusion and fear vanish and Kyle regains the use of his legs. *No, wait! I love her.* He wraps his arms around her, gets lost in her eyes, kisses her lips.

She seems mildly amused, but meets his kiss with hers. He lingers for a moment, enjoying her lips, until she backs away. "You might want to put some pants on, cowboy."

He goes to his bedroom, slips into a pair of shorts and a t-shirt. When he returns to the kitchen, Marci and the man are sitting down for breakfast as if they're old friends. She sets a bowl for Kyle and coffee steams from his cup. Kyle sits.

The man and Marci eat as if nothing in the universe could be more important than paying full attention to their food and the process of eating. Each of them in their own time selects the next bite, picks it up, chews with closed eyes, swallows and takes another bite. Their eating seems to be a holy ritual or a meditation. It would be offensive—maybe even a sin—to speak while eating is underway.

Kyle looks at the man sitting across from him. He's of indeterminate age. In his sixties or seventies, or, just as possible, in his thirties or forties. His skin is clear and his eyes sparkle with an inner light.

"Who are you? Is this real?" Kyle asks.

"None of this is Real." The man continues eating.

Kyle turns to Marci. "I dreamed about you. How can you be here? In my kitchen?"

She stops with a spoon half way to her mouth and smiles like a Cheshire cat. "It's a miracle." She returns her attention to the bowl in front of her.

Kyle stares at the clock on the microwave oven but can't read the time. Its display is flickering in and out of focus. It's still dark outside.

Eventually, the nameless man pushes his plate aside, giving Kyle his full attention. "Don't worry. We're here to show you some amazing things. The first step is helping you realize you're dreaming even when you would swear you're wide awake."

I'm awake. My belly is full. That makes no sense. "Listen," Kyle says. "I don't know who you are." He turns to the woman. "I dreamed I killed you on the beach. Someone almost killed me to get even. I don't know you. But it feels like I do..."

"You didn't kill me. I don't have any broken bones or any limbs out of joint. I appreciate how you wove that green seaweed into my hair, but it's not there now. It wasn't Real. It never happened. You were dreaming. And what you're experiencing right now is just another sort of dream."

"I'm awake. What day is it anyway? What time is it? What's going on?"

"The day and time are meaningless. What's going on? It's your dream, as Aimer told you."

"Aimer? Is that your name?" *Finally, at least one answer.*"

Yes Kyle, that's as good a name as any. But here's what's important for you to know. Once again: You are still asleep. Marci and I are here to walk with you through this dream, to help you wake up and learn what is Real. At times, you'll think it's one of the hardest things you'll ever do, and it might take what seems to be a long time to truly awaken. That's okay too. Time is a slippery thing in a dream. What seems to last for hours might actually be only a split second...or no time at all."

The CoFone in Kyle's bedroom pierced the air with the 6 a.m. news and traffic report, intermixed with the earsplitting sound of the alarm, as it did every morning.

"Just a minute," Kyle said to the two strangers. He jumped up, raced to the bedroom and silenced the alarm. Stillness closed in on him. The entire universe went silent.

He looked back into the kitchen. No one there. No dishes on the table. No pot on the stove. Goosebumps erupted over his body. *Am I still dreaming? Going nuts?*

He went to the bedroom and stared at his CoFone as its clock rolled over to 6:01, then 6:02—as if verifying the passage of time could somehow cancel out what had happened. He slapped himself in the face again. *I need to get out of here. Talk to somebody. Get normal.*

He stripped a tangle of soggy sheets off the bed and tossed them into the washer, then sat on a deck chair in his screened-in lanai. The sun, still not visible above the palm trees that seemed to cover most all his native Florida, cast a gentle first light into the waning night sky.

Kyle gazed into the distance, thinking. He couldn't connect those strangers, nor the nightmare, with anything even half-way rational. Could the stress of his work have brought on these visions, these hallucinations, that nightmare? He pulled out his CoFone, chose a medical diagnostic app and scanned his body. ACTH and cortisol were both high; signs of the stress. Nothing else wrong. *To hell with all of it!*

Kyle was accustomed to thinking logically. He had earned a Master's Degree in Computer Science and another in Physics, then a Ph.D. in Physics, followed by post-doctoral work studying the phenomena known as weak and ultra-weak photons. He'd solved most of the theoretical and practical problems that challenged quantum computing researchers. Only the software he struggled with now stood in the way.

Got to get this software running. That's all that matters. Kyle closed his eyes. *But I'm stuck. There's got to be a better way.* He sat with that thought. *A better way. A better way.* His breathing became regular as he dozed into a light sleep.

The high-pitched beep-beep-beep of a garbage truck backing up roused him. The clock showed eight-thirty. Kyle shook his head and sat up straight. As he did, an image of his long-time friend leaped into his mind.

Rick Huggins. Freckled face and red hair. Maybe he can help. Rick had been Kyle's constant companion, beginning in middle school and continuing all the way through their respective doctoral programs. As middle and high school students, they both loved science and math. The other kids called them Frick and Frack; two nerds.

Things changed when Rick got a motorcycle in eleventh grade. They bought matching black leather jackets and let their hair and beards grow. They went everywhere together, the motorcycle giving them mobility and a "look" the girls noticed.

Rick was Kyle's rock, Kyle was his. After high school their respect and regard for one another matured. In college, they played hard and chased girls for much of their freshman and sophomore years, then buckled down as they focused on physics and computer science as juniors and seniors. From there, they both qualified for Masters programs and, later, Ph.D.'s. They were tight. Roomies. Best friends forever. No matter how bad things got at either of their homes, they had always found something to take the pain away.

Where is he now? Last we talked, he was in Miami teaching college.

Kyle pulled out his CoFone and called Rick. *Need to catch up. See if he can help. Get him involved.* The call went to voicemail. Over the next hour he called twice again, but each call went to voicemail.

Finally, Kyle dressed and drove to his eZo Systems office, where he sat before the computer screen and brought up the program code he'd been working on for the last few months. *Damn this code!*

CHAPTER 2

Rick

Rick Huggins had few habits. Of late though, an early morning swim with his spear gun started most days. He waded into the water, rinsed his mask in the surf and put it on, clamping the snorkel between his teeth. He swam out past the sand bar, approaching a coral reef, and dropped his diver-down flag. A bend at the waist and a few kicks powered him toward the bottom.

Fifty feet away a stingray glided near the reef. Rick followed it, kicking hard to catch up. *Good. Rays are like a kid banging a drum. They scare other fish. Flush them out of hiding.*

As he closed in on the ray, a dark brown fish with a white belly darted from its cover. *Damn! He's got to be three feet long. It's a crab eater. A cobia.*

The cobia swam diagonally across Rick's path away from the reef. Rick aimed his spear gun and waited for the fish to pass directly in front of him. His breath was getting short; he'd have to surface in the next ten or fifteen seconds.

The cobia approached. Thirty feet. Twenty. Rick fired. The gun's triple power bands launched the spear at ninety feet per second. It passed through the cobia. The fish dove toward the bottom in a death struggle to break free. Rick grabbed the line in one hand, held his gun in the other and kicked toward the surface. His face broke into morning air. He pulled the fish to the surface, admiring its continued fight, then grabbed it by the gills and plunged a knife into its head, ending the struggle.

Great catch. This'll be dinner. Love cobia. He waded ashore then bagged the dead fish and dropped it and his gear into the saddlebag on his Harley. He strapped the spear gun to the side of the bike and drove back to his KOA campsite.

"Hey, Rick. Whaddya got there?" a neighbor at the adjacent campsite called out.

"Cobia. Too much for me to eat. You want some?"

"Sure. Thanks, neighbor."

"No problem. I'll bring some over soon as I clean it."

He went to work, scraping off its small scales, gutting it and cutting the fish into man-sized steaks. He finished by nine-thirty.

"Hey Walt, here's that fish."

His neighbor stepped out of his RV. "Thanks, Rick. This'll feed the whole family tonight. Sally said she's gonna grill it. She wants you to join us for dinner."

Rick nodded and put his hand on Walt's shoulder. "Thanks, man. Count me in."

"Good deal. Oh, by the way, I heard a CoFone ringing earlier. It was coming from your pop-up. Someone must have called two or three times in a half hour. I hope everything's okay."

Rick shrugged. "Can't imagine. Thanks." He climbed into his pop-up camper and found his CoFone. Caller ID showed Kyle's name. Three voicemails waited. He listened to the first.

"Rick, this is Kyle. Would you give me a call? It's urgent. Need to talk with you ASAP."

The second. "Kyle again. Ring me when you can, okay?"

The third. "Me again. Hoping I could catch you."

Rick deleted all three and dialed his oldest friend.

"Hey, you all right? I got your voicemails." Rick peered at his friend's face on the CoFone screen.

"Hey, thanks. Sorry about the repeat calls. Yeah, I'm okay. Just had a rough morning. I need to talk with you."

Rick saw a troubled look on Kyle's face. "What's goin' on?"

"I had this God-awful nightmare last night. I thought I was going to die in that dream. I mean actually die, for real. Then this morning I started thinking about you."

"What're you saying? Dying reminded you of me?"

"No. Sorry. That didn't come out right. What I mean is, I couldn't get that nightmare out of my head. So, while I was trying to get my head on straight—I don't know why—I started thinking of all the times we had together. How we could always talk about anything. I felt like I needed to talk with you to get grounded again."

Rick nodded. "Fire away, partner. How can I help you?"

"Thanks, man. I *never* had anything like that nightmare. But screw it. It's so good to see you and hear your voice again. What are you doing these days? Where are you?" Kyle asked.

Rick laughed. "Havin' fun. I'm down in Cudjoe Key. Got a little pop-up camper at the KOA. It's my fun house."

Kyle could see palm trees waving behind Rick on the CoFone video screen. "Yeah, I'll bet. Any women in your life?"

"None that matter. You?"

"No. So, what've you been up to?"

Rick grinned at Kyle. "Whatever I damn well please. I do some fishing. Some scuba. Chase a few women. Simple stuff. Fun stuff. By the way, I have a big ride planned."

"Ride?"

"Yeah. Bike ride. Motorcycle. There's this Ass of Steel group that gives awards for extreme rides. I'm running low on cash so I thought I'd go for it. See if I can win ten grand."

Kyle's face screwed up into a contorted grin. "Ass of Steel?"

Rick laughed at the confused look on Kyle's face. "Yeah. I'm riding from Key West to Alaska and back in thirty days. Eight thousand miles. A third of the way around the freakin' world. The Ass of Steel guys pay ten grand to anyone who does it. It'll be fun."

Kyle stared at Rick and shook his head. "You're as crazy as ever."

"Maybe. What's going on with you?"

"Like I said. That nightmare really messed with my head. Did you ever have a dream, then wake up from it and find the dream characters in your real life? That's what happened. It was like a dream within a dream, and weird as hell. I started thinking I might be losing it."

"What do you mean the dream characters were in your real life?" Rick asked.

Kyle explained the strange man in his kitchen, Marci, and their disappearance when the 6:00 a.m. alarm went off.

"At first I wanted to talk to you to get clear from that damn nightmare. Old friends are the best friends, right? Now though, in the light of day, I want to tell you about a project I'm working on.

I think there's some real money in it. I could really use your help, Rick. I'm thinking we could work together to bring it to life."

Rick's raised his eyebrows. "Tell me more."

"You got time now? I could come down to Cudjoe, or you could come up here. It'll take a while to go through it."

"What's the bottom line? What's it about?"

"I'm building a quantum super computer. I need your help."

"Oh, I thought it was something simple. I don't know. A faster-than-light spacecraft. A time machine. Something easy." Rick sat down on a deck chair next to his camper.

Kyle grimaced. "No, smart ass. This quantum thing is real."

"Yeah, I'm just messing with you. I've got time to talk. Fire away."

"Good. Did you know I worked for Corning for a while?"

"Yeah, I heard that."

"The company makes fiber-optic cable. They wanted to find a better manufacturing process. It was about increasing the reflectivity of the fiber so weak light photons can pass through without being attenuated."

"Okay."

"Well, the more I looked at the problem, the more I got intrigued with some bizarre things about weak photons. I lost interest in the project with Corning and got sidetracked. So, I quit and started my own company to research how to entangle weak photons. You know, quantum entanglement. I thought it could be the basis of a quantum computing system."

Rick shook his head. "You serious?"

"Dead serious. I sold the family house and put the money in the bank. I already had life insurance money from my parents. I started the business with four hundred thousand. My company's called eZo Systems. It's in West Palm. I'm making progress on a quantum system, but I need your help."

"You want to get Frick and Frack back on track?"

Kyle frowned. "C'mon. This is no joke. Yeah, I do. This thing needs some deep programming expertise. I'd love for us to work on it together. I haven't been able to figure it out on my own."

Rick turned his CoFone away from his face and panned it around the campsite, taking in the entire vista. "You want me to give up this fun house? Look at this place. It's got everything a man could want."

"Yeah, I see that. But your little paradise could be destroyed if I can't bring this computer to life."

"Destroyed? What are you talking about?"

"Have you heard about the Doppelganger project?"

"No."

"It's a secret project run by the government. Some details leaked out a few months ago. They're trying to build a quantum computer that can crack Internet cryptography. In their words, they want to 'penetrate hard targets.' And 'own the Net.' They'd know exactly what everyone's communicating, all the time. There'd be no such thing as privacy. No security. Who knows what would happen if they get their system running? I can see OmegaNet and the whole Internet come crashing down. Banks could go under. Worldwide. Everything could change."

Rick shook his head. "I don't see the government doing that..."

"What happens when that quantum technology gets loose into the world? You think the government is the only one working on it? Without security, online purchases, credit card transactions, banking, commerce and trade all become impossible. Transactions will need to be face-to-face with cash. I don't trust the Feds or anyone else with that kind of power. I need to get there first. *Need* to."

"What if you do? You won't stop them."

"Maybe I can. There's more I've got to tell you. Lots more. I don't want to do it over the phone. Can't. It's too risky." Kyle paused for a moment. "If we could work together on this I think we could do something great."

Rick gazed off toward the surf, remembering his life with his best friend that had lasted...how many years? Twenty? "Okay, man. Tell you what. How about I come over to your place. It'll be great to see you again. I'd like to hear more about your quantum computer. I'm not doing anything much this week. I can batten down the hatches here at KOA and be there in five or six hours. Get some wind in my hair."

"Great. I love you, man."

"Love you too. You had better lay in some supplies. I'm not riding' over for the hell of it."

"Name your poison."

"A case of Heineken, a bottle of Jack and a couple of pizzas. That ought to be a decent start."

"You're on, steel ass."

CHAPTER 3

The Black Hole

Rick pulled into Kyle's driveway late that afternoon. As soon as he got off the bike Kyle pulled him into a bear hug.

"Hey! Great to see you, beach bum. You ready for a beer?" Kyle opened the door to his condo and let Rick go in first.

"Damn! This place is tiny. You live here?" Rick asked.

"Yeah. It's all I need. Four hundred square feet. I'm renting it. I'll give you the grand tour. This is the living room and that's the kitchen." Kyle pointed to the stove, sink and refrigerator lined up against one wall with three small cabinets above them. A narrow hallway led to the bedroom and bath.

"I've seen RV's bigger than this at the KOA." Rick looked around for somewhere to put his helmet, and finally set it in the corner on the white tile floor.

"For six hundred bucks a month, it's perfect. I don't spend much time here anyway; I'm mostly at the office. Since I set up eZo Systems I'm living on the cheap, but I'm spending money out the yin yang on computing gear. That four hundred grand I mentioned is down to around three hundred already."

Kyle popped open two Heinekens and sat in the lone chair in his living room. He motioned to the sofa. "That's a sofa bed. I'll put some sheets on it tonight. You can sleep here. I have a lot to show you. It'll take a few days. Maybe more."

Rick sat down, pulled off his shoes and kicked them under the sofa. "Yeah, so what's goin' on with you and this quantum super computer?"

Kyle leaned forward. "I've got a quantum system working, sort of. But I need a software front end for it. You can't just load a program into a quantum computer like you do with an ordinary machine. It needs software that translates the problem you're trying to solve into something the quantum system can work with."

Rick nodded. "That's the programming expertise you said you need?"

Kyle took a swig of beer and nodded. "Yes. We can make this thing happen if we work on it together. Then we can share in the profits when we market it."

Rick emptied his beer and set the bottle on the tile floor. "Is the company paying you anything?"

"Yeah. And it can pay you too. You can be the Chief Technology Officer...or whatever you want to call yourself."

"So, you're offering me a J-O-B? Maybe you don't get it. I was in paradise before you called me."

Kyle fixed his friend with a stare. "So, what have you been doing? I know you worked down in Miami. But it seems like you're just letting your PhD fritter away. Living at a KOA, for God's sake? Riding your bike across the country? What's going on? You spent a ton of money getting your PhD."

"Yeah, I worked at the university for a while. But academia isn't for me. Too much bullshit. I took the job there to do research, but that didn't pan out. So, I said screw it and took a break. I always wanted to see what the Keys are like. It's been great. No schedule. No demands. I do what I want. When I want. If I want."

Kyle nodded. "All right. But listen. I'm not offering you a freakin' job. I'm asking if you'd like to help me change the world. Nobody's been able to build a quantum computer. I'm close. Real close. I could hire someone from the outside to work on the software. But I'd have to show him my proprietary work. I can't risk that with a person I don't know. I want to work with you. We've been together forever. We each know how the other one thinks. We trust each other. We can do this and get rich in the process."

Rick twisted his head from side to side, like a prize fighter cracking the bones in his neck, limbering up before going into the ring. "What's this J-O-B pay?"

Kyle shrugged, knowing it didn't matter what number he named. "I'm giving myself a couple grand each month; more if I need it. It's not much, but it keeps me going. You can have the same. Besides that, I'm willing to offer you ownership in the company."

Rick seemed lost in thought. "We always had fun working together." He took the last swig of his beer and set the bottle on the coffee table. "Yeah, I can cut my vacation in Cudjoe short." His face brightened. "Actually, it'll be good to have something to work on again. Writing code for the front end to a quantum computer sounds like a real challenge. To be honest, the KOA was getting a little old. All right. I'm in. Sign me up."

The two plunged into Kyle's research for the next week. By the end of the week the eZo Systems office looked like a fast food war zone with pizza boxes, burger wrappers and empty beer bottles stacked everywhere.

The leased office space had a lobby, a conference room and an office for each of them. A loading dock at the back of the building opened into a warehouse crammed with racks of blade computers and other equipment. At Rick's first visit to the office Kyle explained what he'd built.

"I've designed a mini-Internet here. A simulation. I bought a few hundred kilometers of fiber-optic cable just like the cable that connects everyone on the Internet. I'm using it to simulate the actual Internet." Kyle described how it served as a proof-of-concept for his quantum system, which when fully operational, would use the Internet as its foundation. They spent a day going through the details.

Over the next few weeks, Rick cobbled together software he hoped would serve as the API—the Application Programming Interface, the "front end" to the quantum system. Software bugs plagued his first efforts. He scrapped his work and began anew, this time using a different programming language. When Rick broke from a coding session, usually after sitting in front of a screen for ten or twelve hours, they talked about how they could validate the computer.

"We need some problems we can submit to the system that shows if it's working or not," Rick said.

"Yeah. I've been thinking about weather forecasting. No one can forecast with any accuracy for more than a week or two. If our system can forecast for, I don't know, let's say a year...well, I'd say that would be all the proof we need."

"Sounds like a tall order."

"Yeah, but think about it. If we can forecast a year at a time, we can have a real impact on agriculture. We can give people advance notice of storms and hurricanes. Those super computers at the National Weather Service cost millions. They use tankers full of water to cool their CPU's and thousands of kilowatts to keep them running. But none of them give us anything better than a fifteen-day forecast. And they only run forty to ninety percent accurate."

"Yeah, that's because they're using brute force computing and they're running up against its limits," Rick said.

Kyle gazed out the window for a moment. "You know what accurate year-long forecasting could mean? Third-world countries where food is in short supply would be the big winners. Our forecasting could let farmers plant with knowledge of the entire growing season months ahead of time. They could shoehorn plots into specific geographies based on the forecast for each area and grow crops where nothing had grown before. During the next season, people could plant in other geographies that weren't viable before. Eventually, we could give them the info they need to feed everyone on the planet.

"So, I've been looking into forecasting and have some code we can test once the API is up and running. But I think there's something easier we can do to test the system."

"Like what?"

"Another kind of forecasting. Sports. Let's see if we can forecast the outcome of some games. If we can do that it'll be a validation anyone can understand."

Kyle sat in the conference room with a half-finished beer in one hand and a carton of order-in Thai food before him. Rick noticed he was gazing into space with a worried look on his face. "What's on your mind?"

Kyle brought himself back to the present moment. "Just thinking about how we're going to protect the system. Once we get it running we'll have to be damn careful about how it's used. It'll be able to solve almost anything. It won't care if it's solving a problem that helps people or hurts them."

"Yeah, like that Doppelganger project."

"Right. But it's more than that. It's more than the government having a quantum system."

"Why?"

"You watch the news lately? All you hear is attack and loss. Terror and war. Death. The same stuff that's been in the news for hundreds of years."

"Yeah. So?"

"I don't know. It just seems like things never change. The world is all about duality. Us or them. Light or dark. Black or white. Right or wrong. Good or bad. Help or hurt."

Rick frowned. "Where's this coming from, man?"

"C'mon, Rick. How many nights did we sit in our dorm room talking about this kind of stuff? You said once you were going to change your major to philosophy. Remember?"

"Yeah, but I didn't mean it."

"I know. But just look at what we've done with computers in the last seventy years. How we've used them to build better weapons and fight wars. To optimize marketing and commerce so banks and businesses can rip more money out of consumers' pockets. Then there's the difference between the rich and the poor. A handful of people and businesses control almost all the world's wealth. It's no coincidence that's happened as computer tech advanced. I've looked at it."

"Never thought about it."

"Then here's something to think about. What happens when quantum computing is everywhere? When everyone in power has access to it. They'll be able to build more dangerous bombs, if that's even possible. To compromise security and get into everybody's stuff. It will give bad actors and crooks everything they need to wreak havoc." Kyle took a couple of bites of his Thai food.

"Here's what I'm saying. Imagine you're a bad actor. You've got a quantum system and you want money. Once you've got it, you want power. Here's how you go about getting everything you want.

"First, you'll be able to crack any online security system and hack into whatever you want. Why not start with the Federal

Reserve Bank? Draw down a few billion dollars for starters. Hold them up without ever leaving your easy chair. That'll get you all the money you need. Then, if you want power, why not hack the Treasury Department and sell off a couple of trillion dollars of bonds. That'll increase our national debt. If you did a good job you could drive the country's credit rating down. If you did a *great* job, you could bankrupt the USA. Hold it hostage with your quantum computer."

Rick stood and gazed out the window. "Yeah, I guess I can see all that."

"Or, what if a dictator and his military gets hold of a quantum system? Or an international crime syndicate? Or even a political candidate? They'd all use its power to serve their own interests. I think those machines and the way people use them to get what they want could spell the end of life on Earth."

Rick cast a quizzical look at Kyle. "I get what you're saying. People are too wrapped up in grubbing around for money and power. But you think you'll save the world by building the first quantum computer?"

"I've got to get there *first* so I can control how it's used. If I can do that, it will become the most powerful system anywhere. It will be able to out-think any other quantum systems that comes along."

Rick scoffed. "C'mon! *Out think*? That's ridiculous."

"You know what I mean. Researchers today are still trying to entangle a few dozen quantum particles. I'm talking about entangling thousands. Tens of thousands. Millions. They won't be able to compete. We'll blow all the others out of the water."

That evening, back at Kyle's condo, they took a seat outside in the lanai. Kyle stared at the clouds drifting past the moon. A deep sigh escaped his mouth as he continued thinking about the dangers he may be unleashing on the world.

"You remember my little sister? My mom and dad? Sometimes I can't get over that they're all dead. None of them deserved it. Life doesn't seem fair. God, if there even is a God, didn't give a shit about them. The cards are all stacked against us. I don't want to bring anything into the world that's going to make the game even worse for people."

Rick stood up.

Kyle stretched and yawned. "Heard enough of me for one day?"

"Yeah. Come here." Rick faced Kyle, pulled him into a hug and slapped his back. "I'm with you, man. I get you. Let's get this computer up and running." A smile spread across Rick's face. The two stepped back inside.

"But I've got to tell you, this sofa bed isn't for crap. It's breakin' my back. I need a room somewhere."

Kyle chuckled. "Yeah, sorry about that. We can go out tomorrow and find one. I'll front some money if you need it."

"Sounds good. But I've been thinking about something else, too. We need a name for this project. One that'll hide what we're doing. We need to keep it under wraps. I'm thinking 'the black hole in the Internet.' That ought to keep people wondering." Rick laughed.

Kyle snorted and punched him on the shoulder. "So be it. We're building a black hole in the Internet."

"Yeah. And if what you're saying is true, it ought to have about the same power as a real black hole. Let's hope we don't get sucked down into it."

"We won't. Not if we can find lawyers to write up the licensing agreements so we control how the system is used." Kyle said.

"Right. Used for beneficial purposes. That sounds like such a simple idea. So benign. But I think we're going to pay hell to find a way to control it. I'm not even sure a licensing agreement is going to be enough to give you the kind of control and protection you want."

"Yeah, but we've got to try."

CHAPTER 4

Ego Box

The two resumed their work and, over the next few months, Rick completed the software API. They got busy building a program that could predict sporting events. Much of the information they planned to feed into the system involved busy work that neither man had time or desire to take on.

"How about we hire someone to collect all the sports data we need?" Rick asked. "An admin assistant."

Kyle pondered the idea. "I guess that would work. We can probably hire someone from a temp agency to pull it all together."

A young woman, Cary Thomasson, came on board to handle the job. Not only did she have a degree in computer science, she arrived at work each day enthusiastic and willing to do any task the men asked of her. They enjoyed her presence in the office. After a few weeks, Kyle hired her as a permanent employee, had her sign a non-disclosure agreement and stressed the proprietary nature of the work they were doing: exploring a black hole in the Internet.

The men ran the sports data she compiled through the quantum system. It accurately predicted scores for baseball, a World Cup and other events that had already been played. They wanted to prove their system by making true predictions for upcoming games. The Olympics gave them just what they needed.

The 2032 Summer Olympics were due to begin shortly, so the two scientists began pouring sporting contestant data into the quantum system only a few weeks before opening ceremonies. They worked days, nights and weekends to load the system with raw data.

Rick shook his head. "I'm busting' my butt here. Databases everywhere. Swimmers, track and field, gymnastics, karate, baseball."

"I know. Kudos to Cary for pulling all this stuff together. Where the hell did she find data on badminton players, for God's sake? Beach volleyball...I can understand that. It's popular. But badminton? Fencing?"

As opening day grew closer they called a halt to their data uploads.

"We don't have to try to forecast *every* event," Rick said. "I think we've done enough to either prove the quantum system...or else we're back at the drawing board."

As the first day of competition began, they flipped the TV from one OmegaNet channel to another, programming various stations to record outcomes of different events.

Kyle sat on the edge of his chair with a stack of paper containing printed forecasts from the quantum system.

Rick shook his head. "Kiteboarding? When did they add that to the Olympics?" A dozen contestants raced across the water on their boards pulled by giant kites soaring above them. They followed a course that spanned a kilometer. "That guy from Greece. He's way ahead. Who did the computer predict to win?"

Kyle flipped pages until he found the kiteboarding predictions. "Spain."

The Spanish kiteboarder, stuck in a pack with two others a hundred meters behind the Greek, struggled to gain on the leader. As the Greek crossed the 750-meter marker, the wind shifted unexpectedly from his back to a crosswind. He and two others tried to adjust, but one sailed into the air, while the Greek and the other kiteboarder crisscrossed, causing their lines to tangle. Both hit the water just as the third man fell from a height of ten meters into their tangled lines.

The Spanish kiteboarder broke free from the pack and raced to the finish line, winning Gold.

Rick slapped his knee. "My God! Did you see that?"

"Unbelievable," Kyle chimed in. "Chalk one up for us."

They turned to an OmegaNet channel that had captured final scores on the golf competition. Another channel recorded tennis matches, while still others documented results for table tennis, rowing, weight lifting and the 400-meter hurdles.

"I think we've done something right."

"Me too. Everything's matching up so far."

"Yeah. We need to find a bookie in Vegas who'll take our bets," Rick said with a half grin. "We could be millionaires by Christmas."

Kyle nodded. "Yeah, but we'd attract too much attention. I'd hate to get on the wrong side of the Vegas bosses, or start showing up in the news. You know: 'Two Florida Scientists Win Millions.' We don't need that kind of headline. We've got to keep our work under wraps."

After a full day's work, Kyle watched Rick drive away from the office on his Harley to the room he had rented. Just when he disappeared, Kyle's CoFone rang but showed no Caller ID.

"You might have a hard time with this," the voice said.

A flush of annoyance ran through his mind. *A telemarketer?* "Who's this?"

"Marci. Like Aimer said, it might take a long time and some hard work to learn this curriculum. This is a perfect time to begin. Are you ready?"

When he realized who he was talking to, a rash of chills broke out across his body. *She's back!*

"Begin *what*?" He might be talking to a ghost.

"Don't worry. I want to show you some things. It's part of your curriculum. Your learning curve. Why don't you come home now so we can begin?"

Kyle realized he had been holding his breath. His shoulders were drawn tight. He breathed a long sigh but the tension didn't abate. "Where are you? You and that guy just disappeared from my condo that morning."

"I'm where I always am, my friend. Just come home, Kyle. You're still *dreaming*."

His shoulders drew higher and he gripped his CoFone tighter to his ear. Anxiety rushed through him as he recalled that horrendous nightmare where he'd killed Marci. He looked around the office once again, then noticed the time. Eight o'clock. "Yeah, sure. I was coming home anyway."

"See you soon," Marci answered.

He drove from the eZo office to his condo. He found Marci sitting cross-legged on his living room sofa with a large cardboard box on the floor in front of her. It was a cube about three feet on a side. He stood at the entry from his one-car garage, staring at her.

"You're here again!"

Marci sat there, smiling at him. "Hi cowboy. Good to see you again."

He didn't move from the doorway. "What *are* you? How'd you get into my condo?"

Marci's smile left her face. "What am I? Now that's a great question." She stood up and faced him. "I can help you answer that question and so much more. I'm your advisor. Your mentor. Your helper."

"What?"

"Don't worry about all that now. I've got something exciting to show you tonight." She pointed to the box. "Come here. Sit down with me."

She patted the cushion next to her, inviting Kyle to sit.

An attractive woman. She looked hot and sexy sitting there. He sat down. "What's in the box?"

" It's a *special* box. Let's call it an 'ego box.' It holds something you'll understand right away. In fact, this box belongs to you. It's your personal ego box."

She slit the box open. He gasped as he looked inside. Brightly lit holographic images, layer after three-dimensional layer of images with everything in motion like waves in the ocean filled every cubic inch. Each image appeared to be a miniature living scene, a live 3-D movie. They were so complete and rich it seemed each one might contain a segment of a real person's life. Kyle's eyes landed first on a scene that showed Marci lying dead on the Florida beach. He realized those scenes were from *his* life.

"That's your dream. Remember? This box holds all of it from start to finish. If you lean over a little to your right, you'll see it from another angle."

Kyle changed his viewpoint and saw himself running down the beach, searching for the indigo and violet splotches of sunlight as he ran. He leaned to the right and saw a part of the dream he didn't remember. He was standing under a palm tree talking to Marci's friend, Aimer. He heard the conversation from his dream: "Marci is here to help you, as I am. You won't want her help at first; maybe not for quite a while. In fact, you might try to get rid of her, to push Marci out of the picture."

Marci pointed to another moving image. "Over here: Those are your recollections of your family before your dad was hurt in that traffic accident."

Kyle winced as he saw his father, young and vital, before he became paralyzed in a car crash. *Oh shit! I don't want to see this.*

It wasn't his dad's fault. He had been driving on the interstate when congestion forced everyone to slam on their brakes and slow down to about twenty miles per hour. A semi tractor-trailer plowed into the back of his dad's car, crushing him against the air bag, with the steering wheel and the dashboard and the engine compartment crumbling as they were designed to do...but still taking his father's legs out of service.

Ambulances arrived on the scene, but Kyle's father eventually left the hospital without serviceable legs, a useless right arm and permanent paralysis below the waist. Kyle was only ten years old. His father, forced to live on disability checks from the government, found they weren't enough to support the family. Kyle's mother had to get a job. Her weekly paycheck and the disability check kept food on the table and, occasionally, new clothes in the closet.

Kyle tore his gaze away from the box, but as he did he caught a glimpse of another scene inside. There, in their front yard, he watched his little sister, Julia, playing catch with him. *Julia! I'm so sorry!*

Kyle's young life had taken a big turn when his mother began working each weeknight. It became his job to care for Julia while his father did the best he could to help from his wheel chair with his one serviceable arm. Kyle made her meals, washed her clothes, helped her get ready for school and put her to bed at night. Julia was two years younger than Kyle. He never questioned the care-taking chores thrust upon him. Kyle watched over and attended to Julia with a maturity and sense of responsibility well beyond his tender age. Of course, all that changed.

Shifting his gaze again, Kyle saw his family in a funeral home standing before a small, closed casket. *Oh God!* Kyle struggled as he tried to avoid seeing the scene again—the one that had burned indelibly into his memory years ago, on a perfect summer's day turned horrific.

He saw himself playing catch with Julia in the front yard. He threw the ball to her, but tossed it a bit too high, just above her reach. She shrieked, "I'll get it" and ran, chasing it into the street. A speeding car killed her almost instantly.

Kyle jerked his head away from that awful 3-D image and let out an angry shout. He jumped up from the sofa and glared at Marci. "Stop this! I don't want to see any more of this. Get rid of this goddamn box."

Marci stood and put her arms around Kyle, comforting him. She held him close. "God didn't damn this box. He doesn't even know about it." She squeezed him tighter. "I can assure you, God has nothing to do with it. It's *yours*." She placed her hand on his chest and, presently, a sense of peace spread through him. Marci sat again on the sofa, guiding Kyle to sit next to her.

She spread her arms over the box. "This box is your entire thought system, Kyle. It holds everything you have ever experienced, touched, tasted, smelled, heard, seen, perceived, believed, imagined, dreamed or thought. You can see it's very busy, always in motion. It's like your mind. It runs constantly from one thought to another without you even noticing."

Kyle sat in silence, eyes closed, shaking his head, wishing the box and its horrors would disappear. Finally, he spoke. "What thought system?"

Marci answered, speaking slowly. "Sometimes people refer to it as your 'ego' thought system. It's the part of your mind that knows you are Kyle and that certain things are true while others are not. Your thought system is everything you think you are, my friend. Your perception of life and the world around you, your memories of the past, worries about the future—all of that's in this box. Here, look at this."

Kyle peered again into the box and saw his mother returning from her night-shift job, opening the kitchen door and sitting down at the table. He saw his father join her in his wheel chair at the table with the flowered plastic cloth. Only the light over the stove shone, leaving the room in semi-darkness. *My God, all that drinking. I hated it.*

He heard his father speak: "How'd it go at work?"

His mother answered with a tired voice. "Same as always. My boss is still an idiot. He had me pull stray shopping carts in from the parking lot. In the rain. I hate my job."

"I'm sorry, honey. I wish to God there was something we could do. Something *I* could do. A better job for you. I don't know..."

Kyle saw his mom open a black plastic bag. She returned home from her night shift around eight-thirty each morning. Her bag usually held a bottle of sherry. She and her husband would sit at the kitchen table drinking wine instead of eating breakfast, sometimes crying, while Kyle poured a bowl of Cheerios and ate before running off to school—or, in the summer time, skipping breakfast altogether so he could escape the house as quickly as possible.

As months dragged on after Julia's death, his mother graduated to a fortified, port wine. That led to port mixed with vodka. then to 750 milliliter bottles of cheap vodka, gin or tequila. Each morning, as Kyle's parents drank, their crying became more obscene. Their parental tears flowed as fast as the alcohol and gradually turned into arguments that made no sense and had no end.

When Kyle was sixteen years old, his mother filed for divorce and took Kyle with her. Kyle's dad was left to the care of impersonal government programs. Eventually, he passed, leaving Kyle fatherless. *What the hell was that idiot judge thinking—putting me in her custody? Mom was a drunk. She didn't do anything for me. And dad didn't deserve to be left alone like that.*

Kyle shifted his gaze again and saw an image of the apartment where he and his mom had lived after the divorce. He saw his best friend, Rick Huggins, knock on the door and watched the scene as he and Rick climbed onto Rick's motorcycle, then drove off to their part-time jobs.

He heard Rick say, "My stepfather's a son of a bitch. He hates me and is always telling me what to do. What not to do. I don't know what my mom sees in him. I've got to get out of that freakin' house."

Kyle heard himself answer. "We should try to get into college. We'd both be able to get away from home. You know. Live in a dorm and have our own lives."

"That takes money. I don't have it. You don't either."

"Yeah, but we've got jobs. I was thinking. If we hunker down and save our money—open bank accounts instead of spending our money on music and games and OmegaNet and stuff—we could save a lot in two years."

At Kyle's urging they each began saving money for college. Their after-school and summer jobs gave them modest bank balances that grew. With respectable scores on the SAT and ACT, both got into college with the help of financial aid and small scholarships.

Marci interrupted Kyle's intent focus on the images in the box. "You're like everyone else on the planet, my friend. Your mind runs on and on, jumping from one idea to another. If you understood that you might laugh and say 'Hey, that's a problem, a disability!'

"It's where your mind rambles on with no conscious control. Aimer and I are here to teach you control so you no longer have to be a victim to all that rambling. To all that remembering. To letting what's happened in the dead past affect your present. Eventually, we'll show you another completely different box. A new way of thinking that will bring more into your life than you can begin to imagine."

Kyle might have been coming out of a trance, "I don't know what you're talking about."

"That's why Aimer and I are here. We're mentors. You're on a learning curve. Taking a course. Learning a new curriculum for your life. What I'm showing you today is a beginning. I'm showing you that the thought system you live with is entirely enclosed in a box like this one here on the floor. It's your dream.

The dream we keep telling you about. Much of who you think you are is tied up in all those memories; things that are over and done. Most of your sadness comes from remembering the past, while worries about the future influence you, too. What you hate about yourself is in this box, too. That's how this thought system works for everyone."

"I don't hate myself."

"Actually, you do. You just don't acknowledge it yet. But there's another thought system that's separate from all this." Marci looked into Kyle's eyes as if she were searching for something. "It's over there to your right, but you can't see it yet. It's one you can *choose* to pay attention to and find a different, better way to live. The Right way. When you do, you'll awaken from this dream." Marci closed the box and pushed it to the corner of the living room. She sat down in the chair directly across from Kyle.

He wiped his hand across his face and frowned. "You keep telling me I'm dreaming. What dream? I'm living my life!" He cast an angry glare at Marci. "I'm *fine* with my life. Sure, it was hell growing up. But when I license my technology I'll be able to..."

"To *what?*" Marci interrupted.

Kyle paused, angry and confused. "To bring quantum computing to market. To start making a difference!" Kyle's eyes drilled into hers.

"There's no doubt; it's a certainty. You *will* make a difference." She stood up from the sofa and took Kyle's hands, pulling him into a standing position. He jerked his hands away. She smiled, then reached out and took his hands again. "Stand up Kyle. no need to be angry. Or afraid." He stood up and glared at her. She wrapped her arms around him, held him close and whispered in his ear. "You're doing just wonderfully. I want you to know that."

Kyle let Marci hold him for a moment. He couldn't help but smell the sweetness of her hair. He felt her warmth with her body pressed against his.

Marci stepped away and gently pushed Kyle back onto the sofa. She touched his forehead and he immediately fell asleep. He dreamed of Julia and of his mom and dad. Then his dreaming morphed into a scene where he killed Marci on the beach once again.

CHAPTER 5

Prototype

6 a.m. Still asleep on the sofa, Kyle awoke to the blaring of his alarm. He turned off the noise and walked through the condo. Marci was gone. The cardboard box on the floor was gone. He looked in the garage. No box. *Was I dreaming again? I'm losing' it.*

He went to the shower and turned the water from hot to cold several times. The scalding water scorched him. The cold water soothed him for a moment, then felt like a stream of ice. Three cycles of hot, cold, hot, cold, hot, cold. He got out of the shower and scrubbed the steam off the mirror. He stared at himself and rubbed his face. *C'mon man. Get real.* He forced himself to think about the work that had become his obsession, then dressed and drove to the office.

Cary Thomasson, eZo's admin assistant, greeted him with a smile as she did every morning: "Good morning. How are you?"

"Um...okay." He paused. "What's on the agenda today?"

"I hope you didn't forget. The lawyers from Palo Alto. They're due in at ten o'clock."

"Right. Did we get the non-disclosure agreements?"

"The NDA's are on your desk. Anything I can do for you?"

"Yes. See if you can order some snacks to go with the coffee."

Kyle went to his office and checked the non-disclosure agreements to be sure the lawyers had signed them. Before eZo Systems' could disclose its technology in even the smallest detail, Kyle and Rick agreed they had to throw a veil of absolute secrecy around their research and their quantum computing concept. The first step was to bind the attorneys with non-disclosure agreements. Then, as eZo approached their first-tier target companies—Google, Amazon, Apple and Zigma—to talk about licensing, perpetual royalties, and other aspects of the deal, they'd lock the company they chose to license their technology into inviolate agreements with penalties for illegal disclosure that could tie even the biggest of them up in court for years.

A rental car pulled into the space near the front door a few minutes before ten o'clock. Two men in pinstriped suits, power ties and wingtips climbed out.

"Hello. I'm Kyle Williams."

"Harmon Hughes. And this is my associate, Miles Bogan."

Harmon Hughes, a tall but slightly built man in his late fifties, presented himself warmly. "I'm glad to meet you, Dr. Williams. Just to get the formalities out of the way, I'm a Senior Partner in the firm and Miles Bogan is the attorney who will be handling your work."

Miles Bogan wore glasses with black frames and Coke-bottle lenses. He had a swarthy complexion and thinning hair with a comb-over. His still-developing hair transplant plugs hadn't yet reached the fullness they someday might. Their ugliness drew Kyle's eyes to Bogan's head even as Kyle realized he was staring. The three exchanged handshakes. Cary offered coffee and snacks. The three men retired to the conference room just as Rick drove up on his Harley and joined them.

Kyle began. "Gentlemen, I appreciate your trip from Palo Alto to meet with us today. Like many entrepreneurs you've worked with, we believe our technology has value. Enormous value. In our case...I don't know how to estimate the revenue we can produce. Let's say multi-billions are not out of range."

Miles Bogan looked away from Kyle and coughed into his hand.

Kyle continued. "Today we want to outline our road map for licensing our technology to any one of four target companies. We need one of them to help us install our tech out across the Internet. Worldwide. In the process, they'll boost their own bottom lines and ours beyond measure."

Rick picked up the conversation. "Right. We know you guys work with plenty of tech firms. You might have some ideas about other companies who could use our tech, but we want to keep focus on those four. They're the only ones positioned well enough to do what we need."

Harmon Hughes replied. "Of course. We're glad to work with you. Our firm works exclusively with companies in the high-tech space. We specialize with firms that work toward solving social issues with their technology."

He paused, glanced at Miles Bogan, then fixed Kyle with a stare. "But I must say, I get worried when I hear you talking about multi-billions of dollars. If you hadn't explained how your discoveries could improve weather forecasting, I'm not sure you'd have caught our attention. Let's get to the point. You said you're making progress on quantum computing."

Kyle nodded. "Correct, and we've come upon this technology from a totally unexplored direction. Researchers at other organizations are going down different paths than ours. Let's get into a bit more detail."

Rick took the floor. "I'll summarize some basic facts. Stop me if I'm covering old ground. Ordinary computers solve problems by running a sequence of steps, one after another. For instance, a computer trying to find the right key to open a padlock has to try one key after another. A quantum computer could try a million keys at the same time. You can't legitimately compare the speed and power of a quantum system to ordinary computers. They work on entirely different principles."

Miles Bogan looked bored. "Yes, that's fundamental, Dr. Huggins. I think we all understand that. Let's not waste time."

Rick continued. "All right. Our quantum system uses light photons. We entangle them as they pass through the Internet's fiber optic cables. We convert them into quantum bits, qubits. Then we use those qubits to do computations.

The attorneys, in a single motion, sat up straight in their chairs and listened intently as if something about using the Internet caught their attention.

"Trillions of photons flow through the Internet every second. If we entangle just a thousand of them from across the whole Internet—which we know we can do—we can work on so much data it takes a number 300 digits long to describe it."

Rick paused and looked at both attorneys, "That's a huge number. Imagine this: The number of atoms in the visible universe is a number that's 'only' 80 digits long. So, we're talking about unlimited computing power."

"All right, I think we understand those basics as well," Bogan said.

Rick shot a glance at Kyle, then continued. "Okay, but there's more you may not know. About fifteen years ago, Google and NASA started working on quantum computing. They discovered that posing a problem to a quantum computer was a hell of a lot more complicated than writing a program for an ordinary machine. Those guys couldn't figure out *how* to ask questions of those experimental systems. What was even more unexpected? They had to sort out what *kind* of problems a quantum computer could solve. They ran up against all kinds of brick walls, but we solved all that."

"Yes," Kyle continued. "Rick has developed software—an application programming interface, an API—that simplifies asking questions of our quantum system. We'd like you to help us protect our API and other components with licensing agreements."

The meeting broke for lunch, then resumed and continued through the afternoon. Kyle and Rick took turns at the whiteboard. They drew diagrams to give the lawyers a sense of how eZo was building their quantum super computer.

Rick explained that one particular component was the workhorse for the entire system. "This here...it's a hardware device we install inside the optical amplifiers that keep the Internet running..."

Bogan interrupted. "You put this *inside* optical amplifiers? There must be thousands of them all over the world, wherever data passes through the Internet."

"That's right, thousands. This piece grabs photons flowing through the Internet's fiber optic cables and entangles them. The more of these devices we put in place the more qubits we have to work with." Rick looked at Miles Bogan. "You get this, Mr. Bogan? It's all about numbers. We want to put our device in every optical amplifier on the planet. We'll have access to more qubits than you can count."

Hughes spoke. "All right. This is impressive. Have you developed any kind of prototype?"

Kyle paired his CoFone to the video projector and projected a slide show onto the screen.

"We have a working quantum computer," Kyle said. "Let me explain. We ran a few hundred kilometers of fiber-optic cable back in our warehouse area. Most of it's still rolled up on spools as it came from the supplier, but it simulates a small-scale version of the Internet. We placed optical amplifiers in strategic locations and installed our technology in them. Then we began flooding the fiber with traffic—that is, with light photons carrying information from point to point. We have a working quantum computer. It's using entangled weak photons flowing through our mini-Internet. Would you like to see some of the problems we've solved?"

Hughes dropped both hands on the table, clearly surprised. "Of course!"

Kyle started a slide show and narrated.

"Rick and I wondered whether we could pose a problem to forecast who would win different sporting events. We started with games that had already been played. For instance, for baseball we fed in data from MLB.com, sources that gave us information on the teams' management history and other factors. At first our predictions weren't much better than chance, but as we tweaked the programming, the predictions got better. Finally, we forecast about forty MLB games in row, and they were all spot on."

Miles Bogan interrupted. "Forecast? How does computing what already happened equate with forecasting?"

"We didn't want to wait around for the whole season to unfold to see if our system was working. But you're right. Forecasting past games seemed a bit hollow. The real proof came with the Summer Olympics. We loaded about a hundred terabytes of data on the Olympic athletes into our quantum system. Here's what our system predicted.

The screen showed outcomes for more than a dozen Olympic events, medal counts and other data.

Harmon Hughes absently clicked his ballpoint pen as he scanned the slide. "You're saying you got these results *before* the actual events?"

"Yes, but here's something better. You won't have to take our word on this one," Kyle said as he advanced to the next slide.

"We decided to see what we could do with weather forecasting. We seeded the system with real-time weather data from the National Weather Service. We added mathematics derived from chaos theory, Lorenz strange attractors, topological mixing and so forth. In a few hours, our system began printing a twelve-month weather forecast for cities across the U.S. Here's what our system predicted, compared with actual conditions."

The slide showed a column of dates followed with quantum computer predictions versus actual weather for several cities. The right-most column of the table showed error percentages on each meteorological factor. Predicted and actual precipitation, temperatures, cloud cover, wind speeds and wind directions over the past several months all matched with less than five percent error.

Kyle paused his presentation to display the current weather forecast for West Palm Beach. It matched closely on all counts with thc quantum system's prediction for today. He closed the slide show.

"Our prototype works. Better than we expected," Kyle announced as he met the attorneys eye to eye. "Our mini-Internet only gives us a modest number of qubits, so it took several computing hours to work out these problems. When we're able to tap into the entire Internet and entangle weak photons around the globe, computations like these we've shown you will be done in seconds...or even fractions of a second."

Hughes smiled, apparently without words to express what he was feeling. Miles Bogan stared at the whiteboard as if transfixed.

Kyle continued. "We'd like you to work up a licensing agreement. The agreement needs to spell out how the licensee will pay eZo Systems for the use of our technology. We want a royalty every time the computer solves a problem. However, the agreement needs to specify the system can only be used for peaceful purposes. Things that advance the welfare of humanity."

Hughes squinted. "That's a complicated request. Have you thought through what those restrictions might be?"

"Yes, in general terms, but we'll need your help to put our ideas into legal language."

Bogan interrupted. "Pardon me, but you've got an amazing piece of technology here. Seems to me you need to be thinking about how to commercialize it so you can start making money."

Hughes turned to his partner. "Hold on, Miles. I see their point. They don't want people using their tech to build better bombs."

Kyle stared at Bogan. "Exactly. Too many people in power are out for their own interests. I can't let this fall into the wrong hands." Kyle gestured at the diagrams on the whiteboard. "This technology will give people the power to solve just about anything. We don't want to be known as the guys who unleashed a computer on the world that does harm or kills people."

Bogan tapped his pen on his notebook. "Yes, but I'm not sure there's a way to put your stipulation into a licensing agreement. There's no legal precedent; no framework for licensing an item for humanitarian purposes."

Kyle stared at Bogan. "Are you saying your firm can't do what we need?"

Bogan's eyes narrowed. "We'll certainly think about this 'good of humanity, peaceful purposes' caveat, but I'm not confident there's any way to do what you're asking..."

Hughes interrupted. "Miles, these two men are right. They can't allow their technology to be used to do harm." He turned to Kyle and Rick. "You two have done what no one else has been able to do. I'm impressed. Let us study the 'good of humanity' issue. We want to work with you. We can get it done."

"All right. Is there anything else we need to discuss?" Kyle asked.

Hughes replied. "Not for now. We'll be in touch within a week if we need anything further."

Hughes and Bogan drove back to the Hyatt Hotel. At six o'clock they met at the restaurant for dinner. Each ordered a drink to fill the time until their meals arrived. Hughes stirred his bourbon and water. "You were a little rough on those two scientists today, Miles. Any reason for that?"

Bogan shrugged. "I don't see any way we can draft a licensing agreement that does what they want."

"I agree it's going to be challenging, but there was no reason to keep pushing back on them. Those two have done something amazing. Accurate weather forecasting for an entire year. Nationwide. They'll revolutionize agriculture once they get their machine running full speed."

“Maybe,” Bogan said, while his eyes stole glances at an attractive woman sitting alone at the table behind Hughes. He returned his eyes to Hughes. "Look at what they want. A licensing agreement that pays them for every job that's run on their system. How does that get priced out? Who's going to keep track of it? Do they want a fixed fee no matter what the computer solves? Or do we need to come up with a variable fee schedule?" Bogan gulped his gin and tonic. "Then there's the *coup de grâce.* They want to put limits on how the machine can be used. How can anyone define what's 'good for humanity'? It's impossible. They need to get their system on the market. Start making money."

Hughes listened to Bogan in between sips of his Four Roses bourbon, then set the glass carefully back down. "I see your point. But let me share an idea with you; something you can keep in mind when we're on first meetings with new clients, like today. We've been talking to Dr. Williams for six weeks. He looked all over the country for a law firm, like ours, that focuses on social issues. He found us and he signed our engagement contract. He gave us a retainer. He bought our airline tickets, paid for our hotel room and that rental car outside. And he showed us something today that, frankly, is far beyond anything I expected."

Bogan ran his fingers over the back of his head where hair still grew naturally. "I understand what you're saying, Harmon, but I stand by what I said. There's no way we're going to be able to draft that licensing documentation."

Hughes shook his head. "Let's not be pessimists, Miles. I know you'll find a way." The server appeared with their meals.

As Hughes buttered a dinner role he glanced at Bogan, "Miles, we can talk about eZo when we're back in our office. We're both under NDAs. We can't afford to talk about them on the plane or anywhere else in public. Right?"

"Got it," Bogan said.

The two men finished dinner and returned to their rooms. Bogan paced the floor for a moment, then sat down and dialed Walter Barbins, a man he'd met many years ago.

Barbins answered. "Talk to me."

"Walter, this is Miles Bogan.

"Yeah," Barbins said with a thick Texas drawl as his face appeared on Bogan's CoFone screen. "What's on your mind?"

"Our investments in Zigma Corporation. They're at risk."

"Tell me."

"I'm under an NDA so I can't say much. I'm in Florida and spent the day with a new client. They could put Zigma out of business."

"How the hell are they gonna do that?" Barbins demanded.

"I can't go into details."

"God dammit. Don't call me and tell me half the story. I've got a million dollars tied up in Zigma."

"So do I. I can't afford to lose it any more than you can," Bogan said, skirting the answer to Barbins question. "Let's just say this Florida company can forecast weather better than anyone else."

"How much better? Are they a threat to Zigma or are you just getting yourself worked up? C'mon Miles. Tell me what the hell's going on."

Bogan looked at Barbin's squinted eyes, bald pate and furrowed forehead on his CoFone display. *He looks better on a screen than he does in person. His head's too big for his body, but he looks almost normal here.* "I told you I'm under an NDA..."

"To hell with the NDA. I know why you called me. You're scared of losing your million dollars. You want me to do something. Right?"

"I called to give you a heads up..."

Barbins cursed and shouted. "Dammit, Miles. Either tell me what's going on with Zigma or call me back when you're ready to talk."

Bogan looked away from his CoFone for a moment and let out a sigh. "All right. This Florida outfit has built a new kind of computer that can forecast weather a year at a time with 95 percent accuracy for the entire nation. Probably for the whole world."

"Damn! Zigma can't do anything like that. You think this newcomer has cracked the code on forecasting?"

"Absolutely. They showed us forecasts for the entire U.S. for twelve months. It was dead on accurate."

"Shit. We're both screwed."

"Listen Walter. That million I put into Zigma? That was my life savings. I busted my ass for thirty years in this law firm to save money, to find smart investments and watch them grow. I'm ready to retire. I can't let this Florida company snatch it all away."

"Don't cry the blues to me, Miles. We're both in the same damn boat," Barbins hollered.

Bogan bristled and held his CoFone closer to his face. "Listen! When you told me you joined that angel investor group down in Houston, I thought you and your investor pals had done due diligence on Zigma."

"Don't blame me for this, Bogan. Nobody coulda known some upstart in Florida would muck up the works."

"I'm not blaming you, but you're the one who brought this Zigma deal to me. You pitched it hard, told me how they were a lock for long range weather forecasting. But I know. I know. *I* made the decision to put in my million. I just wish to hell I hadn't." Bogan paused. "I've got an idea on how we can keep Zigma alive and protect our investments. I'm going to need your help."

"Whaddya got in mind?"

"Turns out the Florida company is thinking about four potential licensees to monetize their computer. One of them is Zigma. I about choked when I heard that. So, bear with me for a minute. What do you think about Zigma getting a tip that the Florida people have stolen some of their patents?"

"Did they?" Barbins asked.

"Does it matter? As far as I can tell, those two guys in Florida don't have any investors. They're probably running the business off their own savings. A complicated law suit for patent infringement could put them out of business."

"What's the name of this Florida company?"

"Doesn't matter now, but tell me, who's that lawyer you use for your business things?"

"Micky Morgan. Why?"

"Because I can't take any legal action here at the firm. I need an outsider. What firm is Morgan with?"

"Not with a firm. He hung out his own shingle; he's got a little office over in the Clinton Drive-Waco Street area. It's a crappy place to live and work. He gets most of his work from the crooks and gang bangers who live there. Not a class guy, but he does what I tell him."

Bogan hesitated for a moment. *Perfect. No big law firm to worry about.* "All right, Walter. I don't want you to do anything yet. Let me do some ground work. I'll get back in touch with you." *I need Barbins' help, but can't let him go commando and screw things up. There's too much at risk.*

"All right. Keep me posted, but don't waste any time. I can't afford for Zigma to go bust."

"Me either. I'll be in touch."

CHAPTER 6

Sin, Guilt & Fear

After spending the day with the attorneys, Kyle returned to his condo. He found Marci sitting on the couch. The big ego box was on the floor once again.

Kyle stood in the doorway for a full five seconds. *Oh shit! Now what?* "Marci, what are you doing here? I have too much going on. You need to quit harassing me."

"Harassing? Well, cowboy, I never thought of it quite like that." She walked across the room and pulled the door closed that led to the garage. "I guess you had a good day at the office with the attorneys. I can tell you now, they're going to work hard for you, up to a point. But you're going to have some ugly speed bumps along the way. Let's see if we can figure out how you can get over those bumps."

"What do you know about the attorneys?"

She laughed. "It's all here, Kyle. In your ego box. Sit down. I'll show you."

He sat next to Marci and peered into the box.

"Look over here." Marci poked her arm deep into the box, through many layers of three-dimensional holographic moving images and grabbed one, lifting it up so Kyle could see it. "That's your meeting today, see? You and Rick and Hughes and his partner, Bogan. Now, over here." She twisted the image as if she were turning it inside out. "These are the attorneys at their office in Palo Alto next week working on your documents."

Kyle threw his hands in the air, palms open to Marci, as if he wanted to push her away. "Now I can see the future? C'mon!"

"Sure. Because time is an illusion that's part of the dream you're dreaming. What's *Real* is Eternity. Some of your philosophers and thinkers say there is only *now.* But even that isn't quite right. There is only Eternity. There is no such thing as time. It's something you constructed as part of your dream. That's why looking at these images and twisting them around a bit can show you what appears to be the past and the future, as well as what you call the present."

Marci smiled at him and touched his hand. "When you understand what's *Real* and end this dream it'll all make sense."

"Listen. I had long day. You're telling me again I'm dreaming my life."

"Yes. Everyone is."

"So, what happens when I wake up?"

"You'll come to the end of dreaming," she said.

Kyle scoffed. "Listen, I'm wide awake. You're starting to piss me off with all this talk of dreaming."

"You *think* you're awake. Remember! I told you this box represents your thought system. It's everything you think is true. That includes your concepts of time. Of the world around you. Of the quantum computer. Of Rick and Cary. Hughes and Bogan. Who and what you think you are. There's nothing in your human existence and experience that's *not* in this box. Of course you believe you're awake. This world is dense. It's hard to ignore or even to imagine that it's all an illusion. I'm showing you those illusions here in your ego box so you can see them with your body's eyes and begin to understand."

"I'm on the verge of something wonderful at work. If we're going to go anywhere with this stuff of yours, I need to know who you are. Why you keep talking about some kind of *thought system*, for God's sake. Telling me everything I do is a dream..."

"Fair enough, Kyle. Get comfortable, sit back and relax." Marci put her hand on his chest and touched lightly, pushing him against the sofa. "Take your shoes off, undo your tie. Lose the suit coat. Let me start by telling you you're an incredible friend I care about very much. More than you can know. You're a wonderful person. You have the potential to change the world. You will, one way or another."

Kyle snorted. "C'mon. Answer my questions. What are you? A spirit woman who comes into my dreams? Into my house in the middle of the night? You say you care about me. That I can change the world." Kyle paused for a few seconds, thinking. "On top of all that, in that dream I had about you, I loved you. Now, with you sitting next to me, I don't know where that comes from. And part of me is terrified of you."

"You're asking me all the right questions. Let me explain.

"When you dreamed of me that night, Aimer warned you that even though he and I are here to help you, you wouldn't want to accept my help at first. You'd be terrified at my appearance in your life. That you might even try to get rid of me. That's what happened in your dream. You killed me. That person with the fear gun? That assailant was your *guilt* for having killed me. Sin, guilt and fear run rampant in your dream world. Want to know how that works?" She looked at him expectantly.

Kyle shrugged. He noticed her nose wrinkle and the smile lines at the corners of her mouth. She looked gorgeous and desirable, like his physics professor, the one who had sponsored him as he worked on his doctorate. She had a cool and professional demeanor, but a hot body. Kyle had imagined bedding her on countless occasions, but never risked it because she was his sponsor. Marci was hot too; nothing cool or standoffish about her.

Marci smiled. "Pay attention! Here's a crash course on the unholy trinity: sin, guilt and fear. If you want to take notes just write a big headline at the top of the page: S-G-F. Because everything you *think* is real comes from those three things. They control everything in your ego box and your life."

Kyle collected himself. "Take notes?"

She chuckled. "No. I'm kidding, but burn this into your brain. Sin. Guilt. Fear. S-G-F." Marci waited, as if she expected Kyle to somehow make a permanent memory of those three letters. "Now, think of a time when you did something you thought was sinful, wrong or illegal or unethical or immoral. You don't have to tell me what it is. Just answer this: Did you, or do you now, feel guilty about having committed that sin?"

Kyle looked toward the ceiling, thinking of the day he tossed a ball to Julia. "Yes."

"Okay, and when you did something wrong and felt guilty, did you feel you deserved to be punished?"

He shrugged. "Yeah, but anytime I did something wrong I always hoped I wouldn't get blamed. You know ..."

"Right. That 'hoping you wouldn't get blamed' feeling...would you say you were afraid you might get caught and punished?"

"Sure. No one wants to be punished."

"That's the unholy trinity. You feel you've done something wrong. That's sin. Then you feel guilty. Then you fear punishment. Sin, guilt and fear," Marci said.

She looked at Kyle, inspecting him from his face to his feet.

"Fear is a powerful force in this dream world. You're worried about how your black hole project might be misused, and you've got reason to worry. This illusory world you live in, this dream world, is a place of duality. Your dream of killing me was all about fear that you carry deep down inside this box, inside your thought system; in this world where everything is two-sided, where fear seems to be the opposite of love. You and everyone else dream of fear. On some rare occasions, you dream of love. Now, sitting here, you're trying to figure out how part of you feels it loves me while another part is terrified. Let me tell you again: This, what you and I are doing *right now*, is a dream."

Marci laughed. "Except that no one is going to accost you with a fear gun here. You can find all the fear you'll ever need, whether it's fear of not licensing your black hole...fear that plans for your life won't work out...fear that your quantum computer will be stolen or misused. Fear goes on and on in this dream."

Kyle sat quietly. Marci gazed at him, waiting.

He choked back a nervous laugh. "I don't like this." He looked around the room and his gaze fell back on the ego box. He took a deep breath, recalling all the horrendous things it held. "Look. I'm a physicist. A scientist. What you're telling me doesn't make sense. But let's just say I accept the idea that I'm dreaming and the world's all about fear. It makes no sense, but for the sake of our talk..." he cocked his head, "let's say I get it. How can I wake up from the dream? And if I did wake up, what would I be waking *into*?"

"Good questions, my friend. There *is* something you can do to wake up. It's what Aimer and I have come to teach you. As he told you in the kitchen that morning we met, it will take time, as you measure it, and you'll need to do some serious work to wake up."

"I remember that."

"Second, when you wake up you'll be waking up into a completely different thought system. A different box. It's called by many names but for now let's call it the Right Mind box. It's the one where you gain *Vision* and *Knowledge* and learn to see what is *Real*. It's one where there is no duality. No fear. Only love. No time. No space. It's eternal. It's infinite even beyond what the word 'infinite' can possibly mean.

"It's a box where you have no wants because *everything* you could ever imagine wanting is already provided in a richness that is beyond words and human understanding. Here's the best part. You have this Right Mind, but you don't know it. Aimer and I are here to help you find it so when you do awaken from this 'life' you think you're living, you'll see your *true function* here in this world. Moreover, you'll get more help than you could ever imagine in taking on that function and operating out of your Right Mind."

"That's too weird. You're talking like I would disappear, like my life would end and I'd be sent on some kind of—I don't know—a *mission* that has nothing to do with what I'm all about. You're describing nirvana or utopia. I've got work to do here and a life to live." Kyle walked to the window and stared outside, his back to Marci. "I think you should leave. And take Aimer with you."

Marci laughed and joined him at the window. "Well, my friend, don't send us on our way just yet. No one gets this the first time around. This will help: You aren't going to disappear or lose your life or make some mystical transit into nirvana. You'll still be the CEO of your company working on licensing your so-called black hole. Every morning when you wake up you'll spend time in your Right Mind; and again, before going to sleep. Eventually, you'll begin spending a lot of time in your Right Mind, and that will bring you many wonderful changes. And what's absolutely the most important: You'll learn about an amazing power that comes directly from your Right Mind box. It's the power of forgiveness.

Kyle snorted. "This is starting to sound like a Sunday school lesson. I'm not much on all that God stuff."

"I know."

"Then you'll understand why I can't see any point in thinking about God. He didn't do squat for my family. They're all dead. None of them deserved it."

"I understand how you feel, but let me give you the scoop on forgiveness. Almost no one here understands what it is. Most people say, 'Oh, he did so and so and it was wrong, but I forgive him.' That's not forgiveness at all. It's what we call judging and projecting. Here's what really happens.

"Let's say a guy named Jack is walking down the street when a truck drives by and splashes water all over his business suit. Imagine that you could read Jack's mind. What would he be thinking?

"Really? Now we're playing what-if games?"

"Sure. You'll learn something."

"Yeah, right. Well, Jack would be pissed. He'd cuss out the truck driver and blame him for ruining his suit. If the driver stopped, Jack would probably give him a piece of his mind, call him names, punch him out. Whatever."

"Right. That's how it seems, but here's how Jack's ego thought system works. Jack gets splashed. He feels that shouldn't have happened to *him*. He's Jack, after all! He's someone special. So, first he *judges* the truck driver as careless or something worse. His ego mind bubbles up an appropriate emotion. In this case, anger. Then Jack *projects* his anger on the truck driver. It happens almost instantly, at the speed of thought. Anger is always waiting in the background ready to be expressed or, as we say, projected. We're quick to dump it on other people, events and all kinds of situations. Now that Jack has projected his anger, he *perceives* the truck driver as a bad person. Maybe Jack shouts out and calls him an idiot. The act of seeing the driver as an idiot, or an enemy is what *perception* is all about.

"You might need to think about this: Judgment and projection always happen *before* you perceive a person, situation or event. In other words, what you see, hear and feel about things in your life don't exist until you project an emotion or thought energy on them. Once you do that, you perceive the person or event colored by the emotion or belief you've projected."

"Yeah, that sort of makes sense. It's psychology."

"Sure. Even philosophy. Emmanuel Kant was one of your 18th century philosophers. He proposed a theory in his day he called idealism. Let me quote him. Kant said 'Our perceptions are not the results of a physiological process by which our eyes somehow transmit an image of the world into our brains. Rather, they are the result of a psychological process that combines what our eyes see with what we already think, feel, know, want and believe. Then we use this combination of sensory information and preexisting knowledge to construct our perception of reality.'"

"Yeah, I read something like that in one of my undergrad classes. I guess it's as good a theory as any."

"It is. Now let's get back to the issue of forgiveness. This time Jack gets splashed. Instead of projecting anything, he simply *looks past it.* He doesn't judge the driver or the event. It's just something that happened. The universe simply unfolded an event and it happened to cause him to get splashed. Okay?"

"Yeah, I suppose. But it probably ruined his day."

"So it seems, but there's something amazing going on here when he chooses to not judge the event. When there is no judgment there can be no need to project anything on the driver, the puddle in the road, or the overall event. Forgiveness begins with not judging the people and events in your life."

Kyle ran the fingers of both hands through his hair and signed a deep breath. "I can't imagine not judging things."

"Yes, it does sound strange at first. Let's imagine another scenario. You're in a boat floating down a river and you have no oars. It's taking you to a place you don't want to go. You want to either get out of the boat or stop the river. You sure can't stop the river. It makes no sense to blame the river or the boat. You choose to not judge what's going on and see how you can best work out your little dilemma. Maybe you'd jump out of the boat and swim to shore. Same thing with Jack and the truck driver. Just work out the dilemma without judgment. Take a moment to realize you are honored to be witnessing this moment in the unfolding of creation. Even a splash from a passing truck. *That* is what true forgiveness really is."

"Unfolding of creation?"

"Yes. I've already told you, part of what you hold in your ego box and believe to be real is time. In the *Real* world, there is no time. Instead, there is Eternity. Nothing comes before or after Eternity. It simply is. Here though, it seems that events unfold on their own over time. If you were to see the unfolding as something that happens naturally, you'd be able to avoid getting emotionally involved in events as they unfold. You'd learn forgiveness."

"So, you're saying projecting our thoughts causes us to perceive the world around us? By not judging what happens we can avoid those projections...and that's what forgiveness is? What's the point? What if Jack were walking down the street and a mugger shot him or stabbed him and took his wallet? How can Jack just 'look past' that?"

"You're asking the perfect question. If Jack were shot or stabbed, he might be challenged to not judge the mugger or the event. But—and this is a gigantic 'but'—over in the other box, your Right Mind box, you have a Teacher whose job is to give you everything you need to look past *anything.* Even being mugged, stabbed or shot. Your Teacher is there to show you how to wake up from this dream. Learning non-judgment and forgiveness is the first step in awakening from this dream."

A Right Mind box. A teacher. Forgiveness. Kyle again laid his head back and stared at the ceiling. After a moment, he stood up and grabbed a beer from the refrigerator. "Want one?" he asked Marci.

"No thanks. Let's stay with this for another minute, okay?"

Kyle sat down and gulped a deep swallow. Marci continued. "We've covered a lot of ground here tonight. Let's go climb into that fold-down bed of yours and I'll show you how you can begin to find that Right Mind box and your Teacher."

Kyle took in Marci's shapely body. *Climb in bed?* A warmth crept over him. He rearranged himself on the sofa in anticipation. Marci watched him scrutinize her body, then took both his hands in hers. A sensation of peace pervaded his body and mind. He felt loved, cared for and worry free as he hadn't since, as a young child, he'd climbed into bed between his mom and dad to escape the memory of a bad dream. "Sure Marci. I'll go to bed with you."

"Let's go, Kyle." They slid under the sheets. Kyle lay on his back and reached over to touch her. "Marci, I don't know what you're doing but I want to hold you and make love with you."

"I'm helping you get ready for your first trip into the Right Mind box." Marci slid over and put her head on Kyle's shoulder, pressing up against him and putting her hand on his chest. She spoke softly into his ear. "I know you like my body Kyle, and I'm enjoying the feeling of having one and being close to you. Now we're going to merge together, but in a different way than you expect. Together we're going to talk with your Teacher and see what He has to say to you. Close your eyes."

Marci began humming a sweet, soft melody, her voice a murmur in the darkness. Kyle closed his eyes and felt he was being bathed in a potion of love that wrapped and filled him at the same time.

His ever-rambling mind quieted down, almost as if someone had turned down the volume of an always-on radio. With his eyes closed he noticed a subtle lightening and darkening through his eyelids. Gradually the brightening took precedence until his field of view was illuminated with a warm glow.

A series of gentle thoughts entered his awareness. *I am here with you at every moment. I am closer than your hand or your heart.*

In his relaxed state Kyle basked in that revelation. Another thought grew into his consciousness: *I have always been here. You haven't noticed me, so I waited for this moment. As your Teacher, I would ask only for your little bit of willingness to call upon me when you make decisions.*

Fully and blissfully relaxed, Kyle understood those thoughts that flowed into awareness, letting them be whatever they seemed to be: unspoken ideas given him by a loving entity he could not begin to comprehend.

Every moment presents you with a choice to turn to me or to rely on your ego filled with fear, danger, disappointment and all the dualities of this world of form. As you awaken in the morning, turn to me. As you fall asleep at night, turn to me. I am your Teacher and I speak from your Right Mind.

Kyle reveled in the feelings of love and comfort. Everything felt loving, peaceful and sweet. He received those ideas in amazement as they filled his mind. It was simple, he thought. Offer a little willingness to seek help from this unearthly teacher who, somehow, seemed to be within him. One who promised to answer his every question; to help with every decision. How unlike anything he'd experienced. Ever. With the warmth of Marci next to him, her hand on his chest and her head on his shoulder, Kyle drifted off to sleep.

He dreamed. Kyle found himself on a sandy beach seated before a small bonfire as the late afternoon sun crept toward the horizon. Next to him sat Aimer and Marci, the three forming a triangle around the fire. The heavenly music Marci had been humming filled the air with rich harmonies, just noticeable above the sound of ocean waves rolling onto shore.

Aimer pointed toward the water. "See that couple walking their dog along the water's edge?"

Kyle looked to his right and watched as a couple approached with a black lab on a leash.

"The woman feels her husband doesn't pay enough attention to her; that he works too many hours. That he cares more about his work than about her. She's been talking with her female friends about it. The man feels it's his job to be a provider and make money. But he spends a lot more time thinking about work than he does about her. He's gone missing from their marriage. He knows it, but doesn't know how to change things. She blames him, and he feels guilty but justified at the same time. It sounds complicated but it's one of the most ordinary situations couples struggle with," Aimer said.

As the trio approached, Kyle overheard the woman's words to her husband.

"I know your job is to make money! I know you love your work, but I'm home alone every night. I'm lonely. It feels like your work is more important than our marriage. What about kids? You always say we need to save more before we can even think about children. My clock is ticking! I don't think you care about our marriage. I'm coming to the end of my rope."

Their voices faded as they passed by.

Aimer spoke. "Did you hear the emotion in her voice? Her ego mind was driven by emotions. They began forming in her childhood as she had thoughts and feelings triggered by people and the world around her. As they were repeated, some of them coalesced into core beliefs. That woman had some reasonable thoughts about what a marriage should be. However, underneath, her core belief told her 'I am not enough!' As a child, she might have been part of a big family with many children and never felt she got enough attention. Or she might have been berated, bullied, criticized or abused for some reason. No matter.

"She believes she 'is not enough.' If she were enough, her husband would pay more attention to her and what's important to her. Not being 'enough' is her 'sin.' She feels guilty for not being enough for her husband to love. That guilt brings on fear. Fear of being left alone, undervalued and perhaps even losing her marriage and having to start over again. In turn, her fear generates anger that she *projects* onto her husband. Did you hear his reply? He said, 'Well, if you were more caring when I'm around maybe I'd be around more often.' He attacked her verbally."

"Yeah, I see that. It's what happens on a dozen soap operas every day," Kyle said.

Marci smiled. "Yes, but there's another way those two could be working things out. It comes straight out of their Right Mind. Can you guess what it is?"

"I don't know. Something about forgiveness?" he asked.

"Yes, but before that, it's about not judging. Each of them *could* choose to stop judging one another. That simple step would defuse almost everything that's happening between them. Not-judging would give them the space they need to communicate honestly with one another. They might even be able to uncover those old childhood core beliefs that give them so much trouble relating. It might even be possible they'd find something like Love."

Aimer chimed in. "The man's response was a direct attack on his wife. He said, in essence, 'It's your fault!' He blamed her. Blaming and attack are never warranted when a person wants to learn forgiveness. They both came out of their ego boxes where everything that brings pain into a person's life actually thrives."

"I see that," Kyle answered.

The three sat in silence for several minutes, gazing into the fire as the sun retired from the sky, casting blends of pink, orange and violet across the high clouds. Kyle felt at ease with nothing pressing on his mind; relaxed and comfortable in the company of these two strange friends sitting with such camaraderie on the beach. As the fire waned into glowing embers Aimer and Marci began speaking. Marci to Kyle's right, and Aimer to his left, each speaking with different messages. As Kyle listened to the cadence of their voices, they began to merge.

"Every time you choose to look past something...*the easiest way to not judging*...forgiveness happens...*is thinking from your Right Mind*...you can choose to ask for my help at any time...*where little errors you make along the way can be corrected without judgment*...my answers to you will always lead you to a Right action...*and you begin to change the world*...helping and teaching all mankind."

As Marci and Aimer spoke, another voice joined, creating a spoken symphony of words in Kyle's mind.

Learning forgiveness is simple because it only asks your willingness to talk with me. Make that choice throughout each day whenever you feel uncertainty about the best course of action. But learning forgiveness may not be easy. Your ego wants to answer your questions and make your decisions. It is your responsibility to choose—either your Right Mind where I can help you, or your ego mind where fear, trouble and pain are in charge. Your choosing decides how the rest of your life will unfold.

The three sat in silence while the harmonies merged with the sound of surf landing gently on the beach.

6 a.m. A sudden buzz followed by radio babble reporting traffic and weather. Kyle awoke and turned to see Marci lying next to him.

"Good morning, my friend. Did you sleep well?" she asked. "Do you remember a dream?"

Kyle gazed at the ceiling. "Yes. You and Aimer were in my dream last night. I bet you knew that."

Marci smiled. "So I do. What do recall?"

"Everything. The couple on the beach, you and Aimer talking to me. A voice that spoke to me about making decisions. Was that the teacher you told me about?"

She nodded. "Yes. Let's take a moment to reconnect with your Teacher. It's a useful way to begin your day. You can talk to your Teacher just as you would to me. If you're troubled you can talk to Him as if He were your advisor, your friend or even your therapist. Or, you could talk with Him as if you were talking to your Creator, to God Himself."

Marci paused and placed her hand on Kyle's chest once again. "Now close your eyes. Think these words to your Teacher as I say them."

"Thank you for this new morning and the happiness of starting my day by talking with you. I would like to hear your thoughts so you can guide me through the day in my Right Mind.

"Thank you for your Love and showing me your wisdom in dealing with situations gracefully, so my words and actions are pleasant to all. I am happy your plans for me are good. I trust your guidance in all things I encounter today. Thank you too for helping me hear you speak to me from my Right Mind. For helping me choose to judge nothing, to forgive everything and to share what you teach me with others I meet throughout the day."

Kyle lay in bed, eyes closed. "Marci, say that again, slowly."

Marci repeated that morning prayer as Kyle's lips moved in sync with her words.

"Giving thanks. That's the true nature of prayer. It's not about asking for things. When you give, you receive; giving thanks always returns God's Love to you." With those words Marci disappeared from the room.

Kyle listened to the sound of his breath. A sliver of morning sunlight shined through an opening in the curtain. It reflected off the beveled edge of the mirror above his dresser and cast a tiny rainbow across the ceiling. *I'm cared for. Watched over. Loved. How can that be?*

CHAPTER 7

Prayer

Kyle climbed out of bed and went into the bathroom. He stood before the mirror, staring into his own eyes. Thirty seconds passed. Sixty. *This body. It's not what I am.* He gazed deeper, leaned close into the mirror, then backed away, still staring. *This feeling! Of comfort. Caring. Peace. Knowing I'm watched over.* He closed his eyes. A quiet whisper of contentment, of exhilaration, filled his belly with a happy tickling. It transformed from happiness to gratitude. He closed his eyes and raised his chin toward the ceiling, expressing his feelings to whatever it was that had entered his life. *Thank you for your love.*

He showered and dressed, then sat on his lanai watching the sun climb above the horizon. Two Sandhill Cranes walked across the grass, majestically, as if they owned the land, their heads down, probing for food with their long beaks. *They mate for life.* He watched their elegant stroll over the lawn. *The way they're together. So perfect. Is it love that keeps them together? Do animals know love?* He thought about love. That love he felt from his Teacher. From spending time in his Right Mind. It was palpable. Tangible. Real and fulfilling. He thought of his black hole project, how it would put food on empty tables. How it would solve social problems and bring people together. *It'll help people. Bring comfort. It can be a catalyst and maybe even bring love.*

He called Rick. "Hey, it's Saturday. Let's forget about work for a few hours and hit the beach." Ten minutes later Kyle piled onto the back of Rick's motorcycle. They drove to the Jupiter Inlet and sat under an umbrella just steps away from the surf that continued its eons-long roll onto the sand.

"I've been thinking about our black hole," Rick said. We'll make a lot of money with it. What're you going do with it?"

"I don't know. Buy a house. Hell, I'll probably be able to buy my own island somewhere. Or a house at the beach or in the mountains. Or all of those, but that's not what I'm thinking about."

"Yeah, I know. I was happy down in Cudjoe Key with nothing but a pop-up camper. Having a bunch of money is better than not having enough, but there's more to life than getting rich."

"Yeah. What I want more than anything..." Kyle turned to his best and oldest friend. "I want a sweet woman I can live with happily ever after. No alcoholics. Nobody dying before their time. No stress. Just comfort, peace and love."

"Sounds good to me." Rick held up his hand and they bumped fists.

Kyle continued. "And with our black hole? If I'm ever remembered by anyone, if I have any kind of legacy, I'd like it to be as a man who made a difference. Someone who brought people together. Gave them a better life. Cut down the stress and worry and fear in their lives." The two sat back and watched a trio of pelicans gliding by just a few feet above the water.

Kyle turned to Rick. "You know, when I was a kid my mother taught me a prayer. I said it every night when I went to bed. I was always afraid if I didn't say it, something bad would happen."

Now I lay me down to sleep
I pray the Lord my soul to keep
If I should die before I wake
I pray the Lord my soul to take.

Kyle snorted. "At first, that prayer scared the crap out of me. I wondered if I might die in my sleep. I wondered and worried: Wouldn't God automatically take my soul? What if He didn't? I was just a child. I hadn't done anything wrong. Yeah, but after a while I added some extras to that prayer. I begged God to protect my family. I beseeched Him to keep my aunts and uncles and cousins safe. Even my dog.

“It just seemed I had to plead with Him to keep everybody safe." Kyle gazed off at the horizon for a moment. "Then when Julia got killed, I knew that praying wasn't for shit. God didn't care. Or maybe He didn't listen. That's about as close to God as I ever got."

Rick shook his head. "So...what's bringing you around to all this? This God stuff."

Kyle turned his gaze to the horizon. *I can't tell him about Marci. It's too weird.* "It's hard to explain. Lately I've started feeling...I don't know how to describe it...maybe like someone is watching over me. And with our black hole? I've been thinking about how it could make life better. Not just for you and me. For everybody."

"I don't know about God and bedtime prayers. But you're right. It can make things better once it's running full bore." Rick sat quietly for a moment. "Something I'm wondering about."

"What's that?"

"You never went to church that much."

"No. Seemed like a waste of time. All that God stuff didn't have any place in my life. Even so, I said my prayers every night just in case. I guess I quit when I was in high school."

"Yeah, so where'd you come up with this thing about helping people in the first place? You want the quantum system to work for the good. That's all great, but I never thought you were that way."

"What way? You mean that I care about people? About doing good things."

"Yeah. Like, why build a computer to solve peoples' problems instead of science and engineering problems?"

"I don't know. Maybe it was all the crap I had to go through growing up. Maybe it made me more aware of what others have to deal with. Besides, I knew God didn't give a damn about me or my family. I guess I felt like it was up to me and all of us to make things as good as we can." He paused and looked up at the sky as if it would stem the emotions he felt. "If only there had been some way to save Julia! I feel like it's my fault. And my parents' problems? I don't think they'd have divorced if Julia hadn't been killed. That feels like my fault, too."

"Don't beat yourself up, man. None of that was your fault. Shit happens. No matter what anyone does."

"I know. I guess I beat myself up because I can't let it go. Maybe trying to help other people is how I deal with all that. You think?"

"Hey, I'm no shrink. Just quit worrying about all that. There's nothing wrong with you, man. That's the only advice I got."

"Yeah, but you know...with the quantum system we have a real chance to change things. This world and the way people struggle sucks in so many ways."

"Yeah. Seems life is nothing more than a game you struggle to get through, and then you die. There ought to be a better way to live."

Kyle turned to Rick and nodded. "Hey, thanks for listening to me."

"You done with all this God stuff and beatin' yourself up?"

"Yeah."

"Good. Let's get back to the office so we can get some work done."

They worked through the weekend. Sunday evening Kyle climbed into bed and repeated the prayer Marci had taught him, then fell into a peaceful sleep. Monday morning at 6 a.m. he awoke to Marci's voice calling from the kitchen as she made coffee.

CHAPTER 8

The Wave

"Good morning. It's time for your morning prayer," she said.

His surprise at finding her in his condo changed to anticipation. He couldn't help getting excited at her beauty and the warmth of her body against his. "You're like a shadow that comes and goes. I didn't expect to see you again so soon."

"No. I'm more like a flash of sunlight. There's nothing dark about me. You should know that by now."

Kyle pursed his lips. "Sorry. That's not what I meant."

Marci snickered. "Don't worry. I'm just messing with you. So, are you ready for that morning prayer? It's best to do before you get out of bed. It'll help you get your entire day started on the right foot. Actually, I should say 'in the right *mind*.'"

She led Kyle to his bed. Together, they gave thanks for this new day.

"Marci, I love the feeling I get from that prayer. It makes me feel...I don't know how to describe it. Maybe 'clean' or 'pure.' As if there is someone I can turn to who might help me live my day. Who might help me in making choices. Who can make life happier."

"You're on target, dear one. Taking a few of your earliest moments each day to connect with your Teacher is a powerful first step in beginning to find your Right Mind box."

"You keep talking about boxes. The ego box. It still boggles my mind when I think about it. Now, another box that's connected with this teacher?"

"The boxes are symbols, Kyle. They let me show you two different ways of living and being. I showed you the ego box so you could begin to understand how your mind works. How everything you believe is in that box. How your past experiences determine how you deal with issues as they come up each moment.

"Think of a wave on the ocean. It's rolling along. There's nothing you can do short of building an obstruction to change it.

Life is like that wave. Life rolls along moment by moment. It might rain today and an avid golfer might be annoyed that he can't get out and play eighteen holes. But weather is just part of the wave. No one can do anything about it; no more than you can keep planets from rotating in space. Fighting it—getting angry at the weather, being disappointed because he can't play today—is pointless. You can't change the wave.

"So, the answer to all this is easy. We all need to accept that the wave of creation, of life, is rolling along. Nothing more or less. Choose to be peaceful with *whatever* happens. Just like Jack who got drenched by the passing truck. Let life happen without judging it. Look past things that your ego mind wants to resist, and decide not to resist them. Choose to live in each moment as it happens. Feel *honored* to be so fortunate that you're here to experience life. That's forgiveness and that's mindfulness and that's some of what we're here to teach you.

"Your Teacher can give you immeasurable help. And as you learn, you'll begin to wake up from this dream world you're living in. Where the Real you, not the one you think you are, will start enjoying a whole new experience."

Kyle adjusted his pillow and turned on his side to face Marci directly. "I understand your words. But I'm hard-wired to react to things as they happen. Everyone is. How can I ignore the things that go on all around me every day? What happens if our black hole technology falls into the wrong hands? Or if the companies we want to partner with try to take over? Or the government begins using our quantum computer to win wars and kill people? How can I 'look past' those possibilities? It doesn't make sense in the real world."

"You're asking about the Real world? I think you forget what we keep telling you, or more likely, you don't believe it yet. This so-called 'real world' you talk about is a *dream*. It's an *illusion*. It's driven by the belief in sin, guilt and fear. It's not the *Real* world."

"Come on Marci. This bed we're in is real." Kyle shook the blankets and rapped its wooden frame. It resounded with the sound of his knuckles impacting the wood. "I can put my arms around you, hold you and kiss you. You're about as real is anything gets." Kyle reached out to embrace her.

Marci allowed herself to slide into his embrace. Their lips met for Kyle's long-anticipated kiss. He adjusted his body to meld more intimately with hers. He stroked her back and pulled her closer, feeling her body press against his. Her softness and fragrance entranced him. His hands began to wander over her body.

"Marci, I love you," Kyle spoke softly.

"Yes Kyle, I love you too. More than you can possibly know. But remember what I've been telling you: You're dreaming. Your body and mine are part of the dream. In the only reality that is Real, we are not bodies at all. We are One. Our bodies seem to prove that we're two individuals; that we're separate from one another. But in fact, in Reality, you and I are One; the same."

Marci drew back with a mischievous smile on her face. "Because now I'll show you what I mean about this dream in terms you can see for yourself. I want you to watch what's about to happen."

Marci sat up in bed. Kyle drank in the view of her sensuous body and her wavy brunette hair as the sheets fell away. "I want you to see that this is a dream, my dear friend."

Marci instantly disappeared from his view and from the bed, as if she had never been there. There was no clap of thunder as molecules of air rushed in to occupy the space she had held. The sheets simply collapsed around where she had been sitting and the depression in the bed from the weight of her body vanished.

A voice from the kitchen: "Hey, Kyle! Come on! It's time for breakfast. Get a move on."

Kyle sat up in bed, then cautiously put his feet on the floor and shuffled toward the kitchen. He found Marci preparing a bowl of fruit that appeared to have a sprinkling of raw rolled oats. Coffee steamed from two mugs, one at Marci's chair and another set for Kyle. Marci poured a dash of almond milk into the two bowls.

He stood at the entrance to the small kitchen. Marci was fully dressed in a business suit: a smart top and jacket with a skirt that modestly exposed her knees. Moderate heels. Her hair was coiffed, giving her the conservative bearing of a corporate attorney ready for an important business meeting.

Marci laughed. "Come on. Get some pants on. Seems like I need to keep reminding you to be decent when we sit down to eat."

Kyle looked at her as she sat down at the kitchen table. He went to his bedroom and threw on some clothes, then took a seat across from her. "How the hell did you do that?"

Marci smiled. She took a bite of mangoes and bananas, chewing quietly with eyes closed. "Well my friend, *hell* has little to do with anything I do. Hell is where you live, in this dream world. I wanted you to see with your body's eyes that it *is* a dream where anything can happen, no matter how real this dream seems to you."

Marci paused as Kyle sat down at the table. "When I talk about dreams and illusions, *I'm not kidding*. There's nothing here in your ego box that's Real. The only thing Real is your Right Mind. The one where you spend time with your Teacher. And with me, pulling you up this learning curve, step by step, so you can see there's a different way to live. A better way. My little demonstration can help you begin to understand what I'm telling you is true."

Kyle stared at her. "What *are* you? How can you disappear from my bed and show up in the kitchen fully dressed?"

Marci took another bite of fruit. "Come on. Stop indulging your ego mind with questions that have no answers you'll believe. Have breakfast. We have a lot to do today. The Palo Alto attorneys have FedEx'd some documents you'll have on your desk this morning. We'll go to your office together and I'll help you work through some of the speed bumps I warned you about. Your black hole technology is a lot like a real black hole. It can suck everything you want in your life down into it and leave you here in this dream world. I can help you avoid that. So, eat your breakfast. It's going to be a busy day."

"What speed bumps?"

Marci stared at him. "You'll see."

CHAPTER 9

There's a Lot I Need to Tell You

Kyle opened the door to eZo Systems and found Cary at the reception desk. "Good morning, Cary. I'd like you to meet Marci. She's here to help today with some of the documents we're getting from the lawyers."

Kyle saw a look of puzzlement on Cary's face. "Hi, nice to meet you," she said.

"Hi, Cary. Likewise." Marci held Cary's handshake for a few seconds as she gazed into Cary's eyes. Cary's puzzled expression melted into a friendly smile.

Kyle and Marci found Rick in the conference room focused on a big-screen computer display. It was filled with code and the whiteboard nearby was covered with math formulas and more code. "G'morning, Rick," Kyle announced as they entered. "I'd like you to meet a friend of mine. Marci."

Rick turned, surprised to find an attractive woman he didn't know standing with Kyle. He stood up from the console and held out his hand. "Nice to meet you, Marci. I'm Rick. What brings you to our office?"

Before she could answer, Kyle said, "She's going to help me with the documents we're getting from the attorneys today."

"Did we get something from FedEx? I didn't see anything come in today."

A chime rang through the office, indicating someone had opened the door at the lobby's main entrance. Kyle peered down the hallway into the lobby. "The FedEx guy is here now."

Rick stared at Kyle with a frown covering his forehead. "Oh. Okay."

How can I explain Marci to Rick? "Marci has been...uh...helping me with some things I haven't mentioned. She knows about our black hole and says there are some speed bumps we're going to hit. I brought her here today to meet you so she can bring both of us up to date on what she thinks we'll be facing."

Rick turned to Marci, looking her up and down, then spoke to Kyle. "What? How does she know about the black hole?"

Marci intercepted the question while Kyle struggled to find words. "Rick, I'm glad to meet you. I know you and Kyle are creating something that can affect all humanity. I've known Kyle all his life and am here to help you avoid some of the pitfalls waiting for you. There are a lot of things that can go wrong. Let's say I can help you look past them, work around them."

Rick glanced at Kyle then returned his gaze to Marci. "Sorry, I don't get it. You said you've known Kyle all his life. I never heard him talk about you. Kyle and I have been friends since middle school."

"No, he wouldn't have talked about me. He's only met me recently, but I've been watching over Kyle for his whole life. For that matter, I've been watching over you, too. You guys together are on the cusp of something that can be used for wondrous advancements or that can produce disastrous results. I'm here to advise you so you get the results you want with your black hole. And with your lives."

"Excuse us for a minute," Rick said. He looked directly at Kyle. "We need to talk." Rick led Kyle to his office and closed the door.

"What the hell's going on? Who's that woman? What is she talking about? She's been watching over us our whole lives? What does that mean? What have you told her about our black hole?"

Kyle put his hands in his lap. "I don't know if there's any way to explain what's going on. I don't understand it myself. Not in the least. It all started with that nightmare I told you about, remember? I killed this woman in that dream and someone almost killed me to get even. When I woke up, I walked into my kitchen and found a man there cooking breakfast. A moment later this woman, Marci, walked through my front door. The same woman I killed in my dream. Since then she's been showing me things I don't understand. She talks about a different way of living. She showed me something she calls my 'ego box.' It's like something out of a sci-fi movie. She knows everything about our black hole."

Rick stared at Kyle. "You been tokin' weed or something? You on drugs? Dream people don't come to life..."

"She did."

“Why haven't you told me about her?" He glared at Kyle.

Kyle rubbed his hand across his face, wondering how he could possibly explain Marci. His first reaction was to scream back at Rick out of his own frustration. Then a feeling of quietude came over him and he remembered he could make a choice to look past conflict. *Let this moment pass. Don't judge what's happening. Let it go.*

He returned Rick's angry glare with a calm voice "My friend, there's a lot I need to tell you. Let's get out of here and go somewhere we can talk. You're not going to believe what I have to say. I have a hard time believing it myself."

Rick and Kyle left the office, passing Marci sitting in the lobby, talking with Cary. "See you guys in a while," Marci said as the door closed behind them.

They drove a half-mile to a restaurant and ordered coffee; it was just after nine o'clock. By eleven o'clock Kyle had recounted everything that had happened since his dream of Marci on the beach. The ego box, the holographic images, Marci's ability to see the future. Their prayer and meditation session, and her instantaneous transformation into a fully dressed businesswoman.

As Rick listened, he sat unconsciously shredding paper napkins into little pieces, then rolling the pieces into a ball. Now, he tossed another ball into his empty water glass, pushed it aside and leaned forward with his elbows on the table. "That's all bullshit. We've got real work to do. I don't care if she can change lead into gold. I can't buy into witchcraft." He grabbed his glass to take a drink but realized it was empty but for the shredded napkin. "Dammit Kyle! I thought we were partners. I'd never drag some stranger into the business without talking with you first."

Rick's loud voice caused patrons at nearby tables to turn and stare. Rick stood up as if to walk away, but instead slapped the table. The smacking noise resonated through the dining room. A

Palm Beach County police officer eating breakfast two tables away approached their table.

"Everything okay here?" he demanded.

Rick sat down. "Yeah. Sorry about that. Just a little disagreement."

"I need you to take it outside if you can't be civil. You're disturbing people."

"Yes sir," Rick said. The officer returned to his table.

Kyle gave Rick a moment to compose himself. "Listen, I don't know what more I can tell you. She knew the legal documents were coming back today and insisted on coming with me. I wish to hell you'd been there to see that ego box filled with living, moving holograms. How she pulled the image of the attorneys out of the box, then turned it inside out. She showed me what they were doing at that moment, and what they'd be doing in a week's time. For God's sake, she can see the future in that damn box."

Rick whispered across the table. "See the *future?* C'mon! That's impossible. I've got a bad feeling about her. Did she drug you? I think you're losing it, man!"

An hour later the two men reached the point where neither had anything more to say, to argue or to debate. They both sat in quiet frustration, avoiding eye contact. Rick looked down at his fourth cup of coffee. It was nearly empty, and cold. Kyle looked off into the distance at nothing in particular.

Finally, Kyle spoke. "That woman, whatever she is, is giving me a new way to see things. She's some kind of teacher. I don't know where it's all going, but I think we need to see what she has to say. Can you deal with that? At least for today?"

Rick let out a long sigh. "I guess I don't have much choice. She's already stuck her head into our affairs."

At that moment, as if orchestrated, the doors to the men's and women's restroom swung open. Marci and Aimer emerged, both striding toward their table. "Hey guys, it's getting close to lunch time. Mind if I join you? My treat," Marci said. "By the way, Rick, I'd like you to meet my friend, Aimer."

Aimer reached his hand out to Rick. Rick looked from Kyle to Marci to Aimer, then slowly extended his. "Hello, Aimer."

Aimer pulled out a chair for Marci, then both sat down. The two scientists sat speechless as Marci motioned to the waitress who cleared the table and, in a moment, returned with lunch menus.

"I guess you guys have hashed this out for a couple of hours now. You're both trying to understand what's happening. I wouldn't expect anything less. Let's save any further discussion until we're back at the office. But for now, why not order lunch? By the way, do either of you follow the Tampa Bay Rays? How about the Miami Heat? The Marlins?"

CHAPTER 10

Clouds

They returned to the office an hour later. Kyle led the way to the conference room, waited for the three to enter, closed the door and sat down.

Aimer spoke to both men. "This meeting has been a long time coming, as you would think of it. Today is a day for answers. It's time to clear up all the mystery you're struggling with so we can get down to work."

Rick spoke in a tightly controlled voice. "Answers? Yeah. You're right it's time for answers. We've been working in secrecy. Our stuff is state of the art. Now you two show up with crazy ideas about ego boxes. Speed bumps. Who are you people? Where'd you come from? What do you want?"

Aimer spoke slowly, almost as if he were addressing a frightened child. "We're the good guys, Rick. We're on your side. We're here to help you, even though you don't realize you need our help. You can think of us as people who care deeply for you and every living soul on the planet. You can think of us as mentors. Advisers. Counselors. Teachers. We're here because you and Kyle are treading on dangerous ground. A slippery slope, you could say. We're here to help you succeed with your project without sliding down that slope."

Rick and Kyle sat motionless, eyes fixed on Aimer.

"We're your team mates," Aimer said. "We're here to smooth the path so you can launch your black hole technology. We can help you over those speed bumps you're going to face. We can give advice and show you why certain paths are the best ones to take."

Aimer continued. "Getting a successful launch of your technology is a huge issue. A lot of people are going to want a piece of it. Some of them, like your government's Doppelganger people, have been working on quantum computing for years. They'll want to apply your system to their own needs. The military will want it, not just here, but in other countries, too.

Not to mention DARPA, the NSA and others. Any of them could maneuver to get hold of your invention. You've thought about the implications that could have."

"Yes, we know all that. That's why we're building in safeguards so the system will only be used for beneficial purposes," Kyle said.

Aimer nodded. "I understand. However, licensing agreements don't *guarantee* it won't be used to do harm. Agreements only establish penalties. You cannot be absolutely certain a legal document will force compliance with the terms it lays out. You'll need something more."

Rick sat listening, flicking a ball point pen open and closed every five seconds or so.

Marci picked up the conversation. "Aimer is right. Politicians will want to use your tech to find more effective ways to get elected, to get new laws passed. To exploit the political system. International politics and economics could take on a whole new face. Once the economists get hold of it, and depending on how they misuse it, there's a good chance the Euro could go belly up. The U.S. dollar, already in a precarious spot, could lose its position as the world's reserve currency.

"Now many of these things I'm talking about are on a certain trajectory. Even without your black hole tech, changes are taking place in the world—wars, uprisings, economic failures, dangerous viruses, crime. Those are nothing more than the natural unfolding of this apparent reality you believe you live in. This hell. We've been telling Kyle it's a dream, an illusion. Even this discussion we're having today is another part of that dream. *But...*"

Marci paused for a full five seconds as she looked from one man to the other. "*But*, you've got to listen to what I'm about to say. If you handle the black hole correctly, it can bring an end to this absurd dream, replacing it with a life of joy, peace and bliss for all humanity that you can't conceive. There are simply no words sufficient to express it."

"That's why we're here, gentlemen," Aimer said. "We're here to show you how you can save humanity centuries of searching, of enduring misery, pain, wars and ultimately finding only worry, fear and finally sickness and death as the payoff. Each person, and mankind collectively, can *choose* a different way of living. Without your black hole it will take thousands of years for that choice to be made. You are the two men who can cut that misery short. Who can lovingly set the world on a new path. We're here to help you snuff out the candle that's burning now and replace it with far brighter light that brings humanity to the place it was willed to be in the beginning."

The four sat in silence for a moment.

Rick spoke first. "Okay. Okay." He seemed to be searching for the words to express his burning question. "That's a wild picture, but I still don't know who you are. Who are you?"

"We're teachers, Rick," Marci said. "We come from another plane. You're a physicist, right?"

"Yeah..."

"Then you know about the work underway to connect the science of the cosmos, the very big, with the science of quantum mechanics, the very small. Right?"

Rick nodded. "Sure. Relativity and quantum mechanics don't play so well together. Everyone's looking for the unified Theory of Everything, the TOE, the M-theory that ties everything together."

"Well," Marci continued, "Then you know that cosmologists looking at the makeup of the universe have found that only about five percent of it is made of ordinary matter. According to your scientists, the other ninety-five percent is made of dark matter and dark energy. Did you ever consider that dark matter and energy come from a place and are made of something no scientist has yet to imagine?

"All that so-called dark stuff isn't *dark* at all. It's Real; you just can't see it yet. It's what God created when he extended His own Love to create All That Is. It's *Love.* I am that. Aimer is that. So are you." Marci smiled at them, her eyes shining. "Relax now and just *be*. I'll show you."

An intangible cloud of color descended on the four and filled the conference room. It cavorted across the ceiling, walls and floor and covered each person with all the colors of the spectrum, and more colors human eyes had never seen. The colors touched each person's skin and permeated into each body. The colors were insubstantial, airy and ineffable. They carried a sensation of Love beyond anything Rick and Kyle had ever experienced. It surpassed any part of their human experience. It replaced every emotion, thought or feeling either of them had ever had about love. It bathed and enfolded them. It brought forth a vision, an image, of a gigantic "Sonship"—billions of people, billions of souls—all united in that wondrous cloud of Love. It offered the sense of an entire planet laying down the issues that separated people from one another; it connected all humanity into one indivisible creation.

"Aimer and I are *that*," Marci said. "We're the energy of Love, although 'energy' is too small a term to describe us, or you, for that matter. It's so ironic that scientists use the term '*dark* energy' to define what is actually Love. According to them, it's 'dark' because you can't see it." Marci laughed.

"We're the exact opposite of 'dark'—as you are experiencing right now. We are the Light. Just as you are once you find yourselves outside this dream world. Come join with Aimer and me for a while. Bask in this, which is your birthright. It's the only thing that's Real. Close your body's eyes and let's commune with our Creator for a while."

A heavenly music—the same that Marci had hummed into Kyle's ear and that he'd heard during the dream of the bonfire on the beach—filled the room. It was a joyful symphony with rich overtones and echoes. It brought overwhelming feelings of peace and the most caring love Kyle had ever imagined. Embraced and surrounded in the music, Kyle couldn't help but feel tears of happiness well up. The feeling grew deeper as Marci's words flowed into his mind, mixing with the heavenly music.

"Aimer and I are like your older brothers and sisters. We live in Eternity and we're here to show you how all the Sonship can move from this dream of being individual bodies to the place you find yourself in right now. This is the Right Mind. It's the place you can help everyone reach without waiting thousands of years and enduring all the horrors of this hellish place you call 'reality.' Your quantum computer is only a tiny wrinkle in Eternity, but it has all the presence needed to accelerate a change from an illusory dream to this Right Mind. You and Rick can bring the Sonship with you to this very place."

A knock on the door. Cary entered and took in the scene of four people sitting, eyes closed as if in a trance, with billowing colors flowing through the room. The cloud immediately enveloped her as she fell involuntarily into a chair, overcome with the same irresistible feeling of Love and peace and beauty. She burst into tears of joy.

"Welcome Cary," said Aimer. "Now the team is nearly complete. We've been waiting for you to join us, dear one. Sit with us for a while and know that you are loved beyond measure, beyond anything you could dream or imagine. Be with us, sister."

Aimer gestured with open arms and a large box appeared before them on the conference room table. Transparent, like glass, it shone with a glow that seemed to be violet, white and golden at the same time. It was completely filled with just one endlessly moving holographic image. Aimer reached into the Right Mind box and pulled it out, holding it in his hands. Kyle, Rick and Cary looked in amazement as Aimer somehow laid the image flat onto the table. It held a moving picture of all five sitting in the conference room. It changed gradually into another image of billions of people. The brilliant cloud of colors surrounded all of them.

"This is what you are here to create, my friends," said Aimer. "It's what eZo Systems and you three are about. You're about to change everything. To make it better than it's ever been on this tired, worn-out, dry and dusty planet; this place where starved and thirsty creatures come to die.* We're here to help you create what you see here: people living from their Right Minds, loving and filled with the joy that is the birthright of every person who's ever lived—but sadly, few ever found."

Aimer wore a Buddha-like half-smile. "We are here to teach you how to live in this Love all the time. What we teach may seem overwhelming at times, but you need do nothing except

---

* ACIM OE W-ST341

offer your willingness to do the work that lies ahead. If you're ready to begin, we're here to work with you."

Marci, Aimer, Kyle, Rick and Cary rested in the cloud.

"Make no mistake. What you're feeling now is only a taste of what is yet to come," Aimer reminded them. "Now let's talk while you still have this wonderful perspective on who and what you are."

Cary eventually broke the silence that had lasted...she wasn't sure. It could have been minutes or even hours, for it seemed that time had been suspended. She turned to Aimer. "I've never felt anything like this. I feel so connected to all of you; with *everyone*. Nothing else matters."

Aimer explained. "What you're experiencing is what some have called a Holy Instant. It gives you a glimpse into Eternity and a moment to know the Love that you Are. This state you're in shows you that everything you've ever thought you needed and wanted is unimportant compared to the bliss you're feeling *now*."

Kyle relaxed into the sensation as Aimer continued.

"People cling to things they desire and try to avoid things they fear. Now, you're without desires and without fears. You're in a place of grace that, as Marci said, is your birthright. A place where you know you have already been given all you could ever imagine. Everything. Because there is nothing else one could want."

Marci picked up the conversation. "Here, while you are in this Holy Instant, take a moment to search your mind and find things in your everyday life you cherish. Think of things that bring you joy and comfort and happiness."

Marci paused while the three sat quietly.

"Now, turn your mind to think of your worries. Your regrets. Your fears. Those dark, secret things you would never share with anyone." She gave them a moment.

"All of those—the things you love, those you fear and your shameful secrets—are illusions of your dreaming ego minds. Not one of them is more important than another. *All* of those things, whether you love them, fear them or hate them, are one. They all mean nothing. *Nothing!* None of them are Real."

Marci touched each person on the forehead. "Ask yourself: Are *those* the things you would choose instead of this Holy Instant? This Peace of God?" She paused as the three sat, eyes closed, with the colors swirling around and through them, and with the sweet sounds of heavenly music filling their ears. Then, the music and colors combined and became something else. A heavenly, artistic creation; a thing of consummate beauty; an indescribable combination of color and music become one.

Kyle watched the beauty as it joined with more beauty. He saw kindness, warmth, peace, joy, certainty, grace, and more he couldn't name. They all joined the beauty that had begun as color and music. The creation, rising far beyond anything that could be described, overwhelmed him when he realized the beauty he saw was Love itself.

Kyle noticed he was pure mind. No sensation of having a body. Love washed through him like a waterfall. The world ceased to exist, even as an idea. It was replaced by an experience of pure, joyous Being extending endlessly into Eternity. Eternity, with nothing before it, nothing after it. For it existed outside of time and space. Beyond the world of form and illusion.

Kyle sat, enveloped in profound feelings of peace. It made words as useless as random noises in the night that carry no meaning. The beauty that flowed through him bathed his mind with Love so intense it outshone the sun.

The illusory world of form continued to mark time as they glowed in that wonder. After a while, Marci spoke to draw the eZo people back to their customary state of mind.

"You can bring this beauty with you by keeping the memory of what you've experienced today. It will remind you that you have a choice to make in every moment. You can choose to live in dreams your ego and this world of form give you. Or, you can choose to live with the Peace of God, in a world where duality, pain and fear are replaced by Love. There is no other decision to make."

As Marci spoke, all three opened their eyes. Cary relaxed in her chair as she basked in the afterglow of her experience. She savored and immersed herself in the awareness of everything being exactly, perfectly right, then spoke to Marci. "How can I choose this? What should I *do*?"

"Cary, do you recall what Aimer said earlier? That we're glad you're here because you're part of this team?" Marci asked.

"Yes, but I don't know what that means."

"It means you're here to play a role that will be an invaluable learning experience for all of you. It will show you in no uncertain terms that you don't need to live from your ego minds. You can come to this place of peace whenever you choose, rather than struggling with almost every aspect of life as it unfolds," Marci explained.

"Play a role? What am I supposed to *do*?"

Marci explained. "Choose your Right Mind, Cary. Offer your willingness to live from it. Don't let your ego mind trick you into believing this experience is something outside of you. That it's something you can't find on your own. It's within all of you and you can always choose to be and live in your Right Mind."

Marci turned to speak to the two scientists. "Now Kyle, Rick. Listen to me carefully. You've built your quantum computer. You're at the starting gate. As we've said, you're also on a slippery slope. You heard what I said to Cary: Choose to live from your Right Minds. You *cannot* live from your ego minds if you expect to bring your technology to the world. Remember too, this place of peace is *in* you.

"Now, it is time to leave you for a while," Aimer said. "Marci and I are by your sides to help you undo your ego thinking and find the peace that is yours."

Then, Aimer and Marci and the glowing box were no longer in the room. The three from eZo sat in the glow of Love for an hour, entranced and speechless in stillness. As the cloud of love dissipated, Cary stood and slipped out of the conference room, walking quietly toward her car as if she were still entranced by the experience.

Rick looked at Kyle, his eyes glistening. "I don't know what to say."

"Me either. I never believed in God. Never trusted Him after what happened to my family. Now, I feel like He has touched me."

After a long silence Rick spoke again. "We've got a lot of work to do. See you tomorrow, bro. I got to let this sink in. Figure it out."

Kyle drove home, trying to understand what had become of the life he'd always known. And what might become of it if the promises Marci and Aim[illegible] came to pass. *What will I become?*

CHAPTER 11

Cary

Cary drove to her apartment in a mellow daze, replaying what had just happened. She had knocked on the conference room door to let Kyle and Rick know she was leaving for the day. It was Friday, with the weekend ahead. She couldn't have imagined the scene before her.

She had found Kyle and Rick sitting with their eyes closed as if they'd been hypnotized. That woman, Marci, and her friend, Aimer, had their hands neatly folded in their laps as if in prayer or meditation. The entire room had been charged with colors, music, and something Cary couldn't define. A feeling. An emotion. She had felt herself being drawn into the room and all but fell into a chair next to Kyle. She was overpowered with a sense of loveliness, of warmth and caring all directed into her, filling her. The beauty of it swept over her with so much power that she could do nothing more than break into tears of joy.

What was that? What did Aimer mean when he said I'm part of the team? What team? What am I supposed to do?

As she walked from her car to her apartment building, still feeling the peaceful mood the cloud of love had produced, a grade school boy raced toward her on a bicycle. She scurried out of his path. He swerved, not sure which way to turn to avoid her. The bike's handlebar slammed into her hip. *Ouch! Dammit! That hurts.*

She screamed at his back as he raced away. "Hey! Be careful. You hit me." The remarkable events of the day vanished as she stood there rubbing her hip, staring at the boy as he drove around a corner and rode out of sight.

Cary limped a couple of dozen steps toward her apartment building. She entered, dropped onto the couch and kicked off her shoes. Her hip throbbed. Her CoFone, stashed away in her purse, began to chime.

She hobbled over to retrieve it and saw the Caller ID. It showed the name of an old college roommate she hadn't spoken to for a few years, despite occasionally staying in touch on Facebook. Sandra Todd's face bloomed on her CoFone. "Oh my! Sandra, how *are* you?"

"Hey Cary! Sooo good to see ya again. Let me tell ya. My husband and I? We were looking through our old yearbook last night. When I saw your picture, hey! I thought I oughta give ya a call. Is this a good time? I'd love to catch up and hear what's rockin' your life."

"Sure. Great to hear from you. I just got home from work. I'm not doing anything. Where are you these days?"

"We live in Dallas. How about you?"

"I'm in Jupiter. Florida. Just north of Fort Lauderdale."

"Nice. I wish we had an ocean here. It's so hot all the time." She moved her CoFone and Cary's screen showed Sandra sitting in an overstuffed chair in a lavishly decorated living room. "My husband, Bob...you remember him? Bobby Jensen? He played varsity basketball? We got married four years ago. Yep. Four years now." Her lips pulled into a tight smile, her white teeth sparkling, but the smile didn't reach her eyes. "Then the company transferred us here last year. Bob's a geologist. He works in the energy industry. You know, oil."

"Oh?"

"Yeah. And hey! He just bought me a new SUV. It's a BMW! I needed something bigger and safer to drive because we've got a little boy now. He's two years old. Here, look at my little angel." Sandra turned her CoFone to focus on her son playing on the floor. "He's the love of my life."

"Awww, he's gorgeous. You're so lucky!"

"I know. Everything here is perfect. How about you? Are you married now, too?"

Cary tried to avoid showing any facial expression. "No. Not yet. Still looking for the right man."

"Oh?" The image on Cary's CoFone jiggled as Sandra leaned over and held a cracker out to her son who was crawling across the carpet. "What ever happened to that guy you were with in college?"

"David? We lived together in our senior year, but after graduation he couldn't find a job. He went home to Virginia to live with his parents. I guess we weren't meant to be."

"Oh, sorry to hear that. You seemed happy with him." Sandra's face drifted off Cary's screen. She heard Sandra saying something to her child, then her face reappeared. "Well, that was a long time ago. Do you have a guy now?"

"Not at the moment. After David, I had another relationship that lasted a couple of years, but it didn't work out."

"You're smart, Cary. And pretty. And fun. I can't imagine you having trouble finding a good guy."

"I thought I did find him. A guy named Robby. We were together for three years. We worked at the same company. It was a little awkward, but we had a lot of fun...for a while. He'd come over two or three nights every week. At first we did a lot of things together..."

Sandra interrupted. "Just a second..." Cary could hear her talking to her child again. "I'm sorry. You were saying...?"

"Yes, just that I could see it wasn't going to work out."

Sandra's lips pressed together and she shook her head. "That's too bad. I'm sorry. You shouldn't be havin' all those troubles. But listen. There's plenty of good guys out there. You'll find one. I know it. Just keep a stiff upper lip and keep looking. Mr. Right is waiting for ya."

"Yeah. Well, I'm on a couple of dating sites. Someone will turn up."

The conversation drifted into an awkward silence.

"What kinda work are you in?" Sandra asked. Her child began to cry, then to scream. His tiny voice filled the air with a shrill racket that pierced Cary's ears. "I'm sorry, Cary. Bobby junior here needs some attention. I've got to cut this short. Let's get back in touch, okay?"

"Sure. I'm glad you called. Glad things are working out for you." Cary ended the call. *Oh yeah. Some catching up. Sandra's living the life and I'm stuck here alone.*

As she sat there, the force of her only compulsive habit took control as it did every evening after work, and a couple of times each on Saturday and Sunday. She logged into the first of the two dating websites she used. She looked at the inbox on the first site. It was filled with garbage. One creepy-looking guy had left her a message: That shirt's be-coming on you. If I were on you, I'd be cumming too. She opened another message: You know what I like in a girl? My dick.

Cary winced as she deleted the garbage and closed the dating site. *Idiots! Isn't there a decent man out there somewhere?*

She opened a can of soup, made a sandwich and sat down to watch TV. Just as she turned on the TV her CoFone chimed and Rick's face appeared.

"Cary, sorry to bother you at home, especially after everything that happened today, but I've been thinking. I'd like you to set up the network server with some new permissions. I'm going to start working some late hours."

"Really? Why?"

"I see now that we can't lose time finishing our project. There's too much at stake. I want to streamline things as much as I can."

"Good idea..."

"Yeah, I don't want you driving here in the middle of the night to help me find some file I need. Set it up so you can access the network from your CoFone. That way if I need your help I can call you."

"Okay. That's super thoughtful. I'll get it set up right away."

"Yeah, and there's something else. I'd like to get you started taking care of the network here. There's a network management class starting next week and another one on IT administration. I'd like you to go."

Cary nodded. "Sure!"

Her job at eZo was growing; becoming more exciting. Yet despite her evolving role, Cary's primary thoughts were about the rest of her life as a woman. She worshiped the belief she'd find a man to love her and whom she could love, to give her children and to live happily together. She knew women were having babies almost into their mid-forties, but she didn't want to be a Medicare recipient when her children finally reached college age. She wanted to enjoy her youth with a family.

CHAPTER 12

Muddy Waters

Harmon Hughes assigned Miles Bogan to work on eZo's licensing agreements, Bogan worked for almost two weeks after their meeting in Florida. He began with reviews of prior high tech licensing deals he thought might be adaptable to eZo's black hole. Yet Bogan struggled. Not only with the intricacies of the task at hand; but with his fear of losing his million dollar investment.

How could this technology be licensed only for applications that would benefit mankind? There was no precedent for such a limitation. Licensing agreements are legal documents. Trying to include language that restricted the use of the technology for only certain purposes was nonsensical. "The good of mankind" simply didn't translate into legal terminology.

Miles Bogan took the elevator up to the penthouse suite where the partners had their offices. He walked down the mahogany-paneled hall to Harmon Hughes' office.

"Harmon, thanks for seeing me. I've got to talk with you about eZo Systems."

Hughes nodded and closed the file he'd been reading. "How are you coming on that?"

"I've looked at dozens of licensing agreements to see if we can use any of them as a model for the eZo agreement. I can't find anything that gives me a clue for excluding uses that don't benefit humanity. The payment scheme they outlined is problematic too, but that's not why I wanted to talk with you."

"Then what is it?"

"When we were sitting in their conference room they explained how their system worked. They put some diagrams up on the whiteboard. Remember that?"

"Yes..."

"Did you notice the Client Interface they drew? Dr. Huggins said it's the workhorse; it's the component that goes inside optical amplifiers across the whole Internet. He said it's the device that entangles photons to make qubits that enable quantum computing. Do you recall?"

"Yes, I remember."

"Good. Because here's what got me worried. It's been bothering me ever since we visited with them. When Huggins drew that Client Interface on the whiteboard he labeled it "Zigma Client Interface." Zigma Corporation is one of our firm's clients."

"What are you saying?"

"I'm concerned that eZo might be using something from another of our clients. I don't know if they are, but why would they write Zigma's name on the board? It makes me wonder what their connection with Zigma is."

"That does sound strange. Have you talked to eZo about that? Asked any questions?"

Bogan prepared to tell the lie he'd practiced for the last two days. "Yes. I put a call into Dr. Williams. I asked him if he'd had any contact with Zigma. He said 'no.' When I asked him about the Client Interface he said he couldn't discuss it over the phone. I pressed him a little further and he pushed back on me. He asked me how the licensing agreements were coming along. He wouldn't talk about the Client Interface. I tried to turn the conversation back to it, but Williams got aggressive. The way the call went made me suspicious. Can I tell you what I think might be happening?"

"Of course."

"I think there's a chance eZo has pirated something from Zigma. Some kind of technology. Maybe something patented."

"Do you have any proof of that? Anything Dr. Williams said that suggests eZo has done that?"

"Proof? No, but Williams was evasive as hell on the call." Bogan rapped his knuckles on Hughes' desk. "As soon as I mentioned Zigma, he clammed up. Didn't want to talk any more. Like I said, he got aggressive, demanding to know why I was asking about Zigma. We need to look into this. Making phone calls to Williams isn't going to give us the truth. We need to put an investigator on the job to uncover what's really going on."

"That seems a bit extreme, Miles. Why would we do that?"

"Because we don't want the firm to be embarrassed if we find that one of our clients is stealing intellectual property from another client. How would we ever explain that? This whole engagement with eZo Systems is too sketchy."

Hughes got up from his desk and went to the window of his corner office overlooking San Francisco Bay. He stood silently for a full minute, gazing outside.

Bogan watched Hughes struggle with the damage eZo could bring to the firm. Hughes' rise to a full partner had only taken place less than six months ago, while Bogan had served as an underling for much of the last thirty years. He had failed the bar exam in California three times and only managed to finally pass the bar by taking the test in Arkansas. His employment at the firm had started as a law clerk. It had taken him years to work himself into a position of trust, a position where he was given cases to handle on his own. Hughes, on the other hand, had a great deal to lose if this exciting, new client turned out to be a patent thief.

"I'm not entirely comfortable with assigning a PI to investigate," Hughes said, "but I can't expose the firm to risking that kind of a scandal. Word would get out and our competitors would have a field day. So, go ahead and do it. I'll talk to the other partners and let them know of your concerns" He turned away from the window and took his seat again. "I hope you're wrong about this, Miles. Thanks for bringing it to my attention. Keep me posted on every step you take. Get to the bottom of it as fast as you can. You can use Paul Glazer. He's the best investigator we have. Have him find out what's happening."

"I'll get on it today. Thanks, Harmon."

CHAPTER 13

Patent Thieves

Bogan returned to his office and asked his administrative assistant, Kathy, to call Paul Glazer.

"Hello Paul. Miles Bogan here. I need to talk with you about a project. Can you meet me this afternoon for about thirty minutes?"

Glazer agreed to drop by later that day, and at 3:30 he tapped on Kathy's office cubicle. "Hello sunshine!" Glazer sang out. Standing just over six feet tall with broad shoulders, a shock of sandy blond hair and a friendly smile, he reached out to meet Kathy's handshake.

"Miles asked to see me. Is he available?"

"Yes, he's expecting you." Kathy walked Glazer to Miles Bogan's office. The men exchanged greetings as she closed his office door.

Bogan recounted the discussion he'd had with Hughes. "It's a possible patent infringement," he summed up. "I don't know much more, but I'd like you to go down to West Palm Beach and look into this for me. At this point the job is simple. We need to know if eZo is playing by the rules. Here's a file of Zigma's patents. I looked up eZo Systems; their address and phone number are in the file too. I'll have Kathy book you a flight, a car and a hotel. How long do you think it'll take to wrap this up?" Bogan asked.

"I don't know. Maybe a few weeks. It won't take long to get the basics on the company and its people. Getting hard data may take a while. I'll send you reports by FedEx," Glazer replied.

Bogan buzzed his assistant and asked her to setup accommodations and a flight to leave the next day.

"This is good timing," Glazer said. "I was planning to go to Florida next month, so this works great."

"How so?"

"I'm tired of dealing with California. I lived in Florida until I was fifteen. I'm ready to move back."

"No problem. I suppose you'll always have work with the firm no matter where you live. But get busy on this eZo situation right away. We need answers."

"Will do."

The next morning Glazer settled into his first-class seat. The non-stop flight would give him plenty of time to tap into the plane's Wi-Fi to do some preliminary research.

A web search turned up almost nothing on eZo Systems. They didn't even have a website. Zigma's site, on the other hand, had a reasonable summary of their research and development work as well as links to the investment group that had funded them. If it turned out eZo had stolen Zigma's intellectual property or infringed their patents, they'd go after eZo like a coven of banshees.

After an hour and a cup of coffee, Glazer put away his CoFone. There was nothing significant to discover about eZo through ordinary web searches. For a minute, he considered logging into the restricted IRB and TLO databases. Both allowed private investigators to identify businesses, their assets, their employees and employees' relatives, officers and owners. The IRB database contained billions of records available only to professional private investigators. The Feds regulated access to both databases to ensure that even licensed investigators could not use the data except for legally permissible purposes. The TLO database held trillions of records and was used primarily by law enforcement officials. However, realizing that public Wi-Fi on the aircraft wasn't secure, Glazer decided to find a private location where he could set up secure VPN access to those data repositories.

Glazer knew that patent trolls—people who endlessly searched the U.S. and international patent databases—usually had financial motives. Often a company would search for patents that infringed on a patent the company already owned, then would go to court to enforce its ownership of that intellectual property and win a financial settlement from the infringing company. Many times though, the patent databases were simply hunting grounds for entities seeking a solution to a research and development problem. Sometimes the solution involved software an infringer could bury deep inside a silicon chip or hide among thousands of lines of programming code that only experts could uncover. The number of patent related lawsuits had skyrocketed in recent years, from around 500 a year at the turn of the century to well over 10,000 this year. Patent trolls, sometimes called "serial infringers," were a persistent problem.

Glazer thought about how he'd approach this job. First, he'd settle in and get some time with the databases to learn what he could about the people at eZo. Then, one way or another, he'd find a way to surveil the company; to infiltrate it and discover whether Zigma's patent had been stolen.

Glazer had done investigative work in several prior patent infringement cases. None of them had been easy. Each time the legitimate patent holder had refused to file a lawsuit until they had definitive proof of theft.

A flight attendant stopped by with trays of lunch. Paul turned his attention to his meal, then put in ear buds and listened to a long, dreamy piece until he fell asleep. In that twilight moment between wakefulness and true sleep, phantom remembrances involving a young college girl flitted ominously through his mind, as they had over many years.

The plane flew eastward into darkening skies where the local time was past eight o'clock. Three dings awakened Paul as the aircraft made its approach into the Palm Beach International airport, touching down five minutes ahead of schedule. He gathered his belongings, deplaned, picked up his rental car drove to his hotel.

He'd get started first thing in the morning, wondering if he'd find a couple of Ph.D. patent thieves.

CHAPTER 14

Research

Friday morning. Glazer awoke early and ordered breakfast from room service. He set up his CoFone with its VPN software and ran a quick speed test to see what kind of performance he could get from the hotel's Wi-Fi. Satisfied with the speed and his secure tunneling connection, he logged into the TLO database.

A banner appeared on his screen: FOR LICENSED INVESTIGATOR PURPOSES ONLY.

He found eZo Systems: a Sub-S corporation registered in Florida with two officers: Kyle Williams as President and Fredrick "Rick" Huggins as secretary. A bit of searching revealed only one employee: Cary Thomasson. He found the "potential subject photos" for all three. They appeared to be taken from driver license records.

None of them had negative information. No warrants outstanding, no arrests or criminal history, no sex offender registrations. Prior and current home addresses and driver license information gave Glazer what he needed to find them at their homes if that became necessary. He didn't find voter registration records, pilot licenses or evictions, however Cary Thomasson's report had a list of previous employers.

Glazer logged into the IRB database to confirm what TLO had reported. He found no discrepancies and nothing additional.

He turned his attention to the three people's social media activities. He discovered a link to a scholarly paper Kyle had published during his work as a contractor with Corning. He noticed Cary frequented online dating websites, while Rick Huggins seemed to have no online profile.

Glazer poured the last cup of coffee from the carafe and stared out the window, thinking about how he'd approach these three people. He wanted to get a glimpse at the whiteboard Bogan had described to see if any Zigma notes were still there. He knew the first step in any investigation involved surveillance. The second was a direct approach to talk with suspects and ask questions while gaining their trust. Unlike uniformed police, who didn't need the subject's trust, Glazer had always been most successful uncovering the facts when he'd achieved at least some smattering of credibility with the people under investigation.

He slipped into business casual clothes and drove to the eZo Systems office parking lot. The company's face to the world was a simple leased office in a single-story commercial building that also housed a printing company, a small machine tool sales company and a half-dozen others. Glazer estimated eZo might have a couple thousand square feet of office space. He drove around to the back of the building and found nothing more than a locked fire door, a delivery bay with a roll-up door at each office suite and two dumpsters. He'd come back after dark to look through the dumpsters. If he were incredibly lucky he'd find evidence he could use to speed his investigation. A long shot, but an easy place to begin.

Glazer pulled out of the parking lot and drove a mile to a fast food restaurant. He dialed eZo's number.

"eZo Systems," Cary answered. "How can I help you?"

Glazer put on a deep southern drawl to disguise his voice. "Hello. My name is Victor and I'm with Office Services. We're a janitorial company and we take care of several offices in your area. Are you the person who decides what janitorial company to use?" Glazer asked.

"Yes sir, but we already have a cleaning company and we're happy with them. Thank you for calling."

"I understand, Miss, but I would like to send you some information about our company. We can usually save our clients at least thirty percent. By the way, who is your janitorial company?" Glazer asked.

Miffed but patient, Cary told him.

"Oh, if you're using them we can do even better. Probably save you forty to fifty percent on what you're paying now."

"Well thank you, but we're not interested in changing companies. Have a good day."

Glazer tapped his CoFone and dialed the number of the company she'd mentioned. Their receptionist answered. "Hi. I'm going to be leasing office space here in West Palm and someone at a company in the same office park told me they're using your services. Can you tell me what your rates are?"

"Yes sir. Let me connect you with Mr. Gentry. He's our sales rep. One moment."

"Sam Gentry here. I understand you're looking for janitorial service."

"Yes. My name is John Lanier," Glazer said. "I was talking to someone at eZo Systems and they referred me to your company. They said you do a great job taking care of their office space."

"Yes, I'm glad they gave you our name. What kind of company do you have? How many square feet? How many restrooms?"

"We're a temporary employment agency. We'll have about eighteen hundred square feet. Two restrooms, a reception area, a conference room and several cubicles. We generate a lot of paperwork that's highly confidential. Resumes, salary information. Proprietary information from hiring companies. We need to be sure it's disposed of securely. Do you have a way to do that?"

"You might want to do what other clients with security issues do. They use Maximal Security Services to dispose of all their paperwork. Do you know them?"

"MMS? I've heard of them. Who's using them?

"In that office park? eZo Systems. They use MMS."

Glazer knew them well. MMS was the preeminent disposal company for classified and confidential information. They provided trash cans with padlocks that could only be opened by MMS's own security specialists. Once the trash cans were loaded into their secure trucks they were taken to high-security disposal centers where the contents were shredded and recycled. If a company disposed of their paperwork with Maximal Security Services, there was no legal way anyone could gain access to it.

"I see. Well thank you, Mr. Gentry. Once we get settled into our new office space I'll give you a call." Glazer ended the call.

He'd hoped to find a reason to do some dumpster diving that night, but with MMS in the picture that option was gone.

Glazer drove back to his hotel room. He opened his CoFone and looked at the notes he'd taken from the databases. Cary Thomasson's driver's license picture jumped out at him. *Nicest DL pic I've*
seen in a while. She's a cutie.

He looked at her Facebook page. One picture showed her with another woman in a restaurant. Another, from the waist up wearing a light green top that made her auburn hair just pop. He sat back and paged through a couple more photos, admiring her from different angles. *And she's single!*

He did a quick web search to find popular online dating web sites, hoping to find her smiling face on one of them. On one site at a time, he laboriously created a bogus profile, placing himself in Jupiter, Florida, twenty minutes north of West Palm Beach and a mere five minutes from Cary Thomasson's apartment. Once he'd created his free profile on a given site he was able to browse women in the area. As he scanned endless head shots, and many provocative images that gave him reason to pause and admire, he saw some that bore some resemblance to Cary. The late morning turned to mid-afternoon before he found her. The site showed she had logged in last night. *Bingo.*

He paid for a 30-day membership so he could communicate with her through the service, then studied her profile.

Hello Guys,

I am an intelligent woman, 33, never married, no kids, ISO a responsible and sensitive guy for a long-term relationship. Yes, that means commitment and marriage and a family. I'm looking for a man who is kind, warm, compassionate and non-judgmental. I'd like a guy who's well educated, height/weight proportional and who enjoys the fun of an outgoing, gregarious woman. I love to laugh, I love life and am seeking a partner who can become the "one" in my life ... so I can be the "one" in yours.

Please! If you're looking for a date or anything other than a committed relationship, don't contact me. You'll be wasting your time and mine.

Glazer considered how he'd adjust his profile before contacting her. He revised it to read:

I'm 35, six feet tall, blond hair, blue eyes. I'm a caring, considerate man. An optimist. I'd like to raise a family, live here in Florida and enjoy life together with an intelligent woman who enjoys the outdoors, movies, concerts and good food. I like to cook (mostly veggies and seafood) and try to keep up a regular schedule of working out. If there's something about me you'd like to know, ping me here anytime. I look forward to meeting you!

Glazer re-read his profile, then posted it along with a picture of himself from his personal photo album. It showed him standing in a California forest, a smile and a beam of sunlight shining down through the branches, highlighting his thick blond hair. Satisfied, he sent Cary a note.

Hello Cary, I'd enjoy chatting with you...or better yet, meeting for coffee. If you'd like to begin with a chat online, I'll be available after 7 p.m. today. I hope to hear from you.

Sincerely, Paul

CHAPTER 15

First Date

Cary logged into the second of her two dating websites. It was the one she usually saved for last because it seemed the men there were a better class of people. *It's probably the $109 per month subscription that keeps out the riff raff.*

Her inbox held two messages: Sammy and Paul. She looked at Sammy's picture and read his profile. Poor spelling and grammar. Delete.

Paul's message caught her attention, though. An optimist. Caring. Considerate. Nice looking. She read his polite introduction a few times and opened her text editor to craft a suitable reply. She never took a chance of entering a note into the dating site's entry screen. It was safer to compose the perfect reply offline, then paste it into the window so every word and turn of phrase was just right. In a moment, she'd written her response:

Paul, I enjoyed your note. Can we chat later this evening? I've got a few things to do, but ping me around eight o'clock if that's convenient. I look forward to hearing from you. Peace to you. Cary.

She set her CoFone on the kitchen counter, took a shower, cleaned up the kitchen and got comfortable, waiting for eight o'clock to roll around.

When it rang, she took it to the couch, sat down and opened a chat window. Her heart beat a little faster as she considered this man, Paul, and whether the conversation they were about to have would lead anywhere. Her fingers poised over her keyboard as she sat upright on the couch. She waited for him to start typing.

Paul: Hello Cary. Thanks for answering my note.
Cary: Hi Paul. Welcome. TY for reaching out.

Paul: My pleasure! I like your profile. Thought we might have some things in common.
Cary: Me too. Where are you Paul?
Paul: Jupiter.
Cary: I'm nearby.
Paul: Nice! How should we begin?
Cary: Tell me about you.

Paul tapped away and, with each keystroke, told her he worked for a law firm; he was an almost-vegetarian who liked to swim and work out as often as he could make time. Cary volunteered that she worked at a local company as an office manager; that she liked outdoor activities; that she'd never been married. Their chat, filled with smiley faces and broken sentences, ran on for ten minutes.

Cary paused a minute, wondering if she should stop typing and convert their chat to a voice call. *Seems like a nice enough guy, but I don't want to give him my number. Not yet.*

Paul: You sound like fun. Maybe we could meet for coffee.
Cary: Okay. Starbucks on Indiantown Road? Saturday, tomorrow, 11 a.m.?
Paul: Sounds good. See you there.
Cary: Good night, Paul.

The chat window closed. *Hope he's for real.*

Saturday morning, she applied makeup to give herself a natural look: a touch of blush, eye makeup and a natural shade of lip gloss. She slipped on a fashionable watch and placed a ring on her right hand. She shook her head to fluff up her hair, sprayed a light mist to hold it in place. The hair spray had a mild scent of lavender. She inspected herself from several angles in a full-length mirror. *Yes. All good.*

At the age of thirty-three she had short brunette hair, almost auburn, thanks to L'Oréal. Her face was slightly rounder-than-ideal; she wished it were more finely sculpted and thinner, but was pleased with her trim figure. Too bad my looks don't get me any closer to a committed relationship, she thought. Is it my face?

She pulled into Starbucks at eleven o'clock sharp. Paul was sitting under an umbrella at an outside table and immediately stood up to greet her.

"Hello Cary," He lowered his head in a shallow bow, smiled and shook her hand warmly. "I'm happy to meet you. I'm glad this morning worked for you."

"Hi, Paul." She noticed he held her hand a bit longer than the usual handshake. His hands were strong, suntanned and warm. He wore khaki slacks, loafers and a light blue polo shirt that complemented his blue eyes. "I'm glad to meet you too." She gave his hand a small squeeze.

They sat at an outdoor table under an umbrella. The breeze flowed in and kept the morning comfortable. Paul went inside to order drinks and returned with two tall decafs. Their conversation, at first tentative and cautious on Cary's part, eventually moved to information-gathering. "How long have you lived in Jupiter?" she asked.

"Actually, I live in northern California."

Cary's eyes widened and she all but fell back in her chair. She could almost feel the blood draining from her face and wondered if she looked pale.

"I'm here on business for a while but my job lets me live anywhere I like. I lived in Naples as a kid. I've been planning to come back to Florida for a while now. California is no paradise. You know: traffic, social problems, cost of living. I'm tired of California. It's great to be back. It feels like home. Sun on my shoulders, the ocean minutes away. One that's warm enough to swim in without a wetsuit. And now, meeting you." Paul smiled kindly. A small frown took over his forehead when Cary leaned away from him.

"How long are you going to be here?"

"I don't know. A few weeks on this job. Maybe longer. I hope we can get to know one another."

Cary let the silence build for a moment. She liked what she'd learned about this guy from their chat last night. Yet the news that he was in Florida only temporarily was annoying, making her feel as if she'd been hoodwinked. She glanced around the parking lot, seeing her car a short distance away.

"I enjoyed chatting with you online. You seem like a nice guy, but a long-distance friendship isn't what I had in mind." She considered her purse sitting in the empty chair next to her, not sure whether to pick it up and leave, or to wait and see what he'd say.

"I get that. I'm not into long distance either. I'm going to move here. I wanted to meet someone while I'm here. Someone I can continue seeing once I've moved. When I saw your profile I wanted to get to know you face to face."

Cary's CoFone rang. She excused herself and took the call. Rick's face filled her screen.

"Cary? I've been trying to add a node to the cluster here, but I can't find the ACL file. Do you know where it's stored?"

"Just a second." She logged into the company network and ran a query. "It's in the second rack on node five. Here, I'll send you a link."

"Thanks. Got it."

Cary put her CoFone away, slowly, taking an extra moment to fumble in her purse so she could collect her thoughts. "I appreciate your honesty. It's not often a man will talk to a woman who's looking for a husband. I don't know what to think about you living in California. Wanting to move here, and now finding out you're only here for a short time."

"I'm sorry, Cary. I didn't mean to disappoint you. Confuse everything. I guess we're not getting off on the right foot."

Cary sipped her coffee and found nothing to say as she glanced at him over the edge of her cup.

"Could I make a suggestion?" Paul asked.

"What?"

"We can talk more while we enjoy our coffee. It seems we've got some things in common. If we get to know each other a little, well...who knows what might come along?"

She watched him carefully as he spoke. Watched his body language. He spoke naturally and easily. He sat upright in his chair, looking directly at her as he talked. No red flags. She liked the sound of his voice, deep and resonant. Even the way he said "enjoy *our* coffee" instead of "this coffee." His voice was gentle. His entire focus seemed to be on her and her concerns, without any sign of defending himself or making her feelings seem wrong.

Paul paused, looking up at the high clouds adorning the sky. "I've got an idea. When we finish our coffee, we could head down to Juno Beach and take a little walk before it gets too hot. The wind surfers will be out today. They're always fun to watch. Besides, walking is a good way to start a conversation, don't you think?"

Cary couldn't get over feeling she'd been tricked by this guy; this potential forever man who only planned to be here for a short time. *Walk on the beach?*

She stared across the parking lot at her car again. She thought of the sandals she was wearing. They were made for fashion, not for walking in sand. *I don't know...I guess it wouldn't hurt. Oh, what the hell "*

She turned back to Paul. "Okay. I'll drive."

"Sure."

They finished their coffee and stood to go. "I'm sorry for confusing things, Cary." Paul took a step forward and held his open arms out to her. She stepped into them and they exchanged a light hug. "Lead the way," Paul said.

Cary parked her car at the Juno Beach public parking lot and retrieved a reusable shopping bag from the trunk—the kind green shoppers use to save trees. She and Paul crossed the A1A highway and walked to the sandy beach. It was crowded, but no wind surfers had come out to race across the ocean on this particular Saturday.

Stepping into the sand, they removed their shoes and put them in the shopping bag. Paul slung it over his shoulder as they walked to where water lapped onto the sand. He rolled his pants up to his knees. Cary wore capris that fell just below hers. They stepped into the wet sand at the water's edge as small waves slid around their ankles.

"This is beautiful," Paul said as he surveyed a distant ship on the horizon. Pelicans skimmed the waves against a sky filled with fluffy clouds, brilliant white and always changing against a pure blue sky. "Did you ever spend time watching the clouds unfold and merge together? They're a lot like our lives, you know."

"What do you mean?"

"I think life unfolds around us all the time. Just like the clouds up there. But we're too busy with all the things we think we need. The things we want. Even things we don't want. Despite all that, life keeps unfolding like the clouds. Same with the ocean. It's the same as it was ten thousand years ago. It rolls in and rolls out. That's what I think, anyway." He looked at her, waiting to hear her reply.

"I never thought of life quite like that. Seems to me it's more about getting things done. You know. Getting through college. Getting a job. Settling down. Having a life, having a family."

"Yeah, you're right about that, but when I get out here on a day like today, it touches me a little. But you're right: We've got to take care of business." He paused for a moment as they walked. "Tell me a little more about you. What do you do?"

"I work for a small business in West Palm. A couple of physicists are working on a computer project. I signed on there a few months ago. I take care of the computers. Make coffee. I run the office so the guys can do their work. They've sent me to school to learn more about IT administration. I think in the long run it'll be good for my resume.

“For now, I'm enjoying the job, even if one of the guys has to call me on weekends once in a while. He used to have me drive down to the office at all hours of the night to help him with some IT issue—finding a file or setting up a file system. Now I can do almost everything from my CoFone. I don't miss all those late-night drives down to the office."

They continued talking about their lives, what they believed and what was important to them. "Have you been in any long-term relationships?" Cary asked.

Paul nodded. "Yes. I was together with a wonderful woman for almost three years. It ended about five years ago."

"What happened?"

Paul gazed toward the horizon. "Catherine passed away. Cancer. She was a real fighter, right up to the end."

"I'm sorry, Paul."

"Thanks. We had a great time together. She was a schoolteacher. Elementary school. She loved kids. We made wedding plans, but when she was diagnosed, she put everything on hold. She said she didn't want to leave me a widower."

Cary looked up at him. "I'm so sorry. That must have been horrible for you."

Paul kept his gaze on the horizon. "It was, but there's nothing to do about it now. Things happen and you've got to deal with them." He turned to look at Cary. "She wanted kids. I did too. We talked about how nice it would be to have a boy and a girl." He paused again and smiled at her. "But that's all in the past. What's important is now. So, tell me about you, about your relationships."

Sadness crept up on Cary because Paul had lost so much, suffered so much. She looked away at the waves breaking onto shore. Her feelings toward him softened. She had let her hand bump his a few times as they walked. When he didn't take the hint, she took his hand in hers. She recounted her loves and what had happened with Robby.

"He wasn't a bad guy. We didn't have enough in common. A relationship needs to be solid. Deep. Respectful. It doesn't work if you have to change the other person to make them fit your ideals."

"Yeah. I agree. We can't change anyone but ourselves. Even that can be hard." He squeezed her hand, wanting to inject a little lightheartedness into their conversation and leave the issue of lost loves behind. "Thanks for sharing. Like I said, now is what's important. And right now, I'm having fun being with you." He noticed a tiny bead of sweat breaking out on her forehead. "Are you tired of walking? Should we get off the sand?"

Cary felt the size of his hand in hers. His palm and fingers almost enclosed her entire hand. She felt sweat breaking out on her hand, or maybe it was his, or both. The gentle swing of their arms as they walked felt comfortable. She didn't want to let go. The story of his fiancé's death—she must have been *so* young—touched her. She wondered whether his loss had kept him from finding another woman; and, whether he was still suffering.

Cary squeezed his hand and smiled up at him, determined to shake off her sadness and perhaps any that he still carried as well. "Get off the sand? Tired? No!" She glanced at him with a flirtatious smile on her lips. "I'm certainly not *tired*." She dropped his hand and poked his shoulder. "A woman my age has lots of get up and go. In fact..." Cary took off running and shouted over her shoulder, "I'll race you to the next lifeguard shack."

Paul broke into a jog and caught up to her. "You know the best thing about a race? It's having a worthy competitor."

Cary laughed and picked up her pace, running down the beach a bit faster. Paul kept pace with her. After a hundred yards, they arrived in front of the lifeguard shack, both breathing more deeply.

"Say there Cary, you *are* one of those, aren't you?"

"One *what*?"

"Worthy competitor!" Paul smiled and put his arm around her waist. They began walking back toward their starting point. "Hey, it's getting hot. I'm hungry. How about you? Ready for something to eat?"

Cary looked up at him with a smile. "Sure."

"Super. I know just the place." He took her hand and waved her arm in a big swing, back and forth a couple of times like two kids, then laughed.

They returned to the car. Cary drove up A1A to a little outdoor restaurant that had ceilings mounted on poles, but no walls. Only lush tropical vegetation separated them from the parking lot and the rest of the world on one side, and the beach and ocean on the other. They took a table in a private alcove overlooking the water. The waiter cleared the two extra table settings, leaving them facing one another. They ordered Thai shrimp lettuce wraps for starters and a bottle of Gewürztraminer.

"This is a perfect wine for sitting and sipping," Paul said. They both picked up the finger food appetizer. "The shrimp go well with it, don't they?" he said.

"Yeah. They're a little spicy. A nice pairing."

"You're right." Paul smiled at her. *She's so cute! Tease her a little. Warm things up.* "And that reminds me of something I need to tell you. Something you don't know about me yet. You see, I'm a special kind of expert "

Cary picked up on his flirty attitude. She put her elbow on the table and cradled her chin in her hand. She held her eyes on him, feigning the anticipation men love when they think a woman is hanging on their every word. "Oh my, what could it be?"

Paul ignored her teasing tone of voice. "I'm not only good at pairing wine and food. I'm an expert at analyzing another person's character."

Cary rolled her eyes and laughed. "Really? Who told you *that*?"

"Nobody told me. I just am. I get a feeling about a person and I'm right about ninety-nine percent of the time. Isn't that amazing?" Paul grinned, his eyes sparkling.

She continued sitting with her chin in her hand. She felt the sea breeze wafting through the restaurant, flowing across her face and fluffing her hair. She shook her head gently, mimicking disbelief. "Oh, sure. Amazing. It sounds like what we call women's intuition. Now I wonder where you got *that*?"

"Here. Let me show you. We met each other a few hours ago, right? Well, I've already learned all kinds of things about you. First, you're a good character. You're not going to tell me I'm wrong, are you?"

She smirked. "Of course not, but exactly what makes me a good character? That's a funny way to describe a woman you just met. Can't you be a little more specific?"

"Okay, Ms. Thomasson," he said with mock formality, "the first thing is that you're direct. I equate that with honesty. The second thing is that you're fun to be with. You're quick to laugh. You're playful. You're intelligent. You're pretty. Not only that: You're a fast runner." Paul smiled. "*There*. Now don't you think I have amazing powers?"

"At least you know how to flatter a girl."

Paul swirled his wine around in his glass. "Yes, but the last thing isn't about character at all." He left his words hanging in the air.

"The last thing?"

"Yes. Are you ready for this one?" Paul asked, putting his glass down and ceremoniously wiping his fingers on his napkin. "I like you."

Cary took a sip of wine, taking a moment to decide how she'd respond. The sea breeze faded as if it were holding its breath, waiting along with her. She felt her cheeks warming. *I like this guy, but I can't tell him too much yet.*

"I'm having fun, too. You're a nice man, Paul."

She watched the water for a moment, afraid the audacious idea forming in her mind was too crazy, and wondering if she'd later regret following her impulse. Without taking her chin from the palm of her hand, she raised her eyebrows and smiled at him. "If you were sitting next to me instead of across the table, I'd share something about me that *you* don't know."

Paul moved to the chair next to hers. He turned to face her. "What is it?"

Cary reached out and took Paul's hands. "I'd like to know you better."

Paul raised his hands to Cary's face, cradling it as he stared into her green eyes. His hands fell away as she leaned toward him. Their lips came together. She took in the smell of sunshine on his shirt and his masculine scent. She leaned back in her chair, her eyes still fixed on his.

"That was *nice*," Paul said as he took Cary's hands. So small compared to his. Yet he felt her strength as she squeezed his. "*Very* nice."

The server brought their meals. They worked their way through the main course, talking with an increasing sense of ease about their lives and whatever else came to mind. Cary relaxed into the conversation as they began exposing more of themselves, their thoughts and beliefs. Yet she felt cautious about going too deep. After all, this man had just shown up today and could be back in California in no time.

"You know, I can't quite believe you're planning to move here. What kind of work do you do that you can live anywhere you like?"

"I do research for a law firm. When they need information that's not easy to find, they ask me to dig into it. I can do that without having to live in the Bay area. I can be on a plane to the next job no matter where I live."

"You're sure about moving?"

"Yes. I'm going to check out some real estate while I'm here."

"I have to be honest with you. The reason I'm asking is because I'm afraid of getting involved with you if you aren't going to be here. I like you or we wouldn't be kissing a few hours after we met. I don't want to be disappointed if your job or something else takes you back to California."

"I understand. Thanks for being straight about how you feel. I like that about you. That honesty. Like I said before, I grew up in Naples. I lived there until I was fifteen. Almost half my life. I loved Florida then. Still do. I'm done with California."

"When will you have to fly back?"

Her CoFone rang again. She reached into her purse and pulled it out. Rick again. *Crap! Now what?* "Hi Rick."

"Sorry to bother you."

"What's up?"

"I tried to reset the ACL file with new permissions, but something's not working. Can you give me a hand?"

Cary closed her eyes. *I thought that remote login was a good idea, but now he calls about every little thing.* She logged into the eZo network and found the ACL file. "I see what you're saying, but I can't see anything wrong from here."

"Could you take a few minutes and drive down to the office? It's important," Rick said.

Cary pulled her CoFone away from her ear, frowning. She mouthed a few words silently to Paul, first pointing to her chest, then pointing into the distance: *I probably have to go.*

"Can it wait until Monday?"

"No. We need to get this thing fixed. We're on a tight schedule."

She held the CoFone away from her ear. Her wavy auburn hair fluttered out of place in the breeze. She took a deep breath and let it out. "Okay, Rick. I can be there in an hour." She ended the call.

"I'm sorry. My boss needs me to come to the office. I don't know how long I'll be there."

"I'm sorry, too, but I've had a great time with you."

"Me too. When will you have to go back to California?"

"I don't know yet. The way things are shaping up it'll be at least a few weeks. If I can find time to look at housing and find something I like, the only reason I'll go back is to move my things here." Paul looked at her expectantly. "How about we get together again tomorrow?"

"Sunday?" On one hand, she wanted to get to know Paul. On the other, there was hardly enough time to build a real relationship in a few weeks.

She again noticed his wavy blond hair, his blue eyes. The muscles across his chest stood out under his shirt. He wore a smile on his face and had a look she would call hopeful. *What the hell! He's a decent guy. Go for it! But I don't want to look too easy, too eager.*

"Sunday doesn't work for me. I've got a lot to do tomorrow, but Monday works. How about dinner at my place? I'm a pretty good cook."

"Wonderful. I'll bring the wine."

CHAPTER 16

Unintended Consequences

Glazer drove to his hotel, took a shower and relaxed in front of the TV for an hour. At seven o'clock he turned on his CoFone and composed his first report to Miles Bogan:

Report #1 re: eZo Systems
Used secure databases to gather information on the company.
There are no records of bank loans, angel investment or venture capital funding. It appears the company is funded by its principals.
The company is a Sub-S corporation registered in Florida with three employees: Kyle Williams, President; Fredrick "Rick" Huggins, Secretary and CTO; Cary Thomasson, office manager and IT administrator.
No criminal, sex offender, personal debt issues or other derogatory information reported on any of these people.
The company is housed in a leased office space with about 2,000 square feet. Access is through the front door and through a fire door and loading dock door at the back of the building.
Apparently the two principals sometimes work until midnight or later and through weekends.
I investigated the possibility of retrieving information discarded in the company's trash, but found they are using a secure disposal company to shred their paperwork. I don't anticipate finding anything of value in their dumpsters.
I met their office manager socially and will work with her to see what information she might provide.
More to follow.

Glazer saved the report to a tiny memory card and placed it in a FedEx envelope to be picked up the next morning. He checked out the mini-bar and opened a two-ounce bottle of Dewar's scotch. Then another. He poured them into a glass, neat, and took a sip. It warmed his stomach. He turned off the lights and opened the curtains to let the evening sun fill the room as the clouds and sky turned pink and orange.

Florida. He loved everything about it. And now, Cary Thomasson. He replayed his day with her. *She's fun to be with. Easy to talk to. She's open and honest. Need to spend more time with her.* He'd have to find a way to get her help, somehow, with the Zigma issue.

Glazer thought about taking her out for lunch on a weekday. That would get him into the eZo office through the front door when he picked her up. But it wouldn't give him any opportunity to prowl around. Maybe he'd be able to meet one of the principals. He might be able to parlay a seemingly "chance meeting" into a visit with Kyle Williams or Rick Huggins. Perhaps to talk with them and drop the word "Zigma" to see what kind of reaction it got.

He knew investigations only proceed one step at a time. Most often, very small steps. Getting to know Cary was the first step in the eZo Systems case. All the rest would follow if he did things right.

Glazer strived to keep his investigations on the up and up. Some PI's, especially those working on domestic and divorce cases, did anything they could to collect information. Some would get close to a friend of the person under investigation. With subtlety and trickery, a PI could learn a lot from the friend. Glazer avoided those shadier styles of investigation. At least he tried to. He'd often worked cases where a lie or a sly trick would have given him useful information. But he'd done that only once. That shameful memory reared up and filled his thoughts once again. He reached for another mini-bottle of scotch.

Early in his career he'd worked a case that haunted him. A man suspected his college age son of dealing drugs. He hired Glazer to surveil the boy. Glazer discovered he had an attractive girlfriend. He began to split his surveillance between her and the boy. She was putting herself through community college working part-time as a nude dancer at a local club.

Glazer began visiting the club. In a week's time he'd become a regular, handing out twenty-dollar bills for dances. After each dance she'd sit with him and talk. Glazer was taken with her looks and fantasized about bedding her. One evening Glazer asked her if she knew where he could score some drugs. She waved across the room to her boyfriend sitting at the bar. He joined them and set a time and place to meet the next day so he could make the buy.

Glazer contacted the boy's father, who asked Glazer to keep the rendezvous. Then, unbeknownst to Glazer, the boy's father called the police and alerted them to the meeting. The local media picked up the story; it was the biggest news to hit their small town in months. "Father Has Drug-Dealing Son Arrested."

The story outlived the usual twenty-four-hour news cycle when it came to light the boy's girlfriend was a stripper attending the local community college; and, that she might have been complicit in using or dealing drugs. The publicity ruined her. She lost her job and dropped out of school. Her parents were stunned and embarrassed. Her younger brother and sister, still in high school, were ridiculed and bullied for having a "white trash stripper" sister. News trucks with on-the-scene reporters parked outside their home for a week.

Glazer hated himself for the unintended consequences. He should have found another way. He'd let his hormones get in the way of doing a professional investigation and damned himself for taking the low road. He should have simply surveilled the boy. He blamed himself for the hardships inflicted on the girl, who was never charged and was working as a nude dancer only because her family couldn't afford to pay her college expenses. The family's reputation was ravaged throughout their church-going community. Glazer fought with himself for months, debating whether he wanted to continue doing PI work. For Paul Glazer, being a PI was a profession. Not a license to lie, trick, use or compromise people.

Now, after spending the day with Cary, he was torn once again. He had considered different ways to surveil or make contact with one of the eZo employees. When he saw her picture, tracked her down on Facebook, then found that Cary frequented dating sites, much of his professionalism flew out the window. In his eyes, she was gorgeous; a stunning hottie. He knew, even as he went about setting up profiles on different dating sites, that approaching a suspect from a romantic angle wasn't right. That road contained too many possibilities of harming the woman. Yet something about having that XY chromosome...something about being a man who'd dated around but had yet to find a woman he could settle down with...something most women would agree is a serious character defect...*something* overshadowed his better judgment.

Glazer felt like he was standing on a precipice with a filthy swamp far below. He feared tumbling off the edge. On one hand, he had a job to do. On the other, he wanted to get much closer to Cary.

CHAPTER 17

Sigma

Monday morning following her date with Paul Glazer, Cary drove to the office and found Kyle waiting for her in the lobby. He asked her to join him in the conference room. Kyle took a seat at the head of the table. Rick was seated to his right.

"Cary, we can't pretend we didn't all have a mystical experience with Marci and Aimer here in this room on Friday. They told us we've got something to do together; all three of us. I don't know how it's supposed to work, but if the picture Aimer showed us of that 'Sonship' living in harmony could actually come to pass, it would be beyond incredible."

Kyle paused, noticing how Cary seemed so attentive, so focused on what he was saying. "It's clear to me that we're on to something a lot bigger than we know. Aimer said our work needs to be a team effort. I asked you to join us today because we need to bring you up to speed on what this project is all about. What eZo Systems is about. I don't think we can do what Aimer and Marci have shown us without having you onboard. Rick, would you explain what we're doing?"

"We're designing a quantum super computer. It'll let us analyze all kinds of complex data and advance scientific understanding in almost every field. People will become more innovative. We can improve public safety. Improve energy efficiency. We'll help researchers discover new bio-markers and drug targets. Medical science will develop cures for diseases. Economists will be able to forecast which strategies will bring the greatest wealth to the greatest number of people.

“All wonderful stuff. But, on the downside, people can use this technology to plan wars, political coups and things we the world doesn’t want. That's what Aimer and Marci meant when they told us there are downsides to our technology."

"Does that make sense?" Kyle asked.

"Yeah, but I don't know what to say. I've heard you guys talking about the 'black hole'. I thought it was some kind of

Internet project. I had no idea you've created something that could affect the whole planet! It's a little scary, if you want to know the truth, but we've got Aimer and Marci to help us. Where are they now?"

Kyle rubbed his forehead. "I don't know where they are, or even *what* they are! They show up when it suits them. First they appeared at my condo. Now they're putting in appearances here at the office. I have no way to reach them. They told Rick and me they've been watching over us for our entire lives. I guess they might be our guardian angels. Probably yours too. I don't know what to think."

"Angels?" Rick said.

"Well...yeah. What else would you call them? They said they live throughout Eternity. What does that mean?"

Rick squirmed in his seat. "There's no use trying to figure out who they are. Let it rest. All we know is that they see our project from a different vantage point. Let's get Cary up to speed on parts of the system she doesn't know about."

"Yeah, you're right," Kyle said.

Rick began explaining the quantum computer. He drew a few diagrams on the whiteboard to illustrate how the Internet itself would become its foundation. "There are three main pieces of our technology that make this all work. The real workhorse of the system is the sigma client." Rick added another box to the diagram and labeled it "Σigma."

"Did you say sigma??"

"Yeah."

"Why are you using the Greek letter?" Cary waved her finger in the air, tracing out the Σ-shape.

Kyle grinned at Cary and touched her hand. "Rick's all about making things mysterious and confusing. He's always trying to keep what we're doing cloaked in secrecy. In fact, Rick's the one who came up with the idea of calling our quantum computer 'the black hole in the Internet.'"

Rick ignored Kyle's remark. "Sigma's a letter from the Greek alphabet. In math we use the sigma character to indicate we're adding up something."

"I know that. I took calculus in college," Cary said as she chuckled. "You guys tickle me sometimes."

Rick shook his head and continued. "Anyway, this sigma client is the device that needs to be integrated with the Internet. We call our device a 'sigma' client because it sums up the state of the entangled weak photons. There are thousands of amplifiers all over the world. We need to put a sigma client into each of them. It's the piece that actually entangles those weak photons and makes quantum computing possible."

"All right, I'm with you on the big picture," Cary said as she took notes on her CoFone. "What do I need to know about all this?"

"First of all, remember that you signed an NDA when we hired you," Kyle said. "Everything we're telling you is proprietary. Trade secret. Make sure you encrypt everything you're putting in your CoFone."

Rick continued. "You need to understand the main components of our technology, especially the sigma client. We're about ready to start running more problems through the system. I'll want you to be able to make tweaks to the software as we go along. How's that sound?" Rick asked.

"Complicated. We'd better get our heads together on this. I'll take notes, starting with your diagrams," Cary snapped a picture of the whiteboard on her CoFone.

"Good. Let's get started."

Kyle stood up. "Okay guys, I'll leave you to it. Cary, we both appreciate you. Once this project goes live we've agreed that you're going to be paid well for your work. You're already doing a lot more than your salary warrants. I wish we could pay you more right now, but brighter days are ahead. I'm glad you're on the team."

Kyle saw a smile grow across Cary's face at the news she'd be making more money.

"Wow! What can I say? Thank you! I love working with you guys. I'll do everything I can to help you get this launched."

Kyle left the two to work through the complexities of the sigma client interface. By five o'clock Cary had taken pages of notes on her CoFone. Her head was swimming.

"Rick, I need to digest all this. Can we get together tomorrow and go over some of it again?"

"Sure. Look it over tonight. See you in the morning."

Cary cleared off her desk in the lobby and walked to her car with thoughts of sigma clients and promises of a bright financial future. As she drove home, the day's excitement about her job mixed with her thoughts of cooking dinner for Paul. What a day! Life is great, she thought.

She had laid in supplies on Sunday and done some of the prep work. She planned to serve two large fillets of smoked salmon on a bed of braised kale and baby bok choy. Asparagus tossed with olive oil, cracked pepper and a dash of sea salt grilled for a few minutes would make the side. Paul said he'd bring the wine.

Her doorbell rang at seven o'clock. She opened the door to find Paul smiling at her with a bottle and a bouquet of flowers. "Hi Cary."

Cary set the wine on the table and found a vase for the flowers. "I love the flowers. Thank you!" She looked at him with raised eyebrows. "How'd you get to be such a gentleman?"

"I guess it comes naturally, or maybe I should thank my parents for raising me to appreciate beautiful women." He opened his arms and gave her a warm embrace. "I'm glad to see you."

"Me too, and I've got a lovely dinner planned for us." Cary flashed a mischievous grin. "But I'm a little worried. I'm hoping I didn't throw you a curve ball with dinner. I mean...it's smoked salmon and I have no idea what kind of wine you brought. Do you think it will work with the salmon?"

Paul smiled. "Oh, I get it. You're testing me, aren't you? Well, you've told me what you like to eat, so I took a wild guess that we might have veggies and seafood. So, I brought a Napa Valley Brut. It's bubbly and sweet." He grinned. "Would I sound too glib if I told you I was thinking of you when I picked it out?"

Cary laughed. "Oh, you're so funny. I like you, Paul Glazer, and I see your powers of observation are still working. Now let's see if we can get that magnum open and enjoy a glass of wine before dinner."

The first glass went right to Cary's head. She'd hardly eaten anything since breakfast, having spent the entire day with Rick, skipping a proper lunch. They ate dinner and each had another glass of Brut. By nine o'clock both were feeling good and a bit tipsy.

They sat on the sofa, talking. Talk gradually turned to touching, then kissing. Cary found herself enjoying the sensation of Paul's strong arms wrapped around her as she breathed in his kisses.

She took a deep breath, wondering again if what she was about to do, what she had thought about and fantasized about all day Sunday, was just too risky. She didn't want him to see her as needy. Or too fast. Or too loose. She had worried over her fantasy. Debated with herself. She nuzzled his ear and whispered.

"My mother always told me I should never drive when I'd been drinking. I wouldn't want you to do that either. So I've made a special place for you to stay over if you'd like."

Paul smiled at her. "A special place?"

"Yes. Come with me."

Cary led Paul into her bedroom and pulled down the blankets on her queen bed. "I always sleep on this side, but the other side happens to be empty."

"There you are, being direct and honest again. I like that. Yes. I'd love to share your bed."

"There's a new toothbrush in the bathroom if you'd like to use it." She'd bought it a day earlier as her plans to have Paul spend the night began to take form.

"Thanks." After taking turns in the bathroom Cary found Paul sitting on her bed, waiting for her. She straddled his lap and began unbuttoning his shirt, then threw her arms around him and leaned in for a long, deep kiss.

The flowers, the wine, the romance. A really nice man—a gentleman. Strong, intelligent and good-looking. Cary felt that hoped-for man she'd been idolizing for years was here, right now, kissing her and holding her in his arms. The two rolled into bed and their bodies joined together.

CHAPTER 18

Σigma

Over the next two weeks Cary's job consumed her during working hours. She often worked long into the evening, making it impossible for Paul to gather any further intelligence on eZo Systems. The weekend gave him his only access to her. From Friday night dinner until Sunday evening they began to learn one another's habits, likes, dislikes and idiosyncrasies. Paul settled into the routine.

On a Saturday morning Cary awoke to the smell of coffee brewing. She put on her robe and found Paul in the kitchen.

Cary put her arms around him. "Coffee smells great."

"You smell good, too."

The two ate breakfast, talked and snuggled. Cary's CoFone rang.

"Hi Rick."

"I was wondering if you can come into the office today. I know it's Saturday..."

Cary paused; she had planned to spend the day with Paul. "I've got a lot on my plate here. Do you need me there today?"

"Mmm, not if you're busy, but I made some changes on the sigma interface. Got a minute to get your notes?"

Feeling torn between wanting to be a team player and wanting to spend the day with Paul, she hesitated. "Sure Rick. What is it?"

"Remember the discussion we had about the sigma client?"

"You mean the sigma client hardware itself, or the interface?"

Paul sat discreetly, listening.

"The interface. I found a problem so I changed how it connects to the server. For now, delete your notes on the interface. I'll show you what I found on Monday."

"Okay. Do you want me to delete everything about the sigma client, or just the part about the interface?"

"Just the interface. Thanks. Sorry for bothering you on a Saturday again."

"That's okay." She ended the call.

"Sounds like your boss makes a habit of working on weekends," Paul said. "Was that an emergency?"

"No. We've been having technical discussions. I took a lot of notes on my CoFone. He called to tell me something had changed; some of my notes are wrong. I need to delete them."

"Is that the 'zigma' thing I heard you mention?" Paul asked casually.

"Zigma? No, it's sigma. Sigma with an 's.'" Paul stood behind Cary as she tapped her CoFone. His eyes lit on the snapshot Cary had taken of Rick's whiteboard diagram with the word "Σigma" clearly visible in a couple of places. As Cary scrolled through her documents a page of text with a bold-faced title "Σigma Client Interface" appeared, with the word "sigma" appearing a few times within the text.

Cary tapped at her CoFone and deleted those pages. "There, it's gone. I can't tell you how excited I am about what's going on at work. This job is turning into the best one I could ever imagine. My boss told me I'll be getting a raise once their product launches. Besides that, I'm learning a lot about IT."

"What's the product do? What is it?"

Cary put the CoFone back in her purse. "I can't talk about it. I'm under a non-disclosure. But today is Saturday. I don't have to work. What would you like to do today?"

"How's Miami sound? Lincoln Park Mall is a fun place to go."

They spent the day enjoying the outdoor mall and made a short run over to South Beach where the "beautiful people" congregate.

Glazer returned with Cary to her apartment for another evening of romance. They were becoming ever more comfortable with one another and ever more intimate. Yet tension filled his belly when he pondered what he had learned about eZo's sigma interface, and how he had come to learn it.

Back at his hotel Sunday evening, Glazer composed a report to Bogan.

Report #2 re: eZo Systems

As noted previously, I connected socially with eZo's office manager who also works with their IT systems. I had the opportunity to see notes she had taken on what the company is apparently making; a "Σigma Client Interface." Take note of the Greek letter sigma ("Σ"). I was able to get a clear view of that document. It also had the word "sigma" repeated several times throughout the document.

Her boss, Rick Huggins, called her at home on Saturday and asked her to delete the notes she had saved on her CoFone pertaining to that topic. I speculate her boss did not want evidence of this "Σigma" on a non-secure device outside the office.

I suggest you talk to your IT experts to see if the term "Σigma Client Interface" is meaningful. I've searched for it on the web but don't find anything relevant.

Seeing this document and overhearing a short phone call discussing what the office manager referred to as "sigma" does not indicate any patent scraping has occurred.

Please contact me once you've discussed this with your IT resource people. I'll await your further instructions.

He dropped off a FedEx envelope containing his report on Monday morning, then took the rest of the day to connect with a local real estate agent. On Tuesday, the agent showed him several properties between Jupiter and West Palm Beach.

Bogan received the package on Tuesday. He pushed his glasses up on his nose and read the report. *What's that?* he wondered, looking at the word that strangely began with a Greek letter. He contacted the firm's IT forensics expert and asked her to look into Glazer's findings.

She did numerous inquiries on the Σigma mystery but found nothing useful. Bogan, ever watchful he protected Zigma from danger, sent a short email to Zigma's CEO, Sanjeev Ramajedran.

Sanjeev,

I am contacting you on a matter that troubles me. Based on preliminary information it appears another of our firm's clients, eZo Systems, may have infringed on Zigma's intellectual property. We represent eZo Systems but have assigned a private investigator to check into the matter. We've received only preliminary information, but I thought it best to alert you to our on-going investigation. Please contact me at your earliest convenience.

Bogan's phone rang moments later.

"Hello Miles, this is Sanjeev. I read your email. What's happening?"

"Like I said, the investigation has only been underway a short time. Let me ask you a question. Does the term 'Zigma client interface' mean anything to you?"

Sanjeev answered slowly. "No...it doesn't. Why do you ask?"

Listen closely Sanjeev; you're at risk, Bogan thought to himself as he began to unfurl his plan to save Zigma.

"I'm asking because our private investigator has seen some eZo Systems documentation with the title "Zigma Client Interface." I should also tell you that I spent a day at the eZo office not long ago. I noticed the word 'Zigma' on the whiteboard in their conference room amid a bunch of diagrams. That's what initially raised our concerns."

"What do you think? Is there something I should do?"

"We have a tricky situation here. You're working on long range weather forecasting. So is eZo. Our firm represents both your company and theirs. If our investigator finds any indication of IP theft that leads to litigation, it would create real problems for our firm. I'm trying to do some damage control for the sake of our firm, and I'm also letting you know your IP might be at risk. I wanted you to know we've been looking into the situation."

"Okay Miles, I appreciate the heads-up. I'll put a call into eZo Systems and take the tiger by the tail. No use spending money on investigators and patent litigation if I can talk to them myself. Who's their CEO?"

"You can do as you like, but keep me in the loop on anything you find. The CEO's name is Dr. Kyle Williams. Here's his number."

Bogan ended the call. *Good that Ramajedran decided to take charge. Best to let him work things out. If litigation is down the road, it it'll be Sanjeev's call.*

Ramajedran called his chief software architect into his office as soon as he hung up with Bogan. The discussion revealed nothing about the term 'Zigma client interface.'

Bogan sat quietly in his office, but his mind raced. He'd planted the seeds with Hughes and assumed Hughes had informed the other partners of his concerns about eZo. Now, Ramajedran was taking action. He called Hughes to give him an update.

"That's where things stand, Harmon," he said. "However, I think it's about to get messy with all this Zigma interface business showing up at eZo. Now, with Ramajedran calling Williams directly, this is a good time to cut the cord with eZo."

"What do you have in mind?"

"I've written a letter to terminate our engagement with eZo. It doesn't say anything about IP theft. I'm about to drop it in the FedEx. Effective today eZo is no longer our client. Then if Zigma decides to file suit..."

Hughes finished the sentence: "...it won't hurt us." Hughes paused, and Bogan saw what he thought was a look of relief on Hughes' face. "Thanks, Miles. I'm sorry to lose such a promising client, but it's better that we don't take chances."

"Right," Bogan said, then hung up.

He printed the letter he'd written on letterhead, then read it one final time.

Dear Drs. Williams and Huggins,

We have appreciated the opportunity of working with eZo Systems. However, we are finding great difficulty in creating protection for your work that will restrict the use of your technology to, as you stated, "only applications that benefit all mankind." That stipulation moves the strict licensing process beyond the field of law into philosophy. Courts around the world would be overwhelmed with lawsuits trying to define which uses for your technology are beneficial or non-beneficial.

Because of this issue and others, and with sincere apologies, we have no choice but to decline to do further work with eZo Systems, Inc. Our personal non-disclosure agreements are in effect for perpetuity subject to the terms and conditions therein specified, and we shall certainly honor them in every respect.

As for any billing you might have received, please disregard it. We do not intend to bill for our services to date and I have notified our billing department accordingly. As well, I have notified our accounting department that the remainder of your retainer should be returned to you.

On behalf of our entire firm, we wish you the greatest success with your technology,

Respectfully,

Miles Bogan, Esq.

cc: Harmon Hughes, Esq.

Satisfied with the believable rationale he offered, he gave the letter to his admin assistant, who placed it in the outgoing FedEx stack.

CHAPTER 19

Password

Cary's office phone rang. "Hello, eZo Systems. How can I help you?"

"Hello, I'm calling for Dr. Kyle Williams on behalf of Sanjeev Ramajedran of Zigma Corporation. Will you connect us?" a woman asked.

"One moment please." Cary rang Kyle.

"Zigma Corporation? What?" Kyle spoke with a rising voice, with no idea why one of the companies he had targeted to license eZo's technology would be calling. "Okay, put him through."

"Hello, Dr. Williams? This is Sanjeev Ramajedran of Zigma Corporation. I'm the company's CEO."

"Yes, I know who you are. How can I help you?"

"It's come to my attention your company may be using patented technology that belongs to Zigma. I'd like to talk with you about that."

What? Kyle's heart missed a few beats, but he spoke calmly. "I can assure you we are not. What gives you such an idea?"

"I'm not at liberty to go into details. However, I'd like to ask you about your Zigma client interface. It seems strange that your work uses our company's name."

"What do you know about our client interface?" Kyle controlled his voice carefully. "And by the way, it's not Zigma. It's sigma."

"Sigma? Can you tell me about your *sigma* interface?" Ramajedran stressed the 's' sound.

"No, I'm sorry. Our work is proprietary. State of the art. We've developed everything here from the ground up. There's nothing we're doing that uses any of your intellectual property, or that of anyone else. I'm sorry I can't be of more help. I'm sure you understand the need for confidentiality on projects under development."

"Of course. I hope you don't misunderstand my call. As I said, we got an alert. I called you so we could speak directly. I don't want to think about a lawsuit and what entails."

"It's hard *not* to misunderstand your call, Mr. Ramajedran. You just accused us of stealing your property..."

Ramajedran spoke over his suspect. "I am not accusing you of anything, Dr. Williams. I got an alert that you might be using some of our patented software. I called you to discuss it."

"An alert? What kind of alert?"

"A phone call. An email. It doesn't matter."

"Look. We haven't stolen from anyone. We've read about the work you're doing. In fact, we've followed your work on weather forecasting." *Crap! I shouldn't have said that. He'll think we're stalking him, for God's sake.*

Ramajedran didn't speak for a moment. "You're following our work? What do you mean?"

"We saw some of your early papers on weather forecasting and were impressed. Nothing more."

"You're saying you haven't used our intellectual property?"

"Of course not! Like I said, we've built everything here from the ground up."

"I know this is awkward, Dr. Williams, but I have to ask. Can you tell me a little about the work you're doing with long range weather forecasting? If you've been following us, as you said, you know we're working on the same thing and that we are competitors."

Oh crap! How's he know about our forecasting? Kyle felt the blood rushing to his face as a potent mixture of anger and worry poured through him. "I'm going to tell you again: We have not used your intellectual property. We read most of those early research papers you published, but we're not doing anything even remotely similar to your work. Do you understand?"

"All right, Dr. Williams. Thanks for your time."

"I hope..." Kyle began as Ramajedran ended the call. Kyle shouted. "What the hell was that about? Something's been compromised here."

Rick rushed into Kyle's office at the sound of his shouting. "What's the matter?"

Kyle paced the room. "The CEO of Zigma called. He thinks we stole his technology. He asked me about our sigma client interface, but he called it 'Zigma.' He knows we did something with weather forecasting. How the hell did he know about it? He said he got an alert. That's ridiculous. We don't need this kind of headache, especially from a company on our short list of licensees." Kyle's face was red.

Kyle hit the button to call Ramajedran back. His call was blocked. "Damn, Zigma's set their phone to 'private only.'"

Cary rushed into Kyle's office with a FedEx envelope, torn open, holding a document in her hand. "Kyle, this just came in. It's from the law firm in Palo Alto."

Kyle read the letter from Bogan and fell into his chair, slamming the letter down on his desk. "Oh shit. Everything's going to hell. Here. Read it. It's from our attorneys. They dropped us."

Rick read the letter. "They're dumping us?"

Kyle spat out his words. "This screws up our whole damn schedule. And Zigma? How do they know we have a sigma client interface? Besides the lawyers, we're the only three who ever heard the term, as far as I know. It's the key to everything we're doing."

"How about Aimer and Marci?" Rick asked. "They know everything. They could have leaked something."

"I have no idea. I can't call them. You know they show up when it suits them."

"All right. Let's sit down and work this through. Cary, take a seat," Rick ordered. "We've got two problems. One with the attorneys, another with Zigma. Let's talk about the attorneys. We need a law firm if we're going to bring our black hole to market. The letter says it's about the 'good of mankind' issue. I didn't know how they were going to address it, but as far as I'm concerned we can't go to market without that stipulation."

Kyle's voice steamed. "Of course not, but maybe we need to find another way to say it."

Rick turned to Cary. "I've got an assignment for you. Make it priority one. Get online and find us a law firm that specializes in high tech ventures and intellectual property. Look for those with a strong social responsibility policy. They're the ones most likely to fit our profile. You'll need to make some phone calls. I doubt if you'll find all the info you'll need at their web sites. See if you can get a list of five or six together ASAP."

"Sure. I'll get on it," Cary replied.

"Yeah. See if you can have a list of firms we can talk to by Friday." Rick said.

"Okay," Kyle resumed. "Now let's talk about Zigma. Ramajedran said they got an 'alert.' I have no idea what that means." Kyle pulled a handkerchief from his pocket and wiped away a bead of sweat from his forehead.

"Aimer and Marci told us we're going to hit some speed bumps. This must be one of them. After the experience we had with them in the conference room I can't believe they leaked anything. There's no way we're going to be able to answer that unless they show up again. Let's table Aimer and Marci for the time being. How else could our work have leaked out?"

"We might have been hacked," Rick said. "I'll look at the logs and run a virus scan across the servers and nodes. Cary, have you noticed anything out of the ordinary?"

"No, but I haven't been watching for attacks. Do you want me to look for security holes?"

"No." Kyle said. "I'll check out our systems. I know we've got everything buttoned down damn tight, but not as tight as we once were. Rick and I used to turn off our routers whenever we left the office so there'd be no Internet access. We went dark. We didn't want to take any chance that someone could get into our systems from outside. Maybe we need to start shutting down again."

Rick and Cary looked intently at one another for a long moment, then Rick let out a deep sigh. The room went silent. Kyle looked from one to another and saw Rick's eyes close as he hung his head.

"What's the matter, Rick?"

"Oh God, *I* might be the security breach here."

Kyle's voice rang out. "What?"

"I asked Cary to set up access to our network from her CoFone so I could call her at home for help instead of asking her to drive all the way down here when I'm working late. She's helped me a couple of times, but I didn't think that through."

"Cary, where's your CoFone?" Kyle asked patiently.

"It's in my purse in my desk drawer."

"Has anyone else used it? Can you think of any way a person could have used it without your knowledge?"

Cary thought for a moment. "No! I don't let anyone use it. I keep it with me all the time. I've got a lot of personal stuff on it too. No one uses it."

"Is there a possibility someone could have used it without you knowing?"

"I can't imagine how that could happen. Like I said, I keep it with me all the time, in my purse. I've never lost it or misplaced it or left it laying around."

"Okay. Go get it, would you?"

Cary left the room and returned with her CoFone in hand.

"Show me how you login to eZo."

Cary laid the CoFone on Kyle's desk and both men watched as she opened a secure VPN tunnel, entered her user ID and her password—a sequence of seemingly random numbers and letters: 33aW4t1.

"Does your password have any significance? Something a person who knows you could guess?" Kyle asked.

Cary blushed. "No."

"It's completely random? Or does it stand for something?"

Cary looked away, flustered and embarrassed. She cast her eyes around Kyle's office as if looking for someone to come to her rescue.

"What's wrong Cary?"

"Well, it's an acronym...but it's embarrassing to tell you what it means." She paused again, then exclaimed, "Oh, what the hell! It stands for thirty-three—that's my age—And Waiting For The One." She clipped off each word then looked away, not wanting to meet either man's eyes.

Kyle repeated her explanation to himself. *33 and waiting for the one*. 33aW4t1. "Ohhhhh, okay. I get it." He paused, then smiled at her. "I'm sorry if I embarrassed you. Actually, that's a great password." Kyle turned to Rick as Cary tried to regain her composure. She could feel her face flush with sweat breaking out on her upper lip.

"I doubt Cary's CoFone has been compromised, but let's get rid of the remote access login. Let's start disconnecting from the Internet whenever we leave the building, too."

"Sure. I'll delete my login profile." Cary's fingers flew over her CoFone, dropping her profile into the trash. "I'll take my login credentials off the server too."

A bell chimed throughout the office. Someone had entered through the front door. Cary walked to the lobby.

Paul Glazer stood just inside the door and smiled at her as she came around the corner. "Hi Cary! Are you ready for lunch?"

Cary froze in position. "Oh! Hi Paul. I'm sorry. We've been in a meeting all morning. I totally forgot about our lunch date."

Glazer laughed. "Out of sight, out of mind, huh?"

"No, don't say that! We're up to our ears with some problems and I need to dig in for the rest of the day. Could we have lunch another day? I'm under a deadline to get some things done. Or we could have dinner tonight," she said, just as Rick walked into the lobby.

He ignored Glazer and spoke to Cary. "Excuse me, Cary. Sorry to interrupt. Kyle and I were talking about the law firms. It'd be a good idea to ask the firms you talk with to give you referrals to a couple of their clients. We'll want to talk with them, too. We need the best information we can get about the firm we finally choose."

"No problem."

"Good. Then go ahead and jump on the web to see who you can find. It doesn't matter where they're located. Anywhere in the lower forty-eight is fine." Rick turned and left the lobby.

"Sounds like you've got your hands full," Paul said.

"Yeah. It's been a hell of a day so far."

"You look stressed. I guess I should leave you to your work."

"I feel awful. I forget our lunch date, but I'll be ready for a good dinner. Why don't you come over? I'll find something to whip up. It'll help me unwind."

"Okay, if you're sure, I'll come over at, what? Six o'clock?"

"Let's make it seven. We can kick our shoes off and relax."

"Until seven." Glazer stepped closer to Cary as if to give her a hug, then stopped. Instead, he held out his hand. "All right Ms. Thomasson, thank you. It's been a pleasure visiting with you," he said with mock formality as they shook hands. Cary smiled at him and winked.

"See you later, Mr. Glazer."

Glazer left the office and drove away, while Cary sat down at her desk and began searching for a law firm that could translate eZo's impossible terms and conditions into a set of binding agreements courts worldwide would understand and enforce.

CHAPTER 20

Rewind

That evening, Cary lit a candle and queued up a series of songs by the GuruGanesha Band before dinner. Lilting and sweet, the gentle sounds of her favorite song, "A Thousand Suns," filled the apartment with harmonies and lyrics that never failed to put her into a mellow, open-hearted mood.

They ate dinner, enjoyed a couple of glasses of wine, then carried the dishes to the kitchen.

"You wash and I'll dry," Cary said. "There aren't enough to put in the dish washer."

Paul filled the sink with hot water and soap, then began washing a dinner plate.

"With everything going on at work I'm glad you came over tonight. I love being with you," Cary said.

"Me too. Know what? Today I looked at houses and condos. There are a couple here in Jupiter I like. I want to live near you."

Cary picked up the plate, but handed it back to Paul, pointing to some food he had failed to wash away. He scratched at it with a spoon, scrubbed it, rinsed it again and gave it back to her.

Cary finished drying the first dish, placed it on the counter, then leaned over against Paul to give him a lingering kiss. "I don't know what's happening. People say it's just infatuation at the beginning of a relationship. It's more than that. I think about you constantly and want to be with you. I love who you are. Everything about you."

"I love you, sweetie. I think this trip to Florida was meant to be. It's brought us together." He scrubbed another dinner plate. "That makes me wonder. Do you believe in fate? Or do you think things happen by coincidence?"

"I don't know. I think it's serendipity. But whatever it is, I'm glad we found each other. Is that fate or coincidence?"

Paul Glazer finished washing the remaining dishes and started in on the pots and pans. He stood without answering. She said she loved everything about him. If she only knew what he'd done; how he'd manipulated her. He thought of the young woman and the family whose life he'd ruined years ago by sneaking around rather than doing his professional job.

He cared for Cary in a wholesome, honest way. He cared about her welfare. Again, he damned himself for connecting with her as a man seeking a long-term relationship as a ruse to get inside eZo Systems. Now he was caught in a trap he had set for himself, and Cary could well become another unintended victim.

He washed the pan inside and out, then inside again, scrubbing hard at a piece of food burned onto the bottom. Finally, he rinsed it and handed it to Cary. "No, I don't think it's fate, Cary. I'm sure there are thousands of men who would make a good mate and give you a happy life. I just happened to come along."

Paul cast his eyes at the table and the stove to see if there were any more dishes to be washed while he searched in vain for the best way to explain himself with the least harm. He wondered if he should keep what he'd done a secret never to be disclosed. What would an omniscient advisor tell him to do?

Finding nothing more to wash, he rinsed out the sink, wrung out the dishrag and took a corner of the dish towel from Cary to dry his hands. He stood before her and took her hands in his. Paul took a deep breath and let it out slowly. "Sweetheart, there's something I need to tell you and I don't know how to do it."

She looked at him intently.

"I told you I do research for my law firm. I'm a private investigator. I can't keep carrying this around inside me. I *have* to tell you."

Cary pulled her hands free and took a step away from him. "A private investigator? What do you want to tell me?"

"The law firm sent me here to find out if your bosses have stolen patents from another company."

"Stolen patents? What are you saying?" She blurted her words out.

"Just what I said. That's what brought me to Florida. I was sent here to investigate eZo on a patent infringement matter."

Glazer paused, unable to continue. Cary backed away until her shoulder blades bumped into the refrigerator.

Paul jammed his hands into his pocket and looked at the floor. "It's worse than that. Private investigators need to find a way to get inside a company they're surveilling. I didn't know how I was going to do it until I found you use a couple of dating sites. So, I set up a profile and contacted you. *That* is how we met.

"I hate myself for doing it because I care about you. If I didn't care I wouldn't be telling you *any* of this. I'd play the game to get what the law firm needs. But I *do* care about you. I did from the first day we met, and I can't go on with the pretext I'm doing a job for the firm. You're so much more important to me than the case I was sent here to investigate."

Cary almost stumbled across the kitchen to the counter, saying nothing in response. She poured another glass of wine, emptying the little left in the bottle. She approached Glazer, stopped a foot in front of him and threw it in his face. Her own face was livid, drenched with anger.

"Get out of my apartment! Don't come back. I don't want to see you again. *Ever!*"

"Cary, please. I wouldn't have told you this if I didn't care for you. Please ..."

"Get *out* Paul. Now!"

Glazer gathered his things and left her apartment, closing the door gently. He drove back to his hotel.

Cary felt as if she'd been slapped. A light-headed dizziness descended upon her as her entire world spun crazily out of control. Cary stormed around her apartment looking for some way to work off the crushing hurt and anger she felt. She scrubbed the countertop, cabinets and floor furiously to remove any stains from the wine she'd baptized Glazer with. *Damn him! He played me. It was about snooping around and getting into the company.*

She'd once again failed to find the man to share her life. Worse yet, she'd been used like a toy. *Paul is no better than the others. Little boys who can't find a job. Men who prefer beer and video games to love. Now, this. A man who sneaks up and uses me.*

Cary's doorbell rang. *Oh God, what does he want now? I told him to go away.*

She opened the door to find Marci smiling at her.

"Hi Cary. Tough evening, huh? Can I come in?" Marci let herself into the apartment. Cary stepped away from the door as Marci closed it.

"Cary, you're right on the crest of one the speed bumps I've been telling you guys about. I'm here to help you get over it. Can we sit down?" Marci sat down on the sofa as if she owned it, then patted the cushion next to her, inviting Cary to take a seat. Cary dropped into the seat, wary and confused.

"Cary, I'm here to help you. Tell me what happened tonight."

Cary shouted as she slapped her hand down on the sofa. "Paul told me he used me to get inside my company. That he's working for a law firm to find out if eZo has stolen a patent. I thought he cared for me, but now I see he's been using me. *That's* what happened."

A patient smile crossed Marci's lips. "All right. Now I'm going to show you how to see tonight in a different light. After tonight you are going to learn how to see a *lot* of things differently. As you do, you'll find more peace and happiness in your life. It can all begin with Paul, believe it or not," she said with authority.

Cary gave her a blank, confused stare.

"Life, in fact all of creation, unfolds continuously all around you. Do you remember when Paul talked about clouds? How they're like life because they're always in motion? That's what you've experienced tonight. Some things simply unfolded before you. Paul was sent here to do a job. He chose the wrong way to do it. He told you he chose the wrong way. He's been tormented inside, trying to find a way to break the news to you without hurting you. Believe me, he's hurt other people before and he spent years beating himself up for it. He thinks he's committed a horrible sin or two, the most recent one being the way he introduced himself to you. He feels guilty about it. He's been unrelenting in punishing himself. Paul is fearful and terrified of losing you. What he's done to you, from *your* assessment of it, is nothing more than your own feelings projected onto Paul. Do you know the feelings I'm talking about?" Marci asked.

"You're damn right. And I *know* what he did to me."

"I'm sorry, sister. You *don't* know what he did to you. Instead, you projected your own fears about not ever finding a man and your past experiences with men onto Paul. Paul bared his soul to you, as best he knew how to do, but you didn't catch that. You chose to project your own fears and emotions onto him, blaming him for 'using you.'"

"Yeah, but... Cary began.

"But nothing," Marci interrupted. "Let's take a moment together." Marci walked over and turned on the music. "A Thousand Suns" began playing quietly once again. "Now, sit back and unwind." Marci put her open hand on Cary's forehead for a few seconds and pushed her head back to rest on the sofa. Cary relaxed.

Under Marci's influence, Cary relaxed into the music. She felt herself transported to a quiet place where the events of the evening no longer took front stage. The music caressed her even as a peculiar clarity descended upon her.

"Look at this, Cary." Marci waved her hands before Cary's closed eyelids. A scene appeared that showed an image of a young child Cary immediately recognized as Paul. He'd heard a cheeping-croaking sound and found a snake in his mother's garden with a frog in its mouth, half devoured. Fearless, he picked up the snake and pulled the frog free. The snake slithered off to find another meal. Little Paul carried the frog to a nearby creek and turned it loose.

Another scene. TV remote camera crews parked outside a house in a middle-class neighborhood. Flashes of TV coverage about the college girl exposed as a stripper and possible drug dealer. An image of Paul sitting alone in his darkened living room, crying, with a glass of scotch in his hand and a half-empty bottle on the table.

Now, a scene of Paul and Cary on the beach at Juno. Laughing. Having a foot race. Paul looking lovingly at Cary when she didn't notice his gaze.

"Cary, all of that is life unfolding. There is nothing anyone can do to keep it from unfolding as it will, on its own, but everyone tries to change it. Everyone *projects* their own stuff onto what they see. They reach conclusions about what is. They judge everything. They blame. They find fault. What happened here tonight was hard for you, but *only because you judged it.* You judged Paul. You don't need to do that. In fact, you cannot project and be judgmental if you want to find the kind of relationship and the man you've idolized for so long. So, let's revisit this evening with a new perspective." Marci again placed her palm against Cary's forehead, holding it there for an entire minute. "This is for you, Cary."

Cary, with her eyes closed, saw nothing but darkness. Then, a lighter spot seemed to appear off to the upper right of her closed-eye field of view. She felt herself drawn into it. She focused her attention on the lighter place, that wasn't a place at all, and was drawn into a stillness where only her own breathing was noticeable. In that quiet place of mind, she understood Paul's apologies, the ones she'd dismissed. She understood the guilt and fear he'd struggled with in revealing his untold story of investigating eZo Systems. Then she saw a clear brightness, filled with loving kindness and caring. She somehow knew it represented the loving couple she and Paul could become.

"That light you see; how would you describe it, Cary?"

With eyes still closed, still feeling the rhythm of her breath, Cary spoke barely above a whisper. "It's...lovely...beautiful...it feels like joy."

"It's yours, Cary. It's within you all the time. Remember the experience you had in the conference room with Aimer and me? We told you this state of mind is a Holy Instant, but it can last far longer. When you don't judge and project, you can feel this way all the time. Even as you go about your daily life. It takes learning and practice to live in this place, and I'm here to help you learn how. Tonight, you're getting a crash course."

Cary sat silently.

"As life unfolds it presents you with situations where you can choose to react by judging and projecting, or where you can choose to deal with the lesson from this place in your Right

Mind. Tonight was such a situation. Now that you're here in this Holy Instant, I'm going to *rewind* a bit," Marci said as she suddenly vanished from Cary's apartment.

Cary once again found herself in the kitchen, preparing to dry the dinner dishes as Paul washed them. "A Thousand Suns" was playing.

"It's only been a few weeks since we met, but I love being with you," Cary said.

"Me too. Know what? Today I looked at houses and condos. There are a couple here in Jupiter I like. I want to live near you," Paul said.

Cary picked up the plate, but handed it back to Paul, pointing to some food he had failed to wash away. He scratched at it with a spoon, scrubbed it, rinsed it again and gave it back to her.

Cary finished drying the first dish, placed it on the counter, then leaned over against Paul to give him a lingering kiss. "I don't know what's happening, Paul. People say it's just infatuation at the beginning of a relationship. It's more than that. I think about you constantly and want to be with you. I love who you are. I love everything about you."

"I love you, sweetie. I think this trip to Florida was meant to be. It's brought us together." He scrubbed another dinner plate. "That makes me wonder. Do you believe in fate? Or do you think things happen by coincidence?" Paul asked.

Cary remembered this exact scene with Paul as she lived it once again. Still in her Right Mind, she turned to Paul. "I suppose it might be fate. I'm just happy our relationship is so sweet."

"Cary, I've got to talk with you about our relationship. It's important to me. I've got to tell you something." Paul again explained the pretext he'd used in meeting her, as he seemingly had already done once this evening.

From her quietude, Cary found it impossible to judge what Paul had said or done. "You made a mistake. We all make mistakes when we're not in our Right Minds. You know that I'll have to tell the guys at work what you're doing, but we can work through that. What's important now, Paul...I love you. Do you love me?" Cary asked, snuggling up to him.

Paul's brows furrowed as his eyes squinted with confusion at Cary's easy acceptance of his confession. As she looked up she saw him relax and his look change to one of relief. "Yes, I *do* love you. Deeply and dearly. I am so sorry for what I've done. I hope you can forgive me."

"It's already done. I accept you and I love you. It's time we get some sleep. Let's go spoon together and drift off." Cary led Paul into the bedroom, marveling how Marci had upended the laws of cause and effect and time and space. How she had rewound the entire evening. *Everything happened twice tonight. How can that be?* But even more, she silently thanked Marci for showing her how to let life unfold on its own without fighting it, and for the peace that brought.

The next morning Cary and Paul climbed into her car and began the twenty-minute ride to the eZo office. "You've got to explain to them what you've been doing, Paul. We'll work it out. Don't worry."

Glazer sat in the passenger seat, still angry with himself and feeling guilty for using Cary to infiltrate eZo. Last night she had described what he'd done as "a mistake." *What's that mean? What's Miles Bogan going to say about revealing myself?*

"I've been hired to conduct an investigation. It's no different than dozens of others I've handled," Glazer said, justifying himself.

"Then you should tell them that. There's no shame in doing what you were hired to do. Be up front with them."

Glazer stared out the window as they drove.

"Besides," Cary continued, "Kyle and Rick are bright guys. They won't like to hear you've been investigating the company. They probably won't think much of you, but none of that matters. You were hired to do a job. You went about doing it. That's all."

"I know, but what about you? They're not going to fire you because of me, are they?"

Cary pulled into eZo's parking lot. "I don't think so." They walked into the office together. Cary called Kyle and Rick to her desk in the lobby. "Guys, I'd like you to meet Paul Glazer."

The two looked at Cary, then at Paul. Paul took a deep breath, deciding to take Cary's advice and cut to the chase.

"Hello gentlemen. My name is Paul Glazer. I work for the law firm that apparently has decided not to handle your work any longer. I'm sorry to tell you I'm the person you can blame for that unhappy development."

Kyle spoke first, looking to Cary then to Paul. He crossed his arms across his chest. "Paul Glazer, is it?"

"Yes. I'm a private investigator hired by my law firm to investigate your company and determine if you've used patented intellectual property owned by Zigma Corporation."

"You're the second person I've talked to that's looking for patent theft. I told the CEO at Zigma and I'll tell you, Mr. Glazer. We have not stolen anything. Everything we do here is the product of our own research and our own efforts." Kyle looked at Cary with squinted eyes and a frown of suspicion wrinkling his forehead. "How do you know this person, Cary?"

"We met through an online dating site. Last night he told me he's been hired to investigate the company," she said with no further elaboration.

Rick, standing with clenched fists at his side dove in to the fray, ready to do battle, "You *told* her you're investigating eZo? That sounds like a damn stupid thing to do, Glazer. Sounds to me like you've blown your own cover." He turned to Cary. "Didn't I see this guy in our lobby yesterday talking with you?"

"Yes. Paul came by to pick me up for lunch, that's all."

Rick spoke as he approached a step closer to Glazer, getting into his personal space. "You've screwed up months of work and put our entire project at risk. What the hell did you tell the law firm that they decided to drop us?"

Glazer stood his ground and faced Rick, his arms at his side. "I'm sorry. I'm not at liberty to tell you what I've reported."

Rick glared at him and leaned in until their noses were inches apart. Without turning his head, he shouted to Cary "Get that law firm on the phone. Right *now!* I'm gonna get to the bottom of this."

"It's only five in the morning in California, Rick. They won't be there," Cary replied calmly.

"Oh hell!" Rick stepped back to face Cary. "You signed a non-disclosure agreement when you joined the company. I can't have you associating with this person. He's investigating us. You're a huge security risk. I'd better not find out you've been helping this..." He spat out two words as if they were a foul taste in his mouth. "This 'private investigator'."

Glazer moved to stand beside Cary, who had a strangely calm and collected air about her. She sat in her office chair, swiveled around to face her two bosses. Her forearms rested casually on the armrests.

Glazer spoke. "All right. This is tense. Here's what I can tell you. First, Cary had nothing to do with my investigation. We've become friends since we met. That's all. She hasn't told me anything about your work here. The law firm had its own suspicion you might be using intellectual property from another company. They hired me to find out if that's true."

Paul faced Kyle. "For me, it's no different than hundreds of other investigations I've done. If there's been no patent theft, I'm done with this investigation. Let's cut the drama. Can you show me you haven't used any software that Zigma owns? If so, we'll be done and you can continue your work."

Kyle sighed. "Come with me." All three followed him to the conference room. Kyle took the seat at the head of the table. "Mr. Glazer, we're working on a project we call 'the black hole in the Internet.' You can Google it and you'll find old articles in Scientific American magazine with that name. You'll find an article in Wikipedia with that title. There's even a project that uses Hubble to find black holes in the Internet. It's not the old Hubble space telescope you're probably thinking about, though. It's a software package. We chose the black hole name because it has absolutely *nothing* to do with the work we're doing here. We use it to conceal our state of the art work."

"What are you doing?" Glazer asked.

"I won't tell you. We consider our work beyond top secret. However, I will tell you we worked in a clean room from day one."

"A clean room..."

"Yes. Clean room is a way of doing research and design. It means we built everything based on our own research. Did you ever hear stories about IBM inventing their first PC? It had a chip with software that made the computer boot up. Other companies started building knock-offs of the PC, but they couldn't use the IBM software without risking lawsuits for stealing their code. They had to write their code from scratch. From a clean room. It's where the programmers who wrote software had never studied or seen IBM's code. What we've done is exactly that. Everything we've done is clean. We've never looked at patents. *Any* patents."

Cary sat comfortably in the chair, hands in her lap, as if the discussion were nothing more than a casual conversation. "May I say something, guys?"

All eyes turned to her. "Bringing Paul to the office to tell you he's been investigating the company...well ... I know it's a shock. I want you both to know I haven't told him anything about the project. Whatever Paul has discovered he's done on his own. I signed an NDA with you when you hired me. I don't talk about the company or the work you're doing with anyone." She hesitated for a moment. "Marci paid me a visit at my apartment last night."

Glazer looked at her, confused. He remembered no visitor last night. No one named Marci.

Kyle's eyes widened. "She did?"

"Yes. She showed me how I could look past what I thought had happened to me earlier in the evening when Paul told me he's investigating the company." She avoided Glazer's stare.

"What?"

Cary focused on the core of the lesson Marci had given her.

"Last night Paul told me he was investigating the company. Marci showed me how to look past it without judging him or what he's done or how he's done it. It's just his job. I got into that same mental place—she called it my Right Mind—we all experienced here with Marci and Aimer a few weeks ago. I saw things as they are, without the fear and anger, even though those were my first reactions. I saw some other things too. I saw that you have not stolen anything from anyone. I *know* that with absolute certainty. It's as certain as the sun in the sky."

The three men were silent. Kyle spoke first. "Of course we haven't." He looked at Paul. "What did Marci say to you?"

Glazer squinted in confusion and shook his head slightly. "Nothing. I don't know who Marci is. Cary and I spent the evening together. There were no visitors. No Marci."

"Yes, we spent the evening together, but that was after Marci came by," Cary explained, avoiding an explanation of Marci's mysterious nature and the bizarre experience. She turned in her chair, looking from one man to another.

"Listen guys, I don't know how you can prove to Paul you aren't using someone else's patents, but there's no reason for him to continue looking." She stared directly at Paul. "I *know* these men haven't stolen anything. The best thing you can do is notify your law firm there's been no patent theft. Close the investigation. Let's end this."

Glazer hesitated for a moment, raised his eyes toward the ceiling and breathed a deep sigh. *How can I drop the case? Walk away? Bogan will have my head.* He turned to Cary. "I don't know why you're so sure about that."

"These men are working on something really important. There's a lot happening here. It's all good. They aren't the kind of people who would steal a patent."

Glazer heard her words. He also heard something in her voice, and noticed her posture as she looked at him with a relaxed face; her voice clear and genuine. Comforting. True.

He took a deep breath, then let it out in a sigh. "All right. I'll recommend the firm close the investigation. I'll let them know I haven't found any evidence of infringement." Glazer turned to Rick and Kyle. "Gentlemen, I don't know what else to say."

Rick tossed his head toward the door. "I think the best thing you can say is 'good bye.' Get the hell out of here. We've got work to do."

CHAPTER 21

Infringement

Paul Glazer wrote his final report. He had compromised his investigation. Really screwed up. He didn't have any evidence to prove or to disprove intellectual property theft. Yet Cary's certainty that eZo wasn't guilty of wrongdoing, coupled with his deep feelings for her, led him to write a report he hoped would close the case without ruining his career with the firm. Glazer sent his final report to Bogan.

Report #3—eZo Systems

I have discussed the issue of patent infringement with the principals of eZo Systems and their office manager. I find no indication of intellectual property theft. The company does have a software component they refer to as a "Σigma client interface." It's understandable that one viewing their documentation, as I did, and as you did, could have misconstrued the "Σigma" notation as referring to Zigma. I recommend terminating this investigation.

He saved the report to a memory card and dropped it in the FedEx. He had nothing left to do, so Glazer called his real estate agent. By the end of the day he had put an offer on a house minutes from Cary's apartment, and only a short drive to Juno and Jupiter Inlet beaches. Glazer felt excited at what the future might hold in his new, sunny environment. Yet he worried what Bogan would say about his final report.

Bogan received it the next day. He read the brief note, then read it again. *There's nothing here but Glazer's opinion. He didn't elaborate or provide any details.* Bogan called Glazer.

"Paul, this is Miles. I'll need something more substantial than what you sent in your report. What have you found?"

"This is nothing more than a confusion between Zigma's name and the Greek letter sigma. The notes on the whiteboard that you and Hughes saw used the Greek letter sigma to describe one of the eZo's hardware components. Those two scientists at eZo take great pains to conceal what they're doing. They use strange names to describe their work that have nothing to do with what they're doing. I know, it sounds a little grade-schoolish, but that's what they do. After talking with them face to face I'm certain they have not used Zigma's patents."

"What *proof* do you have? Did you compare any of their work to what's in the Zigma patent filing?"

"No. I'm not qualified to dig into software code. They wouldn't give me access to their work anyway. I can tell you, though, all three employees of eZo, from my professional assessment, are innocent of patent theft."

Damn! I've never seen Glazer so sloppy. "All right. I'll be in touch if anything else surfaces on eZo. Are you coming back to Palo Alto?"

"Not immediately. I put a contract on a house here. I need to come back to move my things but that will be my last trip to California for a while, unless you need me there."

"No. Take care." Bogan ended the call.

Glazer breathed a sigh of relief, picked up his CoFone and began searching for the best price on moving companies to bring his things to Florida.

Bogan called Harmon Hughes. "Harmon, I've got an update on eZo Systems. Glazer sent me a report that says there's no patent infringement with Zigma. He's basing it on his professional judgment. I'll send you a copy so you can read if for yourself. Glazer's report isn't conclusive, as far as I can tell. Would you let me know what you think after you read it?"

"Of course, Miles. I'll get back to you this afternoon."

Bogan set his CoFone to double-encrypt his next call. He closed the door to his office and called Walter Barbins.

"Walter, now's the time to get our Zigma deal back on track."

"Glad you called. I was startin' to worry. Whaddya want me to do?" Barbins asked.

Bogan held his CoFone close to his face so his face would fill the screen. "I want you to call Zigma's CEO and tell him you've learned there's a company in Florida that has stolen Zigma's intellectual property. Tell him it's a clear case of patent infringement. If he asks how you know, tell him your investment group keeps an eye out for companies it's invested in. You don't need to explain anything more than that. Got it?"

"Yeah, okay."

"Then, I want you to tell Zigma your attorney is drafting a lawsuit against eZo Systems. If Ramajedran talks about using our firm in Palo Alto—he might, because I talked to him a couple of days ago—tell him your own personal attorney can move a lot faster and be more aggressive. Leave my name out of it. Make him understand that time is of the essence. If he pushes back for any reason, just take charge and tell him you've got everything under control. Tell him he doesn't need to do anything now, but that you'll keep him posted."

"All right, but Micky Morgan doesn't usually do white collar crime cases. He's spends most of his time with street criminals."

"Don't get weak in the knees, Walter. Morgan's gotta be our man. Once you're done with Zigma's CEO, get on the line with Morgan. Tell him you need him to file a suit against a company that's stealing IP from one of your investment companies. You've got to make him understand."

"I'll need details. Names, dates, background. All that."

"Don't worry. I'll send you the file with everything Morgan needs to draft the law suit. He won't have any problems," Bogan said.

"What happens if we lose?" Barbins demanded.

"Are you saying Morgan can't do this?"

"No, dammit, but we could lose."

"We're not going to lose. We're going to bankrupt eZo Systems. Make them go away."

Ending the call, Barbins walked to his liquor cabinet and gulped down a shot of Blanton's Single Barrel bourbon. He poured another, this one taller with a splash of water and a few ice cubes. He sat his overweight frame in a leather armchair and looked out the window of his home office into his suburban back yard. The lawn crew was running mowers and weed eaters full tilt, but the noise hardly penetrated his double-paned windows or his concrete and stucco home.

He scratched the arm of his chair to attract the cat lying in the hall. It ignored him. *Damn cat! Not worth a crap. Wish she'd taken it with her.* When Barbins' third wife left him, she refused to take the cat with her. The cat was now the only company Barbins had at home, except for the housekeeper who came twice a week. "Come here, cat," he said, scratching the chair arm again. The cat looked at him briefly, then rolled over and faced away from him.

Barbins took another sip of his bourbon, then dialed Sanjeev Ramajedran. He told Zigma's CEO he had certain proof eZo Systems had stolen their intellectual property.

Ramajedran took the news calmly. "Miles Bogan, one of the attorneys that works with us, told me that might be happening. I called the CEO at eZo Systems and I didn't like what I heard. So, you're telling me they've used our IP?" Sanjeev asked.

Barbins took another drink. "Damn right," he bellowed. "Sanjeev, y'all are still in early stages at Zigma. Hell, you won't be profitable for a couple more years until you get that weather forecasting working. Y'all have done important work and patented some of it. I can't have somebody stealing your patent. I told my personal attorney to file a suit against them crooks. We'll nail 'em to the wall and get you a nice settlement, too. You can't afford to have your work swiped out from under your nose. Hell, I can't afford it either. Sit tight for now. I'll handle things here and I'll keep you in the loop."

Barbins explained the suit wouldn't cost Zigma anything out of pocket, and that awards for patent infringement could reach into the millions. Ramajedran agreed to the suit. Barbins ended the call.

He poured another tall drink and returned to his chair, only to find the cat sprawled out on it. He set his drink down, put the cat in his lap and picked up his note pad and ball point pen from the side table. The cat jumped down, digging its claws into his leg as it leapt. Barbins cursed and threw his pen across the room at the cat. "Damn you! Stinkin' animal!" The pen hit the wall as the cat made a hasty retreat from the room. "Worthless goddamn beast."

Bogan went to the window and peered outside at the landscape workers. They all wore wide-brimmed hats with a drop cloth in the back to protect their necks and ears from the brutal Texas sun. He keyed his CoFone and dialed Micky Morgan.

Once Barbins explained the situation, Morgan said, "I don't do that kind of case work."

"It don't matter. I'll send you a file that has everything you're gonna need. We need to get this thing rollin' ASAP. When we go through the discovery phase you'll subpoena their software code and put experts on the stand to see how much they stole. The company I invested in...they got too much at stake here to let this ride. So do I. And when you win this thing, there'll be a fat percentage in it for you. These patent cases run into millions."

CHAPTER 22

Mind Machine

Kyle struggled to find a moment of peace in the solitude of his condo after the events of the day, but peace eluded him.

Everything's falling apart. The law firm drops us. Zigma's thinks we're thieves. Private investigator snooping around. No help from Aimer or Marci. Everything's at risk.

He turned on an OmegaNet news channel to divert his mind from his worries.

112 Children Dead in New Era Cult "Cleansing"
Death Count Tops 3,000 at Hand of ZX Terrorists
Trading Fraud Cripples International Money Markets
Terrorist Violence Projected to Triple by 2040
New Freedom Party Stalls Bill to Expand Death Penalty

He closed his CoFone. *Same old crap. It never changes. I need to get our system up now. Get it working before the world goes to hell.* Kyle sat in his living room, besieged with the stench of eZo's possible failure.

Money won't last past September. We need a licensing agreement. Else, go bankrupt. Everything we've done will be up for grabs. Everything.

The longer he pondered the situation the more it began to feel like death. Death takes everything away. The people you care about. Your wishes and hopes and aspirations. The things you cling to. All the roles you've played your entire life. Death erases the hopes you have for accumulating money, living a happy life, raising a family. Death puts everything into perspective, especially if you know *when* you're going to die. Kyle knew that date for eZo Systems. It was only a few short months away. October, to be exact.

He wondered how they could start marketing their technology before eZo went broke and died. *We've got to go after our target companies. Get a licensing deal before our money runs out.*

He lay in bed worrying over problems, running what-if scenarios through his mind. He got up and paced around his condo. After an hour of rambling thoughts, he realized his thinking wasn't going to give him the answers he needed. He lay down in his bed again and pulled the sheet up around him. Midnight, yet sleep still refused to separate Kyle from his fears and disturbing thoughts. He recalled Marci's words about his Right Mind: It's where you gain true Vision and learn to see what is Real.

That Right Mind teacher. Marci said it could help. What is it? He was relieved to have a new line of thought.

Throughout most of his life, Kyle had only prayed when he was at rock bottom or overcome with fear of what the future might bring. He couldn't believe God was his teacher, but he did know a mysterious teacher gave him a different perspective on what was happening in his life. On the occasions when he'd connected, he'd found bliss, peace and joy. He had dutifully tried to connect each morning and evening as Marci had taught, but the habit had not taken hold. Eventually, he had let the ritual and the importance of those prayer sessions fade.

Now, exhausted with the cacophony of thoughts rolling through his mind, Kyle adjusted the pillow so his head and neck were perfectly cradled in a comfortable position. He adjusted his body, placing his arms at his sides. He began paying attention to his breath.

In, out, in, out.

He noticed a pleasant quietude as he followed his breath. Each time he exhaled, he noticed a quiet space, a moment without thought, where his mind went empty. Likewise, at the maximum point of inhaling he noticed that same state. He adjusted his breathing to pause and extend the time at the top and bottom of each breath. Kyle's mind became immensely quiet at each point. No thoughts. No worries. No concerns. Nothing at all. Silence. He focused even more acutely, allowing any random fragment of thought to drift away, then refocused on his breathing yet again.

A deep breath in...hold it for a moment, maybe for a count of three. Exhale, slowly, through pursed lips, as if he were breathing out through a skinny straw. Then, pause for another count once all the air is expelled. Now, breathe in again. He relaxed into it, enjoying the quiet state at the beginning and end of every breath. As he did, that state extended to include his entire breathing pattern.

After some minutes, Kyle began to *know*, on a level he'd never experienced, that his thoughts were not what they had always seemed to be. He found himself *observing* the random, what-if thoughts his mind generated. Countless little thoughts, ideas, worries, remnants, shreds and particles of thought constantly bubbled up. He watched from a detached point of view as his mind spit out worries and fears and concerns about the fate and the death of eZo Systems.

In those moments of stillness, a strange idea, an understanding, coalesced. He realized his mind was nothing more than a biological machine, no different than his stomach. His stomach, all on its own, and without any instruction, handled the complex chemical and biological processes involved in digesting food. *It's a food-digesting machine. It converts what I eat and drink into energy. It feeds my body and keeps it alive. My mind just a different kind of machine. It's a thought generator. It works all by itself, but it's not who I am. No more than I am my stomach.*

Kyle saw his mind running an insanely complicated process of creating thoughts. *That's its job. It uses neurons, chemicals, electricity. It releases thoughts that run on and on, one after another. How amazing!*

He realized those thoughts were "tools" his mind used to stay connected with his environment. With other people. Tools that helped him avoid danger. And they could generate strong emotions when he put his awareness on them.

He envisioned a constant stream of thought bubbles floating from his mind into his awareness. *What would happen if they never reached my awareness? If I just let them float away?*

As he continued following his breath, he moved deeper into a quiet stillness. He relaxed more profoundly into the role of observing his mind.

Like his stomach with nothing to digest, his mind became silent when he directed his awareness, his true consciousness, away from it. With eyes closed in the darkened room, the truth suddenly dawned on him: *I don't need to pay attention to thoughts that bubble up. Most of it's just noise. It's about the past. Or what might happen in the future. I can choose to ignore all of that. I can find answers to problems without the ideas my mind generates.*

His ego mind bubbled up a warning. *Don't ignore me. I'm the only intelligence you have. I solve all your problems.*

Kyle let the intrusion fade, then returned to his breath and found the stillness again. An image of that weird ego box appeared behind his closed eyes. Marci had said the ego box represented who Kyle *thought* he was. His ego mind dealt with the world around him, with his life. She'd said he could choose another, better way to live. In his Right Mind. By not judging anything that unfolded. By not projecting his thoughts and emotions on people, situations and events. By acknowledging and enjoying the feeling of being honored to watch creation unfold.

The problems and worries Kyle had struggled with all day began to fall away. He felt a kinship with everything and with the constant creation of the universe. *There's nothing I can do to change any of it. Nor should I try to.*

Kyle listened as his Teacher gently insinuated ideas his awareness could understand. *You are loved. You are cared for and watched over. Marci, Aimer and all the people you think you know...you are all extensions of what your Creator Is. Love. When you work from your ego mind you find only fear. When you work from your Right Mind you find only Love. Everything Real is that. Nothing else exists.*

Another stream of ideas and understandings flowed into him.

I know your ego mind and I know how you use it, but I don't believe what it tells you as you always have. It generates the dreams of your seeming life. It's dreaming what you think you are. Remember only this: Love is All That Is. Your Creator and His creations are All That Is. Your Creator extended and shared the Love He Is to create you.

Following his breathing with a pause at the top and bottom of each breath, he *knew* he was created from Love; that incomprehensible Love Aimer and Marci had shown him when the cloud descended upon him weeks ago. He *knew* it was his function to be happy. To know peace. He *knew* he was cared for.

Kyle lay in the glow of these deepest new understandings. He sent a prayer of gratitude toward the Heaven he had seldom believed in. He envisioned his prayer reaching to the highest place where it would arrive as a gift of thanks and Love for the One who had created him of Itself; a gift of gratitude for being honored to see creation unfold from moment to moment. Kyle felt his gift being received by his Creator, and then sung back to him, along with echoes and harmonies that carried answers to the little dilemmas his ego life seemed to be presenting.

Kyle drifted off to sleep and was awakened by the 6 a.m. alarm. He repeated his newly discovered breathing technique for ten minutes, again thanking his Teacher for everything he'd learned and for the unfolding of creation. He sat up, put his feet on the floor and went to the shower. Speaking quietly to himself, he said "Let's see what happens."

He dressed, ate a quick breakfast and drove to the office.

CHAPTER 23

2 + 2 = 4

Cary scrubbed the Internet for law firms that could take over the job of drafting licensing agreements. After much Googling and many phone calls she found five that might be suitable, but only two of them were willing to provide references to existing clients. Her short list grew shorter.

"Kyle, I've only been able to find two law firms for you to talk with."

"I'll start there. Give the first one a call and let me know when we're connected."

Kyle talked to each of them. He took copious notes and then spoke to Rick about both conversations. By the end of the day they settled on the Lumière, Hansen & Dinor firm in Boston.

Over the following week, the two physicists met with the Boston attorneys. They bound them to NDAs and focused their discussion on the critical "good of mankind" issue. The firm went to work and FedEx'd a package of documentation two weeks later.

Kyle opened the envelope, finding a cover letter and a thick stack of documents outlining the details and terms of the licensing agreement.

Dear Drs. Williams and Huggins,

We are pleased to offer the enclosed licensing agreement for your review. I would like to take a moment to explain our approach in developing the agreement. Please phone me to discuss these documents.

signed: Frank Lumière, Esq.

"Frank, we've gone through your documents. There's a lot here. I'm not sure we understand all of it," Kyle said.

Lumière leaned back in his chair. "We've taken a creative approach here. Your other attorneys were right. The 'good of mankind' issue is a philosophical one. At its base, it's about morality."

"Yes...I guess so," Kyle said.

"It definitely is. So, let me give you a little background on the morality issue. The licensing agreement will make more sense once you understand the ideas behind it."

Rick looked at Kyle and shrugged his shoulders. "Okay, go ahead."

"All right. You know philosophers are fond of debate. They've debated the question of how to define morality for centuries. They've searched for a moral code that assures equal treatment of all people. A code that would be true in every situation, just as a math formula is true in every situation. By the seventeenth and eighteenth century the debate had coalesced into two camps.

"One held that reason and intellect could lead to a moral code. The other believed morality should be defined by one's beliefs, sentiments and feelings. However, for morality to be based on that, the code would have to be as diverse as the people holding those beliefs."

Kyle leaned back in his chair. "I'm sorry. How does this connect with the licensing agreements?"

"Give me a minute, okay? You want to create a morality you can build into your licensing agreements. You want some mechanism that defines what's good for everyone, but throughout history, even to this present day, people can't agree on what's moral across all situations, not to mention from one culture to another. Morality can't be pinned down like a math formula. Two plus two equals four, everywhere. Morality isn't so simple. So, we put our best minds on the case. We consulted with leading ethicists and experts outside the firm. We've concluded you need to take the approach our forefathers used in creating the U.S. Constitution."

Kyle and Rick looked at one another. "What?"

"Yes, they enumerated eighteen roles and duties of the Federal government. They established independent branches of government to counterbalance one another. A framework for government. We recommend a similar approach. We've drafted this so you can create a short list of acceptable uses for your computer. A framework that defines how the computer can be used.

"Next, we recommend creating a Board of Review. It will have the power to approve or deny any proposed use for your computer. This Board should include your company's management, as well as ethicists and people who have demonstrated their dedication to the welfare of humanity through their lifetimes of work. The Board will serve as a final authority, evaluating each proposed problem to be solved on a case-by-case basis. Think of the Board as the gatekeepers to your quantum system. They're like a Supreme Court. They make sure every proposed use for your computer falls within the framework we've spelled out."

Kyle leaned toward the screen. "You're saying this Board would keep the licensee from using the computer for trivial things? Like increasing business profits? Optimizing some marketing plan? Designing weapons?"

"Yes, because those uses aren't part of the framework you'll establish. The Board, which your company will head up, is in the driver's seat. You call the shots on how your computer can be used. But—and this is important—you need a Board to analyze and discuss each proposal. They can't be politically motivated. They've got to be independent thinkers. People who have demonstrated their focus on improving the quality of life for everyone."

Rick frowned and exchanged glances with Kyle. "That's a tall order, Frank. Where do we find these people? How do we pay them?"

"We can put you in touch with some of the ethicists we worked with. They could help you get started with the right kind of people." Lumière held up the index finger of his right hand to emphasize a point. "This is going to be quite a process, but it's worth the effort. As for paying the Board, you would pay them from the proceeds of your licensing agreements."

Lumière sipped from a glass of water, then continued.

"Your licensee would have to submit each proposal to the Board and they would be bound by the Board's decision. That way, your technology remains the sole and unique property of eZo Systems. You would control its use."

"That's a lot to take in," Kyle said.

"It is, and there's a little more. Your licensee could object to the Board's denial for a project. They might seek redress in the courts. We've drafted the licensing agreements recognizing that eventuality. We've given you the greatest possible control over the use of your computer." Lumière paused and smiled at the two. "This is an innovative approach. It would be extremely effective." He displayed the key components of the licensing framework on the screen.

ACCEPTABLE USES FOR EZO QUANTUM
COMPUTER TECHNOLOGY

1. The eZo Quantum Computer and its Licensed Technology shall be used only in applications that promote harmony and goodwill for all humanity.
2. All proposed uses for the eZo Quantum Computer are subject to review and pre-approval by the Board of Review, which in its sole determination, has complete authority to grant or deny permission to use the technology in the manner proposed by each licensee.
3. Applications that would benefit one segment of humanity to the disadvantage of another will not be approved by the Board of Review.

Kyle read the list, then nodded at Lumière's face on the screen. "Thank you, Frank. You've done a great job here. Looks like our next step is building that Board of Review. We'll go through the documents and call tomorrow."

"Good. Any time. We're glad to be working with you."

Rick closed the connection. "This time we're on the starting line. For real."

"Yeah, that's what we thought last time," Kyle countered.

CHAPTER 24

Unfolding

A few days later Cary was at her desk when a uniformed officer entered the lobby.

"Hello, Miss. I am here to see Kyle Williams. Is he available?"

Cary looked at his badge then rang Kyle. "There's an officer here who wants to see you."

"Dr. Williams? I am Officer Kramer. I'm here to serve you with this document. Please sign here."

"What's this about?" Kyle's heart rate ramped up.

"I don't know. I'm only here to serve this."

Kyle took the envelope and signed the acknowledgment of service. Kramer tore the signature page from the outside of the envelope and left.

Kyle sat down in Cary's side chair and ripped open the envelope.

"It's a complaint from Zigma's attorney." He read further, flipping page after page of the document. "They've filed a suit with the Federal district court in San Diego. They say we've stolen one of their patents." He called for Rick.

"Rick, Zigma's suing us. They're asking for injunctive relief. It enjoins us from any further development or deployment of our sigma client interface. Stops us dead in our tracks."

"Cary, get our attorney on the phone. Call Frank Lumière."

"Hello Frank, we've just been served an injunction. A lawsuit from Zigma. They claim we've stolen one of their patents," Kyle exclaimed.

"All right. Send me a copy. We'll look into it," Lumière replied. "Don't do anything. Don't talk to Zigma and don't sign anything until you hear from me."

"Going to court will ruin us, Frank. We can't afford any kind of legal battle. What do we do?"

"Don't do anything. I'll be back in touch as soon as I can. For now, sit tight and carry on."

"Yeah, but this is going to wreck our marketing. We were about to contact our target companies."

"I don't know what to tell you until we've seen the complaint. Just sit tight, okay?"

Lumière called back after lunch. He explained that Zigma was filing suit to stop eZo from any efforts to commercialize their sigma client interface. Further, they intended to file discovery motions that would allow the court to pore through eZo's software and design documents, allowing them to uncover Zigma's patented code.

"These guys want to see our code? Zigma won't find any of their patents in our code, so how can they stop us from marketing? Google and all the others are off the table until this thing is settled," Kyle said.

Lumière summarized. "Gentlemen, this is going to be complicated. Zigma's angel investor is filing the suit to protect its investment. You need to tell me everything we can use to defend you. How you designed your software. We'll need records of what you developed and when. Correspondence with your former law firm. I understand you don't want to be forced to disclose your code, but we need to begin now."

Lumière asked permission to record the call, then began a series of questions about the sigma client interface. Kyle and Rick steadfastly supplied answers. They spoke about their clean room methodology and how they'd developed their software.

"Frank, how does this lawsuit work? What happens next?" Kyle asked.

"It starts with a pretrial phase where Zigma will have to explain to the court what patented property has been infringed. The court will have to determine the claims Zigma made in their patent filing. That's followed by a discovery phase in which each party will have to submit their material to the court. The court and its jury will evaluate both submissions and, ultimately, render a judgment.

"The bad news is that the jury is usually a group of non-technical people. We'll have to explain technical terms and concepts to them in a way they'll understand. It's a roll of the dice once you turn it over to the jury. You can expect this to take a year or more. Based on the work that lies ahead we'll need to establish a retainer for our services. We can begin with $10,000 for the preliminary steps. We'll provide you with time and billing details as the case gets underway."

Kyle and Rick looked at one another. Kyle frowned and sighed.

"Hold on a minute," Rick said as he pressed the mute button. "A retainer? For the preliminaries? We can't afford ten grand."

Kyle stared blankly at the speakerphone. "It doesn't matter. We've got to deal with this mess. We can figure things out after the call."

Kyle un-muted the phone. "Okay, sorry for the hold. Do you have any idea how much this will cost?"

"That's hard to say. I hope we can try this case in a year's time; I think that's reasonable. Cost? I can't give you a figure. It depends on too many factors. The biggest issue is how much financial damage Zigma would suffer due to a patent theft. If the court found you guilty and their damages were under a million dollars, your costs would likely be about $650,000. It could run into a few million if their damages were greater. Please understand, I am not giving you a budget. Those numbers are only estimates."

Kyle closed his eyes and shook his head in disbelief. "All right. We'll have to see what we can do, but we can't afford this case. Is there any chance it could be settled out of court?"

"Not sure yet, but I'm going to start by asking the court for a Markman hearing. It's like a mini-trial. The judge interprets the claims Zigma made in their patent filing instead of a jury. Sometimes the judge will push for a settlement based on his or her interpretation. Your costs would be a lot less if the court agrees to a Markman hearing, but you'd have to show the court your sigma interface material so the court can see for itself that there's been no infringement. The court would probably appoint an independent expert to review your code."

"We cannot give up our code, Frank. There's too much at risk if we disclose it. Give us a day to discuss our options. We'll be back in touch as soon as we can." Kyle ended the call.

Rick slammed his hand down on the table. "Shit! We've already spent a bundle getting a licensing agreement from Lumière and his people. There's no way in hell we can come up with that kind of money. We're totally screwed."

Kyle grimaced. "We're burning through about $20,000 a month to pay for the office lease, utilities, Cary's salary and yours and mine."

Rick leaned forward in his chair. "We could sublet the front part of the office and move all our stuff into the warehouse. Moving the computers would be a bitch. We'd have to disassemble everything, move it, rewire the network and put it all back together."

"No. At best, we'd save $3,500 a month. Not enough to make any difference. This lawsuit is too damn big."

"I guess we could move our computers into your garage and work from there. You know. Stop paying the rent and utilities for this place, and let Cary go."

Kyle stared at Rick. "Yeah. Her salary is almost a third of our monthly nut. That would help. Then, if we moved out of the office we'd cut our expenses in half."

Kyle gazed at the wall for a moment, doing mental arithmetic. "Dammit! No. There's no amount of cost cutting we can do that's going to fix this. The suit will take way more than we can come up with. Today is July sixth. We've got enough to keep the company going for about three more months. We can pay our bills until October. That's it. October comes and we'll have to turn off the lights. Despite that, we'd *still* have to keep paying Lumière and his people to litigate the suit."

Rick stared absently across the room and fumed. "So, we're back at square one. What about bankruptcy? If Zigma knew we'd gone bust over this we could close our doors and re-open somewhere else with a new corporation."

"No. It would only be a matter of time until Zigma's people find out. Then this could start all over again. We're in this thing now and we've got to find a way out, but the money to pay for the lawsuit isn't the only problem. Lumière said this could take a year. It doesn't make any difference if we don't have the money for lawyers. We don't have money to last another year, with or without the lawsuit."

A tap on the door; Cary peeked around the door as she opened it half way. "I'm sorry to interrupt. I'm worried and hope you can fill me in on what's happening. Can I come in?"

The two men exchanged glances. Kyle closed his eyes and gave a slight nod. "We're in a tough spot. This lawsuit could ruin the company and we can't see any way to pay the lawyers to fight it out in court. That's what's happening. We've been going over different scenarios, but this damn thing could end up costing millions. We don't have access to that kind of money."

Rick shook his finger at Cary and scowled. "Yeah. We can thank your private eye pal, that bastard Glazer, for all this shit. You might as well start looking for another job. There's no way we're going to be able to keep paying you."

Cary ignored Rick's glare and relaxed in her chair. "I'm sorry about that, Rick. But you know I didn't have a hand in what he was doing. In fact, I convinced him he had to talk with you two and admit everything."

"All right, Rick. That's enough. Cary's not at fault here. Leave her alone. We've got more important things to do than point fingers."

The room went quiet for a moment. Then Cary leaned forward in her chair and fixed her gaze on Kyle.

"I know it might seem crazy at a time like this, but I think there's something we can do. Let's see if we can look past this the way Marci showed me."

Kyle scoffed. "I don't have time to play mind games with this."

"I get that, but there *is* another way to see what's happening. I think we can choose to not judge what's happening. Are you willing to try? I think it might give you the space you need to see this in a different light."

"No! Like I said, I'm not into mind games at the moment," Kyle repeated.

Cary sat quietly, then spoke again after a full minute had passed. "I told you Marci came to my apartment. She taught me something I can't forget. It changed everything for me. The only way to deal with problems like this is to not judge them."

Rick glared at Kyle. "Hey man! That cuts it. I'm outta here." Rick bristled as he left the room and slammed the door behind him.

Kyle sat nonplussed, staring at her. She seemed so relaxed, as if she didn't understand the danger the company was facing. As he looked at her he recalled how he'd felt when he concluded his nighttime meditation. He'd chosen to ignore his mind's bubbling, babbling stream of thoughts constantly roiling up without control. Kyle remembered the outcome of that meditation and the mantra that brought him peace and relaxation as it had filled his quiet mind. A simple mantra, but profound: *Let's see what happens.*

Kyle sighed. "You may be right. Okay, let's give it a few minutes. Nothing to lose."

Cary and Kyle each sat in high-backed office chairs, their heads leaning back to relax. Kyle began his breathing exercise with a pause at each end of each breath, exhaling slowly through that imaginary, skinny straw. In a few moments, his mind quieted and he began to observe the thoughts that bubbled up. Each time "Oh shit" or "We're screwed" interrupted his focus on his breath, he let it bubble off to wherever it chose to go, and returned his awareness to his breath.

His mind quieted. He once again recognized that Creation was simply unfolding as it always does. Nothing more. He saw Zigma's interference for what it was: an effort by another company to protect itself from what it perceived as thieves. He saw the Lumière, Hansen & Dinor law firm doing what lawyers do at the prices lawyers charge for their services.

Cary sat with eyes closed and found the place of gentle silence she'd experienced when Marci touched her forehead that amazing night at her apartment. She remembered she didn't need to judge anything. There was no need for blaming. For stress. Zigma had taken reasonable steps it felt were necessary based on whatever faulty information they had about eZo. They'd made an error, yet that error would cost eZo time and money to correct. So be it. It seemed to be nothing more than a dilemma they'd have to work out.

After a time, Kyle and Cary returned to their normal, waking states.

Cary nodded at Kyle. "I see Zigma made a mistake in filing the suit. I don't know how, but we'll work it out."

"I know. Let's see what happens," Kyle answered.

"See what happens?"

"Yes. I can't explain it, but it seems we're guided in everything we do here. We don't need to go to battle. We're working on this project to benefit the planet. The outcome is in our hands, but even more, it's in much greater hands. That's what I mean when I say 'let's see what happens.' It's not an expression of defeat or lying down in front of the bus. Or hoping and wishing for a happy conclusion. It's an expression of faith that we can allow things to unfold as they will. We can't change what's already happened. We can't change what will happen next by floundering around trying to come up with millions of dollars. We only need to see what happens next, then work with that."

A knock on Kyle's door. Rick walked in with Aimer and Marci.

"Hi guys," Marci said. She smiled and stood behind Kyle's chair, putting her hands on his shoulders. "Seems like someone's been rocking your boat today. You're dealing with it as two savvy people, though. You're right, Cary. This is a dilemma that needs to be solved. Kyle, you're right too. Zigma's trying to protect itself, even though there's nothing for them to fear from eZo."

Aimer continued. "Think about this. Your brains evolved from ancient times to remember fearful things. Rival tribes attacking. A tiger lurking in the bushes. Minds didn't evolve to remember good things. You're hard-wired to remember scary stuff so you can avoid it and stay alive. Now, when you don't have tigers trying to eat you, you take every psychological fear, every 'what-if', and run it up the flagpole as if it were as life-threatening as being eaten alive. That's your ego doing its finest work to make your life miserable."

"Yes, and let me remind you again: When you *project* fear upon a situation, you *perceive* fearful outcomes," Marci added. "You two are making outstanding progress in forgiving yourselves for what your ego minds project on this lawsuit. No one can win a fight against their ego. You can only choose to forgive it by looking past it."

"What are we supposed to do?" Rick asked.

Marci looked at him. "*Do*? Well, you might want to touch up your marketing plans so they're ready when *you're* ready to put Google and the others in play. You might get started on finding people for your Board of Review. This is nothing more than one of the speed bumps I warned you about. Don't judge it. Carry on with organizing your marketing plans until you hear from your attorney." They both disappeared from the room.

Rick stared at the space the two had occupied. "Those two?" he stammered as he waved toward where they had stood. "Do you think they're right? We're supposed to just sit around and wait?"

"I don't think it's about waiting. It's about not using our ego minds to judge what's happening. They're showing us a better way of dealing with problems," Kyle said.

"I agree," Cary said. "We can choose to see things from a different angle." She looked at Kyle. "So, should we start working on the Board of Review? I mean, we ought to keep busy, right?"

"Right, but I need to step away from this for a while. Let's take a break. Cary, why don't you take the rest of the day off. Go relax. Don't worry about looking for another job. Rick, let's get out of the office for a while."

Kyle and Rick drove to a nearby park where they spent the rest of the afternoon walking trails under swaying palm trees, trying to find a bit of sanity in a world that had been increasingly driving them to points beyond desperation.

"I don't know what's going to happen next," Kyle said. "There's no way to know, and we don't have any way to change any of it."

"I know. I'm trying to look past this lawsuit like Marci said. To forgive it. How the hell can anyone do that? This is *happening*, man, and we've got to handle it. I was thinking about going to the bank to see about a loan, but I don't have anything to put up as collateral except my pop-up camper and my Harley. You don't either. We need to find some deep pockets somewhere. Maybe an angel investor..." Rick's voice trailed off.

"No way. No investors. We can't give up any equity in the company. You want to give away some of your share? Someone else would be calling the shots. We've agreed to keep the company to just the two of us since day one."

"Yeah. I know. I'm just lost for ideas," Rick replied.

"Me too. So, let's enjoy the park and see if we can put the worries away for a while."

Kyle returned to his condo at dinnertime to find Marci in the kitchen. She'd made a meal and invited Kyle to get comfortable and join her.

She had an unexpected smile on her lips. "That attorney threw you a curve ball today. Over half a million dollars, at least. That's enough to put you guys out of business."

Kyle studied her curious expression. "Yeah, it is. I'm trying to forgive this thing but my ego mind keeps telling me I've got to do something to save our butts. Our entire project is going down the drain."

Marci took a bite of dinner and chewed it thoroughly with eyes closed. Then another. Kyle picked up his fork and began eating, silently and without further conversation. Eventually, he cleared the dishes away and retired to the living room.

"Where's that Right Mind box of mine?"

"Just close your eyes and meditate on it," Marci said.

Kyle went to his place of stillness and, in his mind's eye, saw the transparent box glowing gold and violet and white. He mentally reached into it, anticipating the answers he knew it contained. After a moment he opened his eyes to find his Right Mind box materialized on the floor before him. He reached inside and pulled out a living holographic image. "Switzerland," he said. He stared at it. It showed an expansive, formal-looking room with people sitting at a round conference table holding a meeting. As he scanned their faces he saw himself, Rick and Cary seated across from people he couldn't identify.

Kyle changed his view and saw a backdrop of tall buildings with European-style spires surrounding a lake, all visible through the room's windows.

"That meeting is taking place in Zürich, Switzerland," he announced. "Switzerland is one of the wealthiest nations in the world. It was formed in 1291 and hasn't been at war since 1815. It's taken a neutral position in world politics and is one of the world's greatest centers for philanthropy." He glanced up from the holographic image to ask Marci a question. " Did you know 'philanthropy' comes from Greek, meaning 'love of mankind'? That it's an altruistic concern for human welfare and advancement?"

"Interesting," she replied.

"Yes, now I see that's where I'm going to find answers to the problems we're facing."

"Really?"

"Yes. Philanthropy, love...I don't quite see how it happens yet, but I'm certain the answers I've been looking for are there."

"Do you remember the first time we met and what I told you?" Marci asked.

Kyle stared at her.

"I told you this life you're living is a dream, an illusion. It's no different than the dream you had on the beach when you killed me. But in *this* dream you have the God-given power to truly *create*. Now, your learning has taken you to a point where you are creating. Congratulations, brother."

Kyle nodded. "Thank you, Marci."

She continued. "When you rise to the point where you begin to create, you realize you are more than the fragile body you thought you were." She paused and smiled. "You are *magnificent*. A child of *God*, made like Him. You're doing exactly the right thing in looking past this lawsuit and focusing on the good you'll bring to humanity. You still can't conceive what that will be, but I can tell you it's beyond your imagining."

Kyle put the 3-D image back in the box and stood up. "Time to get to work."

CHAPTER 25

Keep Reaching Inside

In the days following, Kyle met with Rick and Cary to map out a plan to connect eZo with the informal network of Swiss philanthropic organizations. Cary discovered the *Fondation Suisse pour la Philanthropie* and began making contact by email with a few select wealthy supporters of human rights, the environment and those focused on advancing medicine. Her efforts led her to others with a history of supporting humanitarian and social causes.

During August, email contacts gradually led to phone conversations. Kyle explained that eZo had developed a new level of computing power that could revolutionize long-range weather forecasting, and other projects aimed at improving the lot of people everywhere. He pointed out the quantum system would give philanthropists remarkable new capabilities to serve the causes each of them addressed. He began to develop traction with a handful of wealthy men and women. He met with them by video to elaborate further on eZo's technology and to discuss a loan that would be repaid from licensing fees once the full system was deployed. Yet he kept his cards close to his vest, not willing to divulge details about eZo's technology.

By late August, those preliminary conversations had attracted three philanthropists who agreed they might pay a visit to West Palm Beach if they could coordinate their schedules. Cary worked with each of them, trying to organize their visit as soon as possible, as eZo's out-of-money deadline was fast approaching.

"All right guys. Let's review where we are and what we hope to accomplish," Kyle began as they gathered in the conference room. "We've identified three Swiss who seem interested in coming here to discuss how our computer can help in their philanthropic work. And to negotiate terms for a loan to carry us through this lawsuit so we can quit worrying about it."

"The first is Hans Seffing, from Zürich. Karla Kensinger is from Bern. Jörg Tritten lives in Geneva. Each of those people has access to multi-millions. We're shopping with philanthropists who have the resources that can keep us operating through this lawsuit and can pay its expenses. I feel good about them. Not just because they can solve our cash problem. I like the kind of work they do. It's consistent with our 'for the good of humanity' approach."

Kyle stepped to the whiteboard and wrote the three names across the top.

"Seffing is an heir to the Bromand fortune. He's fifty-three and donates mostly to advancing medical care in Africa and South America." Kyle wrote those details below Seffing's name.

"Karla Kensinger is the daughter of Fritz Kensinger, who managed the Kensinger Foundation until his death. She's thirty-two years old and has supported humanitarian issues in Eastern Europe and third-world countries." He again wrote details on the whiteboard.

"Tritten comes from a career as a hedge fund manager. He's forty-nine. He's a savvy businessman and has managed investments in scores of high tech companies for over fifteen years. I think he understood the potential of our quantum system right out of the gate. In fact, he's been instrumental in getting the other two together with us. I'm not sure we'd have been able to do that on our own."

Cary interrupted. "What's a hedge fund? What does he do?"

Kyle nodded. "It's an unregulated investment partnership. The members are all high net worth investors. They use all kinds of aggressive investment strategies and look to get huge long-term returns on their money. They're like the cowboys of the investment world. They're super disciplined and aggressive. Tritten is a wealthy man with a lot of connections. He's been making the final decisions on how the fund invests its money."

Rick spoke up. "How do we tell them about the dangers of the technology? And what about the Board of Review? The Board will be controlling how our quantum system is used."

"I've talked to Tritten about the dangers in general terms. I haven't discussed the Board, though. It's a topic we'll have to approach carefully." Kyle wrote "Topics for Discussion" on the whiteboard, then "Upside/Benefits," "Downside/Threats" and "Board of Review."

"Okay, and they do know about our lawsuit with Zigma?"

Kyle wrote "Zigma" on the whiteboard. "Of course. I've been up front with them. I told them we're in court as the defendant in a patent case. I also described our clean room approach and explained our financial position. They all understand we'll be asking them to fund us through the suit and then be paid back from licensing royalties. Tritten and I talked about that at length. As I said, he's a savvy guy. He sees the value we can generate.

"What's more, hedge fund managers don't eat Pablum for breakfast. He's a go-getter. He knows about competitive advantage, which our prototype system gives us. He's all about investment strategy. About sales and marketing, and having a solid risk management strategy. We didn't talk about equity in eZo. That's off the table. We'll never sell off part of our company, but as we pay the Board of Review we can also pay the Swiss what we owe them."

Kyle knew he'd have to offer the Swiss something of real value, something more than interest on the loan, especially because he planned to ask for one million dollars from each of them. That 'something of value' wouldn't be equity shares in eZo, but he had an idea he hoped would take equity off the table once and for all.

"Equity won't be an issue," Kyle continued. "I've figured out a way to make this too good for the Swiss to turn down."

"I hope we're up to all this, guys," Cary said. "I've never been involved in anything this big. I keep thinking with all this planning we're doing—all the mapping out and strategizing—we need to keep reaching inside and asking for guidance from our Right Minds."

"You're right," Kyle said. "Marci keeps saying we've got to work out this dilemma. In fact, she calls it a 'little dilemma.' Seems pretty big to me. We need to solve this with our minds, our intellect. By planning. Thinking things through. By strategizing. But you're right, Cary. We need to come at everything from our Right Minds, too."

"Yes, and to show gratitude for what's happening," Cary added.

Through late August and into the first week of September, only a month away from their end-of-money crisis, eZo continued planning for the meeting they depended on for their very survival. Cary took on the job of setting up lodging and amenities. She drove over to Palm Beach to check out The Breakers, an exclusive and wealthy resort where their guests would feel at home. She researched limo services to bring the three Swiss philanthropists from the airport to the hotel after their flight, and the next morning, to bring them to eZo's office. She gave Kyle a summary of the costs eZo would incur—several thousand dollars once all the arrangements were made, which stressed their dwindling bank account even further. Kyle put most of those costs on his personal credit card.

Rick cleaned up the warehouse area where their mini-Internet was installed and began work to run a protein-folding problem through the quantum computer. Hans Seffing was particularly focused on reining in disease. Rick reasoned a quantum solution to a long-standing medical research problem would win Seffing's support. He decided to attack the protein-folding issue that had challenged organic biologists and scientists for decades.

Meanwhile, Kyle paid Lumière, Hansen & Dinor their $10,000 retainer. With the San Diego Federal District Court being across the continent, Kyle knew the attorneys, with their in-court hourly rates, hotels, airfare, car rental and meals, would burn through the retainer in no time. He decided he'd try to negotiate a smaller payment once the $10,000 was exhausted, knowing any additional payment would move eZo's financial ruin even closer.

CHAPTER 26

Karla

The first time Karla Kensinger heard of eZo Systems was during a phone call with Jörg Tritten.

In Bern, Switzerland, she stepped out of the shower and toweled herself dry. She wrapped herself in a robe and ran to answer her CoFone that rang unexpectedly at ten minutes before 7 a.m. It showed Jörg Tritten's name. She decided to take the call from her friend and sometimes business associate.

"*Guten tag*. Karla *hier*."

"*Wie gehts*, Karla? I am calling to invite you to join me on a trip to Florida. eZo Systems is headquartered there; I want to tell you about them. Do you have time to talk?"

"What?"

"Yes, eZo Systems. Two physicists in Florida are working on a quantum super computer. It sounds like something you should look at."

"Why?"

"They claim they've built a computer that can solve complex problems in agriculture, long-range weather forecasting and medicine. If what they say is true, it could be the answer to some of the things your foundation is working on."

Karla wrapped a towel around her head. "I don't know much about computers, Jörg. That's more your area of expertise."

Jörg told her how the quantum computer could revolutionize the global food supply.

"I see. It would be a blessing to so many people to have enough to eat each day. What about fresh water?"

"I don't know. Dr. Williams—he's the principal at the firm—has been rather secretive about his work, but he's got my attention even based on the little he's told me. Last week he invited me to come to Florida to see the system in action.

"I've worked with hundreds of high tech companies, but I've never seen any that offer what these men in Florida say they can deliver. You told me at the Bundesburg gathering last year you are frustrated and looking for a better way to solve problems."

"Frustrated? Yes. My father accumulated hundreds of millions of Francs over the years. He distributed a lot of it to worthy causes, but I have known for a long time that many of those millions were misspent. Sometimes they were entirely wasted," Karla said.

"Wasted? How?"

Karla pulled the belt on her robe tight and re-wrapped the towel around her wet hair. "It is the whole idea of strategic philanthropy. Philanthropists fill up conference rooms with 'experts' who try to figure out whether a given donation will maximize results. They get bound up in social theories and mathematical models that are supposed to decide whether a donation will be effective. They use statistics to decide whether money will solve a problem, but social problems are too complex. They need to quit philosophizing and abstracting problems and solutions and put their feet on the ground. They need to get on-site to study the problems, then act. That whole strategic approach has wasted more time and money than all the money that's been given to people in need. I am so tired of it.

"Then too, people in the philanthropic community think they can help by giving money to solve local or regional problems. Like the group that gave away free condoms at brothels to cut down on STDs and AIDS. Do you know what happened?"

"No."

"The prices prostitutes charged for unprotected sex raised up because there was such a demand. STDs increased. Free condoms did no good. It was an unintended consequence. No one foresaw it. How could they? So many times we meddle in regional or local affairs and do more harm than good.

Another example. We have micro lenders all over the world giving money to people to setup a business. Maybe they make baskets or weave clothing. The micro lender gives them $1,000 and expects them to create a viable business. Then the lender expects the $1,000 back, plus interest. Is that what people with social conscience do? I don't want to be one of those. *I want a better way.*"

Jörg held his CoFone close to his face so it filled Karla's screen. "I am sorry, Karla. I did not wish to upset you."

"Upset me? No. You did not. You asked me what I meant about wasting money."

"It sounds like you are losing your love for philanthropy. Even more reason to meet those two men in Florida. I think they have found a new way for solving problems."

"What do you propose?"

"Let us clear our schedules and plan a flight over to Florida to see if this computer is real. It will only take a few days. Oh, I have also been talking to Hans Seffing. Do you know him?"

"Not really. I met him briefly once."

"He does philanthropy in medicine and health care. Dr. Williams said they're programming their quantum computer to do work on a protein-folding issue. When I mentioned it to Hans he got excited. I do not understand the science he was talking about, but I see it's a huge problem in medicine. If their quantum computer can solve it, Hans wants to get involved too."

"Those men in Florida sound like latter day saints...if they can do what they say."

"I agree. Anyway, Hans wants to join us on a trip to Florida. My wife will probably want to come too, and bring the kids. So, let us see if we can find a time that works for all of us. The last week of September I am thinking about. Would you check your calendar and let me know if that works? If it does, all three of us can take my plane to Florida to see this quantum computer. With your permission, I will contact Dr. Williams and give him your number so he can tell you more details. *Ist gut*?"

"*Ja*. I want to talk with him. I will call you tomorrow about the schedule for the trip."

The next day Kyle received an email from Jörg Tritten with Karla's phone number and the advice to call her. An unfamiliar European ringing tone sounded in Kyle's ear.

"*Hallo*, Karla Kensinger *hier*."

"Hello Dr. Kensinger. This is Kyle Williams at eZo Systems in Florida."

"Ah, hello Dr. Williams."

"Herr Tritten gave me your number and suggested we talk. Is this a good time?"

"Yes. I am glad to meet you. Jörg Tritten told me about your project. It sounds interesting. Shall we switch to a video chat?"

"Yes, that would be nice," Kyle replied, noticing her German accent but not surprised she spoke English quite respectably.

"Thank you Dr. Kensinger. I'd like to tell you about the work we're doing here."

"Yes. Jörg told to me some fascinating things about your computer. How it might help people."

"Right, that's what I want to talk with you about. We've been working on this for the past few years. At the beginning, it was all theoretical. As we dug deeper, we discovered concepts that led us to build a computer that works on quantum principals. Suffice to say, we've built a proof-of-concept system that's programmable and able to solve complex problems. I've talked to Herr Tritten about solving weather forecasting as well as some medical problems. I'm curious to know what your interest in this might be."

"I have interest to solve problems for people who struggle, but I need to know that donating money will help them. I do not wish to give money unless I know it contributes to a solution. Many philanthropists donate to treat symptoms rather than root causes that underlie the problem. I want to do better."

"Root causes? I like your approach to problem solving. I'm sure we can help your foundation."

"That is what Jörg told me."

"I'm glad he did. I'd like to invite you to join us here in Florida for a demonstration of our system and how you can use it. I promise, we will not waste your time."

"Jörg told me you are a defendant in a patent infringement lawsuit. Tell me about that."

"There's a company that thinks we've used some of their patented code. We have not. All our work has been done in a clean room environment. My partner and I never looked at patents from other companies. We're looking for help from people like you to carry us through this infringement case, and then to recoup your expenses through licensing agreements we arrange with key technology companies."

Kyle went on to explain how he intended the computer to solve problems that benefit humanity, making a point that eZo wanted to solve many of the same kind of problems that philanthropy tries to fix.

"I see, but there must be more. You don't expect us to simply pay your legal fees, do you?"

"No. Of course not. We'd like to contribute to the work you do at your foundation."

"How can you do that?"

Kyle paused. "We have a small-scale version of the system running here. We can submit problems to it and get answers. Of course, it won't have the power of the full system we plan to deploy across the Internet. However, we'll still be able to solve problems with our local version. What are your areas of interest, Dr. Kensinger? I would like to put our computer at your disposal. How can we help you?"

"I was waiting for you to ask me. The business of philanthropy is not working. Wealthy people and foundations like mine give money to many causes, but too often it is altruism without accountability. Personally, I want to protect young girls who are forced into prostitution. I want people everywhere to have enough to eat. Fresh water to drink. Slavery needs be gone from the face of the earth. There is too much pain and suffering in the world. I wish to bring it to an end, but unfortunately, giving money to people does not always solve problems."

Kyle paused to think through the issues Karla voiced. "The issues of slavery and forced prostitution... they're cultural, social and political. I'd like to talk more with you about those. We need to be careful in formulating those problems so the computer can give us usable answers. However, we've already done work around weather forecasting that could have a real impact on availability of food and drinking water. Perhaps that would be a good place to begin working together."

"Yes, Jörg mentioned that." Karla paused for a moment to check her calendar. "Jörg and I are arranging our schedules to visit with you in Florida. Jörg tells me Hans Seffing plans to come as well. We plan to arrive on September 27th if that suits your schedule."

"Wonderful. We'll arrange your ground transportation and accommodations here. If you'll indulge me for a moment ..." Kyle opened a file and studied it for a moment. "...I can tell you our computer has forecast the high temperature here in West Palm Beach will be 80 Fahrenheit—that's about 26 Celsius. We'll have a light southeasterly breeze and clear skies. It should be gorgeous."

Karla laughed. "I can't wait to see if your forecast holds true. Thanks for arranging our accommodations. I look forward to meeting you."

"Likewise."

Karla closed the connection. *An interesting man. I hope he can do what he claims.*

She replayed the video chat on her CoFone. He was forthright when she asked about the patent lawsuit. He seemed to be genuine in wanting to help in the work she did at the foundation. Clearly, he was well educated. Amid those thoughts, she'd also found him attractive. Tall, brown hair and eyes, and with a serious demeanor. She looked forward to meeting him in person, but more than anything else, she hoped his quantum computer could do something to make philanthropy work again.

CHAPTER 27

Barbins

Frank Lumière flew from Boston's Logan airport to San Diego on September 14th to represent eZo. He planned to meet Micky Morgan, the opposing attorney representing Zigma, before they went to the pretrial hearing the next day. Lumière had held several conversations with Morgan, but wanted face-to-face time before court proceedings began. Lumière, relaxing in his hotel room, expected Morgan's call as soon as he arrived from San Francisco.

Lumière's CoFone rang.

"Hello, Mr. Lumière? This is Walter Barbins. I'm with the angel investment firm that funded Zigma Corporation. You got time to meet me in the lobby for a drink?"

"Well...yes, Mr. Barbins. Is your attorney with you?"

"No. He got delayed. Had to take a later flight. He's due in around nine o'clock."

"I see. I'd be glad to meet with you but I'd rather your attorney were present."

"Look. I need five minutes of your time. Right now. There's something I need to explain."

Lumière hesitated. No telling what this person might want to say, he thought. "All right. Give me a few minutes."

As the elevator door opened, Lumière spotted a man across the lobby, pacing, with his arms folded across his chest. The man glanced toward the elevator as Lumière stepped out, then walked quickly toward him. He seemed angry. A big man, probably 240 pounds at six feet plus an inch or two. He appeared to be in his late fifties, early sixties. A fringe of gray hair ringed his bald head and emphasized his frown and grimaced mouth.

Barbins held out his hand. "I'm Barbins. Let's find a place we can talk." He walked briskly toward the hotel lounge and waved at the waitress.

"What'll ya have, Lumière?" He looked at the waitress. "Make mine a Blanton's Single Barrel bourbon. Double and neat."

"I'm sorry, sir. I don't think we have Blanton's."

Barbins grimaced. "You don't *think* so? Well do you or not?"

"No sir. We don't."

"Okay then. Wild Turkey will have to do."

"Yes sir. And for you, sir?"

Lumière smiled at the young woman. "I'll have a Dewar's on the rocks. Thanks."

Barbins rocked back in his chair and studied Lumière. "I guess you're wonderin' why I'm here."

"What is it you want to talk about, Mr. Barbins?"

"The angel investment firm I work with invested a lot of money in Zigma, but Zigma's still a year or two away from showin' a profit. There's a lot at stake here, Lumière."

"Yes, I understand."

"Now listen to me. I can't be having people infringing on their damn patents. When I heard what your boys in Florida did, I told Zigma we'd be damn aggressive in takin' care of it. Whatever it takes to close your clients down." Barbins sat back in his chair and gulped his bourbon down. He waved at the waitress for a refill.

Lumière tasted his scotch then set it down on a coaster and relaxed into his chair. He looked Barbins in the eye and smiled. "I understand your concerns Mr. Barbins. However, my clients have not infringed on Zigma's patents. Tomorrow I'm going to request a joint meeting with the judge and ask for a Markman hearing. Do you know what that is?"

Barbins tossed back his second drink and scowled as he waved again at the waitress. "No."

"It's a special hearing where the judge looks at the claims Zigma made in their patent filing. In a Markman hearing there's no need for a jury. I've determined that's the best way to proceed. It cuts back on litigation costs and can save months. I'll be speaking to your attorney about it if he gets here in time tonight, otherwise we'll talk in the morning."

Barbins tossed back his third double bourbon. "You do what you have to do, Lumière. I'm not here in San Diego for the climate. We're gonna protect Zigma, dammit. I'd rather get it done fast so I can quit worrying about those two in Florida, but if it takes a year to grind them down, that's all right too."

"Mr. Barbins, you seem to be angry about this."

"You're damn right, Lumière. Don't act surprised. If you'd put a million into a company you'd feel the same way. I'm calling the shots here. My lawyer does what I tell him to do, and I've told him to close down your goddamn eZo outfit."

Barbins slammed his empty glass down on the table, stood up and lumbered toward the elevator. Lumière finished his drink, charged his own drink and a tip for the waitress to his room, then gave the waitress Barbin's name for the balance. He returned to his room five minutes later.

Lumière's phone rang just after eleven o'clock. It was Micky Morgan, the opposing attorney. He pleaded exhaustion after a twice-delayed flight and several hours sitting on the tarmac. They agreed to meet for breakfast.

"By the way, Walter Barbins invited me to meet him for a drink earlier tonight."

"Did you?"

"Yes, briefly. He seems to be an angry man out looking for blood."

"Well, Walter can be a bit rough sometimes. He's got a lot of his own funds invested in Zigma and he's protective of the company."

"So he said. A million dollars. But I don't see why he's so angry."

"Barbins made his money in oil down in Texas. The angel investment group he's a member of didn't think Zigma was a good investment. They wouldn't back him or go in with him on the deal. So, he put in a million of his own money and I hear he lined up another million from somewhere else. He probably feels like he's standing alone with Zigma."

Lumière pressed for more. "That doesn't explain his anger."

Morgan hesitated for a moment before answering. "I can't talk to you about my client. I've told you all I can say, Frank."

The two sides met for breakfast the next morning. Barbins was absent. Lumière explained his plan to seek a Markman hearing. They discussed matters and each drove their rental cars to 880 Front Street, the U.S. Federal district courthouse in San Diego.

At ten o'clock the judge called the court to order. The bailiff recited the case: Zigma Corporation versus eZo Systems, Inc. As the pretrial proceedings unfolded Lumière asked the court to consider a Markman hearing. The judge denied his request.

Around noon, Lumière returned to his hotel and called Kyle.

"I'm sorry, the court didn't agree to the Markman hearing. It looks like we're in this for the long haul."

Kyle didn't speak for several seconds. "I'm sorry too. What do you mean by long haul?"

"Well, we're going to have to work this through step by step as I explained. What would you like me to do?"

"Are you going to be in court tomorrow?"

"Yes, but not until three o'clock. San Diego time."

"Okay. I'll talk with Rick and we'll call you by noon, your time." Kyle called for Rick. He explained the what had transpired.

Rick slapped his hand on the desk. "I was afraid of that. We're screwed. We can't pay for the lawsuit. We can't tell the court we can't afford it. Even if we rolled over we'd still have to pay damages to Zigma. What now?"

"I don't know, Rick. I don't know." He paused to think. "Lumière will be back in court tomorrow. Three o'clock Pacific time; six o'clock our time. Let's sleep on it and get back to him tomorrow."

Kyle drove to his condo. His mind boiled with worried what-ifs. *Call tomorrow. We have no money to pay the attorneys. Maybe the $10,000 I paid will keep Lumière going until the Swiss get here on the 27th. Ten days from now. Can we hold out for ten days? What if the deal with the Swiss doesn't pan out?*

He pulled into his garage, got a beer from the fridge and walked into his living room. His ego box sat on the floor in front of the sofa. He searched his tiny condo for Marci. Not there. Aimer? Not there. The ego box simply sat with its lid closed on his living room floor. Kyle felt inclined to open it, yet apprehensive at what it might hold. He sat down on the sofa and stared at it.

It was an ordinary cardboard box. The four flaps at the top were interleaved as if someone had temporarily sealed it by folding the flaps together. A small opening between them revealed moving light inside.

Kyle sat on the sofa and finished his beer, then took a few steps to the kitchen for another. He returned to the living room just as the ego box blasted wide open. A cacophony of deafening screams wailed from it. Tormented shrieks filled the room and shook the windows. The entire contents of the box began roiling crazily around, threatening to spill out onto the floor. Hairs rose on the back of his neck and sent chills down his spine.

He jerked his head toward the kitchen, the bedroom, then the lanai. "Marci!" he hollered. "Marci, are you here?" No answer.

The screams howled louder. The agitated mayhem inside the box spilled onto the floor, surging toward him in a wave. He jumped away, pressing his back against the wall. The beer bottle slipped from his grip and smashed on the tile floor. The foamy mess mixed with the churning holographic images that shot toward him, dragging broken glass across the floor. He tried to back away from the advancing wave, but it rushed toward him as his heels pressed hard against the wall.

The wave reached his feet and began crawling up his legs. The beer-soaked images slithered up to his waist, then to his chest. They enshrouded his body. Forced their way into his ears. His nose. His mouth. They covered his eyes until Kyle could see nothing but horrific images depicting the most fearful events from his life.

He saw images of Julia playing in the yard, then of her closed coffin. Miles Bogan, with his Coke-bottle glasses and hair transplant, merged with Julia's images. His stomach churned.

He tried to suck in a deep breath, but could not, as his heart raced out of control. The room turned gray, then spun before him. With a colossal effort, he put one foot in front of the other to escape the living room. The world went dark around him as he managed to move his body away from the wall. He crashed into the lone chair in his living room. Then, darkness. Covered with moving holograms, unconsciousness claimed him as death beckoned. One hologram covered his entire face. It forced itself into his mind.

Kyle, it hurts! He bent over Julia, laying torn and bleeding in the street. He tried to pick her up. She screamed in agony.

No! Don't! He pulled his arms from under her body. *I can't feel my legs. I can't breathe. Don't let me die!*

Kyle's heartbeat thundered in his ears as he relived Julia's death. He saw the driver open his door and rush to the rear of the vehicle. Kyle shuddered. It was the assailant who had chased him on the beach after he killed Marci. Kyle's eyes fell on the streak of blood that trailed behind the car where Julia had been dragged beneath it. Blood gushed from her nose and ears, then ran down her neck.

Kyle cradled her head in his hands and stared into her eyes as they went blank and empty. *Julia, don't die!*

The driver of the car shrieked a horrific bellowing scream, then pulled a weapon from under his jacket and pointed it at Kyle. A fear gun. He aimed at Kyle and fired into his flesh. Kyle fell to the street next to Julia and her warm blood pooled beneath his head. As the driver poured alien terror into his body, Julia's voice entered his mind.

Kyle! Why did you throw the ball so high? I couldn't catch it.

The driver with the fear gun laughed a monstrous cackle and twisted a dial, turning it to a higher power. Like a maniac, he poured wave upon wave of fear and horror into Kyle's body, dancing around Kyle to guarantee those blasts reached every organ in his body. *See what you've done? You killed your sister. By the time I'm finished with you, you will beg me to kill you. To kill eZo Systems, too, before you destroy the world with your computer.*

Suddenly, silence. Kyle awoke sitting in the living room chair. He sat, barely conscious, with a trail of holographic images, broken glass and beer spread out across the floor between him and the ego box. The gray nothingness before his eyes began to fade, letting in the ambient light of the room. He sat motionless and gasped a deep breath as his diaphragm began working again.

The ego box shuddered and the mess on the floor began a retreat toward the box. The holographic images twisted and removed themselves from his nose, mouth and ears. From his face and his clothes. They slithered to the floor and snaked across the room to rejoin with the broken glass and beer foam.

A minute passed with no further motion or sound. Kyle made a conscious effort to banish the horror from his mind. *Just relax!* He took a deep breath, held it for a moment and breathed out slowly through pursed lips. The wriggling, snaky images on the floor retreated a few inches toward the ego box. He repeated the process and the mess on the floor withdrew a few more inches.

He pulled his feet and legs up under his body, cross-legged, and continued his unconventional breathing. The images moved closer to the box with each breath, then finally began a slow climb up the outside of the box. Within five minutes they were contained once again, all moving gently, roiling around silently within the box. Only the spilled beer and the broken glass remained on the floor.

Kyle got up from the chair and stood cautiously over the box. He dabbed his index finger into it, but felt no sensation. He reached deeper, up to his wrist. Nothing. He stirred the images and noticed they didn't respond with a swirl as a bucket of water would. He reached in almost to his elbow, closed his fist and pulled an image from the box. Mimicking Aimer's act of flattening it, he laid it on the floor and knelt next to it. He pressed the image against the floor and spread it out as if he were spreading pizza dough.

In the image he saw himself driving home and remembered the worries that had burned through his mind. The worries and fear that eZo was in its death throes. All of a sudden, he *knew* the boiling-over ego box was nothing more than a reflection of his own thinking ego mind. His fright and anxiety. His despair and dread at what the future held. His foreboding trepidation at what would happen because he didn't have the money he needed to keep eZo alive.

The image morphed into another. It revealed his office building with only a weathered frontage. The eZo Systems sign was missing. All that was left was the sun-bleached concrete surrounding the place where the sign had been. It left a ghostly, unweathered image of the company's name and logo on the concrete. He saw a "For Lease" sign posted on the glass door at the entrance. He pulled at the image and saw inside the building. The computers were missing. No desks. No people. The mini-Internet in the warehouse was gone. The floor had been swept clean. Only a dim security light illuminated the cavernous space.

Kyle shook his head and stared at the image. *It's an empty building. Not the end. Not death. It's a bad dream. That's all.*

Kyle interleaved the flaps of the box. He closed it, picked it up and kicked it into a corner of the garage, then cleaned up the broken glass and spilled beer. He sat on the sofa. *That can't be my future.*

Kyle paced his living room. *This lawsuit. Money problems. They seem real, but there's got to be a better way to deal with them.*

He looked at the situation anew. He *knew* he had to allow events to unfold on their own. *What the hell? I can't change what's happening. Or might happen. What's the point in obsessing over it?*

An understanding, not made of words, but nonetheless clear and concise, overshadowed Kyle's every thought. He saw and believed deeply in his inability, his inadequacy and powerlessness to change what is. To change the unfolding of creation. He saw himself as a drop of water in the ocean, trying to command the ocean to do what he wanted. He knew his only choice was to accept what is. Without craving and clinging to the hope for success in court, or for the Swiss to bail him out. His sense of relief flooded through him with an intensity that washed his fears and worries away.

He climbed into bed. He began his breathing practice, soon finding himself in his Right Mind place. *Thank you for your guidance. Thank you for showing me the peace that comes by allowing events to unfold on their own. Thank you for creating me of your Love.*

Kyle awoke the next morning and spent time again in his Right Mind, giving thanks and expressing gratitude. He showered and drove to the office.

Cary greeted him. "Good morning. Can I get you coffee?"

"Thanks. Why don't you grab one and join me for a few minutes?"

The two sat in Kyle's office. "Ever since that day you brought Paul Glazer to the office you've been a changed woman. What happened?"

Cary sipped her coffee and gazed into the distance for a moment. "Marci changed me. I no longer feel that I've got to *do* things. That I've got to try to control things. That I have to worry about how things will work out. It's hard to explain, but she did something to me that leaves me feeling peaceful all the time. I know that whatever happens, I'll be okay. In fact, more than okay. I'm happy for the first time in my life. I feel at peace with my life, the world and everything in it."

Kyle looked at her intently. "What did she do?"

Cary tore open a faux sugar packet and poured it into her coffee. She recounted the evening with Glazer and his admission that he'd been investigating eZo Systems. She told Kyle of her hurt and anger and throwing wine in Glazer's face. Of Marci rewinding the entire evening so she could see things differently, with new eyes.

"Marci and her mysteries are everywhere," Kyle said. He told Cary of his encounter with the ego box last night. "I wonder if Marci or Aimer had their hand in that somehow. It doesn't matter. I see now that whatever happens next will be what's going to happen anyway. There's no point in fighting it."

"I follow you. It's hard to describe in words, isn't it?" Cary plunged a plastic spoon into her cup and stirred it absently. "All my life I thought I had to be in control. I mean, it makes sense, right? We've got to watch out for ourselves." She tossed the spoon toward the wastebasket next to Kyle's desk. It hit the edge and fell in. "Now though, it's all different. I guess I still want to take charge of certain things. Like what I'm going to eat for dinner. But all the big things in life? Marci showed me I've got to let things unfold and look past the ones I would normally say I don't like. Stop judging. Forgive everything. Especially myself."

She smiled at Kyle. "The only way I can describe this feeling and what Marci did to me is that I'm a babe cradled in my mother's arms. The idea of being safe rather than unsafe doesn't even come to mind. It's a feeling beyond safety or comfort. It just *is.*" She sat there with eyes closed, rocking almost imperceptibly in the chair.

Kyle watched her and remained quiet for a moment. "Yeah. I guess churchgoers would call that peace you feel the grace of God or something. For me it's a feeling that underneath everything we see and hear, Love is what surrounds us. It's *in* us if we only pay attention to it instead of running around trying to take charge. When I have this feeling of Love in me, nothing else seems to matter. Like, the world and all the stuff that happens isn't real. Doesn't matter."

Rick walked into the office. "Hey man, I couldn't sleep last night. I don't see any way out of this lawsuit. Only option is to button everything up and get the hell out of town. We could start fresh somewhere else. Maybe South America, where no one will bother us."

Kyle got to his feet and looked his friend in the eye. "No, Rick. We don't have to do that. I've thought through the whole situation. We're going forward with the lawsuit. I'm going to call Lumière and tell him to proceed with the case. He said this might take a year. We're going let this thing unfold and see what happens. If we need to wait a year to start marketing...well, that's what happens. If we run out of money, we'll deal with that. There's no point in stressing out about this any longer. I finally realized that last night. What will be will be."

Rick threw his hands open and shook his head. "You losing your mind? We'll be forced out of business, dammit! The money is about gone. We'll be out on the street in a couple of weeks' time. Let's advertise to solve problems. We can use the prototype system. We'll get institutions and governments to pay us. Weather forecasting alone could bring in millions if we do it right."

Kyle stared at Rick. "We're not *ready* to go public yet, Rick. Think about what we have now compared to what we'll be able to do once the quantum system is running across the whole Internet. We'll be using *millions* of entangled photons. No matter what the Doppelganger people are doing or what they come out with, their quantum system won't hold a candle to ours. We'll be in the driver's seat. That's where we've *got* to be."

"Yeah, or we'll be broke if we wait around. C'mon man. We can use the system we already have and put some money in the freakin' bank."

Kyle gazed at his longtime friend, his red hair and freckles. He remembered all the times they'd spent together from around age fourteen, until now. A lifetime of struggle. Of fun. Of living through whatever the world happened to drop on them.

"I get what you're saying, my friend. But our system won't work the way we need until we have it running across the whole Internet. Once word gets out about our system everyone will want to get a piece of it. We can't do this thing half way."

CHAPTER 28

Equity

In his Boston office, Frank Lumière studied the motions Zigma's attorney had filed. One of them didn't make sense. A discovery motion was understandable, but the demand to have eZo's people submit to polygraph examinations? It was a process so foreign to any patent case as to be ludicrous. *That's got to be Barbins. His fingerprints are all over this.*

Lumière paged through the case files he'd built to defend eZo and came to a folder titled "Private Investigator." It was empty. He buzzed his law clerk.

"Sally, I'm working on eZo Systems but I don't find any reports from the private investigator. Where are they?"

"I sent two letters asking for them but we never got a reply from the firm in California."

Lumière frowned. "Okay. I'll look into it."

He called Kyle. "What do you know about the findings of that private investigator the other law firm hired?"

"Paul Glazer? Not much. I never did see any of his reports, but in the end, my office manager convinced him there hadn't been any infringement. That's when he closed the case."

"What do you mean your office manager *convinced* him?"

"It's complicated. Glazer and my office manager are in a relationship. The day Glazer came to the office to tell us he'd been investigating eZo...well, she had told him he had to confess. She pushed him into it. It almost killed me to hear what had been going on. I thought Rick was going to punch the guy out. When Cary spoke up, Glazer just fell in line and agreed there hadn't been any infringement. I can only guess. Maybe he contacted his bosses at his law firm and they dropped the investigation. That's all I know."

"Glazer never got any evidence of infringement one way or another?"

"No. Of course not."

"Okay. Can you get me his address and phone number?"

"Thanks Kyle, I'll be in touch."

Lumière called Glazer. "Mr. Glazer? This is Frank Lumière. I'm the attorney defending eZo Systems in a patent infringement case. I understand you were hired to investigate eZo. I'd like to talk with you about your findings."

Glazer had been arranging furniture in his new Florida house, happily making his new quarters feel like home. He pushed a box of clothing aside and dropped into a chair to relax.

"Yes, my firm sent me here to investigate eZo. I didn't find any evidence of infringement."

"I understand. We contacted your firm twice, asking for copies of the reports you must have sent. They didn't respond. Would you tell me about any reports you filed? Your cooperation could help us defend eZo."

Glazer recalled how Cary had demanded he come clean and tell Kyle and Rick about his probe into the company. How, in the end, she proclaimed she absolutely *knew* there had been no infringement. He remembered why he'd accepted her assessment. It was partly because of the love and respect he had for Cary. Partly because she was so certain and adamant, but mostly because he had felt horrible guilt and shame. He had misled, maneuvered and concealed the truth from her, the woman he'd come to love, so he could gain entry to eZo.

"I didn't keep copies of the reports. You'd have to get them from Miles Bogan at the firm," Glazer replied.

"Can you tell me the gist of what you reported? It's important."

Glazer didn't answer.

"Are you there?"

"Yes. I'm here." Glazer explained he'd been convinced the clean room development process ruled out any patent infringement. He explained his innate ability to separate truth from fiction by reading people, their body language, how they spoke and answered questions. He omitted Cary's adamant assertion that no infringement had occurred.

Lumière pressed Glazer further. "I've heard all that from Dr. Williams. I need to know what you put in your report."

"I told Bogan I had interviewed the principals at the company and determined, in my professional judgment, that no infringement had occurred. I've been doing this kind of work for years, Mr. Lumière. I read people very well. When Dr. Williams asked me to join him in the conference room I realized he was willing to talk. Guilty people don't often invite you in for a chat. Then, when I saw the whiteboard in their conference room, it dawned on me what had happened."

Glazer explained the peculiar similarity between the company name Zigma and the Greek letter sigma used in an otherwise English language word appearing on the whiteboard.

"When I first saw it I read it as a 'Z.' I had to look again to see it was a Greek letter. A couple of attorneys from the firm saw that same whiteboard. They might have assumed eZo had been using something belonging to Zigma. I don't know...it's possible."

"Did you explain that possible confusion in your report?"

"Yes."

"One more question. Dr. Williams told me you're romantically involved with his office manager, Cary Thomasson. He said she asked you to reveal your investigation to eZo's people."

Glazer stood up from his chair and walked around the room with his CoFone pressed to his ear. "I don't see how that could possibly be relevant to your defense of eZo."

"I'm not trying to pry into your personal life, Mr. Glazer, but I understand Ms. Thomasson convinced you to reveal your investigation to Dr. Williams. That she convinced you there had been no infringement."

Glazer frowned and stared out his living room window. "Yeah. I made a serious mistake with that investigation. I got involved with her. But, yes. She did convince me."

"It can happen. Now...I'd like to write a summary statement based on our discussion. It could become a key element of my defense. I'll email it to you later today. Please review it and correct anything that's inaccurate. Then, sign it electronically and send it to me. Will you do that?"

Glazer rolled his head and looked at the ceiling. *What the hell. This thing needs to be over.* He gritted his teeth and sighed. "All right. If giving you a statement can help eZo, I'll do that."

"Thank you Mr. Glazer. I appreciate your help."

Lumière began creating a sworn statement. It confirmed Paul Glazer had been employed to investigate eZo Systems on a patent infringement charge. It emphasized the fact that Glazer had been unable to provide any evidence of patent infringement. Later that afternoon Glazer returned the affidavit, signed and finalized. Lumière then wrote a letter to the opposing attorney.

Re: Zigma Corporation v. eZo Systems, Inc.

Dear Mr. Morgan:

The case of Nurklamu Corporation (Delaware) v. Daynst, LLC is relevant to your prosecution of eZo Systems. On its review you will find that Nurklamu filed an infringement suit against Daynst. The district court found the suit frivolous and without merit because the plaintiff failed to provide any evidence of infringement. The court characterized the plaintiff as a non-practicing entity, which in common language, as you know, is referred to as a patent troll.

While your client is clearly the owner of specific patents, the affidavit (copy enclosed) from the private investigator who surveilled my client provides no evidence that patent infringement has or has not occurred. In essence, the investigation was aborted before a conclusion was reached. Your client has failed to provide any evidence that warrants prosecution. Your case against my client has no merit.

It is worthwhile to note in the Nurklamu case the court ordered the plaintiff to pay the defendant's attorney fees due to similar exceptional circumstances.

You will also note in the MercExchange v. eBay case, the U.S. Supreme Court ruled that injunctive relief, such as your client seeks, requires that the plaintiff has suffered "irreparable injury."

Without any evidence of patent infringement or any indication of injury, the Zigma case you are prosecuting bears all the marks of frivolity.

Therefore, I am filing a motion with the court to dismiss this case. I will consult with my client and advise them to seek redress from the court for recovery of their legal costs to date. I will advise you on the court's decision.

In the meantime, I trust you will advise Mr. Barbins of this development and encourage him to withdraw this suit.

Respectfully,
Frank Lumière, Esq.
Lumière, Hansen & Dinor, LLC

Lumière dropped the letter and affidavit in the outgoing FedEx. As well, he sent the letter to Micky Morgan by email. *He's got no case without evidence. He needs to see that in black and white.* He turned his attention to preparing the promised motion.

The morning of September 26th, Jörg Tritten's flight crew prepped his Gulfstream for the 4,700-mile flight from Genève Aéroport to Palm Beach International. With a long-range cruising speed of 600 miles per hour, the captain filed a flight plan to take them over France and across the Atlantic in a great circle route, with an arrival some eight hours later at the Palm Beach International airport.

The three Florida-bound Swiss philanthropists, Tritten's wife and two children met at the TAG aviation flight center in the C3 complex. They processed through customs and boarded the eight-seat aircraft.

At six miles above the Atlantic Ocean, Karla Kensinger, Jörg Tritten and Hans Seffing enjoyed a cup of tea with Tritten's wife, Corina. The children sat in the two rear-facing seats at the back of the plane, engrossed in a movie. The three had discussed how they might provide money to eZo and what they would expect in return. Those discussions had not yet reached a conclusion satisfactory to all three.

Jörg toasted the three, looking directly at each of them as he touched glasses. "*Zum Wohl.* Here is to a pleasant flight and a family vacation in Florida. Dr. Williams said his computer predicted it is going to be a warm September day."

Karla smiled. "Your children will love the side trip to Disney and Epcot. Just remember to put your CoFone in your pocket. You won't need to conduct business while you're on vacation."

Jörg laughed. "Corina knows I feel guilty about working too much. She says I am...how do you say? *Ein arbeitstier*. You are right, my dear," he said looking at his wife.

"*Arbeitstier.* Yes, the word is *workaholic*," Corina replied.

"Dr. Williams and his partner seem to be workaholics too," Hans added. "They are working on a fascinating problem. I am excited to see what they have done."

"Yes. They have forecast an entire year's weather as well as the outcomes of several sporting events. Those men must *live* in their offices 24/7," Karla mused.

Jörg laughed. "My kind of men. Imagine predicting American football or the World Cup. There is no limit to how much money one could make."

"Only if they would permit that," Karla said. "Dr. Williams was quite specific about using the computer only for humanitarian purposes."

"I do not know how he plans to control that, but I agree. It would be a travesty to use such a machine to win at gambling. I have some ideas to talk with Dr. Williams about. I'm sure he will understand that getting my support will have some strings attached," Jörg said.

"Strings?" Karla asked.

"Let us call them conditions. Here is my strategy. Once eZo Systems is through their lawsuit—and assuming they win the case—they plan to license their quantum computer to large companies who can implement and deploy it across the Internet. They need big companies that can bring it to the world. Today eZo has only a small prototype that proves their technology works. Deploying it full scale will take a great deal of time and money."

Jörg picked up a sweet pastry, then turned to Hans and Karla. "Dr. Williams may not understand. It could take *years* before he receives any income from licensing deals. Any funds the three of us pay to help eZo with their lawsuit will have to be paid back, of course. As years pass, the interest on those funds will continue growing.

"At the same time other scientists are working on quantum computing. A few of them are making progress. By the time eZo completes its licensing deals and starts receiving income, someone else may have come into the market offering the same or even better quantum computing capabilities. We could fund eZo now, but eventually lose the funds we invest. Even worse, they could lose their court battle and be forced out of business." He took a bite of the pastry.

"You have a solution?" Karla asked.

Jörg chewed his pastry then took a sip of tea. He set his tea cup down and nodded at Karla. "A solution? Yes. Dr. Williams has been very clear: He says he won't sell stock in his company. Equity partners he does not want. I intend to convince him that is his only solution. With the network of high tech companies, engineers, executives and experts I have come to know over the years I can take his quantum computer, build it out to a full-scale version and begin using it to solve humanitarian problems."

Karla's eyes flared open. "What do you mean, *take* his quantum computer?"

"A poor choice of words. I want to help eZo *deploy* it. Once it's deployed, we will have access to it by virtue of being equity partners in the company."

Jörg held Karla's gaze. "Would you consider joining me so we can present a united front in our talks with eZo? Think of all the humanitarian work you could do with the power of a full-scale quantum system."

Karla brushed her hair back from her face. "I don't know." She paused. "It could be the better way I've been looking for. Having access to a quantum computer might cut through all the problems with philanthropy. Maybe it could do a better job at finding solutions that actually work."

"I agree," Hans said. "In medicine alone there are countless problems we could solve once we have that kind of power."

"Then it's settled. Let us listen carefully to everything the scientists have to say. We need to understand where they stand in their lawsuit. Let us get to know them as people. However, I may need to take a heavy-handed approach with them. After all, those two men are building something that can make the world a better place. We need to have access to it."

On the ground several hours later, a limo carried the entourage to their luxurious quarters on Palm Beach Island. They toured the grounds and allowed the children to splash and swim in one of the resort's sparkling pools under Jörg and Corina's watchful eyes. As the day wound down they ate dinner and retired to their rooms. Jörg sat with his CoFone, re-running numbers in a spreadsheet, confirming again the vast revenue equity ownership in a quantum computer company could mean.

CHAPTER 29

Groupthink

On September 17th Kyle awoke to his customary 6 a.m. alarm, dressed and drove to the office.

He watched a limo pull into the parking lot at eight o'clock. A uniformed driver opened the rear doors and the three Swiss stepped out. Kyle opened the door as the three entered the lobby.

"Welcome to Florida. I hope you had a good flight." Kyle introduced the Swiss to Cary and Rick. "I'm glad to meet you and want to thank you for taking time to meet with us."

"*Bitte schön*. We're glad to be here, Dr. Williams. We look forward to learning about your work," Jörg Tritten said.

"Wonderful. We have a lot to show you." Kyle led them to the conference room. All six people took seats. Cary sat down next to Kyle. Kyle faced Jörg; Cary and Karla sat across from one another, while Hans Seffing and Rick took facing seats across the table. The chair at the head of the table remained empty. Kyle wanted their visitors to feel this was a meeting of equals with no one staring down the length of the table. They exchanged business cards.

Kyle recounted the history he and Rick had shared in research, the founding of eZo Systems and his hopes their quantum system could bring a new face to humanitarian work. "We believe we have much to offer philanthropic efforts. So, before we begin, I'd like to ask how you each see this kind of technology working to support your efforts."

"Yes, we will certainly want to discuss that in detail, Dr. Williams," Tritten said. "First though, we'd like to hear an update on your legal matters—the patent lawsuit."

"Of course. Our attorney called last week. The lawsuit is going forward despite their efforts to settle it quickly. We could be in court for as long as a year, but as I told you, we haven't stolen any intellectual property. In fact, Zigma is one of the companies we had planned to approach with a licensing offer.

When they accused us of infringing on a patent, it was the last thing in the world we could have imagined."

Tritten leaned forward in his chair and stared into Kyle's eyes. "I have done research on Zigma. They are a small company. Why did you plan to make a licensing offer to them? They appear to be funded by angel investors and may not yet be profitable. How could they license your system and deploy it over the whole Internet?"

Kyle pushed his notepad to the side and returned Tritten's stare. "Good question, Mr. Tritten. A few years ago I hired a market research firm to evaluate emerging technologies. I was looking for those that could create innovative, game-changing services and products that would disrupt the status quo. I wanted to work with technologies that would do more than change the landscape of the consumer market. We wanted to find those that would fundamentally change the lives of people for the better."

"Yes, I understand. And about Zigma?" Tritten asked.

"I had already thought about long-range weather forecasting. It's an extremely complex issue. When the market research people came back to us, weather forecasting was near the top of their list, too. Being able to plant food and feed more people addresses the cause of hunger and starvation in the world. Not just the symptoms.

"As for Zigma, we discovered Sanjeev Ramajedran, who is now Zigma's CEO. A few years ago he published several articles speculating on long-range forecasting. We put a Google alert on his name. When we found he had formed Zigma and been funded, we added him to our list of potential licensees. Yes, his company is small, but we felt working together we might be able to accomplish more than either company working alone.

"Nevertheless, Zigma was our last choice. We are targeting three major players. Google, Apple and Amazon. Any of them could deploy our technology. We feel any of them would accept our terms of use—that our technology could only be used for humanitarian purposes. Not for business advantage and profit," Kyle concluded.

Karla leaned forward and nodded at Kyle. "I appreciate your focus on humanitarian issues and causes, rather than symptoms, Dr. Williams."

Tritten didn't seem to acknowledge Karla's remark. Karla give a small sideways glance at Jörg Tritten, leaving Kyle to wonder about the dynamic between the two.

Tritten continued. "Let us return to your lawsuit."

"There's not much more to tell," Kyle said. "The case is going forward. Our attorney says defending eZo could cost anywhere from half a million to two or three million dollars. We don't have access to that kind of money, but once we get through the lawsuit, which I can assure you we will win, we will repay your loan from the revenue we'll receive."

Jörg Tritten had conducted similar meetings with scores of high tech companies seeking money over the years. His penchant for immediately going to the bottom line on any issue was legend. "I am curious, Dr. Williams. Why do you feel certain you will win the suit? Your innocence is a matter for the court to decide. Not yours. Have you given any thought to what you will do if you're found guilty?" Tritten asked.

Rick answered. "Mr. Tritten, Kyle and I wrote every line of code our system uses. If the court found us guilty, we'd re-code the offending parts. With software you can get the results you need in many ways."

"Thank you. That is the answer I was hoping to hear," Tritten replied.

Kyle, eager to demonstrate the computer's capabilities pre-empted any further discussion. "Wonderful. This is a good time to review the work we've done. Won't you follow me on a short tour of the world's first quantum super computer?"

The group toured the mini-Internet with its optical amplifiers modified with eZo's sigma client interface. They spent the next few hours studying weather forecasts, protein-folding results and sporting event outcomes. Rick described the Quantum O/S. He spent extra time explaining the API written in the Haskell programming language. He showed the Swiss how it facilitated submission of problems to the quantum system. They reconvened in the conference room for a catered lunch.

Hans and Karla became more engaged with eZo's people with each hour and each new insight. Jörg Tritten masked his excitement, not wanting to show too much enthusiasm.

"You have accomplished more than I expected," Tritten said. "Now let us talk about a business arrangement that can bring this to full scale. From a risk management standpoint, I have concerns about funding you through your lawsuit, and then being reimbursed through licensing royalties. We discussed the issue among ourselves, and I want to share our thinking.

"First, you may lose the lawsuit. That could leave you unable to repay the money we spend defending you. At best, it could extend the time until you could make payments. Second, if you win the suit it could take years to build out the Internet's optical amplifiers with your sigma interface. With the acceleration of technological change, competing scientists and companies could come to market with even more powerful quantum systems. If that happens, our money would again be at risk. At best, if all goes according to your plans, we might begin to see repayment several years from now."

Kyle took notes, then studied them for a moment. "I understand your concerns, but I'm curious..." Kyle scanned the face of each Swiss philanthropist before asking his question. "If we put the repayment issues aside for a moment, how do you envision using our quantum system in your work?"

Hans Seffing rapped his knuckles on the table to attract attention. "If I may...There's work underway in Europe and elsewhere on the protein-folding problem. I would apply your computer system first to Alzheimer's research, then follow with work on Parkinson's, Huntington's and other diseases. Faulty protein-folding is at the root of all those."

"Yes, that falls directly into our plan to use the system for beneficial purposes," Kyle replied.

Tritten nodded slightly. "We need a way to rank social problems so the most damaging can be addressed first. Getting them in priority order is the first step to solving problems."

Kyle turned to Karla. "What are your thoughts, Dr. Kensinger?"

"We talked about some of my goals earlier. My major concern is making sure we address the true causes of different problems, rather than trying to put Band-Aids on their effects. Donating money to fix problems does not work unless you understand the nature of the problem at its root. I would like to use your quantum system to make sure we understand the root causes and take the right steps."

Tritten leaned forward in his chair. "I am sure there are many ways your computer can help each of us. However, I would like to know more about the matter of 'beneficial purposes.' How do you plan to restrict the use of your computer? How will you define what purposes are beneficial?"

Kyle felt this was the right time to drop what he thought might be a bombshell. "We've struggled with both of those questions. Now we've answered them. We're going to build a Board of Review. They, and eZo, will be in charge of the quantum system. The Board members will be people who have dedicated their lives to altruistic and humanitarian work."

He leaned back in his chair and looked at each person as he spoke. "Think of people like Mahatma Gandhi. Mother Theresa. Billy Graham. The Dali Lama." Kyle paused when he noticed Tritten's eyes narrow.

"Of course all those people are gone," Tritten said. "Attracting such luminaries could be difficult. Perhaps impossible, considering that each of them have their own objectives."

Kyle stifled a frown. *Don't judge him. He's not an enemy. No matter how he comes across.* Kyle suspected that Jörg was accustomed to getting his own way. He'd probably been on the winning end of most negotiations for the better part of two decades. "Of course, but we'll look for people like them. When they understand how they can advance humanitarian causes, we think they'll join us."

"What will this board do?" Jörg asked.

"It will decide what problems can be submitted to the quantum computer. They'll be the final authority. They'll consider each proposed use of the quantum system and approve or deny each one. The Board will be similar to our U.S. Supreme

Court, or the U.N. International Court of Justice at The Hague. The Board will be the gatekeeper to the quantum computer."

Kyle stood up and went to the whiteboard as if he were about to sketch something to illustrate his point. He picked up a marker, but merely held it in his hand. "There's more I must explain. Over the past week we've been discussing the best way to pay the Board members. That led to some debate about how we will generate revenue. All the discussions we've had with you until now were based on using licensing royalties. In fact, that's been our plan since day one. Now though, we've come to a different conclusion. If we were to license the technology to others—even if we restrict their use of it—we feel certain the quantum system would eventually be used to solve ordinary problems. We decided to use a different revenue model."

Tritten frowned. "Go on..."

"The Board of Review and eZo Systems will have sole access to the quantum system. We will not make our system available for solving just any problem. We want to keep our focus on producing beneficial social outcomes. Each organization that wants to solve a problem will pay a fee into escrow as soon as the Board approves their problem. Those fees will become our revenue stream. We'll repay the loans you make to eZo Systems, as well as salaries for Board members, from those fees.

Kyle laid the marker down and returned to his seat at the table. He looked at each of the Swiss then dropped what he thought might be his second bombshell. "Finally, we have not filed any patents. Nor will we. Ever. Filing patents would expose our work and our secrets to others. What we've done is beyond state of the art. It's completely proprietary. We intend to treat it as a trade secret. We can't afford to let it fall into the hands of people who might use it to do harm."

Karla responded casually, without any visible show of surprise. "Dr. Williams, I understand why you want to restrict the use of your computer."

"Yes. There's no way to know how dangerous this computer could become if we don't control access to it. *That* is why we have decided to restrict and control its use. And most important, we want to work on *root causes* of problems facing us, not their effects," Kyle said.

The room went silent.

Tritten appeared to be deep in thought. He gazed out the window where a flock of white Ibis birds walked through the grass picking at the ground, then returned his gaze to Kyle. "Well, I must say, your new revenue plan sounds reasonable. Of course, it depends on your computer gaining credibility. Many large organizations have tried to build quantum systems for decades, but none have been successful. They will doubt *you* have succeeded where so many have failed for so long."

Kyle ran his fingers through his hair. *Tritten's looking for reasons we're going to crash and burn. Why?* "I suppose other research teams may doubt what we've done, but they won't for long. Once we show the scientific community and the world what we've already accomplished..." Kyle picked up his ballpoint pen and tapped its point on the binder that contained hundreds of pages printed out by his year-long weather forecasting program. "...they'll have to accept it."

Jörg Tritten pushed back from the table, stood up and paced the room. "I appreciate your perspective, but I'm not sure you can guarantee your computer will have such dramatic impact. And I am still concerned about your Board of Review. How do you plan to create that Board?"

Kyle took a deep breath and focused his attention on his body. He let his entire torso go loose and relaxed. His shoulders. Neck. Jaw. A calm and almost happy feeling crept up on him. *We're the same, he and I. Enjoy that. Relax.* He smiled at Tritten. "When our law firm developed the Board of Review concept they consulted with ethicists and others who work in that realm. They suggested a few people to us. Some of those people may give us leads to others who might be suited for the job, but we're only at the starting gate. There's a lot of work to do."

Tritten took his seat, put his forearms on the table and leaned forward. "Dr. Williams, we have talked among ourselves. We agreed that funding your business with licensing royalties was risky. Frankly, while I like your new revenue model, I do not see that it is any less risky. However, we agreed to meet with you on the strength of what you told us in recent weeks. We also concluded the only way we would fund your lawsuit is through buying an equity position in eZo Systems. That would give you the financial strength you need to see the lawsuit through."

Kyle sat impassively. "Mr. Tritten, I'm sorry. eZo Systems is not for sale. We're not seeking equity investors."

"So you've said, but that's the only approach that can work. If you want our support, we need to come to an agreement on buying equity. Speaking for all of us, we have agreed to fund you through your law suit with the three million U.S. dollars you requested. That is in return for a fifty percent ownership in eZo." Jörg folded his hands and leaned back in his chair.

Kyle felt a moment of panic. *He doesn't get it.* He leaned forward in his chair and folded his hands, mirroring Tritten. "As I said, Mr. Tritten, we're not for sale. We've worked for years on this. We can't allow another party to control it."

Tritten stared at Kyle. "I am recommending fifty-fifty ownership, and I must tell you this: In fifteen years running a major hedge fund I bought every kind of high tech company and dealt with entrepreneurs and inventors of all kinds. All of them fell in love with their product, with their company and with their dreams. They were too close to their businesses. You are too close to yours as well. You fail to see the value the three of us can bring."

Kyle's shoulders fell as he realized he was holding tension in his body. He relaxed again, then smiled at Tritten. "This isn't about being in love with the company. It's about providing leadership to the world. Fixing what's broken.

"Look what's happening. The U.N. and world governments are in constant conflict. Wars are. The world economy is in shambles. Terrorists run amok killing innocent people. International crime and slavery are big business. All that's despite our governments trying to fix problems. They don't know how to fix problems. They don't know how to get to the root cause of problems. *The world needs leadership*, Mr. Tritten. We can deliver that. So please don't tell me about all the entrepreneurs you worked with who fell in love with their companies. This is about leading the world."

Tritten's jaw twitched. His lips pressed into a thin line and his eyes narrowed. "So you think eZo and your computer can lead the world? You think you can do better than our world governments? That sounds rather arrogant, Dr. Williams..."

"I have no arrogance, Mr. Tritten. Look at how our leaders lead. They're motivated by money and fear and every one of them needs to win at everything they see. How can anyone expect that to work?"

Hans Seffing stood up, breaking the tension in the room. "I'm sorry. Would you point me to your restroom?"

Cary walked to the door and pointed down the hall, then stood at the head of the table. "This might be a good time to break for a few minutes. There are some refreshments in the next room."

The group stood up and took a break. Kyle excused himself, went to his office and closed the door. He reclined in his chair and breathed in his unconventional style. In a moment, he found the stillness. He sat quietly for a few minutes, then rejoined the group.

He addressed Tritten. "Seems we got off on the wrong foot, Mr. Tritten. I apologize. It might appear that we're miles apart on the equity issue, but I have an idea."

"What?"

"The Board will be the kingpin in everything we do once we get the computer up and running. I'd like to offer all three of you a seat on the Board of Review. You will be its first members. You'll have a say in everything we do."

Surprise covered Karla's face. "We have met only today, Dr. Williams. You do not know us. I think your offer is quite charitable and generous."

Tritten grimaced. "Not so generous. I expected seats on the Board in return for our support. You're asking us for a great deal of money, but you seem to have overlooked my equity offer."

"No, I haven't overlooked it. With all respect, I cannot accept it," Kyle said calmly.

Hans Seffing closed his notebook with a flourish and put his pen in his pocket. All eyes turned to him. He spoke to Jörg

Tritten. "I agree with Karla. Dr. Williams' offer is generous. If we have seats on the Board I do not see any need to own equity."

"Nor do I," Karla said. "Let us leave the equity behind, Jörg. We don't need ownership. These gentlemen have done remarkable work. I would like to join them. A Board seat is quite enough."

Tritten's eyes jumped from Hans to Karla, then to the notepad sitting on the table before him. He gazed at it for a moment and seemed lost in thought. Finally, he spoke. "Dr. Williams, equity rather than debt has been my preferred approach to risk management and business management for many years. Ownership of a business lets me manage risk more effectively. However, considering your remarkable computer and all it promises to deliver, I will make an exception. I will join my colleagues, although I am disappointed in their decision. I pledge my support to eZo Systems through your law suit and will personally commit one million dollars in exchange for a position on your Board of Review."

Kyle stood up, walked around the table and held out his hand to Jörg Tritten. "Thank you, sir. I appreciate your business acumen and your vast experience. You will be a tremendous asset on our Board of Review and I look forward to your help steering the entire organization. I'm grateful for your support and hope we become lasting friends."

Karla spoke with a voice that rang with authority. "Fine then. We're agreed. We will each finance your lawsuit with a loan of one million dollars. In return, you will find places for us on your Board of Review."

Kyle looked at each of the Swiss as he spoke. "Thank you, Mr. Tritten, Dr. Kensinger, Dr. Seffing. Thank you for your help. Welcome to our Board. You are the answers to our prayers."

"And you to ours," Karla said. A smile broke out across her face. She got up from her chair and walked around the table as Kyle held his hand out to her. She ignored it and instead gave a cheek-brushing kiss on either side of his face and a mild embrace. "Dr. Williams, I love your passion for your quantum computer and your dedication to helping people."

Kyle's CoFone rang; a call from Frank Lumière.

"I'm sorry. I must take this call. Please excuse me."

Kyle stepped out of the conference room.

"I've got news. The prosecuting attorney has resigned from the case."

"What?"

Lumière summarized the letter he'd sent. "He called me as soon as he got my email. He said he was glad to resign from the case because Walter Barbins was demanding he take steps that weren't proper."

"Walter Barbins?"

"He's the angel investor who took some part in the initial funding of Zigma. Barbins himself told me he was determined to put you out of business. He's an angry man. Or frightened. I don't know which. He said he tells his attorney what to do, which explains some of the ridiculous motions I've received from him recently.

"Anyway, it turns out the private investigator never filed any reports to confirm or disprove patent infringement. The entire case is without merit. I've filed a motion to have it dismissed and asked the court to require Zigma to pay your legal expenses," he concluded.

"What will the court do?" Kyle asked.

"Based on the evidence I've sent, which includes all the private investigator's reports on your company, the court will have to dismiss the case. I think this was all a fiction dreamed up by Walter Barbins."

Kyle closed his eyes, hung his head and exhaled a deep breath. "Thank you Frank. My friend. I'm eternally grateful for everything you've done. I'd like to share this with the team here. Would you send me an email confirming what you told me? I'm meeting with some new financial partners right now. I'd like to show them something in writing."

"Sure. I'll send it right away."

The two ended their call. Kyle printed copies of Lumière's email for everyone and re-entered the conference room. All eyes followed him as he walked to the head of the table and pushed the chair aside.

"I've got good news from our attorney." Kyle recounted the conversation and passed copies of the email to each person. Upon reading it Rick jumped up and gave Kyle a high five. Cary hugged Rick and kissed his cheek. The Swiss gave handshakes all around, except for Karla, who graced the three from eZo with hugs.

"Congratulations, Dr. Williams. We couldn't have hoped for better news," she said.

"Thank you! I'm relieved. Excited. This changes everything."

"Yes. I think we can help you recruit the best people to serve on your Board."

Hans Seffing interjected. "I have some ideas, too. For example, I think it would be wise to include a medical bioethicist on the Board. We may want to think about ethicists from several disciplines."

"I think Heinz Golamer could be helpful, too," Karla added. "He is the head of the Swiss philanthropic association and has contacts all around the world with the kind of people you're looking for to be on your Board."

Jörg Tritten shook Kyle's hand. "It appears you must have a guardian angel who reserves the good news until the end of the meeting. I must say, I could not possibly have anticipated this outcome, but I am glad the law suit is behind us. Now we can get down to work without any further delay."

Cary stood patiently, seemingly lost in thought. "I think we should talk with Marci and Aimer to get their advice, too."

Kyle nodded subtly, without comment.

"It seems there's work to be done," Kyle said. "Let's close up and have dinner at The Breakers." By the end of the evening they were all on a first name basis.

Part II

Awakening

After much study, the Population Reference Bureau reported nearly 108 billion people had lived on the planet since *homo sapiens* appeared 50,000 years ago. Primitive language, art and music had developed gradually, along with beliefs, or at least hopes, of a life after death. Those beliefs and hopes became cultural universals that led people to offer perhaps trillions of prayers through the ages. They voiced those prayers in forms that ranged from hand prints and artwork left in French caves; to incredible sanctuaries built during the Stone Age 11,000 years ago at Göbekli Tepe in Turkey; to primeval sacrificial offerings; to contemplative study and, eventually, to organized religions.

Many of those prayers reached out to gods of nature; to gods of harvest; to gods of vengeance; and, to gods of salvation. Some feared a judgmental god who commanded love, adoration and obedience, while others chose to ignore and deny the question of gods altogether. Many decided there is no God, or that He is dead, while others simply admitted "I'm not sure ..."

As the decade wore on, a small but growing number who had embraced the 1960s curriculum began to understand the upside-down nature of life and the world. They began to acknowledge the impossibility of harboring two opposite and conflicting thought systems—an ego mind and a Right Mind.

Those followers of the curriculum realized every lethal disease, every perception of lack, every war, every battle, every insurgency, every genocide, every murder, every hatred that ever existed and that exists now—those affecting nations and those afflicting individuals—are signatures of guilt and fear. They understood that belief in sin produced guilt, and that guilt generated fear. To those students of the curriculum, it became clear that life on Earth is profoundly defective and flawed. That it couldn't have been created by a loving God. Instead, it was the making of a mad dream given power by a sleeping, dreaming mind.

Meanwhile, the World-o-Meters website displayed constantly advancing numbers that documented births, deaths and world population growth every few milliseconds. It predicted the world population would stabilize at around 10 billion people by 2062, and that about one of every five people—even after 50,000 years and 108 billion souls—continued to live as atheists, agnostics or "just not sure."

CHAPTER 30

Roots

The Swiss extended their visit to Florida and spent three weeks working with eZo, interrupted only by the Tritten family's tour of Orlando theme parks. Jörg, much to his wife's surprise, left his CoFone in his pocket and enjoyed his children's enthusiasm as they played and laughed through one park after another.

As the Swiss worked with eZo's people, bonds began to grow and deepen. Cary and Karla formed the natural bond most women do; the mend and befriend warmth of the female psyche. They became fast friends. Hans Seffing coached Rick on the finer points of protein-folding and related medical problems, while Rick educated Hans on the capabilities of their quantum system. Jörg Tritten and Kyle worked on business issues: how to create the Board of Review; how to deploy the sigma client interface across the Internet; how much money would be needed to bring the quantum system to full scale; and, a proposed phase-in schedule for its deployment. Three million dollars from the Swiss eased the financial pressure that had built to a crescendo over the summer.

When Kyle was not working with Jörg, he and Karla spent time discussing her philanthropic efforts. Karla appreciated Kyle's intelligence and, as she got to know him, his gentle and sensitive nature.

The conference room had become an occasional lunch room. Karla and Kyle sat across from one another with their sandwiches. Kyle's could have been a salad pressed between two slices of bread. It was stacked high with avocado and tomato with lettuce hanging out over the edges of the bread.

"Are you a vegetarian?" Karla asked.

"Only today. Normally I'm omnivorous." He laughed and took another bite.

"Omnivorous, huh?"

He chewed for a moment. "Yeah. Why? You a vegetarian?"

"No, but I think it is probably a healthy way to eat. It is like working out. The right kind of food and good exercise keep a body healthy," she said.

"Did you notice? I've got some Nautilus equipment in the warehouse. Feel free to use it. It's a good way to work off stress."

"I have used your machines a few times but not for stress; just exercise." She watched him eat the last corner of his sandwich. "Are you stressed?"

"Ha-ha. Not so much now, but I put a lot of miles on those machines while we were beating our heads against the wall to get the computer up and running."

She considered that image for a moment. "May I ask you something personal?"

"Sure."

"For a scientist, you are a mystery to me. Most scientists I know are left-brained. Logical. Linear. Technical. But you have another side. It is warm. Compassionate." Karla hesitated. "I hope you do not mind my saying that."

Kyle wiped his mouth with a napkin. "No, it's okay. I appreciate it. I guess life taught me a few lessons that kept me from turning into a boring professor. Computer code and physics are okay, but there's more to life."

Karla wrapped a leftover bread crust in her napkin and laid it on the paper plate. "I would like to hear about your life."

"And I'd like to hear about yours. What it's like growing up in Switzerland. How about we take a break? Get some sunshine."

Kyle drove Karla to a North Palm Beach park where they sat on shade-covered benches along the waterfront. He gazed out into the channel. "You've probably seen a lot of pain and misery in the work you do. My life doesn't hold a candle to the suffering millions of others have had to face, even though my early years were kind of rough. Everything works out in the end, though. I guess what I experienced motivated me to work at making things better. I was never one for rolling over and being a victim."

He explained the tragedy of his father's auto accident, his disability and early death. He recounted his mother's alcoholism, her death and that of his little sister.

Kyle stood up from the bench and tossed a flat rock across the water. It skipped a few times.

"I was completely alone when my mother died. That was about the time I finished my undergrad work. I knew it was up to me to make something of my life. Somewhere along the way I realized people everywhere were struggling with their lives too. I used to get up each morning and watch the news. You know what I saw?"

He picked up another rock and threw it hard against the water. It skipped a half dozen times before disappearing forever.

"The headlines were the same every day. Murder, disease, suicide bombers, crooked politicians, scandals, failed peace talks. I began to think of the world as an insane place where nothing works right.

"One day I made a conscious decision: I'd had enough. I quit following the news." He laughed. "Big deal, huh? It wasn't exactly a rebellion that would make a difference to anyone besides me, but I felt like the whole world was running with one square wheel on the wagon. Nothing made sense. When you look at all the things we do to one another I started to question that old saying about 'man's inhumanity to man.' Seems to me it should be 'man's insanity to man.' Does that make sense?"

Karla grimaced and shook her head. "It does. Absolutely."

Kyle kicked at a stone half buried in the ground until it broke loose. He picked it up and hefted it in his hand. It was round and wouldn't skip. He threw it far out into the water.

"Look at what's going on," Kyle continued. "Women are still treated like second class citizens, or worse, in much of the world. Theocrats in the Middle East stone people to death and cut off their hands as punishment. Despots like Lenin, Hitler and Pol Pot killed over a hundred million people last century alone."

Karla stood up from the bench and reached out to take Kyle's hand before he could find another stone to throw. "Let us take a walk."

She led the way down a path bordered by palms and thick tropical vegetation. "Not everything is as black as you paint it, although I do see what you are saying. Insanity is all around us but we do not notice it. It just seems to be the way things are. We are like fish trying to explain the water surrounding us.

"When I was a child my father spent millions of Francs on charitable and humanitarian causes around the world. I cannot see it has done anything to change human behavior. Sure, some people were helped. Maybe they could put a roof over their heads or feed their children, but he was not able to deal with the root cause of anything. Philanthropy is nothing more than triage; putting Band-Aids on problems."

Karla stopped and turned her back to Kyle. She stood motionless, looking at the ground in front of her.

"Is something wrong?"

No answer.

He stared at her back. "Karla?"

"I'm sorry, Kyle. There's something I've wanted to tell you. I'm not sure ..."

"Go ahead ..."

She turned to face him and took his two hands in hers. She gazed into his eyes. "Do you remember that old American movie? The one where the woman says 'You had me at hello?'"

"Yeah. I think so."

Karla looked into his eyes. "Well, you had me when you talked about *root causes* and their effects. I am so hoping your computer can help us find a better way."

Kyle laughed. He noticed Karla's eyes, hazel, a mix of green and blue, with smile lines beside them; her blond bangs falling just above her eyebrows. He squeezed her hands and pulled her toward him into a gentle hug.

"Thank you, Karla." He stroked her back for a moment then stood back. "I hope we can, too. I think we've got a lot to talk about. A lot we can do together."

Karla took hold of his hands again. "So do I."

They resumed their stroll. "Listen, I'd like to tell you about something I think goes to the root of everything." He paused to collect his thoughts. "I've been learning something that's changing the way I think. It's helping me find a better way to live. It doesn't rely on my customary way of thinking and doing things."

"What do you mean?"

Kyle watched a pair of sea birds fly overhead, warbling. They traced a graceful arc through the sky until they disappeared beyond the tree line on the other side of the channel.

"Those two birds? They're a microscopic moment in the unfolding of all creation. Their flight was one of uncountable things happening at that exact moment. Those birds did what they did without any advice from anyone. Look anywhere in the universe, Karla. You'll find events unfolding all on their own. We have nothing to do with them. Nothing to say about them. Nothing we can do to change any of them. Yet, by an unimaginable stroke of chance, we're here to experience them."

They continued their walk down the path. "I see that, but where did you come up with that idea?"

"I have two mentors who've helped me understand that, and so much more. They've shown me a new way of thinking. My Right Mind."

Karla's seemed to be confused. "What's that?"

"It's an alternative to making decisions by just thinking about an issue. I guess you could say it's a spiritual alternative. I meditate and wait for my mind to become still. Then answers to questions come to me. Sometimes they come immediately, but usually some time passes. An answer might come as I'm reading something. Driving my car. Taking a shower. Sometimes answers even come in a dream."

Kyle watched for her reaction.

"Meditation? I've read a little about it. People who meditate...aren't they supposed to be more balanced and at peace?"

They stopped walking as they passed beneath a palm tree. Coconuts lay on the ground. Kyle picked one up and shook it, then tossed it back on the sand. It was infested with ants.

"Yes. I've found meditation helps me...how can I say it? It helps me *disengage* from my usual way of thinking. I've learned to stop listening to the constant stream of thoughts my mind plays in my head. I've found a stillness where I can see things differently. Where I can make better decisions. Where I can appreciate all this natural unfolding of events. Of creation. It gives me peace instead of worry. I've learned—or I guess I should say I'm still learning—how to ignore my thoughts."

Kyle explained the parallels he'd discovered during meditation. How the function of his stomach or his liver or his endocrine system and his mind were so similar. They all quietly did the job they had evolved to do.

"I think our minds evolved to keep us aware of our environment so we could avoid danger. Even today, while I don't face life-threatening danger, my mind bubbles up all kinds of stuff. They're based on my life experiences and personality, not external dangers. Lots of them are replays of something that's already happened. Others are thoughts about the future. That's where worrying comes in: thinking about what could go wrong.

"I'm learning to ignore that constant stream of so-called consciousness. In fact, I think calling it 'consciousness' is a mistake. It's more like 'mindlessness.' Anyway, when some thought bubbles up that tells me I need to judge a person or situation or event as bad or worrisome, I'm learning to look past it and let that bubble go."

The curious expression on Karla's face told him she probably didn't understand his point. "It sounds like you are fighting yourself."

"There's no fight. I don't think anyone can win a fight with their own mind. But not listening to it works without a fight. It just takes practice."

"So...do you have to be hypervigilant and watch every thought that crosses your mind? That sounds a little neurotic."

"No. It's not hypervigilance either. It's choosing to let the mind do what it does without following every little thing it bubbles up. I don't choose to focus on those random thoughts. I let thoughts and emotions enter and leave without reacting to them. I guess it might be a sort of mindfulness practice."

Karla listened intently. "That sounds complicated."

"It was, at first. My mind has always wanted to be in charge of everything. How could we live any other way? We think our mind is who we are. Mine has wanted to answer every question I might have. To blast out a constant stream of thoughts. They'd carry me to all kinds of different places. They'd remind me of my little sister's death. Of what could happen if our quantum system falls into the wrong hands. But that's not how I want to live. No, it's just noise from the constant rambling of a mind made to help us stay alive in a dangerous environment. To help us cope and keep our bodies alive. Nowadays, we need to reboot our minds to give us a better tool to deal with life in the twenty-first century. It's too bad we haven't evolved to keep up with the times."

A wry, doubtful smile spread across Karla's face. "You're saying you want to find a way to reboot the mind of humanity? That's a pretty tall order."

"Yeah, I know. Finding the root cause behind wars and all kinds of insane behavior would give me the answers that can help people get to a better place. I'm beginning to understand the insanity itself is an effect, not a root cause. I want our quantum computer to find and solve the root cause that *leads* to our insanity. If we can do that I hope we might be able to eradicate all its effects. Permanently."

Karla walked with Kyle, wordlessly looking at the path ahead as she took each step. Her mind raced to catch up with the idea of multiple levels of cause and effect, of thoughts bubbling up and somehow rebooting the mind of humanity. If insanity wasn't a cause, there must be something much deeper that gave rise to human behavior. "I follow some of what you're saying, but I can't imagine what's lurking underneath the insanity."

Kyle spotted bench at the end of the path. They sat down. Kyle considered telling her about Marci and Aimer, but decided the story was too strange. Maybe someday...

"You're probably thinking I'm a weird man; a little nuts," Kyle said.

She smiled at him. "No, but you definitely have a different view of things. Whatever brought you to this?"

"It's a long story and I'd like to tell you about it sometime." He watched a boat sail down the intra-coastal waterway before them. It created a wake that broke on the shore well after the boat had passed. "Can we get back to the root cause issue and how we can work on it?"

"Sure, but I don't know where to begin."

Kyle turned on the bench to face her full on. "All right. If we agree the problems in this world come from our insane behavior, we need to find its root cause. Now what I'm about to tell you might sound outrageous. I think the root cause is *fear*."

"Fear of what?"

"Fear is an emotion. It's the emotion that appears when the mind bubbles up warnings of threats and danger. What's the greatest fear you can imagine?"

"I don't know. I suppose the fear of pain, suffering and dying. Nobody wants to die, but we all know we will."

"Yes. That's a fear everyone carries around, but I think there's an even greater fear."

"Worse than death? What would that be?"

Kyle thought for a moment to put into words what he had, as yet, never spoken aloud, even to himself. The idea seemed almost bizarre. Unbelievable. An idea that almost anyone would argue with him about simply because it came from so far out in left field.

"I think it's the fear of God. The fear we carry because we have purposely separated from our Creator. We've left God behind and we're terrified He's going to punish us. It's all about our ego mind."

"What is this ego mind you're talking about?"

"Our ego minds are what we think of as ourselves. I'm Kyle. You're Karla. We each have beliefs about who we are. That's how the ego mind works. It's the mind that keeps tossing up different thoughts. It's the mind that tells us we're all separate from one another. The Right Mind is totally different. It's a mind that connects with another kind of reality." Kyle paused and stared at Karla for a moment. "I don't want to intrude by asking personal questions, but I do have one..."

Karla closed her eyes for a moment, pressed her lips together and turned her face toward the sky as she considered what he might ask. She dropped her eyes and looked him. "I guess so."

"Do you believe in a higher power?"

Karla gazed out over the channel, then turned to him. "That's the last thing I thought you'd ask. Yes, I do. Why?"

"Because I believe the Right Mind is a connection to that. I think it's a kind of mind that's literally out of this world. I think if we can find a way to help people get to their Right Mind we can get to the root cause of all the problems in the world."

Karla sat without expression, thinking. Wondering. *What is he talking about? Is this guy an entrepreneur? Scientist and inventor? Or a new age spiritual nut?*

"I've had some strange experiences that have helped me find this new way of thinking. I've never been religious, but lately I've had the feeling I'm being cared for. Watched over. I feel like I walk in favor with something greater than me. That things in my life will work themselves out without me having to worry about them. Without me having to do things or try to control things.

"Like the outcome of the patent trial. It disappeared. Evaporated. I had decided days before I couldn't change anything that was going to happen, so I quit worrying and quit trying. Lo and behold, things worked out for the best. That's the kind of thing that happens when I get into my Right Mind instead of using my ego to worry about everything, trying to do things and control what will happen next. It's what happens when I quit plotting and strategizing and trying to take charge of what's about to happen. That feeling of being watched over...well, I think it has something to do with God."

"You're talking about God? That sounds strange coming from a scientist."

"So be it then. I only know my Right Mind has given me more peace than I ever could have imagined."

The two sat silently for a few moments, watching the water flow through the intra-coastal waterway.

"Here's an idea that might help." He stood up from the bench and reached for Karla's hands, pulling her up to a standing position before him. "May I hold you for a moment?" he asked.

She looked at him, up and down for a moment, not sure what he had in mind. "Okay."

Kyle embraced Karla gently. She turned her head and rested it against his shoulder. Kyle put his left hand at the small of her back and his other on her shoulder blade, then closed his eyes. Karla held him lightly.

"Breathe with me for a moment, Karla." He began his breathing practice, explaining to Karla how to exhale slowly, as if she were exhaling through a tiny straw. Stopping at the top and bottom of each breath. Gradually their breathing synchronized.

"You and I are *the same*, Karla," he whispered into her ear. "We are *one*. We only think we're separate from one another because we use our ego minds to keep us separate. Even our names and the names we give to everything in the world reinforce the belief that we're separate. Behind you is a tree. A river flows by before you. Overhead there's a bird flying. All those are just symbols and ideas. We are all the same, but we believe in separation."

The two stood in an embrace, breathing together. "I think our biggest fear is that we've decided to separate from our Right Mind. From God. We think of Him as some superman in the sky who's judging everything we do. We're terrified He's out to get us for leaving Him to live in our ego minds. Like the prodigal son, we walked away from Him and haven't come back."

Karla searched furtively to express her feelings, to try to understand what he had said as his body pressed close against hers. She breathed along with him. "I don't know, Kyle. You may be right. I don't know what to say."

Kyle continued holding her. He felt her body melded into his. Her chest rose and fell in time with his; her breath moving in and out, her warmth flowing into his body. "We are the *same*. We are one."

Karla backed away from Kyle and stared at him. "I'm not sure what you're saying." She stepped back and crossed her arms over her chest.

Kyle noticed her body language but pressed ahead with his ideas anyway. "I'm saying there are no individual people. We're all the same Right Mind, but in our ego minds, we *think* we're separate from one another and from our Creator. And we're terrified we're going to be punished for believing we separated from Him. *That* is the root cause of our problems on this planet. Fear of being punished for leaving our Creator behind. I think fear is the direct opposite of Love because it leads to attacking, hating, discriminating, judging. Nations fight. People fear other people. There's no end to what fear brings. Can you imagine if the world were powered by Love instead?"

She turned away from him and sat down on the bench. He remained standing before her.

She stared past him toward the water, as if she were deep in thought. His standing and towering over her seemed to make her uncomfortable, so he stepped back. She finally got up from the bench and began walking toward the parking lot. "You've given me a lot to think about. I don't know what to say. Would you take me back to the hotel?"

"I hope I haven't ruined our afternoon ..."

"No. I just need time to digest this. But I must tell you, I can't begin to imagine how even your quantum computer would have any chance at solving a problem as gigantic as the one you've described."

"I can't either. Not yet."

The two drove back to Palm Beach. Kyle dropped Karla off at her hotel.

Alone in her room, Karla sat quietly, thinking of their afternoon together. *Holding on to him and breathing that way felt strange...awkward. But his embrace was sweet, gentle. What a strange man! Er klingt ein bisschen verrückt—he sounds a bit crazy, but is he on to something? A world powered by Love? What can that mean? How does he think he can change people? How can* any *computer do that?*

She ordered dinner from room service, ate her meal then opened her CoFone and replied to messages from Switzerland. After a few hours' work, Karla climbed into bed and lay thinking about Kyle's bizarre ideas. *I liked when he held me in his arms. I respect what he's trying to do, but I don't understand him. I hope he's not some kind of zealot.*

CHAPTER 31

Which Is the Greater Sin?

Marci and Aimer communed with All That Is. They watched creation unfold, but knew "time" and creation's "unfolding" only appeared to exist to those who dreamed their lives.

Marci and Aimer knew without having to think a single thought that all they observed had already happened in the beyond-infinite folds of Eternity. That Kyle struggling to understand the only True Reality was making progress. Yet the "time" for another intervention was coming near. He needed a boost to help him move into another phase of learning and understanding. His team was forming, yet still more would be needed to move them all toward meaningful action.

The one who took the name Marci thought: *Kyle is becoming a teacher, and while he teaches, he learns.*

Yes, Aimer thought. *That's the nature of God's teachers. Even though there seem to be two thought systems in his world, Kyle is gradually making the choice to learn and teach from his Right Mind. He's trying to show his understanding of his Right Mind to others, and each time he does, he gives it ever more surely to himself.*

Indeed, thought Marci. *Teachers and students are the same. He who teaches also learns. This one's understanding is changing, but he has yet to learn the True Cause behind the effects he sees in his dream of his life. He hasn't yet realized his life is not the dream but he, instead, is the one being dreamed. His sleeping Mind that made the world, its universe and all he perceives, continues to sleep in ignorance of Its true being. Yet even while his true mind sleeps, he is beginning to realize what his senses tell him—that he is 'only a man'—is not the Truth. He is not little. He is magnificent.*

Aimer laughed, and his laugh spread joyfully through Eternity. *Yes. Like all his brothers, he believes in the world and all the fears and limitations he made.*

Marci paused a nanosecond or less, for time holds no sway in Eternity. *Yes. He seeks to find a 'cause' for humanity's ills. He has yet to realize there is only One Cause.*

In Florida, Jörg and Kyle hammered out a plan.

"Let's talk about the businesses and stakeholders who built out the European Internet backbone," Jörg said. "You have ICANN and ARIN in the states. In Europe we've got RIPE. It's a group of companies that has invested to build the high-speed Internet backbone—the main pathways for passing Internet traffic around the world. I've talked to them and convinced a few to help us build your sigma client interface into the optical amplifiers that keep the Internet working in Europe. We need to go to them to work out the details."

"Go to Europe?"

"Yes. I'd like you to come to Zürich. We can get things done faster there than we can from America. I've got contacts there who can help us. We can cut months, maybe years, off the deployment of your quantum system."

Kyle met with Rick and Cary. "Jörg asked us to come to Zürich. He's working with people there who can help us roll out the system in Europe. It'll be a first phase."

"What do we do with our business here?" Rick asked.

"We'll need to close it down for a while. Pack up everything and move it to Zürich. Jörg is looking for a place we can set up a European headquarters."

"Who's paying for all this?" Rick asked.

"They are. We'll use some of the three million they pledged," Kyle replied.

"Zürich? Oh my. When do leave? How long will we be gone?" Cary asked.

Kyle noticed Cary's worried look. "Is something wrong?"

She shook her head. "No, I was just thinking about Paul..."

The Swiss returned home while Kyle, Rick and Cary threw themselves into relocating eZo Systems. In a week's time they packed up their servers and IT gear and arranged its transport to

Switzerland. Kyle turned off the lights and locked the door to the office. A few days later the three rejoined their Swiss friends.

Jörg established eZo's headquarters and computing center in the Seefeld area of Zürich, near the eastern shore of Lake Zürich. The building that would become eZo's headquarters had once been a bank, and was fitted with all the customary security features expected in a bank. In addition to an immense vault area designed to hold the wealth of the former bank's clientele, it had ample office space and spacious conference rooms. Rick and Jörg worked together, installing communications equipment needed to conduct Board meetings with their yet-to-be named Board members around the globe. Rick and Kyle re-installed their servers to run the Quantum O/S and the API console in the vault area. It provided the greatest physical security available, short of constructing a new, high-security building.

Jörg took the lead, negotiating with CEOs at Europe's major Internet companies. In Germany, an Internet backbone company capable of handling 10,000 gigabits per second installed sigma interface units in their optical amps. In Amsterdam, a company delivering 8,500 gigabits per second capacity agreed to allow modifications to their optical amplifiers. London, Paris and St. Petersburg followed suit.

"We've got to tackle the Internet one major backbone at a time," Jörg said. "We'll start with Europe and go on from there to the U.S. Then Australia, South America and Asia."

While Jörg and Kyle worked on the technology and deployment issues, Cary and Karla focused their energy on creating the Board of Review. They compiled a list of people who had been recognized for their work in humanitarian efforts around the world.

"I've been speaking with Herr Schlinger in Austria," Cary said. "He's been working with people in South America, especially Colombia, because it's been so war-torn with drugs for so many years. The people there are like you and me. They don't want to live in a place where drug lords run their lives."

"Yes. I have read about him. In fact, my father donated to his cause some years ago. I know he is a person we can count on," Karla replied.

The women built a list of almost thirty people who might be qualified to serve on the Board. They began vetting them, talking with them by video chat and explaining what membership on the Board would require and what it would mean.

Over a few weeks the list shrank to eleven people. Some of the original thirty weren't interested or found the proposal to solve social problems and discover root causes behind mankind's behavior using a computer an implausible idea. Some were in poor health. Yet the final eleven each gained a clear understanding of what was expected of them. They expressed enthusiasm over the project. They were to evaluate, and then to approve or deny approval for each quantum computing project the world petitioned.

It was a heady appointment. It required the best minds and the ability to separate one's self from petty biases and predilections; to think of nothing more or less than advancing the welfare and improving the future of humanity.

Over the next months, Jörg oversaw the installation of eZo's sigma client interface components throughout Europe. The eZo team put the system through tests and found it could solve optimization problems that had stymied traditional computers since their invention. In Florida, the eZo Systems office sat vacant, lights off, while Kyle, Rick and Cary began learning the lifestyle of Switzerland.

In May, the Swiss and American team of six sat down to draft their first memo to the world. They prepared a press release and sent it to OmegaNet, and to the world's few remaining international newspapers.

NEWS RELEASE

eZo Systems' Quantum Super Computer Seeks to Advance Welfare of Humanity

May 7, 2034 - West Palm Beach, Florida and Zürich, Switzerland

eZo Systems, Inc. has deployed a powerful quantum super computer system that uses the Internet as its foundation. To date, the system has successfully used entangled photons flowing through the Internet to create the world's first fully functional quantum super computing system. It utilizes tens of thousands of qubits to deliver the greatest computational power ever achieved.

This system is designed to provide solutions that advance harmony, cooperation and friendship, and to advance goodwill among all nations and people.

eZo Systems is seeking problems to be solved. We invite all governments, institutions of higher learning, foundations, humanitarian organizations, corporations and individuals to submit problems they wish to be solved. Please submit your requests in a petition format, including the names of those people making the request; any organizational affiliations; the funds you pledge to solve a specific problem; and the benefits you anticipate should your project be selected.

All petitions will be studied by eZo Systems' Board of Review. Those submissions not dedicated to advancing goodwill and well-being for all humanity will be rejected. We ask you consider the problem you submit carefully to ensure it addresses issues that will advance the welfare of the planet. We further ask you to submit your petitions using the web form located at our website. Using the requested petition format will improve the likelihood your request receives suitable attention and review.

Please visit eZoQuantumSystems.com for further detail.

Within hours of its release, eZo's inbox went wild. A woman in North Dakota begged eZo to find her child who had been abducted by her boyfriend, an escaped felon. Several scientific organizations blasted eZo's press release, claiming no one had yet been able to build a working quantum computer. A message later traced to a member of the U.S. Federal Reserve Bank sought help in resolving problems of wanton spending—the trillions of dollars in unfunded liabilities the nation had accumulated over decades of political infighting, partisanship, petty squabbling, unfettered spending and misfeasance so profoundly immoral it could no longer be ignored.

The Micronesian nation of Palau, recently overtaken by rising oceans that decimated their islands sitting only a few feet above rising sea levels, sought help for its displaced citizens. A Las Vegas bookmaker asked for help in forecasting the outcomes of upcoming boxing matches. A politician from Virginia sought help in his re-election campaign, claiming his programs would eliminate a plethora of social injustices.

An Indian economist asked for help in reforming his nation's caste system that kept countless millions in poverty and indentured servitude. A child, later discovered to be only twelve years old, touched out a message on his mother's CoFone asking for help with the bullies who made his life hell at school.

The nudist city of Cap d'Agde, France, proposed an initiative that would extend the naturist lifestyle to all the world, claiming nudism would reduce tension and enhance friendship among people. Among their notes intended to justify their plan they pointed out, "People shoot, burn, decapitate, imprison, execute and torture human bodies. Nudists merely choose to forego clothing. Which is the greater sin?"

A young woman in Oklahoma complained that TV shows and movies were too violent; that they promoted hostility, attack and catered to our lowest instincts. She asked for a total overhaul of the entertainment industry to bring it in line with "traditional values."

The NSA and the Doppelganger group met with the White House. The White House consulted with the Department of Justice, but determined, with disappointment, the U.S. government had no authority to commandeer eZo's technology. No patents had been filed to give the government grounds to hijack eZo's technology under the authority of some arcane or esoteric law. The eZo Sub-S corporation had filed all its IRS returns on time. The Fifth and Fourteenth Amendments to the U.S. Constitution presented a major roadblock to government officials who, nevertheless, strongly believed eZo's quantum system should be put into their trustworthy hands. eZo's presence in Switzerland, an armed but neutral nation, further confounded U.S. efforts to make a power grab for eZo's technology. The U.S., Russia, China, Israel, England, Germany and a few nations from the Middle East deployed intelligence assets to Zürich, but found nothing that would give them access to eZo's technology.

The news cycle, usually lasting twenty-four hours for routine stories, picked up the eZo story and carried it for weeks. Reporters found themselves blind-copied on emails sent to the Board of Review. Those emails, sent by entities hoping for publicity on their own pet projects, kept countless channels on OmegaNet jumping with outrageous requests that entertained the masses. Not a day went by without another ridiculous request making its way to the fascinated public. An atheist "mega-church" called for the quantum system to prove, once and for all, that God did not and could not possibly exist. A Christian church group asked for a project to finally locate the Ark of the Covenant and the Holy Grail.

Yet serious bloggers and media outlets picked up on the core message of eZo's press release. They bantered and speculated on eZo's background, both in their op-ed and hard news sections. Who is on that unnamed Board of Review? What qualifications do those boffins have to approve or deny any given proposal? Who or what gives them any authority? An investigative reporter from a London media outlet speculated that Jörg Tritten was involved in re-engineering the Internet, but could not explain how that had happened or his vital role in the project. Another tied Hans Seffing and Karla Kensinger to the story, but again without details or facts that could be confirmed.

The press zeroed in on the financial aspects of eZo's quantum computer. What's the story with their escrow account? They're telling the world to submit problems, but want applicants to commit money? Who can tell what the cost of a solution should be? Does solving "problem A" cost more than "problem B?" The news media speculated on what solving different problems might cost. They went on to consider how eZo was creating a monopoly on solving problems and how they should, therefore, be regulated by some governmental agency. Libertarians and others around the world who stood for smaller government argued eZo should be left alone to work for the betterment of humanity rather than making them subject to government oversight. The debate raged on, just like so many other debates had slogged on for decades with no resolution.

Kyle, Rick and Cary became overnight celebrities as the principals at eZo. Stories appeared worldwide documenting what could be discovered of their lives, their loves, their careers and anything that held even a micron of interest to a fascinated public. The sleazier media outlets filled supermarket checkout aisles with scandal rags using every festering piece of filth they could invent to keep the public frothing. Cary's ex-boyfriend, Robby, gave a first-hand account of their relationship, making it even more lascivious than the paper's disgraceful editorial standards required.

In less than a week, the incoming email overwhelmed eZo's servers. "Rick, we're running almost twenty thousand emails a day. There's no way we can deal with that volume. Can we setup a filtering system to prioritize them?" A few days later, Rick turned it on.

On the second Wednesday of June, Kyle called the first Board of Review meeting to order. Board members who could travel to Zürich met in person and sat at a large, round table with the three Swiss and the three from eZo. Others, dispersed across the globe, joined via video telepresence.

Kyle opened the meeting with introductions from each Board member. A Buddhist monk from Thailand greeted the gathering with the traditional *namaskara* greeting, the gesture holding two hands palm to palm at heart level while bowing deeply to others in attendance to signify his respect for all. An Italian Catholic priest, a Mexican social worker, a woman living in New Zealand who headed a charitable trust that cared for the native Māori aboriginal people—they and others all took turns at introductions.

Kyle addressed the worldwide group. "I am humbled and grateful you have each decided to dedicate a portion of your time and energy to this work. We look forward to collaborating with all of you. Our mission, as you know, is to improve the lot of people living on the planet.

"Our quantum computer can solve incredibly complex problems. It's our role to review the problems and projects various people and organizations submit. Causes always produce effects. It's our goal to keep our eyes focused on the *causes*. If we can eradicate them, their unwanted, damaging effects will evaporate.

"Now, I'd like to ask Dr. Kensinger to review the major categories of projects submitted to date."

Karla stood up from the round table. Kyle remembered just this picture. It was the one he had seen in his Right Mind box months ago when he discovered the solutions he might find in Switzerland. He saw once again the tall, spired buildings visible through the windows of the room, Lake Zürich in the distance and people sitting around the conference table. He marveled how that mysterious vision from his Right Mind box had now come to pass.

Karla began. "Hello friends. We have tabulated thousands of petitions and find many of them fall into the same general categories." She projected a slide for all to see; it ranked the requests they'd received.

1. Humanitarian efforts. More than 800,000 requests ask to solve problems related to poverty, disease and social ills.
2. Sustainability. Some 98,000 seek an answer to how global sustainability can be achieved without contributing to climate change.
3. Clean water was the issue for over 80,000 petitions.
4. Some 78,000 proponents of democratization asked how democracy can emerge from authoritarian regimes and governments.
5. About 1,500 addressed the issue of how ethical considerations can be more prominently incorporated into global decisions.

"Ladies and gentlemen, the list goes on to encompass several hundred thousand legitimate petitions. Yet only a small number address problems that goes to a root cause, to the core, of human discomfort, pain and suffering," Karla continued.

"Please take note of number five. We believe the issue of making ethical decisions more prominent addresses a root cause of many problems. Too often decisions are made for political, economic or financial reasons. We'd like to address ways to bring ethics back into the limelight. When political and business leaders ignore ethics, we see many unwanted effects."

The monk in Thailand raised his hand to comment. "Dr. Kensinger, I agree with what you say. To find the most profound cause behind the ills of this planet we must look deeper. I would submit that *dukkah* is the cause of all problems—the clinging and craving people do to achieve what they want, and to avoid what they do not want. People often place their own wants and desires above ethical considerations."

An ethicist from Denmark seated at the conference table replied. "Yes, I agree. People do cling to ideas, goals and to idols such as wealth and power, and they crave various outcomes to satisfy their wants and needs. However, we may also want to consider another fundamental issue that drives life on this planet. I suggest we give thought to the idea that many people are essentially *fearful*. If we can eliminate fear from our collective mind, we can allow the loving nature of people to express itself in the world. In a world without fear, cooperation and more ethical behavior will take priority."

The discussion and debate began. The Board's first official approvals went to weather forecasting and the protein-folding problems. Next, the Board began discussing the ethical decision-making dilemma Karla had outlined. As they drilled down into root causes, two ideas emerged: one that had surfaced from the Danish Board member—the issue of fear that drove so much behavior. The second was the issue of competition, which pits one against another, guaranteeing an "us versus them" scenario in countless human interactions, both personal and organizational. After a full day's deliberation, the Board laid the groundwork for further discussion on the ethical decision-making problem and established a sub-committee to study it in preparation for next month's meeting.

As the day closed, Kyle took the podium once again. "Thank you, ladies and gentlemen. I'm honored to be in your presence.

I'd like to schedule our next full Board meeting on the first Wednesday of next month. In the meantime, we in Switzerland will study petitions identified in the first four categories Dr. Kensinger outlined. Now, I'm happy to take any remaining comments before we adjourn."

The group listened as each member offered closing remarks, then Kyle ended the meeting. The Board members attending live at the meeting in Zürich departed amid hugs, handshakes and affection. The Americans and the Swiss found themselves alone, with video screens darkened and the conference room empty but for their presence.

"A wonderful beginning," Karla said. The six each stood and shook hands, embraced and congratulated one another. Rick opened a magnum of champagne and poured drinks all around.

"This is way more than I ever thought we could do," Cary said. "Our Board...my God! They're exceptional. We've got some of the best minds on the planet working with us."

"Yes," Jörg said, bringing everyone back down to earth. "It was a good beginning. Now we've got work to do."

The six agreed to meet again the following morning to cull through the submissions made in the first four categories Karla had listed.

Kyle approached Karla as the others left for their homes and their hotels.

"I'd like to take you to dinner if you're not too tired."

"I'd like that."

They caught a taxi to a quiet restaurant favoring the *nach Zürcher Art* style of cuisine at an eatery that harkened back to the sumptuous guildhalls of old Switzerland.

"What is your take-away from our first Board meeting?" she asked.

He thought for a moment. "We've got some great minds working with us. I think everyone agrees we need to focus on root causes. I'm glad the woman from Norway brought up the issue of fear. It generated a lot of discussion."

"What seems to be the next step?" she asked between bites.

Kyle sipped his drink. "With the protein-folding problem Board-approved, Hans and Rick are submitting it to the computer. When we deliver solutions, we can move the money pledged by big pharma out of escrow and into our bank. Several universities, research centers and government agencies are putting up money on protein-folding, too. We'll have about $80 million in escrow. Now it's up to Hans and Rick to find the answers. Rick says the computing power we have with the European Internet backbone is more than enough. It'll be nice to finally put some money in the bank. Then we can continue looking for an answer to the root cause problem."

The waiter cleared their table and brought coffee. "The woman from Denmark talked about fear. How can you hope to eradicate *fear?"* Karla asked as she gazed into his eyes. "That seems like an impossible mission."

"I'm not sure yet. Coding that into the system...I don't know. There's a lot we need to learn before we know how to pose that question."

Karla sipped at her coffee. "That was a good meal, but if I drink this caffeine I'll be up half the night."

Kyle smiled. "Well then, drink up. I'd be glad to keep you company."

Karla leaned forward. "I would like that."

A five-minute taxi ride took them to their hotel. They reached Karla's room and she called room service for a bottle of Galliano and ice. They each took a seat on her sofa with a view over Lake Zürich.

"Zürich is beautiful," Kyle said. "A year ago I never imagined I'd be enjoying this view with a wonderful woman who helped bring our quantum system to life." He peered into Karla's eyes and leaned over to kiss her cheek.

She accepted his affection and leaned toward him expectantly. "*Danke*. Thank you, Kyle."

He set his drink on the table and reached up to cradle her face in his hands. "I'd like to thank you with more than my words."

"I hoped you would," she said.

Kyle and Karla touched their lips together. Gentle touching gave way to kisses that began tenderly, then grew impassioned. Their arms wrapped around one another's bodies as they drew closer. With ice melting into the Galliano that remained in their glasses, and the bottle left uncorked to suffer the ravages of the air, he led her into the bedroom. A few hours later they fell asleep in one another's arms, exhausted and feeling complete.

As the sun began its rise over the mountains, Karla awoke and watched the man sleeping next to her. *Who is this man?* She thought about their lovemaking; his gentleness and sweetness intermingled with their mutual passion. He had loved her as no other man had, ever before. She treasured the way he caressed her, sweeping her hair back from her face and, ever so slowly, finding the customary ways of giving her pleasure, but doing so with such attention, with such caring, with soft touches rather than force driven by so many men's eagerness in the heat of the moment.

Kyle awoke, opened his eyes and met hers. "Good morning, sweet one." He kissed her lips and held her warmly against his body. "I loved our night together."

Karla embraced him even tighter. "Thank you," she responded. "It was lovely. *You* are lovely. I've never known a man like you. I am so happy we slept together."

"So am I." Kyle turned onto his back with his head sharing Karla's pillow. "I'd like to share something with you. It's a morning prayer. It helps me keep in touch with my Right Mind. Would you like to hear it?"

A prayer? Well that's the last thing I expected. She hesitated for a moment. "Okay."

"All right. I'll say it out loud, and if you like you can repeat it in your mind." He began his now-established morning communion:

"Thank you for this new morning and the happiness of starting my day by talking with you. I would like to hear your thoughts so you can guide me through the day in my Right Mind.

"Thank you for your Love and showing me your wisdom in dealing with situations gracefully, so my words and actions are pleasant to all. I am happy your plans for me are good. I trust your guidance in all things I encounter today. Thank you too for helping me hear you speak to me from my Right Mind. For helping me choose to judge nothing, to forgive everything and to share what you teach me with others I meet throughout the day."

They lay quietly at its conclusion. "That is sweet, but I've always thought prayers asked for things."

He smiled. "So did I, for most of my life, but I've found gratitude for what we've already been given is what prayer is truly about. For me, it's a matter of giving thanks. We can't control much of anything in our lives. So, I give thanks for the guidance I get to help me live a better way."

She wrinkled her forehead. "A better way? What do you mean?"

Kyle explained the way of the world: how people judge almost everything; how their never-quiet ego minds bubble up their fears, worries and biases; how people project those on events, people and situations to create each person's own perception; how the act of projecting actually *makes* what one perceives. He told her how his prayer helped him set an intention for each day that changed his perceptions and understandings.

"In spite of everything happening around me, living in my Right Mind gives me a sense of peace. Spending a few minutes giving thanks cements that in place; gets me started off on the right foot." he said.

"What about all the conflict in the world? What do you do about that?"

"I realize it's happening, but at the same time I know it doesn't matter. It's not real."

"Of course it matters! It's real to the person who gets hurt or killed."

"Sure, but I'm coming to see that nothing that happens here is Real. Things only seem to be here for a while, then they're gone. Change is the only thing we can count on while we're alive. I'm beginning to see *everything* in the world as nothing more than change. It's as if change is an entity unto itself. It just is. Putting values on transient things doesn't seem to make much sense. Life? Suffering? Death? Those are all part of the constant change."

"So, are you saying you do not care about suffering and death?"

"Yes. I *care*. That's why we built our computer. To do something about it, but I've got to be sure we don't waste time working on things we can't do anything about. That's why we've got to stay focused on the root causes."

Karla rolled over and put her head on his shoulder. "I don't get it. You're a mystery to me, Dr. Williams."

He chuckled. "Anyway, I say this prayer every morning and night. Well...I have to admit, I missed it last night!"

Karla laughed and gave him a hug. "You might have missed your prayer, but you loved me like no one has ever before." She rearranged her pillow, put her elbow on it, propped her head up on her hand and became serious. "I felt like the most cared-for woman in the world. Like a princess. Like I was the center of your universe."

Kyle smiled. "I'm happy to know that. You *are* a princess to me."

They kissed again, then Karla laid her head on his shoulder as he wrapped his arms around her.

"That 'projecting' thing...is that what you're talking about when you say we need to solve the problem of fear?"

"No, projecting is part of what the ego mind does. It's what keeps us in this dream world."

"Right. Dream world."

"Everything the ego tells us is a dream. None of it's Real."

"Wait. I keep coming back to all the misery in the world. You can't just say it's a dream."

Kyle paused for a moment. "I've seen a vision of what I call a 'Sonship'—all humanity being one. No individual people at all. Just one great Holy Creation our ego minds work hard to hide. It wants us to believe we're all separate people."

"We are! You and me. We're two people."

"Only in this dream. In the Right Mind we're all one," Kyle said. "In the Right Mind everything is peace. I think that's the only thing that's Real. If people could find that, there wouldn't be any more war; any more projecting the fear people carry inside themselves."

"That's why you're so focused on fear being the root cause of our problems. So people can get to that Right Mind?" she asked.

"Exactly. We need to eliminate fear. I think that's what Rick and I are meant to do in this life. I think we're here to put the mystical properties of quantum mechanics to the test. To see if we can reboot humanity and help people get to their Right Minds."

Karla snuggled close to Kyle, squeezed him, reached over to kiss his cheek and nuzzle closer. "You're one of a kind, my good man."

The two held one another in a silent embrace. Eventually Karla spoke.

"What can we do? How can we make this reboot happen? What can we do to get it started?"

Kyle smiled. "Well, I guess the first step would be to get out of bed. Let's head back to the Center and see what we've missed. It's almost ten o'clock! The others are probably wondering what's happened to us."

Karla reached for her CoFone sitting on the nightstand. "You're right. I got two calls from Jörg. I'll call and let him know I'm on the way."

CHAPTER 32

Cause & Effect

"Kyle, I have news," Jörg said. "I have been talking with the tier one companies in the U.S. They provide the major backbone for your country's Internet. They have agreed to let us install sigma clients in their optical amplifiers."

"My God, that's huge. Have you told Rick?"

"No, I wanted you to be the first to know, but there is more. Do you know about FLAG? It is the Fiber-optic Link Around the Globe. It's about 30,000 kilometers long. It connects the U.K., Japan and other countries—India, most of the Middle East, South Korea and some of China. FLAG carries most intercontinental Internet traffic. I do not have figures yet, but I suspect we might be able to install several hundred more sigma clients in the FLAG."

"I'd have to do the math to see how many qubits that will give us to ramp up our compute power. It's going to be incredible," Kyle said.

"Well, do not get too excited yet. It will take money and a good deal of time and work to get them all in place. These people are not doing this out of goodwill. They must be paid. You have to get working on the backlog of petitions we have received through the website. You need to begin giving problems to the Board for approval so you can collect money to pay the U.S. companies and the FLAG group."

Kyle gathered Rick, Karla and Cary together. He recounted the arrangements Jörg outlined. "I'd like to get a recap of problems we've received that fit the root cause issues. Installing a thousand or more sigma clients is going to cost millions. We need to have them manufactured, tested, delivered and installed. Then we'll need to pay the sponsors. I'll get with Jörg on the details. Today though, I'd like to start prioritizing a list of problems we can bring before the Board so we can submit them to our quantum system. Then..."

Rick interrupted Kyle in mid-sentence. "Hey man, there's something you should know. A lot of the problems people submitted came through with no pledge of payment. Maybe we should toss those out and work on the ones that have pledged the most money. We'd get some cash flow going."

Pledged the most money? We need to be looking at root causes. Kyle paused for a moment and thought better. "Okay. Let's take a look at the ones with the most money attached."

Rick gestured at his console and brought up a slice of the database. "The top five problems are all from governments and the UN. Here's one. It's worth $100 million."

A cabal of U.S. government agencies sought to solve optimization problems. On close examination of their supporting documentation it became clear their "optimization" problem involved nuclear weapons. The super computer engineers and scientists had used for years, the second fastest in the world, had helped them build better weapons by simulating tweaks to the weapons' design. Now, they were looking for even more power.

Kyle stared at the projection on the wall with a frown of disbelief. "That's pathetic. They think they can maintain a balance of nuclear power with better bombs? We don't need a Board meeting to answer this one. Mark this one 'dead' and respectfully decline their petition. I can't begin to see how people could think of nuclear weapons in the same breath with helping people."

"Yeah, their $100 million would give us a head start on the money, but building nukes isn't what I had in mind either," Rick said.

"Cary, would you send a suitable reply? Let's move on," Kyle said.

Another petition asked for help solving terrorism. Others wanted help with human rights, torture, slavery, forced prostitution and human trafficking. The day wore on. Climate change. Over population. Proliferation of WMD's. Worldwide economic collapse. Poverty, clean water, protection against meteor strikes on the planet, animal husbandry and the extinction of species. Rick flashed one after another onto the screen.

Kyle struggled with each problem. *None of those are root causes. They're all effects of something deeper.*

They broke for lunch, then continued. Solving the gap between rich and poor. Sustainable development in the face of climate change. Transnational organized crime, the status and treatment of women, renewable energy and a dozen other challenges flashed onto the screen as Rick scrolled through the database. By dinnertime the team felt as if the weight of the world's problems would crush them as surely as the gravity on Jupiter.

"I need to take a break from this. It is too much," Karla said. Her head flopped against the chair back. "I don't know where we're going with this."

Rick turned away from the screen. "It's simple. We're going after money."

"Of course," Karla said. "Why do we not take on a few of the simpler problems that will pay us so we can build out the sigma clients?"

Kyle's jaw muscles twitched and he sighed. "I think you know. All these issues are asking for solutions to *effects.* I want to address root causes. I've been pretty clear about that for a long time."

Karla pushed her bangs back from her forehead. "I suppose many of them are effects, but we need to begin answering people. Accepting their money. Even if the problem they want to solve is not one of your root causes." She stared at Kyle, waiting to hear his response.

Rick jumped into the conversation. "I agree, partner. Let's get some cash flow started."

"Rick's right. We need to see our effort from the Right Mind, like you do. At the same time, we need to generate income, don't you think?" asked Cary.

Kyle looked at his friends. *They're more interested in putting money into escrow than solving real problems.* "I don't know, guys. I don't know. Let's adjourn for tonight and get back together in the morning. I understand we need money, but I don't want to spend a lot of time on issues that don't address the cause of all the misery on the planet. I want to find *real* answers that can cut through all the bullshit." Kyle paused, realizing he might sound like a broken record. "Hey, I'm sorry, guys. You're right. Let's close up shop for tonight and sleep on all this."

The three left the room, leaving Kyle alone. Cary and Karla walked out of the Center together.

"Let's get a bite to eat" Cary said.

"Sure, but I am exhausted. Let us go back to the hotel. We can order from room service."

The two women ate, relaxed and talked.

"Kyle is too stressed out on finding those root causes. I think there's a lot we can do to help people if only he'd agree to take on some of the problems we looked at today. If we can pare down the list we'll have something to work with the next time we meet with the Board," Cary said.

"Yes, I agree. I hope I can survive all this. I feel we have spent the whole day looking at disasters. One after another. It almost makes me ill." Karla kicked her shoes off and let them drop to the floor, then pulled her legs up beneath her. "I wish I had a pill to wipe this all away." She held her teacup in both hands and lifted it to her face so she could breathe in the aroma.

Cary sipped her tea and allowed Karla a moment of silence.

Karla set her cup down. "Strength, sister. That is what I need." She paused. "So, tell me, how long have you been working with Kyle?"

"It's been almost two years now."

"Tell me about him," Karla said, hoping for a deeper understanding of the man who had seemed such a masterful gentleman last night, but who was dedicated, probably beyond practical sensibility, to his root cause ideas.

"What do you want to know? He's a great boss. I really like him, but I must tell you, we've had some strange and amazing experiences together."

"Strange? Like what?"

"I'll tell you some things, Karla. They might not make much sense. What I've experienced since working at eZo has changed everything about me."

"What do you mean?"

"I mean *everything.* I used to worry about where my life was going. About finding a man and raising a family. Now I don't worry about anything. Of course, it helps to have found that man..."

"Oh?"

"Yes. His name is Paul Glazer. He's a private investigator. He's the person I came to know because he was investigating eZo on those patent issues. While all that was happening, we fell in love. He's a wonderful man."

"Where is he? Do you miss him?"

"Of course. He bought a house in Florida so we could be close to each other. He lived in California before his law firm assigned him to the eZo case. Across the country. Now he's just down the street from me. I miss him."

"Why don't you have him fly over? I'm sure we can find a place to put him up."

"Putting him up would be easy. He could stay with me. I'd love that, but I don't know about his work. He's always getting assignments to go somewhere and investigate something."

"Well, if you want him to be with you, let me know. I'll ask Jörg if he would fly him over in his private plane."

"Oh, Karla! You would do that? Jörg would do that?"

"Of course I would. I'm sure I can convince Jörg." Karla sipped her tea. "But tell me more about Kyle. You were saying you and he had some experiences together?"

Cary stirred her tea slowly. "What's happened to me is hard to describe in any way that makes sense."

"What do you mean?"

"I mean we've had some experiences together involving two...'people.' I don't know what else to call them. Their names are Marci and Aimer. They are like angels. The kind of angels who live in Heaven. They're mystical. They're unlike anyone you've ever met. They just appear from time to time to teach us...to give us new ideas...to tutor us, I guess you could say. They're some kind of spiritual teachers."

"What?" Karla's eyes went wide. "What do you mean spiritual teachers? Angels? Kyle mentioned having a mentor. It that who he was talking about?"

"Probably. Aimer and Marci are not of this earth. How can I explain it? They're some kind of spirit beings who visited with us at eZo on a couple of occasions. Then one night Marci appeared at my front door in Florida and changed me forever."

Cary recited the evening she'd thrown a glass of wine in Paul Glazer's face, and how Marci had somehow rewound the entire evening, tossing every law of time and cause and effect out the window. She described how Marci had enfolded her in a meditation that took her to places she'd experienced only once before—when the cloud descended on the conference room at eZo's Florida office.

"My God, Cary! Who are these people? Are they like ghosts? What do they look like?"

"Like real people, but they're the ones, especially Marci, who changed me. I think they've changed Kyle too. He seems to be so much more comfortable with whatever happens than he was before. I was amazed to see him change his mind about the lawsuit. He went from fretting and obsessing over everything that could go wrong to just ignoring what was happening. He told me we need to *see what happens.* When I asked him what he meant, he said he couldn't control anything. Today, I guess we saw his other side. I think he's too focused on his root causes. He's getting too bossy and too preoccupied with it."

"He scares me," Karla said as she picked up her cup of tea from the table, took a sip and replaced it on the table. She stood up and walked to the window. Zürich hung outside her fourth-floor hotel suite like a painting with the moonlight casting silver shards of light across the lake. "I loved being with him last night, but I could not stop wondering if he is entirely sane. Much of what he says makes no sense to me."

"He's completely sane. If you had been there when Marci and Aimer came to us you'd understand where he gets some of his ideas."

Karla left the window and returned to her chair. "Here's what I know about Kyle. He is a fantastic lover. He made me feel like...it is hard to explain. It was like there was nothing else in his universe when he kissed me. As if nothing existed but me. I never felt anything like that before with a man."

"Ha! You and Kyle are an item? I had no idea! I'm glad for you, Karla. He's a good man. You're a good woman. Look at all you've done at your foundation to help people for so many years."

"*Danke.* Despite Kyle's obsession with root causes, I could easily come to love him. Deeply. Maybe I already do."

"You wouldn't be making a bad choice. He's told me a little about his life and I know he had a tough time as a kid, but underneath all that, I know he's sincere about wanting to make a difference. We only have one life, right? Why not do everything we can to live it the best we can."

"Yes, but he has so many strange ideas. Sometimes I wonder if he is a little *verrückt.* Crazy. Has he talked to you about his Right Mind idea?" Karla asked.

"He's not crazy. Yes. He's told me about that."

"What is it about? I do not understand him. Right Mind. Sonship. Billions of people who are all one. Kyle seems strange to me. I do not know what to do about him."

"Marci and Aimer are the ones who brought up the idea of the Sonship. What I learned from Marci one night when she came to my apartment—it's the only way to live. In fact, that's what changed me. I learned in an instant—Marci called it a 'holy instant'—that I don't have to worry or fret or cling to things. I only need to spend time in my Right Mind. Kyle showed me a way to get to that place with some strange ways of breathing. It takes me to a stillness every time I do it."

"He did something like that with me back in Florida. He asked to hold me in his arms and to breathe with him, then said we are the same. That we are one person...but it made no sense. I do not know where he gets those ideas. I wanted to get away from him. I felt like he was living in some kind of crazy land instead of in the world."

"He's talking about the 'Sonship' Marci and Aimer showed us. It's the idea our seeming individuality as people is an illusion—that we're actually one holy Sonship created by our Creator."

The women talked late into the night. Cary explained what she understood of Marci and Aimer, their teachings, and how Kyle had seemed to embrace everything they taught. Karla listened with a sense of awe as she began to understand how Kyle had arrived at such strange ideas.

Finally exhausted from the day's work, the women parted. Cary went to her room and called Paul. His face sprang onto her screen and she realized with a pang how much she missed him.

"Hello, Paul."

"Hey sweetie, I was just thinking of you. How's it going in Switzerland—the land of cheese and money?"

Cary laughed. "It's going well, and I'm calling with good news. My friend, Karla, said she might be able to arrange a private jet to fly you over to Switzerland. You could stay with me. I don't know how much longer we'll be here. It could be months. I'll call you tomorrow if we can get it set up. Could you get a sabbatical from your law firm for a while and come be with me?"

Glazer did a mental jump for joy at thought of flying to Switzerland. He had no active case assignments now and had been enjoying a weekly round of golf in Cary's absence. Otherwise, the uneventfulness of each day, the dawdling clock and calendar, left him with nothing to do but think of Cary and how they might build a life together...whenever she finally chose to return to Florida.

"Of course I can come over."

"Wonderful. I can't wait to feel your arms around me again." She kissed the air sensuously so her CoFone would carry her excitement across the ocean to Paul. "I've got great plans for what I'm going to do with you, Mr. Glazer. I hope you've been working out!"

CHAPTER 33

Oneness

Kyle spent a troubled night in his hotel room. The day had not gone the way he wanted. Looking at proposals that held the greatest promise of money annoyed him.

We need money, but I don't want to whore the system out to anyone who will pay us. Our system is too important to use for effects. We need to work on causes. Why don't they see that?

He climbed out of bed the next morning and made his way to the Center where he assembled the team in the conference room once again. Kyle realized he needed to lead the group, in spite of his internal conflict.

"Okay guys. What we did yesterday was a good start. I'm going to delegate the question of finding the money to you. I'd like you to come back to me by the end of the week so we can get those money makers on the agenda for the Board meeting. But...and this is a big 'but'...I'd also ask each of you to tally up the projects you think will address root causes. I want to be ready to present them to the full Board meeting next week along with your money-making ventures."

Karla frowned. "I do not like to think of organizations that are looking for help as just 'money-making ventures.'"

"I hear you, but remember, the whole purpose of our work is to find the reason the world's so damn infected with all its insanity."

"Yes, the *fear* you talked about. I understand that, but in the meantime, we need to keep money flowing."

Kyle turned away from the group and gazed out the window at a steady stream of people walking along the sidewalks. *I wish we could get on the same page.* He turned to face them. "Yes, you're right. We need to find money. Let's get busy and make a list so we can present it to the Board next week. Now, please excuse me for a while."

Kyle turned and left the room, walked to his office and closed the door behind him. He sat at his desk, wondering why his own people didn't see the project as he did. He leaned back in his chair and began his breathing practice. Even after twenty minutes he'd not found his place of stillness. His mind roiled with annoyance at his friends; their inability to see the importance of their work together.

He opened his eyes. Marci and Aimer sat comfortably on the couch in his office as if they were waiting for him to acknowledge their presence.

"Hey tiger, what's going on?" Marci asked. "You having some problems with the *roots* of the tree? You probably know you can't fix a sick tree only by looking at its *roots*. You've got to look out for pine beetles or whatever. Maybe the tree isn't getting enough sunshine. Maybe the soil is parched."

"Marci! I'm glad to see you."

Aimer had an expectant look on his face. "Are you ready for another new idea, my friend?"

"I don't know. I'm trying to figure out how to fix things. It's not going the way I want."

"Well then, let me ask you this," Aimer continued. "Do you remember we told you your life and the life of everyone here is nothing more than a dream?"

"Of course I remember, but I don't get it. Not deep down." He glanced at Marci. "I've been practicing what you've shown me. Trying to judge nothing and forgive everything. Spending time in prayer every morning and night. I hear you, that we're in a dream, but it hasn't all come together yet. I'm trying to live as if *nothing* is real, but it's hard. I'm trying to find the root causes of our problems so we can fix them."

"It does seem to make some kind of sense to go after root causes," Marci said. "Let me ask you a fundamental question."

"What?"

Marci walked to Kyle, grabbed the armrests of his office chair and swiveled him around to face her directly. She leaned into his face. Kyle shrank back from her intrusion into his personal space. She leaned further into it. "If this is nothing more than a dream, an illusion, why would you spend your time and your quantum computer trying to fix the problems you find in a dream? *What's the point in fixing a dream that isn't real?*"

Kyle sat as if stunned, staring into Marci's face for a few seconds. *Of course I have to fix things. C'mon Marci. Get real.* He pushed himself back on his wheeled office armchair, rolling away from her to put a little distance between himself and her outrageous question.

Marci stood as he rolled away and fixed him with a stare. "You're trying to fix things that are *unreal,* my friend. Why bother? Why devote yourself to your quantum computer? Your Board of Review? There's no point in trying to fix a dream. Once you wake up you'll realize it was all a silly illusion."

"C'mon Marci. There's bad stuff going on in the world. I'm trying to get to the underlying causes so we can fix things. That's been my goal since day one."

Marci took a few steps back and sat down again on the couch. Aimer leaned forward with his elbows on his knees. They both stared at Kyle. He felt a peacefulness fall over him.

Aimer spoke. "We told you a long time ago it would take some 'time' to understand what we're teaching you. You've made great progress. Today we're here to give you another bump forward."

Kyle sat, gazing at them.

"Here's some new guidance for you Kyle: Forget about what you want. Forget about who you think you are. You're setting up false idols by pinning your hopes on something in this illusory world. *You can't fix this dream with your computer.*"

Kyle jumped up from his chair. "What are you telling me? After everything you've said and done to help me get to this point...That's crazy! I'm not buying it. We've got entangled photons from half the continent at our disposal. We can damn well solve almost anything."

Aimer and Marci sat passively while Kyle ranted. Then Marci spoke in a quiet voice. "You're still using your ego mind. Your personality is getting in your way."

Kyle distanced himself from the two and paced the room. He huffed. "What does my personality have to do with anything?"

"It's part of the stuff in your ego box. In fact, it's what holds most of it together." Marci looked at him carefully, up and down, as if trying to find some sign of a defect on his person. "Now settle down and take a seat between us. Let's see if we can help you understand what we're talking about."

Kyle sat on the couch between the two.

"Your personality, the one you invest so much in maintaining—it's *nothing.* That personality you think of as yourself is only those bubbling-up things your ego mind sends up."

"Yeah, I know about stuff bubbling up."

"Sure, but what you don't know is a bit more complicated. There's an entire *constellation* of those thoughts connected to one another like a web. Countless little events in your day can trigger one bubble, and a whole bunch of them follow along in lockstep order. It's a *network* of those bubble thoughts that create your personality," Marci said.

Aimer jumped in. "A personality is nothing more or less than a group of tightly connected thoughts that trigger one another over and over again. Each of those thought bubbles has countless facets and interconnecting links to others. They operate through well-worn neural pathways in your brain. They're like super highways. Like grooves or rivers, where water flows and cuts its path deeper year after year."

Marci explained further. "You might have a specific thought that bubbles up based on what's happening at a given moment. That thought drags the entire network along with it. You might not notice it; it can be subtle. But that entire constellation of thoughts represents your habitual way of responding to events in this dream. It's your personality."

"What are you saying?" Kyle asked. He got up from his place between the two on the couch, confused and annoyed, and stood next to his desk frowning at Marci and Aimer.

Marci fixed him with a stare. "Here's an example. Do you remember the girl Rick dated a couple of times? Sandi? The one who liked to party? Remember what you did when the two of them stumbled half-drunk into your guys' dorm room, ready to have sex?" Marci asked.

Kyle looked far away. "Yeah. I told her to get the hell out and leave Rick alone. I told her Rick had too much important work to do to waste time messing around with a drunken slut."

Marci smirked and broke into a chuckle. "Exactly. I guess you were Mr. Personality, huh?"

Kyle grimaced.

"Well, that little event *was* your personality. It was your expression of what you believe. Your mom became alcoholic when you were young. You've known but hardly admitted to yourself that she looked for another man and slept around after divorcing your dad. One part of your personality—a whole array of thoughts—surrounds your dislike for drunks and loose women. Seeing that girl stagger through your door was enough to trigger those old neural pathways and kick loose a brigade of bubble-up thoughts.

Aimer continued. "Then they connected with another flock of thoughts: the ones that tell you Rick has important work to do. Years ago, you pushed him to stick with you through school. To get a job. Open a bank account. Save money for college. To study physics and computer science. You felt like Rick was one of the few people you could trust. You tried to take charge of what Rick was going to do. To control him so you'd have a sense of order in your life."

Aimer took hold of Kyle's arm, guiding him back to the couch. "Dozens of things happen every day to trigger a flood of thoughts. Those thoughts are almost always consistent. They come from your ego mind. Ego is the seat of your personality."

Marci studied Kyle again, inspecting him from head to toe. "I notice lately you've been almost beating up your friends to find those 'root cause' issues. What's going on there?" she asked.

"It's simple. I need to find causes. I don't want to waste time on their effects."

"Right," Marci continued. "Let's see if we can figure this out. Let's go back to where your personality began, during childhood. Your father was disabled and later died. Your mother became alcoholic and died. Your little sister was killed. You blamed yourself for her death. You built some core beliefs that 'life isn't fair' and 'God doesn't care about me.' In fact, you feared God as someone who would steal your soul away in the night. You begged him to save you and your loved ones, even your dog, but never believed He would listen unless you pleaded."

Kyle listened, but said nothing.

Aimer walked across the room, then turned to face Kyle. "Your personality is based on the core beliefs you built as a child, my friend. Everyone on the planet builds a set of core beliefs. They become touchstones, the stories they tell people, and themselves, repeatedly for their entire lives. You've build a set of beliefs based on the hardships you experienced. You believe God has forsaken you; He's not to be trusted. So, instead of giving Love and respect to the One who created you, you seek for solutions *within* this dream. That's what you're doing with your quantum computer. *You're trying to fix a dream. How insane is that?"*

Marci picked up the lesson. "The fact is that your ego mind, your personality, your so-called 'life' is nothing more than an *electrical event.* The electricity generated in your brain by biochemical interactions uses up about one-fourth of all the energy your body consumes. Your brain is a huge energy sink. It creates a 'field' that *you* call your mind. Your so-called mind is nothing more than an electrical, biochemical *event* you interpret as 'reality.' *That* is why I keep telling you this world you perceive is nothing but an illusion.

"I'll say again: It's only an electrical event. If your body didn't convert glucose from your food into energy to feed your brain, and if your lungs didn't give you the oxygen you need to burn up that glucose, your body would cease to function. You're a very efficient glucose-burning organism fed by the oxygen to create an electrical field you think is your reality. *That* is what your personality is, in truth."

Kyle shrank back into the couch.

"Yes," Aimer added. "As you perceive the world and the universe around you, you interpret it as reality." Aimer paused. "Who is it that *does* that perception, that interpretation? Who is it who *thinks* they understand the universe around them?"

Kyle gave her a sideways glance. "I suppose you're going to tell me it's my ego."

Marci continued. "It *is* your ego mind, your personality. That electrical event, that tiny field you call 'mind.' But, when you find the stillness of your Right Mind, you're operating outside of your

tiny personality. In the stillness you don't project and perceive anything. You have true *Vision* that sees Truth without using your body's eyes."

Kyle sat, trying to absorb her words.

"So, here's the question of the day, my friend. How do you get true Vision? Where does your true Vision come from?" Marci asked.

Kyle sat answerless and confused by the rapid-fire questions and answers that almost seemed to make sense.

"It comes from the God-ness within you," Aimer said. "It is the Knowledge God placed within you when He shared Himself to create His Sonship—all of us. It is His Mind. It has nothing to do with who you think you are or what you think is important. Nor does it have anything to do with those neural pathways that always seem to bubble up your ego thoughts. The *real* you is God-created. The real you is your *awareness*. The *witness*. It's the part of you separate from your ego mind."

Kyle looked from one to the other but found no words to speak.

"Relax. Let's do this for a while," Marci said. She and Aimer placed their hands on Kyle's forehead and watched as he slipped into a deep quietness. His shoulders relaxed and fell as his head leaned back on the couch. With Marci on one side and Aimer on the other, they spoke to him as they'd done once before, at a bonfire on the beach.

Marci: "Your ego mind plays tricks on you. Every time you think of something in your past or worry about the future, your ego gets involved.

Aimer: When your ego plays things in your mind, it bubbles up the same tired network of thoughts.

Marci: They're the core beliefs you've always carried with you; that network of thoughts your ego mind has so intimately woven together to give your life some rational meaning and consistency. Those same old neural pathways are activated whenever you recall the past or worry about the future.

Aimer: You might think of your family and of Julia. Her death. Your ego brings those thoughts up with a thousand other connected thoughts. Millions of neurons fire to generate emotions and feelings about her death and the guilt you feel for it. Their action gives you much of the same pain you felt at the time.

Marci: Your ego wants a consistent memory, Kyle. It wants you to feel the pain all over again.

Aimer: Your ego is a *false idol*, Kyle.

Marci: You want to find root causes? As a child you tried to find ways to get rid of the pain *you* felt. Now you've generalized your need. You want to do away with that pain for people everywhere so you can eliminate your own. Your own fear. Your own doubt that God loves you. Your own fear that He wants to punish you.

Aimer: Your pursuit of root causes is nothing more than an aspect of your ego's personality.

Aimer and Marci stopped speaking as a new understanding insinuated itself silently into Kyle's mind, like silk sliding over naked flesh, making no sound but leaving its gentle sensation.

Your personality isn't necessary. It's a creature of your ego mind. You have no need of it. Continue turning to me within for the answers you seek. Your old neural pathways and your ego have no role when you turn to me. Your Right Mind holds the answer to every question. You need not feel any sense of separation between yourself and any other. As you have said, 'we are One.' You can choose to touch everything lightly, with Love, with no differentiation and no separation between any of the things you encounter. With that comes true Vision.

Marci performed another lingering inspection of Kyle's person. "Now we'll go to the stillness so you can *see* with true Vision what we've been telling you." She and Aimer each adjusted the placement of their hands on Kyle's head and over his heart.

Kyle found himself floating in what, at first, seemed to be the featureless darkness of space. He heard heavenly music, just as he had during his bonfire episode on the beach. Yet he was alone. He moved from the place where he found himself, wondering if 'place' had any meaning within the infinitude he occupied. He moved at such a speed it caused him to wonder if 'speed' had any meaning either. There was no place to go, and yet no place he could not. He had no body, no eyes, no ears; only awareness. Yet with that newfound awareness he *saw* the entire universe laid out before him. Not just the universe astronomers peer into with their tiny instruments launched into earth orbit to gaze at the heavens. He saw a multiverse with, way off in what one might say was a small corner—if such a vision could have a corner—the physical universe he knew.

Countless billions of stars and galaxies filled his vision as he hurtled past that universe, into what something unknowable. All around him, as he skimmed through space that wasn't space at all, seeming to take time that he knew was only a construction and had no reality of its own, Kyle noticed brilliant, glorious "strands" floating through and connecting all the multiverse in a network that glowed like an infinite webwork of divine colors. Yet, they were far more than colors.

Kyle "looked" at the colors and realized they could just as well be music, poetry or visual art. Scholars could spend centuries discussing it, for it defied and transcended definition.

His awareness was drawn to a particular aspect of that web and he found himself inspecting its every detail as if he had all eternity to complete a thorough analysis. He was drawn inexorably into it. The closer he scrutinized it, the greater detail he saw. He thought of a Mandelbrot fractal image that replicates and connects with finer and finer aspects of itself without end, with each tiny portion of itself somehow holding the whole of it. Yet this web moved inwardly and outwardly through Eternity, filling Everything with its infinite replications of itself. Then he saw the most salient feature of that beauteous web of strands: an infinite Intelligence that permeated Everything.

As he delved deeper into it, he realized the web, no matter how it might be named, was All That Is—the very Fabric of Everything. It embraced him, moved through him, encompassed him. A deep, full knowing struck his awareness like a thunderbolt. Kyle suddenly saw All that Is with true Vision and knew its name: Love.

He understood the web of Love *is* the only Reality. He saw an image of everything in the multiverse *being* Love. Intertwining with Itself, connecting with every aspect of Itself, growing and yet growing again into ever more complex combinations, but never changing from Its only true nature.

He basked in Its eternal unfolding. A bright spot seemingly appeared an almost unimaginable time and space away at the center of everything Kyle could survey with his newfound vision. It glowed with a brilliance he could not describe, nor could he ignore its beckoning. He moved through Eternity toward the brilliance.

As he approached it, the music became more salient, diffusing everything with its harmonies. Its rich overtones and echoes wound in and out upon themselves endlessly. Kyle *saw* these heavenly sounds intermingled with the fractal web. He understood that, somehow, the web of color and Love and the music were one and the same. A unique and boundless creation, a form of art and beauty, it defied definition or description. The mellifluous web of Love warmed and bathed his essence with an impeccable, consummate feeling of Oneness. It was so absolute, so limitless and so vast that nothing else could possibly exist. The Oneness—composed of unfathomable Intelligence, brilliance, sound and Love and endless joy—gradually seemed to take on a greater density as the warmth and a growing feeling of unfettered peace and happiness penetrated his every level. Kyle continued moving toward the brilliance as those sensations magnified.

After an unknowable time, he merged into its depth. To its very center. He found and rested in a place where the sublime Oneness reached out with incomprehensible Love and touched all universes. He *knew* he was in the presence of his Creator. He *knew* he was That, the stuff of his Creator.

After what could have been centuries or eons, Kyle noticed more fully how the multiverse seemed to be in a constant state of creation. It had been so throughout Eternity, continually extending itself in floods of beauty. He thought of the things he had made during his earth life and realized nothing man makes endures. No house stands forever. Even oceans, deserts, planets and stars disappear with the eons.

Yet, with nothing more than a thought, Kyle *created* a new ripple in Eternity that changed the music and the brilliant webworks. He created what appeared to be a waterfall gently falling over, under, through and within All That Is, christening it with the profound Love he felt in his soul. Creation sang back to him with thanks and peace and Love as he watched his creation expand ever further to touch and become part of Everything. *What beauty!* he thought. With that thought it became even more resplendent.

Like a giant wave washing over a village, a torrent of understanding fell upon him. He *knew* God had lovingly extended what God Is to create the iridescent web of Love, the music, the art and beauty. God had extended and shared Himself to create All That Is. Kyle *saw* himself as part of that—even knowing it had no "parts" because it was an unlimited Oneness without boundaries or separations. Kyle *saw* how God had created the Sonship that Marci and Aimer had described to be what God Himself Is.

For an instant he wondered how the world, so small and insignificant and imperfect, could have been created in such contrast to all this wonder. He *saw* how the Creator had imbued the Sonship with all His endless power at the moment of the Sonship's creation. He *saw* how the Sonship had an absurd, crazy what-if thought that imagined something not part of the Oneness. *How could that be? The Oneness is All That Is. Nothing else Real exists.*

He *saw* how, in a flash, the Big Bang produced a physical universe, the one he'd seen at a far, small corner of his vision. It became the home for humanity and countless other living beings who lived in worlds with form. Hard surfaces. Water. Air. Corners and angles. Heat and cold. Time and space. Duality.

How limited. How small. How unlike this eternal beauty, this Oneness! As Kyle considered the crazy, insane what-if thought that had made the world and the physical universe, he *knew* there could be nothing that is not of the Oneness. Only the Oneness is Real, he thought. With that thought, his vision of the universe the Sonship had made was no longer. He understood that, in fact, it had never been. It was a dream; the dream of life separate from the Oneness, from God; a dream of life in the ego's mind.

The Intelligence spoke to Kyle. *By not supporting the dream, Love replaces all illusions which quietly fall to dust.* Kyle joined with his Creator.

Marci and Aimer removed their hands from Kyle's head and chest. He remained motionless except for the heaving of his chest, eyes closed, with tears flowing down his cheeks, dribbling down his face and chin onto his shirt. Great sobs of awe, joy and happiness racked his body.

"His human body cannot withstand long exposure to All That Is," Aimer said to Marci. Turning to Kyle he spoke softly. "My friend, now you Know. Please rest. We are here with you."

Kyle couldn't stem the tears of joy, nor the wondrous, inexplicable Love he felt for his Creator, for all life, for all universes; for his experience and the web of Love that filled everything. Marci and Aimer sat with him for an hour, holding him in their arms, stroking his body, extending their calming energies into his soul. His tears subsided and he eventually wiped his face and regained a fraction of his normal sensibilities.

"That was the Peace of God, my love," Marci said simply. "It's the one and only Reality. It's your birthright. It's what all life truly is. It's what you are despite this earthly dream. You've now experienced a true and loving Revelation."

Kyle sat without words, as if his tongue had been put out of commission.

"Relax for a bit," Aimer said. "We're here with you."

Kyle fell into a dreamless sleep. Marci reached into the empty air and retrieved a down comforter, which she arranged over his body.

"Now he Knows," Aimer said again.

"Yes," Marci replied. "Knowledge is. Now, let's get the rest of the team connected."

CHAPTER 34

Team-Building

Kyle awoke hours later, finding himself on the couch in his office, covered with a down comforter. He walked to his desk and sat with a blank expression on his face. He gazed out the window at the late afternoon sky with the sun slinking toward evening.

After a time, he heard knuckles rapping on the door to his office. He made no response.

Karla opened the door and looked inside. "Kyle! Are you there?"

No reply. She walked in. "Are you all right? What has happened?"

He raised his eyes to gaze vaguely at her. He walked across the room and embraced her in the most tender fashion, cradling her in his arms. She held his embrace for a few seconds, then pulled herself away.

"Kyle, what is wrong? You do not seem yourself."

"I'm not." He raised his arm and pointed to the sofa.

Karla turned and sucked her breath in with a gasp. A man and a woman sat comfortably on the couch as if it were their normal resting place.

"Hello, Karla," Marci said. "My friend Aimer and I are here to help Kyle. And you. We've taken Kyle on a journey he'll remember forever. He's still feeling its effects, but don't worry. He'll be fine in a while."

Karla stared at the two strangers, confused and with no words coming to mind, then at Kyle.

"It's all right, Karla," Kyle said. "These are my friends. Marci and Aimer. They're the mentors I told you about. They're here to help us."

Karla looked at the two, then returned her attention to Kyle. "Help with what?"

"With everything," Kyle said. "Would you please do me a favor? Would you get the entire team together? Jörg. Hans. Rick. Cary. Would you bring them to the conference room?"

"Cary left early today. She's with her friend, Paul Glazer. He just flew over from Florida."

"Can you find her? It's important." He paused. "Ask her to bring her friend so he can join us too."

"I will try. Are you sure you are all right?"

"Yes. I'm fine. Let's meet in the main conference room at six o'clock." Kyle said.

Karla left his office and called Cary. "You must come here. Now!"

"What's the matter?"

"Kyle is...I do not know. He is acting strange. A man and woman are in his office with him. He said they are those two strange people you told me about. The mentors."

"Oh my God. I wonder what's happening. Okay. I'll be there as soon as I can."

"Kyle said to bring your friend Paul with you." She ended the call, ran to the other end of the building and rushed into Jörg's office.

"Something weird is happening." She summarized Kyle's behavior and told him of the man and woman in the room with Kyle.

"Here? In the Center?" Jörg walked purposefully to Kyle's office, opened the door and stepped in. He saw the two sitting on the couch and Kyle leaning back in his chair, contemplating the view through his office window. People outside were scrambling out of office buildings into buses and cars, heading home for dinner.

"What is going on? Karla said you called a meeting." He gestured at the couch. "Who are these people?"

"Jörg, I'd like you to meet Aimer and Marci. They've shown me some things I want to tell everyone about."

Marci and Aimer faced Jörg. "Hello Herr Tritten," Aimer said. "I am called Aimer and this is Marci." They each nodded respectfully. "We've been working with Kyle for some time to help him with his project. I'm sure he'll tell you all about it when we meet in a short while."

"Yes, I will," Kyle said. "Now, if you'd be so kind as to excuse us for a few minutes, we'll see you in the conference room at six o'clock." Kyle opened his office door and stood aside for Jörg to exit.

Jörg looked disapprovingly at the two strangers. "What is this about? This had better be good." He left the room as Kyle closed the door.

At six o'clock they assembled with Kyle, who sat impassively in a conference room chair, apparently still under the effects of his journey. He made his way around the room.

"Paul, I'm glad to see you again. It's been a while. I hear you're living in Florida now." Kyle shook hands warmly. He greeted each person ceremoniously with hugs for each of them. He paused when he came to Jörg. "Jörg, you have become a wonderful friend. Without your help and connections, we could never have come to this place today."

Jörg, embarrassed at the physical affection and sentiment Kyle piled on him, returned the hugs with caution and a pat on Kyle's back, as men normally do.

"What is happening here?" Jörg asked.

"I'd like to introduce you to my two friends. They have helped me see why we're all here together." Kyle called out: "Marci, Aimer, would you join us please?"

The conference room door opened. Aimer held it open for Marci, who sat down next to Kyle. Aimer took a seat across from Jörg.

"Who are you people," Jörg demanded. "Why are you here?"

Kyle answered. "These are my friends and mentors, Aimer and Marci. They've helped me for the last year or so; maybe for my entire life. I thank them for all they've done in bringing us together."

Kyle haltingly explained how he'd met them; how they'd confirmed his fears about the dangers of the quantum computer; how they'd helped him navigate problems along the way. "Today they've taken me on a kind of journey I can't begin to describe. It's shown me where I've miscalculated and, most important, what we need to do."

Kyle gazed into space at nothing for a full thirty seconds. The group sat expectantly, looking at him, each with their own thoughts churning through their minds.

"Are you all right?" Cary asked. "Kyle?"

He focused his eyes on Cary's face. "Yes, I am...all right." He turned his attention to each person in the room, moving his eyes from one to another.

"I'd like to suggest we go ahead with as many projects for the quantum system as we can. As quickly as we can, but I am withdrawing myself from the efforts to make money with it. I'd like to suggest a new mission for our computer."

Every eye was fixed on Kyle as he once again gazed off into nothing at all for ten seconds.

Jörg broke the silence, squinting, furrowing his forehead. "There is nothing wrong with our mission. What are you talking about, Kyle? What are you thinking?"

Kyle dropped his hands into his lap and leaned back in the leather upholstered high-back chair and closed his eyes.

"I have had an extraordinary experience today that gives me new insight into the work we are doing with quantum system. I will try to say this as best I can." He opened his eyes and continued. "My friends, I have been only half-right about fear being the root cause of man's problems. The universe is...endless. It is filled, *completely* filled with an energy Marci and Aimer have shown me today. Fear has no place anywhere in it. Fear exists only in the dreaming mind of man. There is no place in the entire universe where fear exists, except here, where life exists. The universe is filled with its opposite. Today I have experienced the ultimate truth. The opposite of fear is Love. Love rules the universes. It is All That Is. We have forgotten that. Perhaps from the moment of each of our births we've forgotten where we came from—a place where Love is All That Is. The people on this worn-out planet...they don't know that."

No one spoke. Cary stole a glance at Karla and saw her worried expression as she stared at Kyle. Hans Seffing sat near the end of the table, slowly stroking the top of a ballpoint pen across his lips as he watched Kyle. Paul Glazer wore a nameless expression on his face, something between a half-frown and total confusion.

Rick walked over to stand behind Kyle's chair. He put his hands on Kyle's shoulders and gave him a small shake. "Hey partner, what's happening here? Looks to me like you're out of it. Was it one of those cloud things again?"

Kyle looked up over his shoulder at Rick. "No. No clouds today. It was much more than that."

"You are saying what, exactly?" Jörg demanded.

Kyle smiled at him and his eyes sparkled. "I'm saying we need to use our computer to bring Love into the world. It's the final solution. Where Love is, nothing else can exist. All problems disappear."

"Oh my God. What are you talking about?" Jörg shouted. "We've got thousands of problems to solve. Now you want to forget them and, in your strange mind, find a way to compute Love into the world? I'm sorry, but that's insane. What have these people done to you?"

Kyle sat without expression and closed his eyes. "They've shown me the Truth. It may seem I'm insane, but it's fear that's insane. Love is what we need to compute, my friend."

Kyle opened his eyes and pushed his chair back from the table. Rick stepped away as Kyle faced him and began to speak.

"You and I have been in this from the beginning. Everything that's happening is the outcome of the work we've done. We've always had the best intentions to keep our quantum system away from people who would misuse it. So far, we've done that, but today...only today, I finally *know* where our work is leading. Marci and Aimer have always been right when they told us we can't imagine how we can change the world."

Kyle walked authoritatively to the head of the table with all signs of hesitation gone and stood before the group. "I'll be leaving for a while, but before I do, I'd like to see if we can make some arrangements to put our quantum system to work."

"Leaving? Where are you going?" Karla asked, seeming to be confused and suddenly afraid.

"No need to worry," he said as he walked briskly to a whiteboard and picked up a marker. "Until now we've been building our system and running the few problems we can solve with only the European backbone as our foundation. Clearly, we need to continue our expansion. To prioritize the problems people have submitted and review them with the Board. We have another Board meeting on Wednesday. I'd like to ask each of you, as the core members of this team, to put your heads together and formalize each of your roles. Here's what I suggest you do during my absence." Kyle wrote each person's name on the whiteboard and scribbled a short note after each one.

JÖRG Expand to the US backbone and the FLAG network. Develop a budget for each phase. Work with Karla.
KARLA Handle the money. Work with Jörg on budgets.
RICK Run the quantum system; solve problems!
KARLA & CARY Find solutions we can deliver. Co-chair the Board meetings while I'm gone.
RICK & HANS Finish up the protein-folding problem and deliver the solution.

Marci and Aimer watched silently. "Paul, I've got a special mission for you if you're willing to take it on," Kyle said.

Paul Glazer sat among the team, seeming thoroughly confused. "Mission? What would that be?"

"I would ask if you'd be willing to work with the group here and find the role that feels most natural to you. Perhaps you'd like to work with Jörg. Or Karla and Cary on Board matters. If you can arrange your schedule to stay here in Switzerland with us, I think you'll find a way to move our project ahead."

Paul scanned the room, pausing to see a smile on Cary's lips and her nodding approval. "Sure. I'll see how I can arrange things, then get acquainted with everyone. Thanks for asking."

"Good." Kyle sat down in the chair at the head of the table. "Aimer, would you and Marci talk to us a bit? I'd like everyone to know you."

Aimer leaned forward and placed his open hands on the table. "Marci and I have been helping Kyle with this entire project for quite some time."

Jörg interrupted. "Who are you? What's your role in this?"

Aimer turned to Jörg with a smile and nodded acknowledgment. "We're mentors, Jörg. We have a greater view of what the quantum computer can mean for humanity than Rick and Kyle initially imagined. We have helped them solve certain problems along the way. We stand outside your organization and see things from a different perspective. We're here to help. That's our role."

Cary turned to Jörg. "Marci and Aimer *are* here to help. They've changed everything in my life. It looks like they've done something like that for Kyle today."

Jörg frowned.

"This will help," Marci said. "You asked who we are, Jörg. We are teachers who appear when and where it is helpful to do so. We are two of many who teach and help people who seek to find the Truth of life. Some have called us the teachers of the Teachers of God. We have been working with Kyle and Rick for many of your years, knowing where their lives would lead and what they would try to accomplish."

A glimmering light shone on Marci as she spoke. The room remained silent as she continued. "Now, today...Kyle is placing the quantum system and all the problems it can solve into your hands. There is great help you can deliver to billions of people. Please do so without worry whether you're addressing causes or effects. Kyle is correct in saying that Love is the solution to all problems. In the meantime, though, you have incredible resources to improve lives all over the planet. For this moment, we would only ask that you begin."

Aimer reached into the air and withdrew a giant globe, a three-dimensional image of the planet. Three feet in diameter, it hovered over the conference room table, lazily rotating. Except for Kyle and Cary, everyone gasped at what could have been magic.

"Do not be afraid," Aimer said. "I'd like you to see how you might begin to use your computer." He pointed to the planet, covered with patches of color. "Each of these colors shows you a kind of map you can use to visualize the physical effects people struggle with. This ocher color represents areas where fresh water is a challenge. These gray areas represent areas of conflict and war. Orange shows environmental problems."

Aimer continued as Rick pulled out his CoFone and began to video Aimer's explanation. As the image of the planet turned, Aimer discussed the state of the atmosphere protecting the planet from the freezing depths of space. He mentioned phosphorus depletion that would eventually decimate food production as fertilizer became scarce, perhaps even by the next decade of the 2040s. He expounded on dozens of challenges facing humanity for an hour.

"Perhaps this survey of the world will help you as you sort through the problems people have submitted to your computer. Marci and I wish you the best, and trust you will work together in peace and harmony."

Aimer, Marci and the globe vanished from the room. Only the muted sound of cars on the city street outside could be heard.

Rick jumped up from his chair. "I got it! The video. It's all here." He synced his CoFone to the projector and the group watched video of Aimer and Marci -with the globe floating above the table. "My God! This is fantastic."

Part III

Connecting

As creation unraveled through the 20th century into the 21st, the hopes and dreams promised by the love-infused Aquarian New Age failed to manifest. Wars and ancient hostilities continued well into the 2030s. Humanity's predilection to judge and find fault with one another continued with historic strength. Endless tensions between nations, cultures, lifestyles and people persisted. Terrorism continued to steal headlines. Global economics fell into disarray. The rich became cosmically more wealthy, while the chasm between rich and poor grew to indecent proportions.

During those same years, the Internet grew enormously. Diverse forms of wireless communication became ubiquitous, blanketing the planet with high-speed connectivity. Computers and cell phones gradually morphed into inexpensive mass-produced CoFones. These pocket-sized computers with terabytes of crossbar memory made PC's, tablets and smart phones obsolete. CoFones provided phone, video communication, specialized apps and computing power that exceeded even the multi-core PC towers that preceded them. They connected the five billion people who had no access to the Internet with the three billion who already did.

Telephone service, cable and satellite TV, and even broadcast radio, each made their gradual transition to the Internet, much as Netflix had done decades earlier. A regional Internet company known as OmegaNet sprang up and began providing services to media outlets. OmegaNet grew through the 2020s and eventually subsumed thousands of entertainment, news and media outlets around the world. North American radio and TV networks were the first to move their entire broadcasting resources to OmegaNet. The BBC, TV Azteca, Indus Vision, Rusiya Al-Yaum and countless other networks and media outlets around the world followed. By 2030 OmegaNet had melded the planet's major news and entertainment channels into one massive, multi-lingual behemoth. It educated and informed the majority of people who inhabited planet Earth. Simple cultures, from the Ecuadorian jungles of the Amazon, to savvy investors at Wall Street, Tokyo, Moscow and Geneva—all of them consumed information delivered by OmegaNet.

The world changed as the entire planet became more intimately connected. Each ripple of change birthed even more change.

Small discomforts formerly suffered in silence by billions of people grew to blaring proportions, aided by the always-on, instant communications OmegaNet and the Internet offered. Governments that had ruled over people for centuries began feeling the effects of individuals. People began reclaiming their sovereignty over their governments, seeking to put governments back into their proper subservient role. They asked questions and demanded answers. *Can't* we the people *solve economic and social problems? Can't* we *work together as a global family? Why do we allow bickering, entrenched, shortsighted career politicians to impose rules they expect us to live by? Can't* we *put an end to conflict?*

This revolution, the dawning age of the individual, began to build momentum. Ordinary people went viral to impress the world with their feats and their thoughts billions of times each day. The Internet became a collection point for uncountable zetabytes of video, blogs and ideas. Social media became a convenient platform to communicate trivia, as well as profound ideas, instantly, around the globe.

People unknown outside their own communities began to spawn big ideas; truly disruptive, game-changing ideas. The long-awaited brain-computer interface made its way into medicine. Highways that captured solar energy eliminated much of the need for gasoline and oil. Plasma rocket engines cut robotic missions to Mars to a matter of two weeks instead of months. Agricultural protein, bio-engineered from hemp, edamame, chickpeas and quinoa gave the world a viable substitute for animal flesh. Big ideas proliferated through OmegaNet and into the world at a dizzying rate.

As technology accelerated, the sum of human knowledge doubled each year, then every few weeks, promising to reach the near-vertical portion of the exponential growth curve. Operators of cloud storage services and massive server farms recognized that the electricity needed to run their hardware would outstrip available resources, leading the largest among them to spend millions on renewable sources from solar, wind, oceans and geothermal power. The Millennium Project, recruiting thought leaders from around the world, sought to promote harmony and plan for the future. The Greater Good Science Center at Berkeley educated millions on happiness, compassion and gratitude.

Small, diverse groups from more than a hundred countries—only a few million people at first—continued studying that mysterious curriculum dating back to the hoped-for Aquarian Renaissance of the 1960s. People organized study groups. Some produced videos, books and movies. Some went on speaking tours. Yet others studied it deeply, quietly, on their own.

Students of the curriculum, at first, thought it was a guide for living better, where forgiveness, not judging others and being careful of what they projected upon others seemed to offer more comfort and peace amidst the cacophony of twenty-first century living.

As they studied further and looked deeper, a more profound teaching surfaced. It became clear that simply living better didn't hold a candle to the immeasurable peace, joy and love the curriculum promised. Yet, even the most devout students of the curriculum found it difficult to put its teachings into full practice because the world felt so dense, so real, so inescapable. Most people remained overwhelmingly dedicated to believing in their own egos and the many fears ego so readily manufactured.

CHAPTER 35

Meditation

Kyle saw that Rick had captured Aimer's presentation on video. He left the conference room and returned to his office. Karla rushed to follow him.

"Where are you *going*?" she asked.

"I'm not sure. I have a lot of thinking to do. I need some place quiet where I can be alone."

She frowned at him. "You don't have to *go* anywhere. You can take all the time you need to work out whatever it is right here in Zürich."

"No, I can't. I need to get away for a while."

"How long?"

"I don't know."

"Let us go back to the hotel," she urged him. "I want to hear what happened to you with Marci and Aimer."

Hans, Paul, Rick and Jörg sat dumbfounded in the conference room. Cary broke the silence.

"I've been with Marci and Aimer on two other occasions. There's no way to understand who or what either of them are."

Hans scrubbed his face with his hands and drew his fingers back through his hair. "I feel I've been in a holy presence...or else it was some kind of magic."

"No, it wasn't magic," Jörg said. He stared at Rick. "Why haven't you told me about those two?"

"What could I have said? That they're spirits? That they appear and disappear at will? You'd have thought I was crazy."

Cary broke in. "Marci said they're teachers. Teachers of teachers, or something like that. She said they come where help is needed. I can attest to that."

She turned to the others to make her point. "We must be on to something really *gigantic*. It's a lot more than the quantum computer. They've told us many times we don't know how big our project is. This isn't something trivial, like the way the Internet changed things. Or the industrial revolution. Or the wheel or even the use of *fire*. Not like anything that's ever happened in history. This project is way bigger than we know. It used to frighten me when I thought about it, but after what happened here today...I know we're walking in favor with someone much greater than we know."

Jörg listened, then spoke solemnly. "That means we have a lot of work to do. I'm satisfied with the job Kyle asked me to do. How about you?" he asked the group.

The team discussed the roles Kyle had written on the whiteboard, finally leaving the Center well after the moon and stars had taken over the sky.

At the hotel, Kyle poured himself a glass of water and sat down on the bed next to Karla.

"What happened to you, Kyle?"

"Nothing less than speaking with God." He described his experience, which brought tears to his eyes once again. Karla reached for a box of tissues as Kyle sat cross-legged, remembering his journey to the Oneness.

"I need to process all this, sweetheart. When the time is right, I'll come back." He gazed into her eyes. "Do you remember when I told you we are *One*? Now I know what that means. I was only beginning to understand it when I said it. Now I *know*: There is no separation between any of us, except for the illusion that we've each got separate bodies and separate names for everything. We really are One. All of us. All One."

He put his arms around her, holding her gently. She returned his embrace and felt his warmth and peacefulness. "Come. Lie down with me for a while." They talked quietly.

"I cannot understand what you experienced. It is beyond me. I was not with you, but I can see it is a wonderful thing for you." She thought for a moment with her head nestled on his shoulder. "There is a place in the Pyrenees; Lac Ilhéou. The mountains overlook the lake. This time of year it is deserted except for a few hikers. One of my friends has a cabin there at the south end of the lake. I can arrange for you to use it while you think about your experience."

"Thank you. I'd like that. Very much."

Karla dialed her friend and, in a few minutes, made the arrangements.

"Okay. You will fly to Toulouse, then rent a car and drive the rest of the way. It takes about three hours. You should buy food and things you'll need in Cauterets. It's the last town of any size before you reach the lake. It's beautiful, but primitive and secluded out there. You will be alone, but not lonely, I hope."

Kyle pulled her closer. "The way I feel...I don't think I could ever be lonely again. Will you watch over our project while I'm gone? Despite all my ranting about cause and effect, I see now there's a lot of practical good we can do to help people with our computer. Then...if I can figure out how to compute Love into the world, we can do even more."

He went to the closet and began choosing clothes he would take on his trip. Karla opened his roller bag and put it on the bed.

Kyle pulled a few shirts off their hangers. "Marci and Aimer told me there's no point in trying to find root causes for things that happen in a dream. All this time I've been telling you our lives are a dream, but I never thought things through. Now I see our computer and the work we're doing is trying to fix the dream." Kyle shook his head. "I can't believe I didn't realize that. Now though, I see we can solve problems to make a better dream. A *happier* dream. That's what I'd like you to oversee while I'm gone."

"I don't know about dreams but I know we can make things better. Of course. Yes. I will watch over the team while you are off...thinking."

"Good. Because our final and most important job is to bring Love into the world. That's what the quantum computer is really all about. I don't have any idea how it all fits together. I feel that getting away from everything for a while will give me some answers."

Karla stood folding his shirts and jeans, then placing them in his roller bag. "I hope you are right."

She took Kyle's hands in hers, embraced him and kissed his lips. "I wish you the best. I love you. I shall miss you while you are gone." A tear ran down her face as she left his room.

The cabin had a wooden sign nailed to the front door with a single word: *Waldeinsamkeit.* A word sometimes considered untranslatable, but that mixes the ideas of nature and solitude and perhaps even joy and peace. The cabin was Spartan and even smaller than Kyle's tiny condo in Florida. A wood-burning fireplace and a cord or two of wood stacked outside kept the place warm at night.

Mountains towered far above and surrounded the lake, which he estimated might cover thirty acres. The water reflected a deep, brilliant blue. He'd been confused as he'd left the city limits of Cauterets, his car loaded with food and provisions. A sign proclaimed "Lac Bleu 12 km." He had backtracked into the city to ask for directions. A store clerk told him Lac Ilhéou was also known by its second name due to the rich color of the water tinted by the clear blue sky over the French mountains. He drove along route D290, a twisted mountain road, past ski resorts and, finally, arrived at the deserted cabin.

It nestled among snow-tipped, craggy mountain ridges. Except for a lone backpacker who soon disappeared through the mountains on the far side of the lake, he was utterly alone in a mountain paradise.

On the morning of his first full day, Kyle lay in his cot while the forest around Lac Bleu chittered with the sounds of life. He stepped outside and surveyed the area.

With appreciation, he watched gigantic *lammergeyer* buzzards with nine-foot wingspans fly over his cabin, occasionally dropping bones from their latest kill to break upon the rocks; then landing with a leaf-blowing *swoosh* to stand and voraciously pick out the marrow. In the distance he saw chamois, a kind of mountain goat, standing securely on impossibly narrow ledges overlooking the valley. A band of groundhog-like marmots occupied a rocky stretch of turf a couple hundred feet away, calling out alarm signals, beating their tails on the ground and chattering through their teeth whenever Kyle approached. He enjoyed their antics. In a week's time, they acclimated to his presence and seemed to tolerate his proximity to their elaborate underground community.

Days became complete with mindful walks around the lake and through the rugged foothills. *I am walking now. The clouds are drifting. The air is pristine. I am breathing.* No detail of the present moment escaped his notice and attention. Days and weeks passed, then grew into an entire month of solitude. Then two months, then a third.

While Lac Bleu was beautiful, nothing on the planet could compare with what he had experienced on his journey into the Oneness. Kyle sat on a rock and gazed at the reflection of clouds on the lake. In the mirror-like stillness of the water, their reflections looked as real as the clouds themselves. *When the sun sets, the clouds remain in the sky, but their reflections disappear. If I look only at the reflections I am perceiving a dream image. Just as I perceive the entire world in this dream. How can I learn true Vision?*

A thought from his Teacher entered his mind. *Vision is not perception. Ego uses the body's eyes to judge what you perceive. You perceive a world filled with danger and lack that ends in death. What you perceive with your eyes confirms who and what you think you are—a body separated from God, alone, living in a fearful place. That is not what you are, and that is not Vision.*

His Teacher continued. *Vision is not a function of the body's eyes. Vision gives you true Knowing, for it looks out through the eyes of the Right Mind God placed within you. Vision is direct Knowing, a certainty, that shows you holiness, innocence and sinlessness. With Vision you focus on those loving aspects of other people, understanding that all behavior that is not Love is a cry for Love.*

Kyle understood the words and the ideas, but still lacked an answer to his question.

His Teacher responded. *Seeing with Vision cannot be learned. Learning applies only to perception, and the ego mind that believes in separation between itself and others, between subject and object. Learning, as well as forgiveness and faith, are important because they help you focus away from your ego mind and begin living from your Right Mind where I exist. None of them are needed when you see with true Vision. To claim true Vision, which is your natural sight, just choose to spend time in your Right*

Mind. The ego, accordingly, will fade from prominence and your mind will open to Knowledge. Knowledge is a certainty that allows no possibility for question or doubt. Knowledge gives you direct experience of God.

On a cloudy evening with rain threatening, just before the time Kyle ate his single daily meal, a sound aroused him from his contemplation. Two men appeared a quarter mile away, walking toward him; the first sign of human life he'd seen in almost three months. Curious, he watched them stumble over rocks and rough terrain at the foot of the mountain. Neither of them carried a back pack. They were empty-handed except for a tall staff in one man's hand. Kyle stood up from the boulder he'd been sitting on and faced them.

As the they approached within twenty yards, the man on the right called out. "*Salut. Qui etes vous?*"

Kyle answered in one of the few useful phrases he'd learned while in Switzerland. "*Je ne parle pas Français. Parlez-vous Anglais?*"

The man on the left answered. "*Un peu.* A little bit English."

The two continued walking toward Kyle until they stood ten feet away. Both men wore dirty clothes that suggested they'd been trekking through the mountains for quite some time. Kyle noticed their shoes were slip-on cloth with rubber soles, certainly not made for hiking. Neither man carried anything except the one who held a staff in his hand. It was as if they had been out for a walk on a warm summer day wearing only their street clothes, but found themselves lost.

The two spoke to one another in French. The man on the left faced Kyle and asked in a demanding tone. "Who you are? What you do here?"

Kyle pointed to his own chest. "My name is Kyle. I am here on vacation." He remembered movies with just such encounters: Two rough-looking men confront a lone vacationer in a remote place. Or, because Hollywood likes to keep the stakes high, a family with one or more women who instantly become suspicious, if not frightened, of two strangers asking questions. Kyle turned to the man with the staff, a thick branch, probably three inches in diameter and every bit of six feet long. The man's face was smeared with dirt and covered in stubble. He glared at Kyle and, without breaking his gaze, spoke to his comrade in French.

After their exchange, the man without the staff asked, "Who with you? You have car?"

"No one is with me," Kyle said, sizing up both men and calculating how far the man with the staff could reach if he used it to attack. Maybe eight or ten feet. Kyle turned and walked toward the cabin to put distance between him and the staff. "Come with me" he called over his shoulder.

The man with the staff ran to get in front of Kyle, stopped and held his ground as he stared into Kyle's face. "*Nous avons besoin de votre voiture. Maintenant!*"

Kyle stood firm and stared back at the man. The other man came up behind Kyle and grabbed his shoulder, trying to spin him around. "Car keys. Now!"

Kyle kept his eyes fixed on the man with the staff. My life could end here, he thought. As he stared at the man's ungroomed face and tattered clothes, the voice of his Teacher swept into his mind. *Attack is never warranted. In your defenselessness does your safety lie.* He recalled what Marci and Aimer had told him repeatedly; what he had experienced first-hand in the Oneness: that all people are one eternal Sonship created by God. These two men can take from me, hurt me, kill me, he thought, even as his face softened and a half-smile crossed his lips. But they cannot hurt what is Real and eternal.

Kyle spoke to the men. "Come with me. We'll eat." He continued walking toward the cabin a hundred yards away. The two men followed him, muttering in French.

As they approached the cabin the man with the staff ran inside. The second man, a few paces behind Kyle, reminded him: "Car keys!"

Kyle heard anxiety in the second man's voice, or maybe it was fear or a sense of urgency. Kyle walked through the open door of the cabin to find the man who had been carrying the staff ransacking his belongings. The man had torn open the cupboard, ripped the meager blankets off the cot, rambled through the bathroom. The second man grabbed Kyle by the shirt and demanded once again: "Car keys."

The rental car was parked next to the cabin, in plain sight. *Where do they need to go?* He watched as the man with the staff continued to tear the cabin apart. Kyle opened his suitcase sitting in the corner of the room then retrieved his car keys and his CoFone. He set it to "Translate."

He held up the car keys for both men to see and spoke through his CoFone. "I have the keys, but I am hungry. I will cook for us, then you can go wherever you want." Kyle tossed his CoFone to the man with the staff.

The two men glanced at one another, then one spoke through the CoFone. "We need to go only a few more kilometers."

"Okay." Kyle nodded, opened the pantry and filled a pan with canned vegetables, potatoes and dried MeatSub, then turned on the propane stove. He stood there, cooking, while the two men watched him. *Sitting down to a hot meal like brothers might calm these two down. Give them a moment of peace.*

The aroma of food filled the cabin. Kyle motioned to the tiny table where he had set three plates. Steam curled through the air above each of them along with three cups filled with black coffee. "Come. Eat," Kyle said. "Please."

As the meal progressed Kyle asked, "Where do you need to go?"

"We go to Ayet," the second man said as he finished his meal. "Let us go now."

Kyle led them to the car and set a course for Ayet. The man left his staff laying on the ground, and his comrade climbed into the back seat. The man in back explained the two were brothers who had escaped from a French work farm, a kind of low security jail for minor offenders, and had trekked many kilometers through the Pyrenees. They were trying to make their way home to tend to their mother, who was dying.

They arrived at the mother's home. The two men climbed out and walked toward a house perched a few hundred feet away on a hillside. Kyle opened the glove compartment and retrieved some cash he had stashed there. He counted out all but a few bills, got out of the car and called to the brothers. He ran a few steps to catch up with them, then handed them his cash, pulled each into an embrace and called out, "*Bonne chance!*"

During the next morning's meditation, Kyle sensed the Oneness touching him as if it were a blanket of Love that enfolded Everything. He walked to the edge of the lake and part way around it, mindfully aware of each footstep and of each thought that slipped into his awareness. *Forgiveness empowers us while we're here. It isn't needed and doesn't exist in the Oneness. There, it's impossible there would be anything to forgive. During this dream though, it's the foundation that leads to Vision, Knowledge and Love.*

He pondered how forgiveness could be restored to the world. How can the world even begin to understand what forgiveness is? How can the world choose to see with the eyes of forgiveness?

His Teacher spoke from his Right Mind in its always-certain voice. *Forgiveness begins with not judging. It is silent and does nothing but choose to ignore illusions of the ego. It restores the Peace God gave you when He created you apart from time. It allows Love to reappear, while all thoughts of conflict and fear fade away. Forgiveness brings a new light to the world. The light of Love.*

That afternoon, Kyle paused to sit on a large boulder in meditation. As he did, an image formed in his mind. He saw a vision of his body standing relaxed at the shore of Lac Bleu. He looked at it from above and behind, as if he were hovering a dozen feet in the air, looking at the back of his own head. All at once a small streak of energy rocketed through the air. Like a bullet, it flew from Kyle's mind downward to enter the back of his body's head. Kyle saw the vision of his body tremble involuntarily.

Why did that streak of energy leave me, he wondered. Maybe it misbehaved, as a child might break his parent's grip to run off and play. Or perhaps it was simply exuberant.

As he watched, that energy bundle formed into a tough shell that encased the image of his body. Intuitively, Kyle knew the energy had a purpose all its own. It wanted to isolate and protect the body from life and all its dangers. He realized it wanted to command the body, to tell it what to do, what to believe, what to think.

Kyle understood what he was seeing. It was the birth of his ego. A spark of energy that left the sleeping mind of the Sonship and took up residence in a body. He *saw* how intensely the ego wanted to make the body real; to make real what the body's eyes perceived and what its ears heard.

Now, the ego spoke to him. *You will hurt and suffer, get old and die. I can live in this body and help you.*

Kyle looked past that cunning promise, knowing the ego delights in generating thoughts of fear.

Live in this body? Kyle understood his body as an abstraction that has no particular meaning, except as a means for communicating with other bodies. He thought: My body is a neutral thing, yet the ego takes command of it. It tells me I will suffer and die. It tells me what it wants me to believe. Ego tries to grab everything it can for its own benefit, always trying to hide my true awareness from me. All the while, the ego says it is protecting me from dangers of the world around me. Yet it spends its time projecting fear onto everything. It *makes* the dangers it says it will protect me from. My entire life has been about being this body, and believing things the ego tells me are real.

Kyle fixed his attention on the image of his body standing near the lake with its tough-skinned ego enclosing it. He moved his perspective inside the body and peered out through the ego shell. He saw through that body's eyes, but also *saw* into the Oneness with his mind's eye.

He heard a voice that was trustworthy. Kyle had no doubt it was his Teacher, the Voice Who spoke for God. It was honest, pure and unemotional. Clear and kind.

It said, "Hear the difference between my voice and that of the ego." Ego instantly interjected a thought. The ego's voice had a different tone. It was demanding, devious. Tinged with emotion with overtones of hidden agendas.

Kyle asked a question and the ego answered immediately. A few milliseconds later, the Voice replied. Kyle listened carefully to the subtle difference between the two. He asked another question, then another. The ego and the Voice answered each time. With each repetition, Kyle learned to distinguish the differences between the Voice and the ego. My Teacher, the Voice for God, is teaching me to hear It and know Its Voice.

He pondered the exuberance of that streak and its efforts to command his life, then looked past it with total forgiveness. Kyle knew none of what the ego had seemed to do was Real.

As Kyle's third month at Lac Bleu neared its end, he lay down on a patch of grass and sank into the stillness with a straw hat over his eyes to block the sun. Speckles of sunlight shone through the straw weave and played on his eyelids. He went deeper into meditation, the place of no thoughts, and found himself reliving his journey into the Oneness.

A voice aroused him from his reverie. "There is something you must do, my friend. Your waterfall needs your attention."

Kyle tossed his hat aside and looked around, expecting to see Marci, but found no one present. "Where are you, Marci?"

Her voice seemed to come from somewhere above Kyle's prone body. "Close your eyes and turn your attention over here," she said.

He followed her instructions and saw the magnificent waterfall he had created with nothing more than a loving thought. It played and frolicked throughout Eternity, constantly unfolding ever more fully into an omnipresent webwork of light, color, music, art, boundless energy, Love and beauty. Kyle rejoiced at his creation, his contribution to the Oneness. He reached out with his mind and merged with its vibration. He resonated in it, then found himself gazing at that tiny corner of the multiverse that was the physical universe in which he seemed to live.

He stood up, threw his arms open wide and turned his face to the sky. In a clear, resonant voice he called out: "Thank you for the peace and Love and joy You gave us at our creation. It is what we Are. Let us know it once again!"

His waterfall creation broke into and rippled through the physical universe made of galaxies, suns and planets. It bathed the universe with something ineffable, ethereal and unlimited. In his mind's eye Kyle watched it surround and infiltrate galaxies, solar systems and planets. It rolled through billions of light years in an instant, an effervescence that knew nothing of space or time. It seemed to light everything with a flash of color and beauty. *Yes! Fill us with your Love. Let us know it again.* He *saw* the effervescence connecting with the dark matter, dark energy and with the ordinary matter that made stars and planets and rivers and mountains and bodies.

His waterfall of Love that had frolicked joyfully in the Oneness now also joined into the world of form.

Kyle bowed his head in thanks, standing in silent prayer for nearly an hour. Eventually, he walked toward the cabin, passing through the marmots' territory without being challenged. Entries into their burrows surrounded him. He marveled how they had created their home beneath a hardscrabble, rocky surface. *They hibernate nine months of the year. Just as I have been hibernating inside my ego mind my entire life. Goodbye, my friends. Until another time.*

Kyle walked to the cabin, swept it clean, loaded up the car with the few provisions that remained, then drove to the airport in Toulouse. He picked up a ticket for Zürich and boarded the plane.

CHAPTER 36

I'm No Illusion

Cary entered Karla's office. "I talked to Rick this morning. He said we've given him enough work for about three months. The logjam isn't the computer. It's getting the problems formulated so they can be submitted," Cary said.

"I know. Rick has been living in the vault with his head bent over the console, writing programs. Jörg said there are not many people who use the Haskell language, but he found a few who might be able to help. They're at Utrecht University in the Netherlands. He is meeting with them this week. He will get some help for Rick so we do not fall off schedule."

The Board of Review had held its second meeting and its third during Kyle's absence. The members had proposed, debated and discussed dozens of key problems. They narrowed the field to what they came to call the "Primary Vectors." Those problems each addressed an aspect of 21st century living and the trajectories they might take in coming years if not resolved.

Each of those generated a host of specific problems. Karla and Cary worked long hours with the Board members to organize and prioritize the details, giving them to Rick as quickly as they could define each one. Rick did the creative work of transforming ideas into discrete computer code that ran in the Haskell-based API.

Unlike coding a program in C++ or Java where instructions follow one another lockstep, Haskell is a "lazy" language with a purity other languages cannot match. Each piece of logic stands alone, but none are executed until they're needed. Rick had studied a dozen computer languages before deciding to write their API software in Haskell. Its beauty and elegance was embedded in its basic design: it could be extended by adding new functions whenever they were needed.

"Our Haskell language API lets me drop whatever I need into its core programming," Rick explained to the Board during their second meeting. "The API doesn't care how much I add. It's like a

Lego toy. You just snap a new part into it. Because Haskell is lazy, those extra functions just sit there. They won't be called upon until and unless they're needed. Eventually, I suppose, the API could hold functions that would let us submit almost anything to the quantum system. This week I might be working on a Global Ethics problem. I'll add the functions I need to submit that specific problem. Next week ..." He paused and smiled. "If I'm lucky enough finish any given problem in a week's time, I can add brand new functions to deal with a population growth issue. The API doesn't give a damn."

Back in Zürich, Kyle called Karla from his hotel.

She found herself standing and beaming smiles into her CoFone, almost unable to contain herself, noticing how Kyle's face seemed thinner. "Oh, my God! I am glad to see you, to hear your voice. Where are you?"

"At the hotel. Room 819."

She wondered if he had changed, whether he'd want to see her right away. *Does he still love me?* She smiled at his bearded face on her CoFone screen. "I like your beard. Are you going to keep it?"

"No, I don't think so."

"Oh. Well, would you like me to come by?"

"Of course. I've missed you, sweetheart. I've got so much to tell you, and I hope you can catch me up on what's happened at the Center."

Kyle's absence for three months had given her time to think about him, to wonder about how, of if, their relationship might develop further. *He's just back. I don't want to rush in on him,* "Wonderful. Shall I come now?" she asked.

"Yes, please," he replied.

Kyle showered and shaved three months of beard away. He unpacked his clothes. He'd been washing them in the lake. They were only vaguely clean, so he tossed them into a bag for the laundry service to deal with. He found a pair of khaki shorts and a t-shirt he hadn't worn during his chilly stay at Lac Bleu. He scrubbed a pair of socks in the sink then dried them with the hair dryer. He glanced in the mirror and laughed to himself. *Feels like I'm dressed for Florida.*

A tap at the door. "Kyle! Oh, how I have *missed* you. It is so wonderful to see you again." She stood before him, waiting. Kyle opened his arms, pulled her into his arms and kissed her lips. "You look like you have lost weight. Are you feeling all right?"

He held her in his arms and nuzzled her neck. "Yes, I feel great." He pulled her tight against his body. "I missed you, sweetheart. I love you."

Karla pulled him tighter, feeling his strong arms encircle her. "I love you too. I am so glad you are back."

After a few moments he leaned back and took her hands. "Come, sit down. What's happened at the Center? How's the project going?"

He is still all about business. Even after all these months. Karla brought him up to date on the problems Rick was running through the computer and his obsession with writing code. "Jörg is trying to find more programmers to help him."

Kyle showed no sign of concern. "What problems has he solved? Are we collecting any money? How's Jörg made out on expanding the system to the U.S. and the FLAG network? How are our people getting along?"

"Hey, slow down!" Karla touched his cheek and laughed. *He is like a boy on Christmas morning. Cannot wait to discover everything that has happened.*

She pulled Kyle into an embrace, then occupied herself with the long-awaited kisses she'd imagined showering on him when he returned. She pressed her body against his, drawing him close and realized her heart was beating fast against his chest. *His lips are sweet! Strong arms. Open heart. I love this man.*

She leaned back and gazed into his eyes. "It's been too long, darling. Did I mention that I love you?"

Kyle kissed her again. "Yes, you told me. All the way back I've imagined this moment with you, *liebchen.* I love you, too."

The two sat down facing one another on the sofa. "What's been happening here?" Kyle asked.

"Be patient, my good man. I will tell you everything.

"You and Rick had already started working on the protein-folding problem in Florida. Then Jörg had an $600 million idea. He found several petitions the big pharmaceutical companies had submitted. They all asked in one way or another for a solution to protein-folding. We contacted them and approved their petitions. With help from Hans, Rick finished the code and ran the problem. We sent our solutions to the universities and more than two dozen pharmaceutical companies. They're in the U.S., Japan, Australia, China and all over Europe. I have details in my office. We finally collected $600 million from the escrow account.

"Then, Hans created a problem for us. He argued that licensing the solutions only to those who paid would exclude dozens of other pharma companies. He said the solutions needed the widest possible dissemination. He and Jörg decided to place our findings into the public domain. That way everyone who can use the data can have it equally. The pharma companies grumbled for a while; in fact, they made some legal threats, but it all worked out."

"How so?"

"We worked with the media and told them why we thought the public domain was the right place for medical information. Cary and Paul argued that even while those organizations paid money, the solutions the quantum system found shouldn't be limited only to them. After the news of a possible lawsuit got out there was international public backlash against big pharma. It seems ordinary people agreed with us. After a couple of months of public uproar, the pharma people finally agreed. We setup a wiki with all the data. I must tell you: Hans was ecstatic at what your computer did. He's predicting new drugs will enter clinical trials in a year or two instead of ten. We've cut hundreds of millions off the development cost for each of the pharma companies and years off their research."

Karla shifted on the couch and took a moment to plant another kiss on his lips. *You are a hero, Kyle Williams. Wonderful things are happening because of you.*

"But the clean water issue got really exciting. We had petitions from nations all over Africa, Asia and South America to find a solution for clean water. They pledged a total of $175 million. Rick wrote some code that scanned the entire Internet and all of OmegaNet for solutions, then collated the results. He was down in the vault for days. He worked all night long a few times. One morning he called us together and said he had found a solution for supplying clean water to the planet.

"It uses some kind of carbon allotrope to filter water. Rick said the filter can desalinize seawater and remove bacteria. That alone will cut death from water-borne illness by eighty percent worldwide. The Board is ecstatic. Oh, and the filter can be made as small as a cooking pot, or as large as you might want. Individual people will be able to purify water where they need it, without the cost and delay of building giant purification plants. We placed the solution into the public domain, too."

Kyle nodded and smiled at her. "Sounds like our project is turning into a series of crowd-funding campaign, but that's fine. We're solving problems."

Karla pretended to grimace. "Why are you not more excited! This is wonderful news for millions of people. But there is something even more fantastic. The computer gave Rick some *extra* information. He doesn't know where it came from. He swears he didn't write any API code for it."

"What kind of information?"

"Information that can be used to build what Rick calls a 'nano-replicator.' He thinks the quantum computer can control this replicator. If that's true, the replicator will be able to make copies of itself."

Kyle sat without expression. "What does that mean?"

"It means the nano-replicator could make copies of virtually *anything*. Imagine if everyone had a replicator. People could make whatever they need. They could replicate food. Gold. Anything!"

"What have you done with that information?"

"Nothing yet. Rick says maybe later we can set up a project to see if the quantum system can actually make a replicator that can reproduce itself. For now though, we decided to keep it to ourselves. Do you realize what this means?"

"What do you think it means?"

"What I think? Ha! I think it could spell the end to economics as we know it. Individual people would be able to make the things they need, whether they live in a tar paper shack or a mansion in Dubai!"

"I agree," Kyle said calmly.

Karla thought back to the afternoon they had spent in a Florida park; the day he embraced her for the first time and asked her to breathe with him. She remembered thinking he was a strange man. *He has not changed. He should be amazed at this!*

"Do you not understand? This is *huge!"*

"Yes, I get it. It's wonderful." He smiled. "Tell me, how's Jörg making out."

What is it about Kyle? Nothing seems to surprise him. Is he still connected to this world? What happened to him at Lac Bleu? Karla looked at him with a puzzled expression. "Well...okay. He...he is working to install your sigma interface across the U.S. backbone and the FLAG fiber cable system. He says the work will be finished in a couple of months. He has a whole battery of spreadsheets with the numbers, and he says it all looks good."

"How is the team getting along? Did the duties I suggested for each of you work out?"

She desperately wanted to feel a normal reaction from Kyle instead of his flat reaction about most of what she said. *Now he wants to know how we work together? What about everything that happened since he left?* "Yes, your assignments all worked out. But you know Kyle, I must step aside for a minute and tell you some things."

"Sure."

"You've impressed everyone here far more than you know. Jörg was angry with you when he found Aimer and Marci in your office that day. Then, when you started talking about computing love...well, we all thought you had gone *verrückt;* lost your mind. But everything we have done—all the problems we have submitted to the computer—they have not only been solved. We have seen side effects, like the replicator. I don't know what else to call them."

"Interesting. Maybe it's something in the API Rick forgot about. I'll look at it with him."

Karla put her arms around him. "I am not done yet. I was going to say everyone here considers you a genius. Our Board is probably ready to crown you or recommend you to the Nobel Committee. The clients we have helped are beyond ecstatic. The UN and more than a dozen governments have publicly applauded eZo, I doubt if anyone in the civilized world does not know your name." Karla's eyes sparkled as she kissed his cheek. "And besides all that, I *missed* you. I am so happy to have you back again."

The two stood and hugged silently, cuddling and rocking gently back and forth. After a time, Kyle pulled away and sat down. "Thank you, sweetheart. Thanks for bringing me up to date, but I won't be looking for any crowns or prizes. It sounds like you and Rick and the whole team are doing a great job."

Karla sat in his lap again with her arms around him. He had lost weight, she noticed. His knees felt bony against her. "All right, my good man. It's your turn. What have you been doing for three months?"

Kyle took a deep breath. "I've been meditating and learning what it means to be in my Right Mind." He paused. "The experience Aimer and Marci gave me changed everything. Now I *know* I'm living a dream life. The quantum computer and everything it does is part of that dream. This entire universe is fiction, an illusion."

Karla sat up straight on his lap. She kissed him and stroked his face. "I'm no illusion, Kyle. What are you saying?"

He took her hands. "I'm saying the nature of reality is different than we experience here. It's filled with and made of Love. There is nothing else. All these problems we have—they all happen because we have built so many barriers to Love."

"How did you come to that conclusion?"

Kyle began pacing the room as he spoke. "Much of what I learned seemed other worldly. One day an image slipped into my head. It showed the planet Earth spinning in the blackness of space. I saw myself standing on its surface. My right foot was standing on India; the other on South America. I must have been five thousand miles tall, straddling the Atlantic Ocean.

"I had to laugh because my gigantic body looked like a cartoon man; a mimicry of a person. A mockery. I realized I had been living my life on a false and unreal stage that appeared to be a planet. I knew that huge body I saw was an imaginary character on an imaginary world. It meant nothing and had no more reality than a cartoon. That image kept me thinking for days because it was showing me that life is all illusion."

Karla walked to the sink and drew a glass of water. "Do you really believe that?" she asked, wondering how anyone could truly believe life isn't real. The water glass in her hand felt hard and smooth against her fingers. The water was cold.

"Yes, I do. That cartoon man was living a dream, and I knew he represented me. It was clear that nothing he thinks or believes is real. He goes about his life with fears and worries. Loves and hates. With preferences and attitudes and beliefs. With perspectives that sometimes seem profound and deep. None of it's *real*. He's a puppet of the ego. He *is* the ego. I was so huge, standing on the planet with each foot on a different continent. So silly. So insane."

Someone knocked at the hotel room door. A guest services rep had come to collect Kyle's laundry. Kyle gathered up his bag of dirty clothes and handed it to the rep.

Karla squinted into the late afternoon sun pouring through the window. Everything outside looked normal. How could Kyle have reached such a conclusion when everything her senses told her disproved his weird view of life? The polished marble windowsill felt cool on her hands. Solid. Substantial. Nothing like strange images that come unbidden into a person's mind while they meditate. *If he thinks everything is a dream, what will he want to do now?* She ran through a mental list of problems the team was working on. *Will they be solved, or will he set off in some other direction?*

Karla turned from the window to face Kyle and sat down at the desk. He was gazing off at nothing. "What else did you learn?" she asked.

"I realized any time I try to judge anything from ego's perspective, I am judging wrong. What I judge as 'good' today may seem not so good tomorrow. So, I have to give up judging anything," he said.

Karla opened the desk drawer, took out a piece of hotel stationery and absently wrote: Everything is illusion. Judge nothing. *It took three months to find that?*

"How is that possible, Kyle? We must make judgments. Like deciding what problems to run through the computer. Or what to eat for dinner. What to wear. Making judgments is part of living."

"I'm not talking about what to eat or wear. It's about judging other people. Events in our lives. Situations. People always want something they don't have or have something they don't want. Without judgment, we don't have to put values on what we have or don't have. Think about how many times your foundation thought it was right, without ever realizing you judged wrong? There's no wisdom in using an arbitrary basis like the ego for decision-making.

"Wisdom is the relinquishment of judgment. Our Teacher's judgment is perfect. He knows all the facts, past, present and those yet to come. He knows all the effects of His judgment on everyone and everything involved in any way. He is wholly fair to everyone, There is no distortion in His Vision. I'm choosing to follow His judgment instead of my ego's."

Kyle brushed a blonde lock of hair from her face. "Sure. I feel your lovely lips. I care for you. I want to be with you. I love you, but nothing we do here has the same endless certainty I found. That's what I mean when I say this is all illusion. I've realized while I'm living here in this dream I can choose at every moment what thoughts I'll pay attention to. I don't need my old way of thinking anymore."

"You're worrying me with this talk of illusions."

He squeezed her hands. "No need to worry. I'm the same man you've known. I've found a different way of seeing things."

Kyle explained his waterfall of Love and color and beauty. That it was his creation. How it merged with and ran inward and outward and within All That Is. He tried to explain the webwork he'd examined and merged into; the brilliant Oneness and his overpowering experience as he snuggled securely within It.

"There just aren't any words. It's so beautiful. So, in the Pyrenees I meditated almost constantly. I found a way to get into my Right Mind and stay there. The more I practiced, the easier it became. That's what I mean when I said my old way of thinking doesn't work anymore."

Will I ever understand what he's saying? I want to. "I'd like to learn what you've learned," Karla said.

"I'll help you."

Karla glanced at the clock. "I cannot think about this anymore tonight. I'm hungry."

"Let's go out to eat. I'm ravenous. I haven't had a real meal for months."

She looked at him, dressed for a sunny climate in shorts and a t-shirt. "Ha! It's cold outside! Let us settle for room service so you can tell me more. Then we can snuggle up in bed."

CHAPTER 37

137.036

Kyle returned to the Center the next morning and called a meeting that brought the entire Zürich team together. He welcomed Paul Glazer and discovered he and Cary had taken on the public relations role, working with the media. After an hour of catching up, Kyle followed Rick to the vault, where Rick worked and lived most of every twenty-four-hour day.

Rick looked Kyle over. "Hey man, it's great to have you back. France agrees with you? You know, when you walked out of here a few months ago we all thought you'd lost it."

Kyle stood looking at Rick, seeing him anew. Brilliant red hair, more orange than red falling toward the front of his head. A wide grin with robust white teeth. A sprinkling of freckles besmirched his face and arms. A best friend since Kyle's earliest days.

Rick Huggins. The guy who'd followed Kyle to college to escape his stepfather. The guy who'd maxed out his undergrad GPA, then went on to earn a Master's and a PhD. The man who'd helped Kyle build the quantum system. Now, the man who sat, uncomplaining and loving his work, in a bank vault in Zürich, writing code that defined the world's greatest problems, then watching as the quantum computer delivered solutions that promised to remake the planet.

"I'm doing fine, my friend." Kyle stared at Rick, taking him in. "You're a genius. I love you." Kyle threw his arms around Rick and pulled him into a hug. Rick patted Kyle's back.

"Uh...thanks. Love you too, man."

Kyle chuckled. "Listen. Karla told me the system has been giving you some kind of extra information. The replicator."

"Yeah! I don't know where it came from. I wrote some functions for the clean water problem. Did she tell you what we got back?"

"Yes. The filtration system, but Karla said you got more than what you asked for."

"Yeah, it was weird as hell. A snippet of code showed up on my screen. Didn't make any sense. So, I dissected it. It took me hours to figure out what it was. You ready for this?" Rick asked.

"Yes."

"It's a new kind of Haskell function. It's like the quantum system wrote a new function and sent it along attached to the clean water solution. It has a recursive feature. You know: It calls itself repeatedly. I couldn't figure out exactly what it does. I played with it for a few hours. When I ran that function, it gave back something weird. A number. 137.036. Know what that is?

Kyle scoffed and shook his head in surprise. "Yeah. It's the alpha constant, the fine-structure constant from quantum electrodynamics. Sommerfeld's constant. What do you make of it?"

"No freakin' idea. So, I thought, what the hell. I put the function right into the Haskell API and ran the clean water program again. When I ran it the second time, I got the replicator design info. *It* came out with another weird set of functions attached. I fiddled with them for a while and finally decided the only way to see what they'd do was to run them too. It was about four in the morning by that time. I plugged *that* new function into the API. It came back with data that shows us how we can harness the quantum system to have the replicator start making copies of itself."

Kyle grabbed Rick in a bear hug. "Outstanding work! Freakin' wonderful."

"Thanks, but I can't take credit for it. It happened on its own."

"Yes, but you did the work." Kyle held out his hand for a fist bump. "What would it take to make the first replicator. What kind of raw materials do we need?"

"Carbon nanotubes."

"That's all? I'll get with Jörg and see what we can do. Once we have a replicator, if it can reproduce itself...Wow! Two become four become eight become sixteen and so forth. We could have eight billion of them after ..." Kyle consulted his CoFone "after thirty-one generations. That would be enough to give one to every person on the planet."

The two men looked at one another in silence. "A replicator that can make anything? Marci and Aimer are right. We *can* change the world," Rick said.

"Yes, but there's something a lot deeper we must do. I've meditated and prayed for the last three months and this is what's been given me. We've got to begin thinking about how to compute Love."

Kyle let the idea sink in for a moment and watched a curious look cross Rick's face. "I know. It sounds strange, but maybe the replicator is part of the solution. It can eliminate poverty. It can even give people food. Who knows? Even gold. Diamonds. But it can hurt, too. What will happen to all the fiat currency of the world when people start making their own gold? The world could fall into chaos. "

Rick gazed into the distance. "The banks could fail, for sure. We might be forced back into a bartering and trading economy."

"Yeah, international commerce could crash. We've got to do some serious prep work before we release this replicator. We'll need to get the full Board involved," Kyle said.

"Yeah, I see that. That's why we decided to keep it locked up. No one outside these walls knows about it."

"Good. So...let's get back to my issue. Computing Love. It's the *main* thing; it's what we *really* need to be working on. I'm convinced we've got to do it now. Not later. I think there's a way to establish Love as the motive for everything on the planet. Before Project Doppelganger or someone else comes along and screws everything up even worse than it is today."

Rick put a hand on each of Kyle's shoulders and stared into his eyes. "Hey, I don't know how we're going to compute love. You've been off in the mountains. You had an epiphany with Marci and Aimer. I've been sitting here in this vault for the last three months. What are you saying? Computing love? I don't get it."

"I did some things while I was gone. I *created* something. I'm sure Marci and Aimer had a hand in it. It's like a waterfall of energy, of Love. I don't know what else to call it. It's bubbling through our universe. What I created might be the source of the extra information the quantum system gave you. It might also help us find a way to compute Love."

"*Created* something? What are you talking about?"

"It's something I did when I was in a super deep meditation. I have a Teacher like Marci and Aimer, but without a body. I think of the Teacher as the Voice Who speaks for God."

Rick gazed at Kyle without expression. "Okay...so what did you do?"

"I *created* something. It's like an effervescence, a natural frothiness that bubbles through the universe. I can't explain it, except to say I created it. I know I had Divine guidance. At first it didn't enter our physical universe. But now it has. I think it's changing things. Somehow, I know you and I are here today because it's our job to compute Love for the world. If we can do it, everything else will work itself out. Everything."

Rick stared at Kyle. "After what Marci and Aimer showed us I can believe just about anything, but where do we begin?"

"Give me a moment." Kyle clasped his hands together, fingers interlocked as if in prayer, and placed them in his lap. Rick sat silently, watching and waiting.

"I can't see the whole process yet. But the first step is to get the world thinking about Love." He paused for a moment. "Okay. Karla tells me most everyone knows about eZo and our quantum system."

"Right. Every news outlet in the world covers eZo. OmegaNet starts every day with stories about what we're doing. We're usually on the evening and late night news too. China even uplinks news to their little colony on the moon. Everyone is on board with eZo. Oh, by the way, Paul Glazer has become our PR guy. He and Cary feed the media almost every morning. Paul's a cool guy once you get to know him. Those two are good at working the media."

"You could say the world knows eZo. Now we need to up the ante. Get those all those eight billion people to start thinking about Love. Get them connected with it. We can start by meeting with ICANN to setup a new top-level domain for the Internet. It's going to be 'dot Love.' You know, like 'www.Love.Love.'," Kyle said.

"Then what?"

"Then we'll start building our infrastructure to bring Love to the world."

CHAPTER 38

www.Love.Love

Kyle sat down with Jörg. "Do you know anyone at ICANN?"

Jörg, in his office at the eZo Center in Zürich, pushed his chair back from his desk and put down his pen. "A few people. Why?"

"I want them to approve a new top-level domain: dot Love, but it needs to be restricted, at least for a while."

"Restricted how?"

"It needs to be registered to eZo Systems so we're the only entity that can use it."

With several emails and a few phone calls, Jörg made contact with ICANN's board of directors, bypassing their New TLD Advisory Group and other internal teams that normally consider grassroots efforts to add new features to the Internet. A week later he and Kyle flew to ICANN's headquarters. They emerged with confirmation the dot Love domain would be rolled out to domain name servers around the globe, giving people access to eZo's yet-to-be-built websites and other resources using the dot Love domain.

Returning to Zürich, Kyle pulled the team together. "Paul, would you tell me more about the work you and Cary have been doing with OmegaNet."

"Sure. We hold a news conference every Monday, Wednesday and Friday at 9 a.m. There's a whole battalion of reporters camping out here in Zürich. We hold briefings in the lobby upstairs, but the crowds got too big. We finally had to cull the crowd down to a few dozen. Now the media people have a lottery system. They decide among themselves who will be able to attend any given conference. It's working out."

"What's the outcome of those briefings?"

"We're at the top of the news every day. I don't think anything less than another world war could get as much media coverage as we do."

Kyle turned to Cary. "So, what's been your role in this, my friend?"

"Paul and I have made some good connections with OmegaNet. Meg Winters for one. She flew here back in May, the day after we announced the quantum system to the world. She's from Australia and she's well-connected with the top brass at OmegaNet."

"Connected how?"

"She used to work in programming. She oversaw the schedule for most of the major entertainment programs that go out around the world. We had lunch together and she said she was burned out on her job. When she heard about eZo she turned in her OmegaNet badge and came to Zürich to freelance for them."

"Burned out?"

"Those weren't her exact words. But, yeah. She said she was tired of all those shows that revolve around strife and combat and battle and revenge. She said 'entertainment' is the wrong word to describe what OmegaNet puts out. She speaks her mind, that's for sure. She complained that almost all their programming appeals to our lowest instincts. Murder. Crime. Disaster. Revenge. War. Attacking and killing the bad guys. Rendering some kind of so-called justice."

Jörg interrupted. "I see why. In all the years I ran the hedge fund there was nothing more important than making money. I bought and sold and rebuilt dozens of high tech companies. Making money was at the core of everything I did. Those entertainment people are no different. They are always looking for the next movie or program advertisers will pay for.

"Entertainment executives figured out what people want a long time ago. They know murder and death and war and sex and conflict all sell. We cannot change what kind of entertainment the industry produces. It is all money-driven. If sex sells more designer fashions, or stories about crime or terrorism or revenge sell more cars during the commercial breaks, then so be it. That is what they are going to give the public."

A wry smile crept across Kyle's face. "You are correct, my friend. Most of that so-called entertainment is based on fear instead of Love. I'd like to change things around a bit."

He turned to Cary. "I'd like to meet with Meg Winters. Would you arrange a meeting with her?"

"Sure. I'll give her a call."

Kyle spoke to the entire group. "Good. Now here's what I want to share with you." He leaned back in his chair and closed his eyes for a moment. "When I was away I realized there's a perfection people are missing in their lives. It's the awareness of Love as the foundation for what we each think and do. Our new dot Love domain can become a 'channel' for people to begin learning how to think from their Right Minds. It can become a teaching platform.

"I'm not talking about programming that goes for the lowest common denominator, or that high drama or silly sitcom stuff you find on OmegaNet. We can use our dot Love domain to *show* the difference between fear and Love. We'll give people programming that *teaches* instead of just entertaining their egos."

Jörg frowned. "Are you talking about building a production studio? Starting a new OmegaNet channel? Hiring actors and directors? I don't see how we can do that."

"I'm not sure yet. We need to let things unfold and see what happens."

"See what *happens*?" Jörg stared at Kyle, who returned his gaze warmly. The room fell silent. After a moment with no reply from Kyle, Jörg sighed. "Okay, Kyle. Let me know how I can help."

"I will."

All right, my friends. Thanks for bringing me up to date." He turned to Rick. "Let's go look at our API and see if we can figure out what's going on with those weird Haskell functions that came from nowhere.

CHAPTER 39

Replicator

Rick and Kyle retreated to the vault downstairs.

"Here's the first of those Haskell functions that came through. It calls itself over and over again. Somewhere along the way it goes quiet, but if you watch over here," Rick pointed at a corner of the display, "you can see another function coming alive. I can't find any rhyme or reason for that."

"Is this thing running behind a firewall?" Kyle asked.

"No. It's live. It's running inside the API."

"Is it asking the quantum system to do something?" Kyle asked.

"Yeah. It's where we're getting Sommerfeld's constant from. 137.036. It's coming back from the quantum system."

"Okay. Show me how you got to the final step. The one that showed you how the quantum system could cause a replicator to reproduce itself."

Rick leaned over the console and made some adjustments. "There. All three of those strange functions are running. Watch."

The display came alive with activity as LED indicators on the bank of Quantum O/S servers blinked outrageously faster than normal. "The quantum system is running something. I don't know exactly what," Rick said.

Kyle watched the display as one Haskell function after another came to life. He closed his eyes and relaxed into stillness. He felt the effervescent waterfall he had created foaming up, becoming activated and taking on new shapes and dimensions as it melded with the endless strands of the webwork he'd experienced in the Oneness.

"Here," Rick called out.

The screen suddenly went still and displayed a link to a file with a notation: UNIVERSAL COMPUTER SERVICES.

"That's what I got last time. See this file?" Rick said as he gestured at the link. "It's filled with hundreds of pages of Haskell functions. I've only looked at a few of them so far, but there's no way I'm going to put them into the API. They're so nested together and recursive it would take me years to figure out what they might do. Too dangerous."

Kyle sat patiently, looking at the code. He enlarged one function on the display and pointed to it. "This is a maze all twisted around on itself." He pointed at another few lines of code. "Here it looks like it's all tied up in a knot, calling itself again and again. Then, down here, see where it passes its values onto another function?"

Kyle closed his eyes and slipped into stillness. Rick relaxed in his chair and waited. He glanced alternately at the console, then at Kyle. Minutes passed in silence. Rick walked to the break room to pour a cup of coffee. He walked upstairs, leaving Kyle alone with his meditation.

A perception grew in Kyle's mind. *This code. These functions. They're not separate. They're all part of one another. Like the webwork I saw in the Oneness. Each one is a tiny piece of something bigger. Each piece contains the whole.* His understanding sharpened slowly. It slipped into his awareness quietly and unobtrusively, yet with clarity that grew, dawning on him like a sunrise brightening the horizon.

These functions let the entire quantum system connect to my waterfall. To the brilliance and the Oneness. These functions connect our quantum system to the Love flowing through the universe.

Kyle sat in stillness, sensing his effervescent waterfall of beauty penetrating. Intermingling. Merging and extending itself throughout the physical universe. He *saw* its beauty as he communed with it in stillness. After a time, Kyle opened his eyes, and stretched.

He walked to the API console and sat down in Rick's chair. He touched the link to the massive file of Haskell functions and moved it into the core of the API, giving the API thousands, perhaps millions, of new computing capabilities. New storage units came on line instantly to accommodate the morass of new Haskell code. A message appeared on the console: API LOAD COMPLETE.

He called Rick. "Would you come back downstairs?"

Rick appeared with coffee in hand.

"Okay. I've updated the API with those new functions," Kyle said.

"What? Oh God. Roll them back out! We don't know what they are or what they do."

"It's all right, my friend. I see now what they do."

"What?"

Kyle stood up and put his hand on Rick's shoulder, gently guiding him to sit down in his chair at the API console. "I *know* what they do. They connect the quantum system and all of us to what I created. Love and beauty and everything we've been searching for. Now, if you would, please run the routine again. The one that gave you the replicator data."

"Hey, man. I can't run it now. You mucked up the works. We need to back that stuff out of the API. We can't run *anything* until we clean it up."

"It's already been loaded." Kyle pointed to the message on the console display. "Trust me, Rick. It'll be okay. Would you please run it again?"

"Oh my God!" Rick crossed his arms over his chest, closed his eyes and sighed. Kyle watched as Rick mumbled "oh my God" under his breath a half-dozen times. "I hope you know what you're doing."

Rick gestured at the console and it came recklessly alive as one function called another, then another, each wrapping around inside and outside and through countless lines of code. Sigma clients throughout the Internet captured the state of millions of entangled, super-positioned weak photons, then fed results to the Quantum O/S. Activity indicators on each rack of computers flashed and illuminated the entire data center to quasi-daylight levels as water pumps whined faster to chill the CPU's in each rack.

Jörg entered the vault, his eyes immediately drawn to the flashing console and the two men staring at it.

"What are you doing?" Jörg asked.

Kyle replied, "We're running some new functions the quantum system gave us. We're using that 'extra information' Rick told you about. It's pretty interesting ..."

Rick stared at the console, as if mesmerized by the intermediate results that were beginning to appear on the display.

"We've set the quantum system to work on the replicator. I don't know how long this is going to take," Kyle said.

"Hey, look at this," Rick called out. He pointed to a link titled UNIVERSAL REPLICATOR, then opened the file.

They all peered over Rick's shoulder at the screen. It displayed an animated diagram of a strange-looking container, a weird bottle. The animation rotated on the screen, giving the onlookers a complete view of the bottle shape; front, back, top and bottom. The mouth of the bottle seemed to disappear into itself and merge with its outside.

"What's that?" Jörg asked.

Kyle said, "It looks like a Klein bottle."

"A what?"

"It's a topological peculiarity. It's a bottle that contains itself. It has no inside and no outside. And zero volume. However, a *real* Klein bottle can't exist in our three-dimensional world. It can only exist in four dimensions."

"Is this some kind of computer game?" Jörg asked.

"It's the result of the problem we ran on the quantum system. I think it's giving us the detail we need to build the universal replicator Rick discovered." Kyle pointed at the image. "There...do you see that feature at the bottom? It's some kind of electrical connector..."

"Just what does it 'replicate'?" Jörg asked.

"We don't know yet, but we think it might be able to replicate anything we give it," Rick said.

"We talked about this 'replicator' when Rick discovered those unexpected API codes. If it actually worked, it would be dangerous."

"I know, but I think we owe it to ourselves to see what it can do," Kyle said. "Don't worry, we'll handle it carefully. I agree with you."

"I haven't agreed to anything," Jörg said. "We need to erase this thing right now. Can you imagine what would happen if people could make their own money? The banks, commerce...everything would become chaos. We need to delete it from the computer."

"Don't fear it, Jörg. Besides, it can't be destroyed. The programming is part of the quantum API now. I know it's been computed for a reason. I want to find out what it does," Kyle replied calmly. "I understand your concerns, but this is something I've *got* to look into. Will you give me that opportunity?"

Jörg looked thoughtful as he stared at the rotating image for a moment. He moved away from the console and grunted. "Yes, but be damn careful with it."

Kyle held out his hand. "Thank you. I appreciate that. I will." They shook hands.

The console displayed the replicator image rotating slowly on the screen.

CHAPTER 40

Klein Bottle

In the closing years of the twentieth century the Nobel Committee awarded the prize in chemistry to three men for their discovery of a new form of carbon. Subsequent work at universities and manufacturing companies refined the manufacturing of carbon nanotubes. By the 2010s, carbon nanotubes were readily available in bulk for use in electronics, optics and other applications. Engineers found them especially useful because they could serve both as extraordinary conductors of electricity or as semiconductors, depending on how they were shaped and formed.

Kyle worked with Rick and Jörg to construct the replicator. Jörg brought people from his personal network of technology experts to work on the project—PhDs from universities and research organizations; engineers from companies he'd worked with over the years. Frank Lumière provided the non-disclosure agreements that bound all of them to absolute secrecy.

The design team came together, then gradually transitioned into a manufacturing team, working to translate the quantum system's instructions into a working replicator. They completed the job four months later. Those who took part in the project were paid handsomely with money earned from problems the computer had solved. Jörg thanked them and reminded them sternly of their obligations under the terms of the NDAs each of them had signed as they returned to their home cities.

Rick carried the finished replicator to the conference room as he turned the strange device around in his hands. "This still surprises me. There's not much to it." Dark gray, almost black, but with a certain sheen to it. About ten inches tall, it looked like a wine flask, or perhaps a hand-blown glass bottle that failed to form properly. It had a hole at one end, but the hole seemed to connect both the inside and the outside of the bottle. Rick handed the replicator to Kyle.

Kyle hefted it in one hand. "It only weighs a few ounces."

"That's about right. It weighs in at exactly one hundred grams," Rick replied. "Its dimensions are interesting, too."

"How so?" Kyle asked.

"It's all about the ratios. I measured it. It's just over twenty-five centimeters tall, and a little more than forty in diameter. Divide one by the other and you get the Golden Mean, 1.618. That seems more than coincidental."

"I see," Kyle said mildly. He cradled it in his two hands, gripped it tightly, then tossed it into the air and caught it."

"Yeah. It's super strong. You can throw it against the wall and it won't be damaged. Yet each of those nanotubes is only one atom thick," Rick explained.

The three men stood looking at the wondrous device. It had a tiny electrical connector at the bottom of the bottle shape. A network of countless nanotubes fanned out from the connector to reach every part of the bottle.

"Are we ready to connect the power source?" Kyle asked.

"Yeah, let's see what we've got," Rick replied.

Kyle called for Paul, Cary, Hans and Karla to join them. Kyle placed the replicator at the center of the conference table.

"All right, my friends. We're going to see what we've made. Rick, would you turn on the video cam? Set it up to capture the visible image as well as the infrared and ultraviolet. Oh, Karla? Would you and Cary take a position on opposite sides of the table so you can each see the replicator from a different angle. Hans and Rick, would you stand at opposite ends of the table?"

Jörg handed Kyle a tiny battery pack with a wire that plugged into the connector at the bottom of the bottle.

"All right. Here we go." Kyle plugged the power source into the replicator.

Nothing seemed to happen. After a moment Rick looked away from the replicator to the video cam display screen. "We're getting all kinds of infrared patterns. It's getting warm."

"Would you project the video up on the screen?"

All eyes turned to the image. The infrared view of the replicator showed myriad spots of red, blue, yellow and green, each representing different temperatures on its surface. They flowed into one another like watercolors mixing together, but with no apparent pattern.

Karla stared at the projected infrared image. "Look! The hole on the top of the bottle...it's disappearing, but I can't see where it's going."

Kyle gazed at the replicator sitting on the table, then at its infrared image. The IR image showed the bottle morphing into an new shape. Rick adjusted the display to show the ultraviolet portion of the spectrum. It revealed the same. Yet the device on the conference room table sat innocuously unchanged. Doing nothing. The colors in the IR image washed over and through one another. Kyle reached out his hand to touch the replicator.

"I don't feel any change in temperature, but something's happening." he said. "Let's put it to the test. Let's see if it can replicate this."

Kyle pulled a coin from his pocket and dropped it into the hole at the top of the bottle. The video showed the coin falling into the bottle. It was visible in the infrared view due to the heat it had absorbed from being in Kyle's pocket, from his body. Yet it simply rested at the bottom of the replicator.

Kyle took hold of the replicator and swirled it around. The coin rolled around inside, still visible in the IR video projection.

"I don't get it," Rick said. "Nothing's happening. We must have missed something. Built it wrong."

"Maybe," Kyle said quietly. He stood watching the replicator. "Karla, Cary, do you see anything happening? Hans?"

They answered in unison: "No." Cary crossed her arms over her chest. "It's pretty clear in the video that *something's* going on. We just can't see it." She paused. "You said this bottle is a projection of a four-dimensional object; that it can't really exist in our 3-D world. I don't understand what the video is showing us, but I wonder if it's trying to show us how the bottle looks in 4-D."

Rick interjected. "Well, you've got to remember, Cary. The video we're seeing is a 2-D image the video cam is projecting on the flat wall. What we're seeing is twice-removed from 4-D."

Cary frowned. "What?"

"Yeah, but Cary may be on to something," Kyle told Rick. "See how the IR and UV images no longer show the hole in the mouth of the bottle? In a real 4-D Klein bottle the bottle doesn't intersect itself at all. There is no hole," Kyle said. "That's the mystery. There's no possible way to visualize the 4-D bottle in our world. It just can't be done."

Jörg stared off into space for a moment. "Here's an idea. Let's pour water into the bottle. First cold water. Then empty it and fill it with hot water. Let's see what that does to the infrared image. It should change with both cold and hot."

Hans left, then returned with two glasses of water. Kyle upended the replicator and shook it until the coin fell out. Hans poured in the hot water. Nothing changed. After a minute, he poured the water back into the glass.

"Okay. Pour in the cold water."

Again, nothing changed.

"That's crazy," Rick exclaimed. "We should have seen a change in the IR imaging. How is it that hot and cold don't affect this thing?"

The team experimented with one approach after another, trying to induce activity or change in the replicator. The video cam recorded a constant change in the IR and UV wavelengths, but nothing more. The images showed a continuously flowing waterfall of color moving over the replicator's surface. The Klein bottle shape on the table sat motionless and featureless.

By eight o'clock the team could think of nothing more to do.

"All right. Let's sleep on this tonight. We can start again in the morning. Rick, keep the camera rolling and leave the lights on. Let's call it a night," Kyle said.

The team retreated to their respective hotel rooms. Kyle and Karla discussed the mystery on and off all evening. "What do you think this means?" she asked as she and Kyle slid under the sheets.

"I don't know. Maybe we don't understand what the quantum system gave us. We might have made a mistake in our engineering."

Kyle and Karla closed their eyes. Karla followed her breath for a time as Kyle was teaching her, then mentally repeated her evening prayer.

Kyle did the same and slipped deep into the stillness. As he had experienced during his time in the Pyrenees and every day since, he felt that fine blanket of Love touching him. He relaxed further into it, then reached out to touch Karla's now-sleeping face and caressed her cheek gently.

He slipped out of bed, slipped into his clothes and walked to the Center. He faced the retina scanner and placed his access card into the reader. The door gave a soft purring sound as multiple locks activated. The door opened to his touch. He locked it behind him and walked to the conference room to find the replicator still sitting idly on the table. The camera displayed the same colorful effects flowing across its surface. He sat down in front of the replicator and found the stillness once again.

Kyle sensed the waterfall he had created while in the Oneness. It tumbled, swept and emanated through All That Is. He again felt the wonder of it as the waterfall seemed to commune with the webwork of all creation, and even with its Ultimate Intelligence. He lifted the replicator onto his lap, holding it with both hands, drawing it to his chest in an embrace.

My creation is in this. The effervescence. The waterfall. It flows through this replicator as it flows through Eternity. It blesses all it touches. Thank you Father for your Love. May It now reach all your children.

Kyle sat with the replicator for hours, then, entirely by accident, discovered what the replicator was meant to do. Eventually, Kyle put the replicator back on the table and returned to his hotel room, reveling in the knowledge that he had been given the same creative powers as his Creator. He expressed his gratitude for being blessed with the same Will as that of God: the Will to Create and extend Love. He expressed his thanks for being shown how to undo all blocks to *knowing* that Love is All That Is.

CHAPTER 41

Remove All Blocks

The team gathered at the Center the next morning.

Jörg had lain awake much of the night. His wife had called from their home in Geneva, pressing him about his long absence in Zürich, complaining about the children's behavior, as well as problems she was having with the gardener and their children's nanny. She said the children missed their father. She told him she wanted him to come home for at least a weekend, reminding him he was living up to his workaholic reputation. Jörg knew, from long experience while running his hedge fund: No business matter could ever take precedence over family issues. At least he'd never found one that did. He agreed to return home that weekend.

Then, still trying to fall asleep, he thought about the replicator, how it appeared to be a failed experiment. One that, after paying the engineers and buying raw materials, had cost three million dollars and four months of time that, now, may prove to have been wasted. He didn't fall asleep until three-thirty in the morning. He arose at seven, walked to the Center and took his place at the conference room table for their eight o'clock meeting.

"I am concerned we have made errors in building the replicator," Jörg said, examining the device on the table. "Or, maybe there's another explanation for why it does nothing."

Kyle sensed Jörg's negativity despite the man's quiet tone.

Jörg lifted his eyes from the device. "I hope I am wrong, but I worry the entire idea of a 'replicator' is a dead end. Besides that, I must still consider what chaos it could cause if we do find a way to make it work. Either way, I have trouble feeling confident about it."

"May I share something with you?" Kyle asked. "Last night I discovered what the replicator does." All eyes turned to him. "It erases all the blocks we hold up against knowing what Love is. It puts us in our Right Mind."

Jörg stared at Kyle.

"Let me tell you what happened. I returned to the Center late last night and sat with the replicator for a couple of hours. I held it in my arms and meditated."

"Meditated?" Jörg asked.

"Yes," he said, then turned to Rick. "Would you replay the video from last night? Start at around three in the morning. I'd like to see what it recorded."

Rick projected the video showing Kyle seated with the replicator in his arms, eyes closed, sitting motionless. The IR and UV images showed phenomenal activity as colors merged and sloshed together in a waterfall that covered the entire surface of the replicator. Then, visible colors began pouring forth from the mouth of the bottle, filling everything in the camera's field of view. Kyle himself was bathed in colors as he sat quietly in meditation, yet with a rainbow flowing through him as if he were made of nothing more than air. Violet, white, gold and all the colors of the spectrum flowed around, into and through him.

"Oh my," Karla exclaimed.

"That's *beautiful*. What happened?" Cary asked.

Kyle smiled as he looked from one person to another, finally resting his eyes on Jörg. "I knew Love."

Jörg leaned forward in his chair and stared wordlessly at the video replay.

"I was in the lap of Love. And I was given to understand the replicator isn't meant to manufacture objects. It won't make gold. Or food. It's much more than that. It generates something palpable and magnificent." He nodded at Rick and Cary. "It's what we experienced in Florida when Aimer and Marci filled our conference room with that cloud of Love."

Cary's eyes flashed open in surprise. She saw the replicator sitting on the table in front of her. "Oh Kyle, can you turn it on again?"

Rick interrupted. "How does it work?"

"Yes, I can turn it on. How it works? I don't know. All I know for sure is that the creation I told you about is bubbling through our universe. I think it's connecting with the replicator through our quantum computer."

Kyle looked around the room, meeting each person's eyes, sensing feelings that ranged from doubt to fear to excitement. "I think you'll find this device eliminates fear and all the blocks to knowing Love. Every problem disappears, to be replaced by the only thing that is Real."

Jörg cracked his knuckles. "You are saying this device ..." Jörg scrambled to find words. "... this device erases fear?"

"More than that. It removes *all* the obstacles to knowing Love. To knowing what we all Are."

Kyle picked up the replicator and held it once again to his chest. "I sat with it in my arms for hours last night. When I put it back on the table I accidentally disconnected the wire from the battery pack. As soon as the power disconnected I felt an overwhelming sense of Love. The same I had on my journey to the Oneness. Maybe leaving the batteries connected all day yesterday charged it up somehow. When the connection came loose, it began creating what I can only call a field of Love."

Cary relaxed in her chair, her hands folded together in her lap. "I'd like to know that again. Would you turn it on, Kyle?"

"I can. Does anyone object?"

No one spoke. He turned to Jörg. "Is that okay with you, my friend?"

Jörg nodded.

"Let me know when you're ready. I'll disconnect the battery pack."

Everyone in the room rolled back from the table. Kyle waited until each person signaled readiness, then unplugged the battery pack. The replicator came alive as a graceful pattern of colors—a waterfall of color, at the same time both brilliant and mellifluous—flowed forth into the room.

It washed through everyone, penetrating and embracing each person, giving them all the hues of the rainbow. Karla looked toward Kyle and saw the waterfall flowing over and through him. An effervescence bubbled throughout the conference room like light from a prism cavorting gracefully but purposefully out of control. Each color mixed with another, then another, until it became impossible to distinguish where one began and another ended.

Paul and Cary embraced and stood motionless, wrapped in one another's arms. Michelangelo could not have captured the essence of two people in love any more elegantly. A tear of joy leaked from Paul's eye, meeting Cary's tears as their cheeks touched.

Rick stood and walked slowly around the table. He held out his hand to Kyle solemnly, then shook hands and pulled Kyle toward him in a giant hug. Hans joined in the embrace.

Kyle sat down and basked in the presence of Love. Presently he spoke.

"Jörg, my friend, this is what we've been working for."

Jörg sat, eyes shining, the worry lines in his forehead erased. A small smile graced his lips and smile lines appeared at the corners of his eyes. "Yes. It is wonderful."

Kyle rolled his chair next to Jörg's and looked at him intently. "So, brother. How shall we bring this to the world?"

Jörg shook his head slightly, but found no words. His face softened. "People need this. It will change everything. I only suggest we study this replicator—like a clinical trial—to make sure we understand what it does."

"Yes, that makes sense." Kyle placed his hand on Jörg's shoulder and gave a friendly squeeze. "Thank you, brother. For all you've done. We wouldn't be knowing what Love is without your help all along the way."

Jörg smiled, closed his eyes and leaned back in his chair to let the sensation in the room flow further into him.

The team sat in silence. Traffic hummed outside the building. Clouds swirled in the sky and Lake Zürich rolled with effects of the weather. World leaders struggled with the same tired issues of the day that separated people and nations from one another.

To Kyle and his team, those "problems," were they to think of them, would all appear as nothing more than ego insanity; people trying to solve problems that don't truly exist, and constantly making fearful new ones that didn't exist either.

Jörg stood up and stared out the window. "Why does it take the magic of a quantum computer to know Love? Why, in all these centuries, have we not learned of this?"

"Our Creator gave us His mind," Kyle said, "but we've listened to our tiny ego minds instead. Now though, this replicator opens us to choose again." Kyle paused for a moment as the rainbow of color flowed through him. "So, my friends, how shall we will take this Love to the world?"

Part IV

Fulfillment

Aimer and Marci communed in the Oneness, where time is not and where communication occurs so naturally and continuously that even the concept of "instantaneous" has no meaning. Communication simply *is*.

They are ready for their next leap ahead in learning, Marci thought.

Yes, they have the tools that can show the world how to choose again, Aimer replied.

What might have seemed to be a nanosecond passed. *Indeed. Changing humanity's perception of itself and its world will awaken the Sonship to its rightful place with our Creator.*

Aimer and Marci momentarily lost their seeming individuality as they merged together into the Oneness. *We shall soon reach the end of this work, for time will collapse and end as their perception changes.*

Yet to eight billion people, time seemed quite rigid, real and impossible to "collapse." Time continued to pass as it always had, but often with leaden, lethargic indifference to the people who lived within its bounds.

As long ago as 1714, a free black man born near Baltimore, the son of a former slave and a white English woman, studied the heavens. He became a brilliant astronomer, a wealthy landowner and writer of "almanacks" that were much loved in their day. That man, Benjamin Benneker, called for the nascent country to establish a Department of Peace. He proposed it should have equal footing with the War Department, and equal resources.

Some 300 years later, the United States Institute of Peace Act was signed into law, possibly bearing some slight relation to Benneker's recommendation. By 2011 its annual budget hovered at less than $40 million, a nearly invisible fraction of the nation's trillion-dollar spending on national defense. The U.S. and other countries around the world continued to fund their fears before anything else.

A woman in Houston posted her problems to Harriet Savant, a little-known OmegaNet lovelorn columnist. The woman admitted to loving another man despite being engaged to her future husband. Savant advised her to choose her path carefully, because what many assume to be love is often little more than the seeking for a "special relationship" to fill the holes in one's own psyche and bring the illusion of happiness. Love, Savant said, runs much deeper than that. Hundreds of people posted comments, many asking what Savant meant by "special relationship." One woman pointed out how she valued her special relationship with her husband and family members. Savant replied: "People often seek love from others rather than acknowledging they are already unconditionally loved by God. Seeking 'special relationships' is a maneuver people use to seek for love away from God, and to deny and ignore His love." Her remarks stirred a firestorm of misunderstanding and vitriol. Harriet Savant's slight popularity grew even smaller.

The makers of artificial meat—a bio-engineered substitute made from hemp, edamame, chickpeas and quinoa—dubbed their product "MeatSub." It could be made to taste like beef, pork, chicken, turkey, fish—and even dog and horse for cultures that consumed such animals—depending on how genetic modifications were applied to each of the base ingredients. MeatSub embroiled the world in a firestorm of controversy.

Giant agri-business companies controlling seventy percent of the world's food market filed suit against the small consortium of companies that invented MeatSub. They claimed its name confused consumers who thought they were buying meat. Another contingent of beef, pork, chicken and seafood farmers joined the suit, claiming the genetically modified substitute posed health risks.

Animal rights activists filed counter suits. They argued big agri-businesses had filed suit only because MeatSub threatened its market domination; that their suit against the makers of MeatSub was frivolous. Environmentalists joined with the animal rights contingent. They argued for eliminating cattle farming, pointing out it would reduce methane greenhouse gas from animal flatulence, thereby mitigating the persistent climate change problem. Those concerned with the treatment of animals argued the horrific treatment of creatures, force-fed in tiny cages for their entire lives only to be killed for their flesh, was inhumane, and that MeatSub solved the cruelty problem. Others who extolled the consumption of non-GMO, organic foods condemned MeatSub as a dangerous substance likely to cause untold damage in the long term.

The EU banned MeatSub for years. Contentious combatants, each with their own perception and strong beliefs about the danger or value of MeatSub, continued to attack one another. Yet, MeatSub's makers grew more and more profitable as people outside the EU embraced the product. When the world's largest fast food restaurant chain began moving away from its traditional beef, fish and chicken supply chain, all but the most resolute allowed their legal battles to fade. MeatSub became the versatile and economical protein that fed the world.

A heartthrob Hollywood movie star nearing his mid-forties denied he was the father of a love child. The woman carrying his child filed a paternity suit seeking half his fortune. He offered her twenty-five million dollars to have an abortion. When news of his offer went viral, it triggered a battle between the pro-life and pro-choice forces. That conflict led to felony charges claiming he was conspiring to pay for the murder of a human being. The pro-life forces sought an emergency hearing with the Federal courts. When the court found no legal basis for conspiracy charges, the movie star paid the woman. She had the abortion. One fewer infant body was born into earthly life.

The ZX terrorist groups developed a new kind of suicide bomb that not only killed, maimed and caused horrific injury; it relied on an explosion of fluoroantimonic super acid—thousands of times stronger than mere sulfuric acid. A nineteen-year old boy detonated himself near the Eiffel Tower, killing 121 people as his body vaporized. The spray from the acid damaged the Eiffel Tower, closing it to the public for months while workers made repairs that cost eight hundred thousand Euros.

Fears of death shadowed professional wrestlers and the fans seated nearest the ring when a 340-pound wrestler known as "Psycho Man" was diagnosed with a new flesh-eating bacteria he had unknowingly passed to his opponent. The media speculated on whether the referee or others in the pre-fight locker rooms had also been infected, and how many fans sitting in ringside seats might have been infected by sweat and spittle that spattered out of the ring. Las Vegas shuttered its doors for three months while the Centers for Disease Control sent hazmat experts to investigate the physical facilities for traces of the bacteria. The U.S. Army sent teams of specialists to supervise and enforce the total quarantine of the city. The gross domestic product of the Vegas gambling and tourist industry fell from its typical 120 billion dollars per year to less than one-fourth that as jobs were put on hold and money stopped flowing. Until the crisis was declared over, three million people living in the area survived on food, water, healthcare and assistance provided by the Red Cross, FEMA and other agencies.

OmegaNet reported certain of its latest online gaming services would be suspended in the face of UN sanctions against a San Francisco game developer. The UN claimed the game developer routinely scavenged the web to find people with felony criminal profiles, then excluded them from game play. Those ex-cons found they could no longer play the fully immersive virtual reality game "Carnage, Blood and Annihilation" series on their CoFones or gaming systems. The company responsible for the game debated with the UN, saying, "It's more than a game. It simulates true attack, murder and torture on a grandiose, mesmerizing level. It is in society's best interest to restrict violent criminals from such game play. We do not wish to be responsible for increasing the recidivism rate of felons, however we do invite those over eighteen years of age to enjoy our Carnage, Blood and Annihilation game."

At the Chinese colony on the moon, nine people died when an insignificant asteroid known only as 4179 Toutatis crashed into one of the bubbles separating its inhabitants from the vacuum of space. Only six survived.

The Pope once again blessed throngs of seekers at Vatican City and renewed his plea to end the inter-tribal genocide that had killed or displaced hundreds of thousands in a tiny agrarian African nation.

Occasional slices of world news he couldn't avoid hearing troubled Kyle. He knew the wars, genocide, disasters and horrors that dominated the news only masked the insane workings of the ego mind. The mind that judges everything. The mind that projects its fears upon the world, then seeks for a solution but never finds one.

We need to act, he thought. To awaken the world. To let the light of Love shine away the darkness.

CHAPTER 42

Prison Time

The team met daily to develop a plan that would bring replicators to the world. As they sat in discussion, their replicators emanated rainbows of color into their bodies and minds. Their communication became more open. The flaws, judgments and tired criticisms each person carried in their ego minds receded further each day as the awareness of Love became more profound. Egos were coming undone.

Karla awoke to find Kyle gazing at her from the vantage point of his pillow. "Good morning, love," she said as she reached out to cuddle with him. Snuggled in his arms, she smiled and kissed his cheek. "Know what?"

"What?"

"I am feeling the effects of the replicator almost all the time now. If I dream at night, it is always a happy dream. When I wake up, I feel happy. Peaceful." She squeezed him tight against her body.

Kyle brushed her bangs away and kissed her forehead before moving to her lips. "The replicator is putting us deeper into our Right Mind. It has affected all of us."

"Yes, especially Jörg. Have you noticed? His eyes sparkle and his worry lines are fading. The effect seems to be cumulative."

"Seems to be. It has an immediate effect, too. No doubt about that. Just one experience of the replicator changes a person. It's been...what...two weeks now since we first turned it on? Look what's happened. Our business meetings are totally different. There's never any conflict. Everyone works together."

"I know." Karla plumped her pillow and changed her position, then continued. "I had to laugh at what Rick said. You know how he is always coming up with a silly-sounding name for things? He said he wanted to plot a graph to show the changes we are experiencing. He called it the 'Ego Deflation Curve.' He said once we release the replicator to world governments, he would use the graph to predict how long it takes for them to quit fighting and retire their armies."

"Well, that might take a while, and only Rick would think of making this a science project." Kyle paused for a moment. "But he's probably right. If everyone's affected by living near the replicator the way we've been, it may well be something he could graph."

Kyle's CoFone sounded an alert and notified him of today's meeting with the manager of prisons for the Zürich canton.

"You're going with me?" he asked Karla.

"Of course. I wouldn't miss it."

Herr Peter Langendanch was the manager of prisons in the canton of Zürich. Each of Switzerland's twenty-six cantons manages its own law enforcement and prisons. Kyle and Karla arrived at his office at the appointed time. A steel desk stood in the center of Langendanch's office. Cold and efficient, inboxes and outboxes sat at its left edge. A keyboard and monitor sat behind him on a credenza. The monitor was dark. The two from eZo exchanged greetings and pleasantries, then got down to business.

"Dr. Williams, I am honored to meet you, and you Dr. Kensinger. It is not often I have such distinguished visitors. How may I help you?" Langendanch asked.

"We've been working with our quantum computer system to find ways to enhance peoples' lives, as you may know," Kyle said.

"Yes, I follow news of your organization every day."

"Thank you. The work we're concentrating on lately is not in the news yet. I'd like to tell you about it, in confidence, and ask for your help. We'd like to conduct...I guess I would call it a 'field test' of a new technology."

Langendanch raised his eyebrows expectantly. "What kind of test?"

Karla replied. "The Swiss prison system is one of a kind throughout Europe. You have painted cell walls pink because it is calming. You permit the use of marijuana among inmates."

"Yes, that is true," Langendanch said with pride. "The shade of pink is tranquil. Inmates fall asleep faster. They are less violent. As for the marijuana, it is not legal, but we know taking it away would cause more problems than it would prevent. Banning it would create a black market inside our prisons and turn them into battlegrounds."

Kyle nodded. "We applaud you for that. Other countries would benefit from your approach to incarceration. In the U.S. we have ten times as many people in prison, proportionately.

"We are here today to ask for your help in testing a device we've engineered using our quantum computer system. It creates some rather remarkable effects. I suppose you could call them psychological effects. It is calming. It promotes cooperation. It allows people to work together as they're not often able to do."

"What exactly is this device, Dr. Williams?"

"It is a device that generates a field of Love."

Langendanch sat immobile behind his desk, staring at Kyle. His eyes narrowed a bit as a frown grew on his face. "A field of love?"

Karla smiled at him. "Yes, it sounds extraordinary ..."

"Dangerous is the word that comes to mind. We do not want our inmates in love with one another!" Langendanch paused, shook his head, then recovered his usual staunch composure. "I am sorry, I do not mean to ..."

"It is all right," Karla said. "Our device isn't about sex or physical love. The field of Love we are talking about is something that brings people together so they gradually begin to realize they need not judge others. Or themselves. They don't need to attack others. Instead, they learn they are all loved as themselves because of what they are."

"Do you mean who they are?" the warden asked.

"No. I mean *what* they are. Let me show you." Kyle opened the case he carried with him and took out the replicator, placing it on Langendanch's desk. "This is the device. May I turn it on so you can know what it does first-hand?"

Langendanch looked suspiciously at Kyle and Karla, but found no sign of concern. No mask of pretense or deception in their eyes. They both sat gazing warmly at him. "What happens if you turn it on?"

"The room will fill with colors and you'll feel the sensation I am calling Love," Kyle said. "There is no danger."

Langendanch sat up straight in his chair and placed his hands on his desk. "*Ja*, go ahead."

Kyle disconnected the battery pack from the replicator. Rainbow hues of colors flowed gracefully through Langendanch's office. The sensation Kyle and Karla had felt so many times permeated the room. They both relaxed even further into their chairs. Langendanch, at first wary, leaned back in his seat and dropped his hands into his lap. The calming scent of lavender and lilac from childhood days spent in his mother's garden recalled themselves to his memory. After a few moments of silence, he noticed that Karla sat with her eyes closed, while Kyle simply gazed at him.

"*Lieber Vater Gott!* This is unlike anything I ever have known," Langendanch said with a smile on his lips. Not being a man overly invested in emotions, he found himself saying, "If this is love, then I have never known what it is until now." His face relaxed even further as he sat back comfortably in his seat once again. The colors flowed around and through him.

"Herr Langendanch, what you're feeling is the sensation our device generates. We would like to install these in your prison," Kyle said.

"Yes," Karla added. "We would like you, your staff, your prison psychologists and other professionals to study its effects."

Langendanch turned a warm gaze to Karla. "Why did you choose my prison in Zürich? Do you plan to put these into other prisons after your field-testing?"

"Yes, but more than that. We want to give these to everyone on the planet. But we want to begin locally, with men whose reactions can be measured."

The three spoke for more than an hour. Langendanch explained in more detail how the Swiss prison system operates. Life sentences without the possibility of parole were exceedingly rare. Even violent criminals became eligible for parole after serving fifteen years. Psychologists played an important role in evaluating inmates. They looked for behaviors and attitudes that would justify release into society, sometimes after only ten years. Recidivism rates in Switzerland fell far below those of other countries. The Swiss focused on rehabilitation rather than punishment.

With promises of financial support from eZo to fund the study, Langendanch agreed to meet with the prison psychologists who, he cautioned, would want to treat the test scientifically. He predicted they would want to set up a control group and conduct the test as if it were a psychology experiment. Langendanch promised to contact Kyle within a week.

Kyle packed the replicator back into its case and returned to the Center with Karla.

He met Rick in the vault to find four people sitting at consoles, programming the quantum system. Jörg had been busy. The two men and two women were Haskell programmers from Utrecht University. They gave Rick the extra manpower eZo needed to keep up with the demand to solve the problems that were still being submitted by organizations and governments around the globe, then studied by the Board of Review.

"Our meeting went well. I think we'll get a go-ahead from the prison to let us test our replicator with their inmates. We'll need to build more. They'll need about fifty replicators."

Rick ignored Kyle's remark. "Yeah, but our replicator doesn't actually 'replicate' anything. We need to find a new name for them. I've been thinking 'L-Gen.' You know, Love Generator."

"It doesn't really generate Love," Kyle said. "It puts us in a state of mind where we can experience the Love that we've always kept hidden and banned from our awareness."

"I know, but I think people will understand the concept of a Love Generator," Rick countered.

"Me too. So be it. We need to get busy building more replicators...I mean L-Gens."

Rick gestured at the four programmers, all hard at work. "With these people on board, I've finally had time to dig into those Haskell functions we got. I found a group of them that work together. I'm not sure yet, but it looks like we can use our original L-Gen to make copies of itself."

"Our L-Gen doesn't reproduce physical things," Kyle said. "Not any that we've tested."

"I know, but let me show you what I found ..."

CHAPTER 43

Love Channel

Back in the vault, Rick opened the universal computer services file. "You see this set of functions? They're all connected. They're recursive." He pointed to one after another.

"Let me have a look," Kyle said. He fell into a quiet, mindful state as he worked, and again began to sense the effervescence of his waterfall creation. After a while he spoke again. "I see what you're doing here. It's brilliant, Rick!"

They worked into the night and resumed the next day. "Okay, Rick. Put some carbon nanotubes into the L-Gen."

Rick stuffed a handful of fluffy nanotubes into the mouth of the L-Gen. "I put in about half a kilo."

"All right, I think we're ready to submit the problem. Would you launch it?"

Rick took his seat at the console and launched the new application the two had written through the night. Instantly the original L-Gen fused millions of carbon nanotubes into a perfect replica of itself. The new L-Gen simply appeared on the tabletop as if by magic.

Rick jumped out of his chair and picked up the new L-Gen, an exact replica of its parent. Dark gray, nearly black, with a curious sheen to it, shaped like a Klein bottle. He set it back on the table. "Amazing!" He peered inside the original. "There's more carbon still inside the bottle. Should we run the program again?"

"Sure," Kyle said calmly.

Rick re-launched the program and another L-Gen appeared next to its partner.

Kyle picked up the two copies and filled each of them with a handful of carbon nanotubes. "One more time, Rick."

Immediately two more sat next to one another on the table, a total of five.

Damn!" Rick exclaimed. "There's no end to this!"

Kyle closed his eyes and slowly bowed his head. "Yes. It appears so. Let's put them all on battery packs overnight. We need to be sure they all work the same way."

Over the next week the entire team traded L-Gens. Everyone agreed that Rick's christening them "L-Gens" was perfectly appropriate.

Hans Seffing took a different one home each night. He and his wife basked in its field during every waking hour and through the night. Jörg took the original L-Gen back to Geneva for a long weekend with his family. His children, often given to bickering and arguments, enjoyed the entire weekend without a single squabble. His wife, Corina, fell into a peaceful mindset and put aside the complaints she had planned to voice about Jörg's constant absence from their home in Geneva.

Cary and Paul met with the media three times that week, but withheld any mention of the L-Gen. Yet the L-Gen in their hotel room gave them time to explore.

"Living with the L-Gen near me at work and here at the hotel every night, I've realized something important," Cary said.

Paul sat next to her on the sofa. "What's that, sweetie?"

"The past is absolutely gone. It only lives in our memories. Can you imagine if we could forget everything about the past except the things that brought us love? If we could forget our ideas of what the world is for? All the ideas and beliefs we have about what things mean and what their purpose is? What would that be like?"

"You don't mean forgetting how to talk and eat and things like that, do you?"

"No. I mean forgetting about every judgment and every decision we ever made about *anything*. Just think. People try to figure out what life is. How it works. Why we're here. Unfortunately, we spend all our time judging things. If we could forget all those judgments and remember only Love, it would be like re-learning the purpose of our world and our lives."

Paul stared at her for a moment. "I don't think that's possible. You'd have to forget everything that makes you human. You'd be...I don't know...lost."

"That's right. We would need to choose again. To choose what life is meant to be. That's what the L-Gens are doing for us. They're putting us in our Right Minds so we can let the dead past and all the judgments we made vanish along with the perception of time. To me, it seems like the past is nothing more than a dream. We paid attention to it most of our lives. Now though, it's fading."

Paul looked away, staring into the distance. A few minutes drifted by as they each sat in silent thought. "I see what you're saying. Things that happened in my past don't bother me like they used to. They don't matter. I used to blame myself for them. Beat myself up. Feel guilty. But I hear you. The past is fading."

"Right. It's nothing but a memory. Marci said we're dreaming everything. That makes the past even less important. What's the point in remembering things that happened in a dream?"

They sat together for a while longer. "I love you, Paul."

Herr Langendanch spoke with the chief prison psychologist and her team. Kyle and Karla made another visit to the prison. The psychologists wanted to experience the L-Gen themselves. eZo got approval to proceed with their test.

The prison staff defined the parameters of the experimental design and how data would be collected. eZo gave them permission to publish results in scientific journals, subject to eZo's timing.

eZo delivered fifty L-Gens to the prison. A procession of psychologists and counselors observed inmates throughout a three-month cycle. They reviewed videos the prison routinely recorded to document any act of violence. Now, they turned their attention to analyzing interpersonal behaviors caught on video. Much like court reporters who document every spoken word, the psychologists built a journal of events that captured the behaviors of fifty inmates.

Their report at the end of the trial period showed a dramatic reduction in violence and anti-social activity. The inmates' behavior and demeanor was more calm, friendly and relaxed. The team found the transformation so astounding they identified several inmates as candidates for early release. Langendanch's team prepared academic papers for submission to the scientific journals, yet were bound by their agreement with eZo to withhold them until eZo gave permission.

Kyle met with Cary and Paul. "Our L-Gens have done what we hoped for at the prison. It's time go public. I'd like to get a press release together. It should tie in with the journal articles Langendanch and his team are going to submit. Will you work on it?" Kyle asked.

"Sure," Cary said. "A while back you asked me to setup a lunch meeting with Meg Winters from OmegaNet. I think she could help get the press release into the right hands. Would you like to meet with her?"

Kyle met Meg Winters at a local restaurant where they could linger and talk privately. She had a disheveled look about her; a woman who had struggled daily with a worldwide network trying to please everyone on the planet with the content it disseminated. She had thinning brown hair, a worn expression and exuded a no-nonsense, hard edge. They exchanged greetings, then found a table in a private room.

"Cary told me you left Australia the day after we announced the quantum system. What happened?"

Meg took a moment to reply. "Your press release. You made some huge promises. I had to come see what you're up to."

"That's why you left your job at OmegaNet?"

She nodded. "I was the President for the Entertainment Programming sector. I had VPs from more than two hundred countries reporting to me, but I was fed up and burned out. What OmegaNet has been putting out isn't entertainment. It's garbage."

"That's pretty strong." Kyle paused, waiting for her reaction. When she said nothing, he continued. "Didn't you have any control over the programs?"

"Of course. I could cancel a show, launch a new series, promote an event. All of that. But what would you do if you had to make a choice for dinner between a bowl of worms and a pot full of boiled insects?"

Kyle grinned at the analogy. "I get your point."

"Maybe you do. My point is that almost everything OmegaNet calls entertainment these days is rooted in violence. Crime. Abduction. Sex. Perversion. Hatred. Attack. Revenge. Terror. Even the so-called family shows that try to have redeeming value end up with people fighting, killing or attacking one another. Shall I go on?" she asked.

"No, I understand." Kyle sipped his water as the waiter delivered their lunch orders.

"I don't have any gripes with OmegaNet. I've been with them for ten years. They've been good to me, but they're at the mercy of what the studios make."

She brushed a few crumbs from the table, then began buttering her dinner roll. When she finished, she laid her knife down perfectly aligned across the top of her plate and took a bite of her roll.

"I'd like to talk with you about a press release we're going to write and about starting a new channel on OmegaNet."

"What kind of channel?"

"A love channel."

Kyle watched as she scooped up a bite of food from her plate. It seemed as if she'd not heard his reply. Finally, she swallowed and looked at him. "Love channel? Tell me about it."

Kyle dabbled at his meal. "I'm talking about a channel that shows people how Love can change their lives. It's the perfect opposite to all the crappy programming you've been telling me about."

She wiped her butter knife on her napkin, cleaning off any trace of butter, then plunged the knife into her MeatSub grilled chicken breast. She sliced off several bite-sized pieces then took a moment to arrange them on her plate next to the vegetables. Meg laid her fork down, sipped her drink. "Tell me what I need to know."

"We've found a way to experience what Love is. We'd like to share it with the world. I've set up a new domain. Love dot Love. I'd like to distribute it through OmegaNet, and I'd like you to be our consultant in making that happen."

Meg leaned back in her chair and studied Kyle. "Adding a new channel to OmegaNet isn't that difficult. I could talk to the people there, but I need to know more."

"Like what?"

"Like what it's all about."

"It's about Love. We live in a world ruled by fear. Love is its opposite. I want to show the world what happens when people live from Love rather than fear."

Meg scoffed. "That sounds like a pipe dream. How do you think you can accomplish that?"

"It doesn't matter. Let's just say we've found a way to help people understand the difference."

"All right, but I need more than that if you expect me to help you."

Kyle pushed his unfinished meal to the side and met Meg's eyes full on. "This is off the record. What I'm about to tell you isn't for publication. Anywhere. I need you to treat me as a confidential source. Do you agree?"

Meg Winters, like journalists everywhere, understood the question. It was fundamental to journalistic ethics. "Of course."

Kyle leaned forward to speak in a low voice. "We have a device. It generates what you might think of as a field of Love. We've been field-testing it for the last few months at a prison. The psychologists and prison officials conducted a study that's about to be submitted to several scientific journals. Our device changed those prisoners. The prison may release some of the inmates solely on the changes our device brought about.

"We have a press release to announce our device. We've named it 'L-Gen.' Love Generator. I want to distribute it through OmegaNet on our Love dot Love domain. I'm hoping you can help us."

"Love generator? That's mad!" she said, as if the idea was beyond believability. "You want to sell these things?"

Kyle realized she was puzzled. "No. We're not selling anything. They're free, but there's more. I want eZo to have top billing all across OmegaNet. I want our Love dot Love website and our L-Gens to be the first thing people see on their CoFones every morning. And the last thing at night."

"Let me understand this. You have a device you want to give away. For free. You want everyone on the planet to know about it."

"Yes, and to have one."

Meg turned her attention to her lunch and took a couple of bites. "OmegaNet has never given any organization top billing. They don't do that. They've democratized the Internet. It's up to people to choose what they want."

"I know about *choosing*, Meg. But people have been making the wrong choice." He stared at her intently. "I'm not talking about the choice of what they consume on OmegaNet. I'm talking about people choosing fear instead of Love. It's about the fear in all that so-called 'entertainment' programming you're so tired of, when they could be choosing Love."

Meg sat with her hands resting on the table, folded over one another, as she returned his steady gaze. She seemed uncertain what to say.

"It's a choice we all make every minute of the day, but making the wrong choice is the cause of all the problems people have. I want to help people choose again. For Love instead of fear. It will change the world. We need to begin right away." Kyle leaned forward and spoke quietly. "Can you help us change the world, Meg?"

Kyle watched her gaze off into space. A preoccupied look on her face remained, even when the waiter came to clear the table and ask if they wanted dessert. As he left, Kyle interrupted her ruminations. "Would you come back to the Center with me? I think this will all make a lot more sense if you experience what our device actually does."

"Yes, I'd like that, but I don't know how OmegaNet could justify giving you a preeminent place in the global network. I don't think it can be done."

CHAPTER 44

Love Generator

After her experience sitting with an L-Gen, Meg made personal appeals to OmegaNet's chairman. He agreed to meet with eZo. Kyle, Karla and Jörg flew to OmegaNet's headquarters in Sydney. Jörg decided to forego his customary negotiator's role. Working, sleeping and living with an L-Gen nearby had reframed his thinking.

"Sometimes things happen faster when strategy and tactical planning are put aside," he told Kyle. "We need to approach OmegaNet openly and sincerely."

Jörg began the discussion with OmegaNet's chairman, Arthur Benet. "We've come to talk with you about top billing for our new dot Love domain. As we discussed, we have nothing to sell. We won't advertise and we will collect no money. We'd like you to help us because what we are doing will benefit everyone, including you and OmegaNet."

Chairman Benet stared at the three celebrities. "Mr. Tritten, OmegaNet is the ultimate democracy. As I have explained to Dr. Williams, every person on the planet can choose what he or she cares to consume. News, sports, entertainment, education, politics, religion, art, music, science, mathematics, technology. It's all there. Thousands of genres. No one has what you call a 'top billing.' Your dot Love domain sounds interesting, but we cannot favor one domain or any one channel over another."

Karla adjusted her position on the sofa, gaining Benet's attention. "With all respect, dot Love is far more than 'interesting,' Mr. Benet. Our dot Love domain is essential to the evolution of the planet."

"That's quite a statement, Dr. Kensinger. What do you mean?"

"Look at OmegaNet, Chairman Benet. You said you distribute thousands of genres and information in every conceivable category people could want. OmegaNet, and the ultimate democracy you referred to, reflect the diversity and—I would even say, the *wonder*—of humanity."

"I agree."

"We're here to magnify your impact on your audience a thousand-fold," Karla said with a friendly smile on her lips and warmth in her eyes.

Kyle chimed in. "Perhaps even more than that. Our dot Love domain has only one purpose. We want to distribute Love to your audience. To everyone. We want them to awaken to Love each day when they access OmegaNet, and to savor it throughout each day and night. Love is the only thing that matters in our world. It solves every problem. We need your help in giving Love away so every person can experience it personally. People will find when they give Love, they receive Love. Unlike giving away money and material things, giving Love returns Love to the giver. People will learn that giving and receiving are the same."

Kyle explained the L-Gen, its magnificent effect on people and dwelled on some of the details from the prison studies. He handed Benet a copy of the articles that would soon be published. "L-Gen is a product of our quantum system. We intend to give an L-Gen to everyone on earth."

"To *give* them away?" Benet asked.

"Yes. We're not asking to commandeer OmegaNet. All we need is a temporary Internet redirect to our Love dot Love domain when people first access OmegaNet each day. They'll begin asking for L-Gens, whether out of curiosity or just because they're free. In a matter of months, we'll be able to blanket the world. Will you help us with a redirect for a few months?"

Benet studied each of them intently. They sat ultra-relaxed with calm expressions: on Kyle's face, a slight smile. Jörg looked kindly on Benet. Karla's face was placid, serene. Benet felt no sense of pressure; only a gentle expectancy.

He stroked his chin. "I would have to speak with our entire Board. We would need to discuss it thoroughly before I can give you an answer."

"We understand. Would you allow us to make a presentation at your board meeting? We would like to introduce the L-Gen to you and your associates," Kyle said.

Within a month Benet had arranged a full board meeting at OmegaNet's headquarters in Zürich. eZo footed the bill for transportation from each board member's home country and brought them together for the presentation. The L-Gens had their usual dramatic effect and led to an agreement. OmegaNet consented to making the necessary technical adjustments. Upon eZo's request, Love dot Love would begin appearing on the opening screen of every audience member's CoFone or other device.

On the return flight, Karla pondered the raw material they would need to supply the world with L-Gens. "Each L-Gen weighs 100 grams. That means we'll need 800,000 metric tons of raw carbon nanotube material to produce an L-Gen for everyone on earth. I can't even imagine that."

"Actually, Kyle and I have already done those calculations," Jörg said. "There are several ways to look at the problem. First, we supply one L-Gen to every household. There are just over two billion households worldwide. They average close to four people each. So, 200,000 tons will put an L-Gen in every home."

"What about the workplace and government offices? College dormitories? Prisons? Hotels? We need to make enough L-Gens to put them wherever people live or work. I think we are should stay with the original plan. One for every person," Karla countered.

Kyle looked up from his CoFone. "That's what we finally agreed on, but with a twist." He let his words hang in the air as they cruised at 600 MPH toward Zürich. "Let's ship every L-Gen with a kilo of raw nanotube material. That will allow everyone who receives an L-Gen to make ten more. That will cut our distribution problem by a factor of ten. Everybody likes to get something for free. Letting people replicate ten more...that should be an added incentive for people to order L-Gens. Not to mention the way L-Gens reproduce themselves; it's almost like magic. That alone should be enough to get everyone's attention."

Karla's eyes popped open. "I did not know people could make their own L-Gens."

"They can. Just like Rick and I used our original replicator to make the first few, then fifty more for the prison study. We did that by stuffing nanotube material into the original while the universal services program was running."

"Yes, you told me something about that..."

"The universal services program on our quantum system connects to the effervescence, that thing I created at Lac Bleu. As long as it's running, any L-Gen anywhere can replicate itself. I think we could even replicate L-Gens on the moon. Or anywhere else in the universe, for that matter.

"People can do the same thing. It doesn't matter where they are. We'll give everyone who gets an L-Gen enough material to make ten more. We'll dedicate the quantum system to running the universal services program continuously. Day and night. Maybe for a whole year. Anyone with an L-Gen will be able to make ten more, then give them to friends, family, co-workers. Anyone they choose. People in prison, homeless people. They'll spread like wildfire," Kyle said.

"Yes, that's brilliant," Karla said. "If we run it all the time, will we have enough power to keep working on other problems? What about all the backlog of problems we're working on?"

"Shouldn't be a problem, but honestly...I don't think there *are* any other problems that need to be solved, my dear. This is the ultimate problem we've been trying to solve all along. Computing Love," Kyle said.

Kyle and Jörg had worked out the physical distribution problem as well. They began by contacting UPS, FedEx, the Swiss Post and major logistics companies to explain the challenge of distributing an unnamed product to every person on the planet. Eventually, a solution emerged, but the numbers were staggering.

The plan called for establishing warehouse facilities on each continent, with several in Asia, Australia, India, Europe, North and South America. With the quantum system running full time, L-Gens could be replicated at each location. The plan called for massive deliveries of carbon nanotubes, shipping cartons and battery packs. Battalions of workers could be hired to package a kilo of carbon nanotubes with each L-Gen, then to box and ship them along with their battery packs. However, robotics could be used at far lower cost. Over several months Jörg and the team made arrangements with a dozen logistics companies that could handle the intake of huge shipments of raw material; that could provide physical space to accommodate the nearly endless replication of L-Gens; and, that could automate packaging and shipment.

While planning for the distribution of L-Gens was underway, the Board of Review continued to meet each month and the quantum system continued to work out solutions to problems the Board approved. Cash flowed into eZo's escrow account like a wild river swollen over its banks as medical, environmental and social problems fell to the incredible power of the quantum system. eZo's revenue grew from hundreds of millions of dollars to billions, then to tens of billions during the two years following eZo's announcement of its quantum system.

eZo prepared a press release. With gratitude, Kyle sent it to Meg Winters, thanking her for her help and asking her to do the honor of breaking it to the world. Kyle included many side notes to Meg, giving her background details, inviting her to use them as she saw fit to further publicize the L-Gens to an unsuspecting public. He contacted Herr Langendanch at the prison and asked that his team submit the psychological studies to the relevant journals and to publish them on the web.

NEWS RELEASE

eZo Systems Announces *Free* Love Generators, Available to All, Worldwide

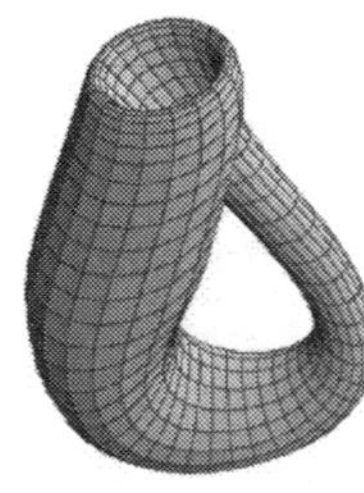

May 17, 2036 - West Palm Beach, Florida, and Zürich, Switzerland—eZo Systems, makers of the much-discussed eZo quantum super computer, in concert with OmegaNet, are excited to announce a new Love domain and immediate availability of Love Generators from eZo Systems.

According to eZo's CEO, Dr. Kyle Williams, "The extraordinary capabilities of our quantum system have given us results more exciting than we ever expected. The system guided us to build a device that generates a field of Love anyone nearby can experience. We have named this device a Love Generator, or 'L-Gen' for short. We are making these Love Generators available to everyone, worldwide, free of charge."

OmegaNet Chairman, Arthur Benet, reports that OmegaNet assisted eZo Systems to make it easy for anyone to learn about L-Gens and to place their orders. "Our entire Board of Directors has worked with eZo. We are convinced the L-Gen devices will be of great interest to all. So, pursuant to our discussions with eZo Systems, OmegaNet has agreed to display the www.Love.Love channel on every CoFone and connected device, automatically, at the beginning of each day. While you may certainly opt out of this new service, we at OmegaNet highly recommend you learn more about the L-Gen."

L-Gens are available, worldwide, at no cost whatsoever, by visiting www.Love.Love. Our goal is to provide a free L-Gen to every person on the planet.

OmegaNet will provide an automated worldwide redirect to www.Love.Love beginning tomorrow at 00:00:00 UTC, and continuing for 180 days. You will find answers to your questions about Love Generators at our website. However, those interested may visit www.Love.Love at any time, as it is a permanent domain.

Dr. Williams added: "Because delivering some eight billion devices to the world community poses many logistical challenges, we have decided to ship each L-Gen with one kilogram of carbon nanotube raw material. Insert that material into the mouth of the L-Gen bottle when you activate it. Your supply of nanotube material will allow you to make an additional ten (10) L-Gens. We encourage you to give those L-Gens away freely to your family members, friends, co-workers and others, including those less fortunate than you who may be struggling."

We wish only Love to you and yours. With Love, all problems pass away. For further guidance and information, please note the following, which you will also find at www.Love.Love.

INSTRUCTIONS

· To order your L-Gen, look here. We will send you an L-Gen at no cost whatsoever.

· For help making ten (10) additional L-Gens, follow these easy instructions. You'll learn how to insert the carbon nanotube raw material we've provided into your L-Gen, and then make copies of your L-Gen. We encourage you to share those L-Gen copies with others.

LEARN MORE

We now understand the so-called "dark energy" in our universe is not "dark" at all. What has been called dark energy is the energy of Love. It fills the universe and all universes. We've also learned an "effervescence" connected to that Love energy is bubbling through our physical universe and has connected with our quantum computer system. This coupling has allowed the quantum system to reproduce L-Gens no matter where on the planet you may live.

The L-Gen device extends an energy field that allows anyone nearby to experience Love. While we have not yet decoded the physics involved with L-Gens, we do understand their impact on people.

We are all infested with beliefs about our lives and life on this planet that are incorrect. In fact, many of our most accepted beliefs lies at the root of human suffering. The L-Gen allows you to see past those misperceptions and to know Love for what it is. The L-Gen removes all blocks to knowing Love and to learning Love is within you. It is what you Are, rather than something you search for outside yourself.

Meg submitted the news release to OmegaNet's chairman first, as a matter of formality and courtesy, then reached out to hundreds of journalists, bloggers, producers, editors, friends and associates around the world. She added her own personal commentary. She wrote additional press releases that included an abstract of each of the articles from the prison study, noting which journals would carry each one.

People began visiting Love dot Love within minutes of the news release. A woman from Cuenca, Ecuador placed the first L-Gen order. A few milliseconds later, dozens of additional orders arrived, followed by hundreds, then thousands. eZo's computer systems parsed the orders out to each distribution point and the first shipments began just hours later.

Rick looked at Kyle solemnly. "This first batch of orders we're sending out? They're the Genesis batch."

"What do you mean?"

"They mark the beginning of changing the way people live. You know, like, 'In the beginning.' We need to memorialize this first batch of orders somehow. I think of them like the Genesis of what's to come. The dawning of a new generation and a new way of living."

As the day wore on, the order rate continued to skyrocket. By evening Rick had tallied more than ten million L-Gen orders. "That's only about one in every thousand people," Rick said. "Still, not bad for less than a day."

Jörg entered the room and projected a newsfeed from his CoFone onto the wall for everyone to see. "Yes, but some people are pissed off with us. I cannot believe this happened so fast," Jörg said. "This could get tricky."

"How so?" Kyle asked.

"I just picked this up from OmegaNet. The U.S. Food and Drug Administration wants a ban on L-Gens until they can study them to assure they're safe and effective. The head of the FDA is calling on your Congress to impose a ban until their scientists can conduct a thorough study of the L-Gen. He's asked your President to issue an executive order to ban L-Gens until Congress can act."

"Makes no sense," Rick replied. "The FDA regulates food and drugs and medical devices. The L-Gen isn't any of those."

"Of course not," Kyle said. "If it wasn't the FDA trying to slow things down it would probably be some select committee in Congress that wants to put their mark on what we're doing."

Kyle closed his eyes for a moment. "We're going to find all kinds of entrenched interests who want to take charge of this. Some will want to put a stop to what we're doing. Not only in the U.S."

Jörg interrupted. "There's more, Kyle. Some of the member countries have called for an emergency session at the UN. The leaders of North Korea and Rwanda are already declaring import bans on L-Gens as well."

Kyle stared into the distance for a moment. "There's nothing we can do about that. Once L-Gens start reaching people and replicating, their effects will overcome what any government or dictator can do."

"I agree," Karla said. "When people understand L-Gens, they will do whatever it takes to share the experience with others. I can even see people smuggling them across borders." Karla paused to think. "What if we were to air-drop L-Gens and nanotube material into countries where they are banned? They would spread quickly."

"I suppose it might work, but in the long run I think the dictators and regulators and politicians who are afraid of this will one day sit with an L-Gen at their sides," Kyle said.

"For now, let's suspend our press conferences for a few days so these events can unfold on their own. Would you ask Cary and Paul to cancel the conferences for Monday and Wednesday?"

"Sure."

"Thanks. Let's watch and see what happens."

Jörg frowned. "Let's hope this doesn't get ugly."

CHAPTER 45

Infested with Beliefs

Reporters from around the world flocked into Zürich following eZo's L-Gen announcement. Calls and emails besieged Cary and Paul. Some asked politely and some demanded a seat at upcoming news conferences. After some deliberation, eZo rented a grand ballroom at a nearby hotel that would seat up to nine hundred people. They set up a lottery to allocate seats and contacted *Stadt Zürich Poleizi* to hire a team of off-duty city police to provide security.

After almost a week with no news briefing from eZo, the room filled to capacity. A mere six days had passed since eZo shocked the world with its L-Gen announcement. It had captured the world's attention just as surely as the discovery of aliens from another planet. OmegaNet's Zürich affiliate arrived with a full complement of equipment to broadcast the briefing live.

Cary looked around the room from the side of the stage. "I see our regular people out there, but I don't know most of them. We've got a full house."

"No surprise there. Everyone wants to know more about the L-Gens," Paul replied.

At nine o'clock Friday morning, Paul and Cary strode across the stage and stood at the podium, which was modestly decorated with the eZo Systems logo. "Good morning. Before we take questions, I have a statement."

She looked out on the crowd. "On May 17th, last Saturday, we broke our press release announcing the L-Gen and our plans to make it available to the world. Since then we've taken orders from more than seventy million people. Each of them can replicate ten more L-Gens. That equates to seven hundred and seventy million—about nine percent of the world population. Orders have come in from more than two hundred countries. Dr. Williams and all of us at eZo Systems are extremely happy the L-Gens have been so well accepted."

Paul stood at Cary's right, just a step behind her.

"Those orders are in fulfillment as we speak. We've setup distribution centers on every continent to facilitate speedy delivery. We want people to experience Love in its fullest incarnation. L-Gens give just that experience. Paul Glazer and I will now take your questions."

A pandemonium of voices filled the room. Paul stepped forward and pointed to a woman standing in the front row.

"Mr. Glazer, you announced your Love Generators last Saturday. Why has the world had to wait almost a week to learn more about them? Is there some sort of problem?"

"There's no problem. We wanted to give people a chance to learn about the L-Gens on their own. As Ms. Thomasson said, millions of people are getting acquainted with their L-Gens, and we've posted all the important information at our Love dot Love website."

Another reporter stood. "There've been reports from North Korea that they will not allow your love generators into the country. Do you have any comment on their position?"

"Yes. We're not sure why any government would choose to withhold L-Gens from their citizens. We hope, over time, the leadership will reconsider their position," Cary answered.

From the right corner of the room: "You're also aware the U.S. President has signed an executive order to postpone L-Gen imports into the country until the U.S. Food and Drug Administration can evaluate them. What plans have you made in that regard?"

Paul Glazer answered. "Yes, we're aware the administration and Congress have some concerns. We believe the leadership will rethink the issue once it experiences the effects of the L-Gen. Until they do, we won't be able to fulfill orders from U.S. citizens. However, we have an order from the FDA and we shipped that unit via special courier. I think it's worthwhile to note: the FDA doesn't have any jurisdiction over the L-Gen. It is neither a food, a drug nor a medical device. We hope they will come to that realization soon."

Paul recognized another reporter. "Brian Faultney, Canadian Broadcasting. We have had some reports of L-Gens crossing the U.S. border from Canada. When you chose to let an L-Gen reproduce itself into ten more units, did you intend that such cross-border smuggling incidents might take place? In effect, their ability to replicate can make a government's embargo irrelevant."

Paul hesitated for a moment. "I don't believe an occasional unit being smuggled across borders will make an embargo irrelevant. And, no. We didn't anticipate that would happen. Our goal in distributing L-Gens that could replicate was a matter of logistics. We were able to cut back our distribution by a factor of more than ten. As you can imagine, distributing eight billion of anything is a massive job. The replication feature let us cut distribution back to around 730 million units."

Another reporter: "On your love dot love website you said people are—and I quote—'infested with false beliefs' that are the cause of human suffering. Would you explain what you mean?"

Cary stepped up to the podium. "Yes. We can choose in each moment whether we will give attention to the thoughts of our ordinary mind, or to approach daily living differently. Ordinarily, people spend a lot of time and energy trying to get the things they want and get rid of the things they don't want. However, once we know Love, those wants and desires no longer hold importance. We realize we have been given everything we could ever imagine wanting and nothing we do not want. Our ordinary ways of thinking prevent us from knowing that Love can change our perspectives.

"Here's an analogy: Astronomers and cosmologists who peer out into the universe agree dark matter and energy exist, but they can't see it and none of their instruments can detect it. Love is much the same. We all generally agree that Love is real, at least as an idea, but we don't have direct experience of it any more than the scientists can see dark matter and energy. We're blind to the experience of Love that's within each of us and all around us."

Cary noticed many reporters were using their CoFones to translate her English words into their native languages. Some wore headphones while others pressed CoFones to their ears. *I've got to make this clear to everyone,* she thought.

"The L-Gen is a remarkable tool," she said. "It removes the blocks and barriers we as humans erect against experiencing what Love truly is." Now she spoke slowly and distinctly to dramatize her words: "L-Gens show you how to *change your mind about the way you see the world*. It helps people find a new *way* of thinking that dissolves the problems we have always dealt with. We no longer need to keep trying to change the world—whether through politics, diplomacy, war or our own personal efforts. We need only change our minds, and that's what the L-Gens help us do."

Cary looked out over the audience. When the finished speaking, no one stood up or jockeyed for position to ask the next question. *Good, they're listening, they're thinking about what I said*. "Our lives and our world are filled with Love. The L-Gens allow us to know and experience that. When we do, we learn new ways of living and understanding."

A murmur broke out and swept through the room. Cary caught a movement from the corner of her eye, turned, and saw Kyle coming toward her. They exchanged a few words off mic, then Kyle took a place behind the podium.

Ladies and gentlemen, I would like to introduce our CEO and the creative force behind eZo's quantum computer, Dr. Kyle Williams.

Applause broke out across the room. Kyle let it run for a moment, nodding and smiling at the crowd. He held up his hand until the room quieted, as if he were a pastor calming his flock.

"Hello. I'd like to add a little to what Cary said. Each of you here today—and everyone in the world watching—want happiness and comfort. We want to live a life of ease and joy and plenty. Why is it so few of us find that?" He paused to wait for a reply to the unanswerable question. The room fell silent for a several seconds as he surveyed the room.

A small smile crossed Kyle's lips. "I know. We all want to earn more money. To be more comfortable. To be happier. Here's the truth only the L-Gen can reveal to you: You have already been given all you could ever want or need. It is there, waiting for you to recognize it. Removing the blocks you have built to experiencing Love will open the curtains you've kept closed until now. Once that happens, you'll find chasing after and worshiping false idols like wealth, comfort and success is what distracts you from what is Real. If you understood that, you would put aside those idols and readjust your life to let Love guide you.

"The L-Gen helps you do that. Once you have the direct experience of Love, you'll begin to see everyone around you as brothers and sisters. You'll *insist* nothing ever be done to any of them that you would not have done to you. You'll live in a world built upon Love as its foundation. Love for everyone, no matter who they are; no matter what culture or group or ethnicity they come from. *That* is what the L-Gen does. It allows you to *choose again* which part of your mind you want to live from. When you choose your Right Mind, you'll no longer find it necessary to try to change what happens to make your life work for you."

Kyle scanned faces in the crowd and saw a man shaking his head and grimacing. He pointed to the man and asked, "Do you have a question, sir?"

"Yes, thank you. I'm John Carceroma of the Baptist Convention. With all due respect, I feel you're preaching to us about another false idol. The word of God is all we need to know. Your device may be remarkable, but it's not a substitute for the Bible and the Holy Word of God. If you distribute these L-Gens to the world and people start worshiping them, your L-Gens could destroy organized religion. They'd beguile people and prevent them from hearing God's Word."

Carceroma's voice rose as he became more emotional. "Personally, I'm not certain we need to change *how* we look at life. Our churches and our clergy provide all the guidance people need. How do you reconcile those issues?"

Kyle stood calmly, nodding slightly as Carceroma spoke. "Mr. Carceroma, we respect the churches and religions of the world. The L-Gen is a tool that allows people to look past the 'me and mine, you and yours' mentality that has infected us for thousands of years. The L-Gen lets people see that you, brother Carceroma, and I, are one and the same. We are each Creations of the One who created us in His image.

"During the time we seem to live here as bodies, as individual people, we're also here to *care* for and love one another. You see, everyone in this room seems to be an individual. In truth, there is really only one of us. One Sonship. When we care for anyone who seems to be separate from us, we are actually caring for the entire Sonship. As we do, our Creator returns our caring and Love to us magnified. That kind of Love doesn't come in degrees. It's a miracle that descends on you so you have no doubt what Love is. Here...let me illustrate that idea..."

Kyle projected his CoFone on the jumbo screen behind him. It showed a picture that might have been a Rorschach inkblot. "See this picture? It looks abstract. There's nothing identifiable at all. Yet, when you see the hidden picture—what it *really* is—you'll never be able to see it again without absolutely *knowing* what it is."

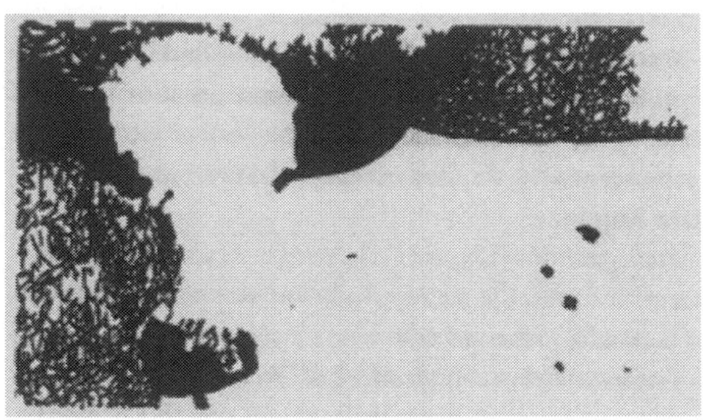

The entire assembly stared at the image. The room fell silent as all eyes focused and minds raced to figure out what the image might be. A moment passed with only hushed whispers among the crowd of reporters. An occasional laugh broke the near silence.

"Can anyone tell me what this is?" Kyle asked.

A man at the back of the room spoke. "It's a man lying down. His head is the white part on the left."

Another held up his hand. "No, it's a woman lying down."

"It's not a person," Kyle said.

John Carceroma stood up. "Is this important, Dr. Williams? This feels like a child's game."

"It may seem so," Kyle said, "but I'm showing you this picture because it illustrates an important point about what L-Gens do for people. Let's take another twenty or thirty seconds with this."

"It's a cloud." someone said.

"Is it a computer-generated image?" another asked.

The OmegaNet team focused their main broadcast camera on the image, turning other cameras to the audience as each person offered an idea. Kyle surveyed the crowd.

"All right," he said, finally. He held his CoFone in his left hand and dragged a finger across the display. "I'm adding a line. That one single line will show you what this picture is. You'll never be able to see this image again without *knowing* what it is. Here." He held his CoFone up and projected the altered picture onto the jumbo screen.

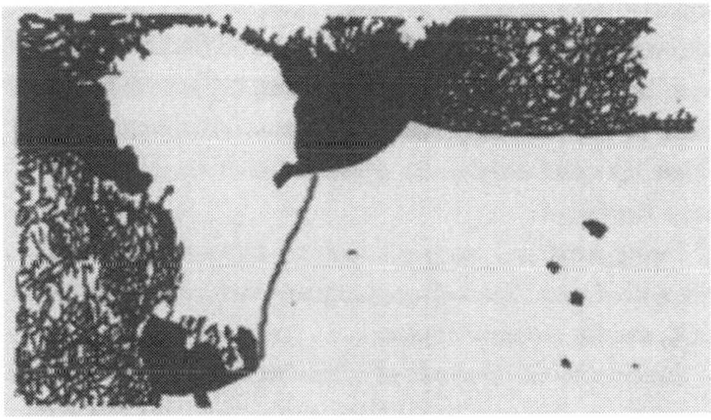

A murmur spread across the crowd. "Do you see what it is now?" Kyle asked.

John Carceroma all but sneered. "It's a cow. That's a cute trick, but I don't see the point of it."

"Mr. Carceroma, that single line I added cements the picture in your mind forever. You'll always know it's a cow whether the extra line is there or not. Whether you look at it tomorrow or in twenty years." Kyle scanned across the entire audience. "The L-Gens are like that single line. They show you what Love is so you can't misunderstand it. With certainty. With no doubt. With no questions remaining. The L-Gens open your minds and hearts to knowing Love in a way you'll never question, forget or doubt."

A man standing at the periphery of the group jumped up and screamed. "That's blasphemy, Williams! God damns you." He pulled a pistol from his pocket, fumbled with it for a second, then aimed at Kyle. Paul Glazer lurched toward Kyle and knocked him to the floor. A bullet whizzed past the space Kyle had occupied and lodged in the wall.

Panic and chaos erupted. Reporters fell to the floor. The shooter took aim and fired again. The bullet struck the podium. He began running toward Kyle with his arm outstretched. He fired toward Kyle and Paul. Three Swiss security officials standing nearest sprinted toward the shooter, tackled him and knocked him to the floor. They struggled and the gun dropped from the shooter's hand. The police subdued him, rolled him onto his belly and slapped on a pair of handcuffs.

The OmegaNet video team captured every moment of the crowd's pandemonium.

Kyle brushed himself off and stood up again behind the podium. He pulled the battery pack from an L-Gen on a shelf below the podium. The entire room filled with brilliant colors as the L-Gen began broadcasting its field of energy. Every hue of the rainbow permeated the room from floor to ceiling. It saturated each person's body with an iridescent glow both beautiful and calming.

Kyle looked at the crowd, then focused on the Swiss security agents. One had his knee in the shooter's back while the other two held the man prone against the floor. Kyle tapped on the microphone to get the crowd's attention. "All right. Everyone? The danger has passed. Please take your seats."

People began picking up overturned chairs and taking their seats again. The screams from a moment ago transformed into a quietude that descended on the room. Faces carried expressions of wonderment; some had huge smiles, a few people were hugging one another while others wept quietly. Kyle called to the group, "Is anyone injured?" With no one reporting injury, Kyle dragged the podium back to its proper position.

"May I see by a show of hands how many of you have experienced the L-Gen before today?" Kyle asked.

Only fifty or sixty hands raised.

"Fine. Then for the rest of you, please relax into this, your first experience of Love." Kyle spoke to the security police. "Would you please bring that man to the podium?"

The shooter walked, subdued, alongside the guards—one on either side holding his arms. The shooter's head hung down toward his chest. When he reached the stage, Kyle spoke. "Please, undo this man's hands."

With his hands free, the shooter stood before Kyle then raised his head to look into Kyle's impassive face.

"What's your name?"

"Gorbeck. Christian Gorbeck."

"Where do you live, Mr. Gorbeck?"

"*München*. Munich."

"Mr. Gorbeck from Munich. Are you all right?"

He stood before Kyle with his shoulders slumped and his head bowed toward the floor, eyes closed. The colors of the scintillating waterfall flowed through his body. His face was blue and green and violet as the L-Gen floated all its harmonies into him. Gorbeck opened his eyes, raised his head and said, "I am sorry. I did not understand." His face wrinkled and a sob escaped his mouth. "I am *so* sorry. I did not understand. Please forgive me."

Kyle held out his hand. Gorbeck hesitated, then reached out. The two men shook hands and Kyle pulled him into an embrace.

"I do not judge you," Kyle said. "You are already forgiven." Kyle stepped back and lifted the L-Gen from its place in the podium. "Please accept this L-Gen as a gift. Take it home with you."

Kyle stood next to Gorbeck and spoke to the audience "No harm has been done. This L-Gen will help Mr. Gorbeck find a new perspective, as I hope all of you will experience, too." Kyle surveyed the crowd and marveled in spite of himself at the L-Gen's effect upon them. Only a handful of these people have experienced this before, he thought. "Ladies and gentlemen, we would be pleased if those of you who have not yet received an L-Gen would take one home with you today. You can pick one up at the room next door after the news conference. Thank you for coming today. I'll turn this back over to Paul and Cary."

Kyle motioned to the Swiss *poleizi* to follow him, then left the stage and walked across the street to the eZo Center. Kyle refused to press charges. Gorbeck was arrested for discharging a firearm in a public venue and reckless endangerment. He was released on his own recognizance pending a court appearance.

The reaction from viewers around the world was immediate. L-Gen orders poured into Love dot Love. The order rate doubled in the next hour. Viewers around the world played and replayed the news conference on their CoFones. Hundreds of OmegaNet channels carried the story to every nation. U.S. reporters covering the White House sought comment, but got none. Others tried to pry a reaction from the FDA, but to no avail. However, Congressional Representatives and Senators were a bit more verbose.

A reporter thrust a microphone into U.S. Senator Harry Dornedo's face as the Senator walked from his house to his limo. "Senator, the events today at eZo Systems' press conference seem to show that Love Generators have a beneficial effect. Yet the administration and Congress have banned their import. What's the rationale for that action?"

Dornedo kept walking. "No. Congress has not taken any action. However, the President did issue an executive order."

"Yes, but Congress is considering the matter. We've had reports the Senate committee on Health and Human Welfare is taking up the matter as we speak. You're on that committee, so I'll ask again: What is the rationale for banning L-Gens in the U.S.?"

It's clear the L-Gen does something," Senator Dornedo said. "For the safety and welfare of the American people, we cannot allow a few hundred million unknown devices into the country until we've determined they are safe."

"Are you concerned about health issues?"

"Of course, but there's a lot more than health to consider."

"What else?" the reporter asked.

"I don't have time to go into all the details now. I'm on my way to a meeting. However, there are concerns that eZo's device might cause people to behave in unpredictable ways."

"Unpredictable?"

"Yes. That eZo device might be far more damaging than addictive drugs. People might find that sitting with an L-Gen is more desirable than going to work. The economy could collapse. Damaging our distribution of food, fuel and other commodities would paralyze the nation if people don't handle their job responsibilities. Of course, there are also concerns about exposing our military to it. We need to have our troops under control and constantly ready to respond to a crisis, not sitting in *zazen* meditating."

Bloggers debated L-Gen issues. One who used the handle "darkside" concluded: "I find it too convenient that Williams shook hands and embraced Gorbeck moments after Gorbeck tried to take his life. I think the whole event was staged to promote L-Gens."

That post fired ugly remarks and acrimony. Thousands responded to the blogger, each expressing their own thoughts on the matter of L-Gens:

gendarmo.de: Your an idiot darkside! Get a life! eZo is giving those things away. There's no profit motive. I ordered an L-Gen. You should too.

Billybob: Forget that crap. What's all that shit bout seeing the world different? My world rocks. If yours sucks, tough shit.

sarahsarah: I'm w/ u gendarmo. I got one. It's wonderful.

Billybob: text me sarahsarah & i'll show u sumthing wonderful.

palinskor: Convenient? Right on. That whole shooting thing was a setup. Profit motive or not, eZo is up to something. Smells rotten.

dualcore: why you say dat? Cuz nobody luv you?

Jessica_Ohio: you don't no nothing palinskor. Why would a company give away billions of those for free? Wish I could get one!

churchman: I think the devil has a hand in this. How else could those L-Gens make new ones out of thin air? Scare the crap out of me. Time to pray.

bocso_girl: Ditto. something's stinks about this Lgen thing. I'm going to church twice this week.

ANONman: c'mon churchman. get real. there ain't no devil. and you ain't gonna get no love at church. get you a L-gen and get real. I' still waitin 4 mine. ne day now.

CHAPTER 46

Nothing Matters

Kyle spoke to Gorbeck. Kyle found he was like any of countless billions of people living on the planet. He projected his own fears on the world around him, then decided to take matters into his own hands to "right the wrongs" he had projected. After a couple of hours talk with Kyle as they sat in the field of Love, Gorbeck came to realize that projecting judgments on others and the world always precedes perception, rather than the other way around. He realized attack is never useful or justified. After all, Kyle explained, "We are all One. When you attack another you are attacking the entire Sonship of which you are part. In fact, when you attack a brother, you attack God Himself. For we are One with God."

Gorbeck, sitting with his newfound L-Gen grasped close to his heart, understood. "Sending your machines to everyone in the world? I thought it was dangerous. A plot. I was convinced you were trying to take over the world. I had to stop you. I was wrong. Very wrong. Thank you, Dr. Williams. Thank you for your love and forgiveness."

Kyle gave Gorbeck a kilo of carbon nanos so he could replicate his L-Gen, embraced him again, then allowed him to go on his way.

The team gathered around Kyle. Karla threw her arms around him and pulled him close.

"We didn't need that drama," Kyle said. He looked at Paul and pulled him into a hug. "Thanks to you, everything's okay now."

"No problem, my friend, but why'd you let Gorbeck go free? He's a troubled man."

"He's afraid, that's all. He'll be all right now that he understands."

"It looks like the entire world has been watching our press conference. OmegaNet's replaying it on every news channel," Cary said.

"Good. It will help get our message out. Actually, I couldn't have asked for things to turn out any better," Kyle said.

Jörg interrupted. "I'm not so sure things are as cozy as you think. There's a firestorm brewing."

"What's happening?" Kyle asked.

"The trending news on OmegaNet. One faction thinks you staged the shooting incident to advance your own objectives. Another is afraid you're going to kill organized religion when people choose their L-Gens over going to church. And, your government announced they're putting an embargo on L-Gens coming into the U.S."

Kyle smiled at Jörg. "That's okay. Those things don't matter."

"What do you mean?"

"You know how our L-Gens work. They start removing all the blocks a person has built up against knowing Love the instant they're turned on. Those old fears begin to fall away as soon as anyone sits down with an L-Gen. They begin to experience Love. Love overcomes everything because it's Real. What seem to be problems are only illusions. They don't mean anything. They'll resolve on their own."

"Perhaps," Jörg said, "but removing those fears takes time. You cannot just sit with an L-Gen one time and erase things you have believed your whole life."

Kyle nodded. "Sure. It takes time. A few repetitions, but as more people around the world get their own L-Gens the process will accelerate. It won't be long until people begin seeing their lives are illusory. As they do, they'll realize all the troubles of the world mean nothing. They'll see that nothing matters."

Jörg put his CoFone in his pocket. "Getting L-Gens out to the world matters. You can't say *nothing* matters."

Kyle's eyebrows raised up and he gave Jörg a warm smile. "Nothing matters. I'm certain of it. Long before we met, Marci and Aimer drilled an idea into me. They said our lives are an illusion. We're dreaming. I heard it so many times in so many ways. I couldn't ignore the idea. At first it was just an *idea*. Over time I began *imagining* that life is an illusion. I played with it.

"It became more than an idea. It almost seems as if my imagining added some kind of energy to it, because it led me to the point of *believing* nothing matters. Now, for me, it's a certainty. Nothing that seems to go on around us is Real. That's why I say these events that seem to take place in the world don't matter. That experience I had at Lac Bleu where I was a giant cartoon man standing on the planet...that showed me in no uncertain terms that this is all illusory."

"I hope you're right," Jörg said. "A lot of people are against us and they're coming from every angle. Political, religious ..."

Cary reached out and put her hand on Jörg's. "Can I share something with you?"

"Sure."

"All those people coming at us don't matter either. That's just how things are unfolding. Let me tell you a story about how things unfold. You might not know this, but the Florida Everglades used to be filled with alligators. Now they're gone. Know why?"

Jörg shook his head. "No, but I think you're going to tell me."

"Snakes. Twenty or thirty years ago, people who kept pythons and boa constrictors as pets got rid of them when they grew too large. They dumped them in the Everglades. Over time they became the apex predators. They killed off all the gators and now the Everglades are filled with snakes."

"So?"

"The news media back then kept running stories about the *horror* of those slithering monsters. A lot of them grew to three meters and longer. They kept beating the drum about how we needed to find a way to kill the snakes and 'restore the Everglades.' How family pets were being killed and eaten. Everyone was horrified when their dogs and cats got killed, not to mention a few children. Today the snakes are still the top predators. The time for gators came to an end. What *was* became what *is*.

"That was despite all the hunting parties sent down there to trap and kill the snakes. There were news reports over the years about all the snake hunts and other efforts to save the Everglades. None of it worked, though. People began calling the snakes a tragedy—you know, the way they took over."

Jörg grimaced. "Alligators were bad enough. I hate the idea of snakes everywhere."

Cary smiled. "Sure, but that whole event was nothing more than the universe unfolding and changing the landscape. That little transition was no different for the gators than for people. I mean, just think of the countless tribes and conclaves of humanity that were snuffed out over tens of thousands of years. Now, releasing our L-Gens into the world is going to put another wrinkle in the unfolding. This time it will bring people to their Right Minds where they can know Love."

Kyle nodded. "Marci once told me our quantum system has all the presence needed to change the world. Now, by delivering our L-Gens, that prophecy is happening. None of what happens in the world, pro or con, makes any difference. In fact, there is no pro or con. Whatever appears to be good or bad is illusion. It's all the same. None of it matters.

"I can imagine the world wrapped in a virtual cloud of Love. Where no one projects *anything* on other people. Where looking past things and offering forgiveness are the orders of the day. Where no one allows *anything* to be done to a brother that they would not have done to themselves."

"That all sounds wonderful," Jörg said, "but at least for now, we're fighting a losing battle in your country. Your customs people are going to impound L-Gens. They're serious about their embargo."

"Like I said, it doesn't matter. We'll continue shipping L-Gens to the rest of the world. Shipping L-Gens into the U.S.? That, and everything else, will unfold on its own."

In the following days and weeks, the question of exactly *what* was unfolding became more clear.

While extremist terror groups had evolved over decades of the 21st century, their core beliefs remained unchanged: They believed killing people with beliefs different from theirs was a solution.

Shortly after the L-Gens began shipping, the current incarnation of Middle Eastern extremists isolated more than two thousand people in the small town of Dubok. They declared jihad against the citizens of Dubok, for the town's residents believed and worshiped in a manner the jihadists found despicable.

They surrounded the town, then cut off water and food supplies. After three weeks without nourishment, children and the sickly began to die. During the fourth week, jihadists began executing leaders among the town's people. A man who had been unwillingly pressed into service of the jihadists smuggled an L-Gen into the town and gave it to Abdul Aleem, a cleric. Aleem quickly replicated ten new L-Gens and passed them to other clerics still alive.

Under cover of darkness, citizens of the town met and sat in fields of Love. They discovered what it felt like to *know* their God's love. They sought to share it with their captors. At dawn on a Monday they arrayed all eleven L-Gens together in a tiny shack at the center of town. The clutch of L-Gens emitted waves and colors of Love far beyond their usual range. It flowed out into the town, enveloping everyone, then into the surrounding perimeter. The captors fell into the experience of Love, and soon came to understand that all people are One. They began laying down their arms. Executions ceased. They realized attack is never justified, and especially when the reason for attack was nothing more than two groups holding different beliefs—beliefs that were nothing more than illusions in a dream world. That event became known as "Dubok's Monday of Brotherhood."

As word of Dubok reached the media, people throughout the Middle East began collecting their L-Gens together to produce the amplified effect. Soon, entire cities became swaddled in clouds of Love that gave no credibility to fear, violence or attack. Astronauts aboard one of the orbiting space stations reported seeing aurora-like light displays surrounding entire cities and towns. Dubok's Monday of Brotherhood was later to be heralded as the beginning of a new era that, at long last, brought an end to the region's centuries-long conflict. Violence caused by people projecting conflicting ideas came to an end. The new idea of Oneness became more than just an idea; it became actuality.

Politicians and military strategists took a wait-and-see attitude. Government officials, their intelligence communities and military leadership in Washington, Berlin, London and capitals of other world powers agreed to ground their offensive drones flying over the Middle East. Yet for a while, they left surveillance drones roaming the skies. As the aurora-like light show spread across the region, they brought those drones back to earth as well.

Heads of companies that supplied military hardware went on record, fearing for the profitability of their businesses. The Chairman of the Board of America's largest military aircraft manufacturer wrote an open letter.

If this season of love brought on by eZo's so-called love generators continues, we may be facing the end of our nation's need for military power in the Middle East. Events there show that eZo's device can bring peace to even the most war-torn region.

While I do understand that love is preferable to war, I am deeply concerned about the millions of people who take part in the supply chain that allows us to build the world's most advanced military aircraft and weaponry. Manufacturers, many of which are smaller businesses, will close. Technology companies who supply the chips and computers we use in our aircraft may be the hardest hit, while our own highly skilled workers at each of our manufacturing plants may face unemployment.

In spite of my preference for peace over war, I am at a loss to see where all this may lead.

CEOs of "private military companies," contract mercenaries, which accounted for nearly forty-five percent of all U.S. military and intelligence forces, expressed concern to their troops that their services would no longer be needed in the Middle East. One mercenary organization scrambled to deploy men and women to other hot spots to avoid massive layoffs. Italy, Germany, Poland and Saudi Arabia pressed the U.K. and U.S. to, at long last, adopt the International Convention against the Recruitment, Use, Financing and Training of Mercenaries—an international treaty dating to the beginning of the century that sought to ban mercenaries, but which the U.K. and U.S. had chosen to ignore.

Meanwhile, the entertainment industry began morphing into something new. Media stars with mega-fortunes traveled the world as a matter of routine when they weren't involved in a project. Many of them managed to find L-Gens. Some were successful at having them delivered or carried back into the U.S. A new paradigm began affecting writers, producers, directors and performers. While movies and other forms of entertainment had focused on attack, revenge, partisanship and violence for as long as the industry had existed, new productions took on a gentler tone.

Meg Winters called. "Hi, Kyle. I thought you might want to know: Your L-Gens are making their way into the States. Hollywood and New York and Chicago, too. A movie is going into production in the next few months. It's about eZo and your L-Gens. Did you authorize it?"

"No. First I heard of it."

"I had lunch with the producer the other day. He said your L-Gens are showing up everywhere in and around LA. A group of screenwriters got together and have been sitting as a team with a few L-Gens. He said they've been really moved. The writers put together a screenplay. The producer likes it. He's trying to get one of the major studios to back him. It's not clear yet if he'll get the funding. If not, he's going to crowd-fund it and go indie."

"What's the premise? Does it have a title?"

"Their working title is 'A Love Affair with God.' It's a story about Christian Gorbeck."

"What?"

"Yes, Gorbeck. He had a checkered past before he tried to kill you. Funny his first name is Christian. He was a 'Christian' in name only. He was in and out of jail a few times. He frequented the Munich whorehouses on Leierkasten regularly. He was married twice and fathered a couple of kids, but managed to avoid paying child support. An all-around SOB. Now, he's a changed man. The story wants to cover Gorbeck's life and show how that event at your press conference changed everything for him. You and your L-Gen will be a big part of the story."

"Sounds interesting. I hope it all goes well."

"There's more. Your L-Gens are showing up at the other entertainment centers. Vancouver, Tokyo, Sydney, Paris, Toronto, Rome, London. My contacts at each of them are telling me L-Gens are giving them a new understanding of what entertainment should be. Maybe all that junk entertainment I complained about is on its way out."

Kyle and Jörg sat together, eating breakfast. "These events in the Middle East have ramifications. Most of them are economic," Jörg said.

"Guess so, but what matters is that peace has finally come to the region," Kyle replied.

"I understand why you say that. However, one event triggers another. Companies that make military hardware and supplies may fail, putting millions out of work. The economy may not survive such a failure. It could fall into recession, or worse."

"No telling what's going to happen. Things will have to unfold. Here's my guess: There's a lot of technology tied up in the military industrial sector. Maybe those companies will find something better to make. Things that help people instead of killing them. If the Middle East is any example, the need for armies may well disappear," Kyle said.

"Yes, but this thing is going to spread beyond the military industry. I'm seeing all kinds of reports and they all predict hard times."

Kyle gazed at Jörg for a few seconds before speaking. "Many people are worried, but worry is nothing more than fear of a possible future, right? There's no need for anyone to worry. We're watched over, my friend. Soon people everywhere will know they're watched over as well."

Jörg nodded. "Yes, but as people move deeper into their Right Minds, I wonder if the foundations of society will survive. I can see competition becoming obsolete. No one will want to put themselves ahead of anyone else. Companies will stop working to maximize their profits; they'll fall into malaise where they barely get by, or even fail. Competition and the profit motive go hand in hand. The profit motive has driven economic progress for centuries."

Profit motive. Kyle gazed off into the middle distance. It's humanity's desire to acquire, accumulate and save money. It's a scorecard. A false idol. He recalled a conversation he'd had with Aimer months earlier.

"Imagine a world without money. How do you think that could possibly work?" Aimer had asked.

"I suppose people would have to barter," Kyle had replied.

"No. Barter would still be a form of exchange. That's not what I'm asking. Try again."

"Well ..." Kyle had scratched his head. "I guess people would need to have a different motive for working. After all, if people don't work there won't be any output from companies. With no output there wouldn't be any consumer goods—food, commodities, fuel. That sort of thing."

"Right. Most people work to get money. What kind of motives would they need if there was no money?" Aimer asked.

"I can't imagine a world without money. I don't know."

"Well then, let me tell you a story about a man known as Hillel the Elder. He was a great Jewish scholar who was born long ago—about 110 BC by your reckoning. A man once came to him with a chip on his shoulder. He was a non-believer. He wanted to aggravate Hillel, so he asked him a question. He said, 'Explain the Torah to me while you stand on one foot.'"

Kyle shrugged. "And?"

"Hillel said this: 'What is hateful to you, do not do to your fellow. This is the whole Torah; the rest is explanation and details. Go and learn.'"

Kyle continued staring at Aimer.

"That's the Golden Rule. Plato, Confucius and Aristotle all spoke of it. Do unto others as you would have them do unto you. Nothing could be simpler or easier to understand. So, let's get back to the issue of motives. Imagine everyone was motivated by doing for others what they wish were done for them. What do you suppose would happen?"

"I guess people would do what's right. They'd work together for the common good. They'd form some kind of socialist society."

"For the common good? Yes, but socialism is just a platform to share wealth, and it still presumes there will be money. It equates money with wealth and well-being. Socialism is so wrapped up with ego thinking and philosophy that it can't stand on its own. It never has for very long. It's one of the ego's rambling ideas that goes nowhere," Aimer said.

"So, maybe the motive to do what you'd have done for yourself would prevail. Is that what you're suggesting?"

Aimer nodded. "Yes. Let's say you want to have a place to live. If you're living in a world motivated by money you'd have to save so you could buy a house. If there were no money, you'd have to find another way. Perhaps you'd find someone who would build a house for you simply because you need a place to live."

"Okay, but they'd need to pay their workers and buy materials."

"Not if there were no money. The workers would do the work because they understand what Hillel said. The Golden Rule: Do unto others ..."

"Sure, but they'd still have to buy all the materials—lumber, nails, concrete."

"Right. The people who make lumber and nails and concrete would be doing it because they are doing for others. Not for money. Same with all the others who make the things you need to build a house."

"That sounds like utopia, Aimer. It could never happen. It's a do-gooder's fantasy."

"Remember, we're talking about motives. What could replace motivation driven by money. Do you think the Golden Rule is a fantasy? Why do you suppose it's even called a 'rule?'"

Kyle had stood up and looked out the window toward the mirror-smooth surface of Lake Zürich, and toward the roads where people rushed along sidewalks, into shops and offices; where cars clogged the roadway; where people were engaged in every possible aspect of living.

"I don't know. It sounds too fantastic. People aren't made to follow rules like that."

"You're right. Because their egos drive them every moment. If they could undo their egos the Golden Rule would become the motivation that replaces money and competition. Once you awaken from this dream you're dreaming, everything changes. Money falls away. Then you begin living in a world where giving is the same as receiving. The world thinks giving depletes what one has. Just the opposite is true. Giving and receiving are one." Aimer had paused for a moment. "*Everything* in this dream world falls away."

Kyle realized he was gazing into space while Jörg sat, waiting for his reply. Kyle let his recollection fade and looked at Jörg. "Sorry. I was recalling something Aimer told me. So...you were talking about the profit motive and competition? About companies falling into some kind of malaise?" He explained what Aimer had said.

"I hope you're right, but to me it is only wishful thinking" Jörg said. He took another bite of breakfast and changed the subject. "Karla said we've delivered more than 400 million L-Gens. After replicating, almost four-and-a-half billion people could have L-Gens. Half the world's population. But the U.S. is still refusing to let them into the country."

"I know, but that doesn't matter, either. They'll come along in due time."

CHAPTER 47

Money, Competition

As months passed, L-Gens blanketed the planet. The Chinese who survived the asteroid impact at their base on the moon began reporting an earth glow. It was visible through their telescope when the planet was in darkness, even from a quarter million miles away. The glow was brightest in heavily populated areas of the globe. Toronto, London, Paris, Beijing, Rio de Janiero, Mexico City, Tokyo, Sydney—they all glimmered in subtle washes of color. Still, patches of the earth showed no colors of Love. Most of the U.S. remained in darkness, in contrast to its neighbors to the north and south. People living without L-Gens struggled with the traditional issues of life and lived in the darkness of their ego miscreations.

Kyle's CoFone rang. OmegaNet's chairman, Arthur Benet, appeared on the screen. "Have you been watching the news this week?"

"Arthur. Good to hear from you. No, I can't say I've seen much news lately."

"You need to. The U.S. is falling apart. People are terrified. They're rioting everywhere. Troops are in the streets trying to restore order. People are dying. It's all about your L-Gens being embargoed."

"I did hear about some of that."

Benet stared at Kyle's image in his CoFone for a long moment. "Well, it's getting worse every day. I called to ask if you had any plans to break the embargo."

"No. Not really."

"Why not?"

"Because there's not much I can do. We haven't heard anything from the FDA about the L-Gen we sent them. It's like they're avoiding making any statement, and while we wait around for them, the government won't let L-Gens into the country. But the problem isn't getting past the embargo. It's the people in power who don't want to *lose* power. They're fighting to keep it. Both government and businesses. They want to keep the old status quo. They think L-Gens will force them to give up everything and make unimaginable sacrifices. They don't understand they have nothing to fear."

Arthur's face wrinkled into a grimace. "Try telling that to people who see the rest of the world leaving them in the dust. The U.S. is alone. Trade with the U.S. is disappearing because the world doesn't work the way it used to. The U.S. economy is a disaster. Their money is next to worthless. It's *your country*, Kyle. I'm sure there's something you can do..."

Kyle nodded. "I understand. The rest of the world is working *with* one another instead of chasing after money. If power and money are both at risk, I can see why people running the U.S. are terrified. Their *fear* is what's behind the embargo. That's what all the unrest is about."

Arthur Benet pulled his CoFone closer to his face. His image filled Kyle's screen with the intensity of his glare. "Listen Kyle, I have been lobbying your President and Congress but they're not listening. People want L-Gens. Can you find some way to get L-Gens into the country?"

Kyle gazed off into the distance for a moment. "All right, Arthur. I'll look into it. Thanks for calling."

Kyle sat in his office looking out the window, squinting to read the Seefeld-Quai street sign in the distance. He saw motorbikes parked across the street and a couple walking toward the floating bathhouses known as the *Zürcher Badis.* They had attracted tourists since the 1920s. For less than ten Francs entry fee, a person could enjoy an entire day swimming in Lake Zürich's exceptionally clean water; or, sit back and sip a glass of wine while sun bathing, chatting and swapping stories with others. He went to Karla's office.

"Hey sweetie, let's take a break over at the *badis*. It's a beautiful day." The two left the Center, picked up swimsuits at their hotel, then taxied to the *badis*. The boards in the floor of the men's changing house had centimeter-wide gaps between them. Kyle watched fish swimming below as he changed. He walked outside, found Karla and they took seats beneath an umbrella. Several L-Gens placed around the sitting area cast their glorious colors into the air.

Kyle relaxed on a chaise lounge with the sun beaming down upon his body. He drifted into a reverie triggered by his talk with Arthur Benet. The U.S. was struggling because people in power were clinging to the old way of living where competition and money ruled everything. Money, of course, was nothing more than an exchange people used to get things they wanted or needed. People and companies and even governments competed with one another to get more money so they could get more of what they want. Competition and money went hand in hand, and together, they allowed people and organizations to acquire power.

What's going to happen when all that disappears, Kyle wondered, trying to put himself in the mindset of the U.S. leadership. He tossed ideas around for a while, but finally the obvious answer surfaced. Losing the comfort that money, competition and power deliver scares the crap out of the leadership. They're afraid to sacrifice what they hold dear, even though they would discover that living a life based upon Love is the furthest thing from sacrifice one could imagine.

Kyle adjusted his chair to an upright setting then reached over to take Karla's hand. She had been scanning the area, taking in the beauty and peacefulness of the *badis*.

"I love what's happened here," she said. "It used to cost ten Francs to use the *badis*. Now they're free. look around. Isn't this place the same as it was the first time I brought you here? It's clean. Well maintained. People take care of it just as they did when they got paid to work here. The wine is free for the asking. The taxi that brought us here didn't charge us, either. L-Gens have changed everything."

"They have, and it's wonderful, but I'm thinking about the U.S." Kyle told her of his call with Arthur Benet and his own thoughts about the fears that kept the U.S. leadership tied in knots over the L-Gens. "We've got to do something, sweetie. We need to reach out and help the U.S. get with the program."

"How many L-Gens have found their way into the U.S.?" Karla asked. "Hundreds? Thousands?"

"I don't know but it's probably in the thousands. Why?"

Karla relaxed in her chair, enjoying the warmth of sunshine hitting her body. She adjusted her straw hat to keep her face in shadows. "What if all those people replicated their L-Gens a few dozen times? If they had carbon nanotubes they could do that. It would not take long until many people had an L-Gen, and not much longer for everyone to have one. We must do something bold to help the U.S. If they do not stop the old way of doing things, they will not survive."

Kyle thought for a moment. "What if we get in touch with the head of the New Freedom Party in Philadelphia. We can suggest they setup a fundraiser or a crowd-funding campaign and collect money to buy carbon nanotubes. Then ship them to New York, Chicago and LA. That's where Meg Winters said most of the L-Gens have surfaced."

He thought for another moment. "I'll get in touch with Meg. She knows some of the people there who've been able to get L-Gens into the country. Once they get the carbon nanos they can start replicating more L-Gens. It'll take a while to replicate enough for everyone, but it's a start."

"Why don't we send them money? We could send them enough to get all the nanotubes they need."

"Good idea. We can contribute to their fund raiser. We'll let the New Freedom people know we're with them, but they need to take charge of this thing. I don't want eZo to be seen as the only contributor. It needs to be something driven by the will of the people. That's how America is supposed to work."

The New Freedom Party arranged a crowd-funding project and, within a few days, had collected enough money to buy carbon nanotubes that would provide L-Gens for nearly one-fourth of the U.S. population. Within a week deliveries started dribbling out to select people in the entertainment capitals of Los Angeles, Chicago and New York. Those people replicated L-Gens they had kept guarded in secrecy. They handed out new L-Gens to families and friends. Those people replicated more and passed those along.

One of them found its way to U.S. Senator Bob Freidlander. A member of the New Freedom Party, he represented the state of New York. After a week of sitting with his wife and children in a field of Love, Friedlander came to a decision. He carried his L-Gen into the Senate chambers and turned it on. A spectrum of color filled the hall. It enshrouded and affected everyone in attendance with the energy of Love. Security guards rushed to the chamber floor, but stopped in their tracks and sat calmly in empty seats as the L-Gen opened their minds to a new way of thinking. The Senators in session fell silent as each person understood Oneness. What they'd heard about the illusion of life and the Reality of Love now made sense.

A week later, the FDA published its review of the L-Gen it had received via special courier. Its evaluation of the L-Gen, they noted, had revealed "no harmful effects." The administration lifted its embargo. A pent-up ocean of L-Gens flooded the nation as eZo's distributors began making deliveries to people who had placed orders months earlier. L-Gens ran day and night in homes, schools, hospitals, government offices and businesses throughout the country.

People everywhere found their first experience with L-Gens wonderful, yet shocking. A woman in Cleveland, Ohio blogged about her experience.

"I got my L-Gen Thursday. I turned it on and peace filled me. I sat down, closed my eyes and let it wash over me. The troubles in my life just fell away. It was overwhelming. All the barriers and blockades I had built over a lifetime melted as I experienced that indescribable, pure Love welling up within me. I understood, for the first time, the Oneness of all people.

"It wasn't like reading about something. Or watching something on TV. It was an experience that reached inside me. I knew with a clarity I couldn't question that we are all one creation. There was no possibility it wasn't true. If you have an L-Gen...you already *know*, don't you? It's hard to explain...

"Sitting with an L-Gen running doesn't teach you anything. It's not about learning something new. It's about *knowing*. It gives you a certainty that's deep and pure and clean. Boundless, certain knowledge. That knowing is so far beyond anything I ever thought I knew...

I always "knew" the sun would come up tomorrow, but that's nothing compared to *knowing* Love and the Oneness of humanity. The sun is a simple fact. L-Gens give you a knowing you can't question. It's like God speaks to you and then you know.

"What else happened? My prejudices fell away as walls of fear evaporated. I no longer think poorly of others. They're all the same as me. I can't judge anyone any more. Even my boss, who I hated before. I realized he was living with fear, just as I had been before I got my L-Gen. My biases fell away as I discovered *everyone* is my brother or sister. Above everything else, there's this sensation of Love that's so pure. So complete I can't even talk about it. If you have an L-Gen, you know there's no way to put it into words."

CHAPTER 48

Attack, Never Justified

With the U.S., and even North Korea and Rwanda eventually accepting L-Gens, the world continued to change. New trends began to unfold.

The World-o-Meters website began showing a drop in the global birth rate. Graphs and charts that had predicted a leveling out of world population in 2062 began to change. Over a period of months, the graphs showed the leveling would occur in 2056. Then, within a few more months, it moved to 2051. As people moved deeper into their Right Minds, increasingly working together for their common welfare, their focus changed. Bringing new bodies into the world no longer held the survival imperative it always had.

Ordinary people made it a point to express gratitude for what was unfolding in their lives. The purpose of their lives took on new dimensions. New motivations replaced those that had always given life its meaning. People no longer sought material wealth or power. They no longer competed with one another to somehow win at any expense. The birth rate continued to fall as new motivations drove people in a new direction.

Karla sat in bed propped up on pillows on a Saturday morning. She set her empty teacup on the nightstand. "What are we going to do with all the money we've collected? We've got enough to start our own nation."

"It doesn't have a place here anymore, does it? The last time I checked we had eighty billion dollars, but that doesn't mean anything. They're only numbers. Just like when we used to wave our CoFone at the checkout line or pay a bill on the Internet, it's all electronic. Dollars, Euros, Bitcoins—they're all the same. They're just numbers. Bits and bytes."

"I know, but we've got lots of bits and bytes in our account. I don't see any use for it."

"I don't either, sweetie. Let's leave our money in the bank. Soon there won't be anyone on earth who will want it or even care about it."

Karla seemed, for a moment, to be lost in thought; the kind of thought that springs to mind with a question that has no answer, or perhaps a question with an answer she didn't want to hear.

Kyle noticed. "What's the matter?"

"I just had a weird thought."

Kyle moved closer to her. "What is it, sweetie?"

"What is *next* for us? What do we do now? L-Gens are everywhere. We have all this money but it is basically worthless. The L-Gens changed everything."

Kyle looked at her for a moment. "I suppose we should let things continue to unfold."

Karla waved the sheets, flapping them up and down around her. "Unfold? We can't keep going to the Center every day and waiting to see what happens next." She stared at him and pulled the sheets all the way up to her neck. "Rick is down there every day working on the system. I cannot imagine what he is doing. Cary and Paul aren't holding press conferences any more. They were planning a trip to England. Hans and Jörg have gone back to their homes. What is next for *us*?"

Kyle moved over in bed and slid his arm under Karla's stack of pillows, drawing her into an embrace. "We've got some time left in this world, wouldn't you say?" he asked rhetorically. "I'd like to spend all of it with you, my dear. I love you."

"What are you saying?"

"I'm not saying. I'm asking. Will you marry me, Karla?"

Karla's eyes turned moist and she hugged him close to her body. "Yes! I love you, Kyle."

Their bodies came together in a gentle hug. Kyle kissed her lips and whispered into her ear. "What kind of wedding would you like, sweetie?"

"One that happens right away. We do not need a big wedding, unless you want one, but I would like to have our friends here for it. I will call Cary. Will you call Jörg and Hans?"

"Sure, *liebchen*. Of course. When should we ask them to be here?"

"Let me make some calls first. Maybe next Saturday or the one following. I would like us to be married in Rapperswill-Jona. It is a gorgeous little medieval town with a chapel. Roses grow everywhere. A most romantic place. I will just check if the chapel is free."

"Sounds beautiful. All right. I'll tell Rick, too."

"Yes, of course!"

The team returned to Zürich a few days before the chosen Saturday. Jörg and Hans brought their wives with them. They sat together in one of the conference rooms at the Center, each updating the other on what had happened since their last time together. As their conversations deepened, Jörg pulled Kyle aside.

They left the room and sat in the office Jörg had called his own. "It seems there are still people who don't have L-Gens."

"Yeah, I don't think we'll ever get to one hundred percent. I don't know what will become of them ..."

Jörg interrupted. "I am talking about terrorists. In spite of all the L-Gens we have delivered, there are still people who use violence to get what they want. I have not told Corina, but an OmegaNet report on the trip over here said they bombed an Internet company in Berlin. Some people died. Attacks in St. Petersburg and Tokyo did more damage. Those are all companies that let us install sigma clients in their optical amplifiers. They are Internet backbone companies. Terrorists managed to coordinate attacks all over the globe within minutes of each other."

"What? Who are these people?"

"Wait a minute. I'm getting another alert." Jörg pulled his CoFone from his pocket. "There's been another attack in New York."

A rumbling sound, almost sub-sonic, surged through the air. Kyle and Jörg got up from their chairs. Kyle turned his head to hear it better. They scanned the office and stared through the open door into the lobby. "What the hell is that?" Jörg shouted. A deafening explosion muffled his words. The walls shook. The lights in the Center flickered off.

Kyle turned and bolted toward the conference room. Emergency lights flicked on and cast sharp shadows on the furniture, the walls and the hall leading to his destination. He reached the conference room to find Karla huddled under the conference table with Cary and the two wives. Flames and smoke outside the window filled the air as people ran down sidewalks. Paul and Hans stood together near the window, looking out.

Kyle saw bodies in the street. A woman's legs twitched spasmodically as a man leaning over her, himself bloody, tried to comfort her.

"What the hell happened?" Rick screamed as he sprinted into the room.

Paul Glazer answered. "We've been bombed, for God's sake. Get away from the windows." He moved to the opposite wall, dragging Hans with him. "Everyone. Get down to the vault!"

They followed as Glazer hustled down the stairs. Once inside, Rick closed the vault door and turned on the TV. An OmegaNet reporter showed a world map with red "X" marks on Tokyo, St. Petersburg, Berlin and New York City. He reported:

"... bombings seem to be targeting companies that have been working with eZo Systems and their quantum computer. It's not clear yet how many casualties...Wait! We have another report. A bombing in Zürich at eZo Systems headquarters. The ZX terrorist groups claims responsibility. Here, video is coming in ..."

The screen showed a man dressed in black with his face concealed but for his eyes. "The day of retribution has arrived. God is Great! Today we have struck a deathblow to eZo Systems and its demon L-Gen machines that corrupt the world. eZo will no longer pervert God's people with its satanic ideas. We have destroyed the quantum computer that desecrates the world. We have restored the world to what God created. All glory to God.

Rick shouted over the sound of the TV. "Who the hell are these people?"

"How much damage did we take? Is the entrance secure?" Jörg asked.

"The security cams aren't working. The blast must have taken them out," Rick said. "I'll run back upstairs to see what's happened." Rick ran from the vault and up the stairs. Kyle raced after him.

"Hey, Rick, wait! It might be dangerous up there," Kyle shouted.

The two scrambled up a flight of stairs and entered the lobby. An entire pane of bullet resistant glass in the windows of the former bank laid shattered on the floor. Black smoke billowed into the lobby through the missing window, turning daytime into an impenetrable cloud of darkness. An acrid smell permeated the room. Rick ran to the security door and tried to rattle it, but found it solid and secure.

Kyle stood behind Rick, choking as he inhaled the thick smoke. He put a handkerchief over his mouth and nose. He heard a sound outside the missing window. An object flew into the lobby. It clunked as it hit the floor, then exploded. A white fog pushed its way into the blackness surging through the missing window. The smoke in the lobby instantly became thicker.

Rick broke into a lung-shattering coughing fit. Kyle felt he was about to be smothered, but grabbed Rick and dragged him from the door.

"That's tear gas! They're right outside!" Kyle shouted.

A dark form hovered just beyond the missing windowpane. A spray of automatic weapons fire with the unmistakable sound of an AK-47 burst into the lobby. Bullets pinged off walls, desks. The furniture at the front of the lobby, riddled with bullets, toppled over with a crash. Kyle dropped to his knees and pulled Rick to the floor.

With visibility almost zero, Rick's racking coughs gave the intruder a direction to fire. Bullets hit the floor next to Rick and Kyle.

Rick screamed. "I'm hit!" Kyle tried to get a clear view of his partner, but couldn't see in the blackness. He grabbed at Rick and caught the shoulder of his shirt, then began dragging Rick toward the stairs. They reached the first step and fell down the entire flight, banging heads, knees, spines and arms all the way to the bottom.

Paul Glazer saw a scramble of bodies careening down the smoke-filled stairwell. He got hold of Kyle's arm and jerked him to his feet.

"Rick's been shot. Somebody's in the lobby with a gun."

Glazer let go of Kyle and scooped Rick up off the floor. Carrying Rick like a child in his arms, he led Kyle back to the vault. Once inside, Kyle slammed the door and locked it. They heard weapons fire and shouts.

The scream of sirens pierced the air. In a few moments the weapons fire stopped.

Jörg stood holding his wife, Corina, in his arms with his CoFone smashed against his ear. "*Polizei kommt!* Police are on the way! I've got them on the line."

"Call an ambulance. Rick's been shot," Kyle demanded.

"They are coming too," Jörg replied.

Rick lay gasping on the floor. Blood covered the left side of his chest. Cary ran to him, tore open his shirt and pressed paper towels against the entry wound just below his armpit.

"You're going to be okay, Rick. Hang on. Medics are on the way," she said, visibly terrified.

She pressed hard on Rick's wound then looked up at Kyle and jerked her head at him to get his attention. Kyle leaned down to hear her voice. "Rick's hurt bad. Real bad. Do something, Kyle!"

Kyle stooped down and placed a folded jacket under Rick's head. "Hey partner, stick with me. We've got more work to do. I need you. The world needs you."

Rick grimaced and with each cough more blood spurted from his wound, soaking the paper towels and running onto the floor. "Yeah, okay man. I'm not goin' anywhere." He choked out a gigantic cough mixed with a shriek of pain. His eyes jammed shut and his body shuddered. His breathing became fitful. Every breath ended with a moan of agony.

"They're here," Jörg said as he closed his call to the police and shoved his CoFone into his pocket. He touched the access panel and the vault door swung open. A team of police and medics rushed into the room. The medics began working on Rick. They bundled him onto a stretcher and carried him up to the lobby and through the missing window to an ambulance. Kyle nearly tripped over a body lying just outside the vault door. He ran alongside the stretcher until a police commander intercepted him.

"*Komm mit mir! Der Krankenwagen nimmt Ihren Freund, Universitätsklinik*"

"What? Speak English!"

"Dr. Williams, I am with *Nachrichtendienst des Bundes*. NDB. The Federal Intelligence Service. Your friend is on the way to University hospital. Now, come with me."

"No. You come with *me*!" Kyle demanded. He led the commander back into the vault and slammed it shut. "What's happened?"

The NDB agent scanned the vault room. It had a large table in the center. Racks of computers filled one side of the room, each with their activity indicators flashing. Computer displays covered every wall. The biggest screen had a leather-backed chair before it with the words "Rick—Chief of Quantum" stenciled across the back. The chair was empty. The commander's eyes scanned the room. He saw men and women—the entire team that had brought quantum computing and L-Gens to the world. He cast his eyes around the room to each of them, then returned his gaze to Kyle.

He spoke to the entire group. "Dr. Williams, you have been attacked by terrorists. Innocent people in the streets have died and many are injured."

Karla spoke to Kyle. "We should have been *done* with terrorists. Almost everyone has L-Gens..."

"I know, but this won't stop what we're doing." Kyle turned to the NDB agent. "What happened to the people who attacked us? Did you capture them?"

"*Ja.* One is dead in the hall outside. Two others are in custody."

"I want to speak with them. Will you arrange that?" Kyle asked.

"I will see. Those people committed acts of terrorism. The government will deal with them," the NDB agent said.

Cary faced the agent and interrupted. "Commander, thank you for your help. Now if it's safe we need to see what damage has been done to the quantum system."

"Nein, Fräulein. Emergency personnel will be working in the streets for the next day or two. We have placed a security team around your building, but you cannot remain here, nor return to your hotels and homes yet. We are arranging temporary quarters for all of you." The commander made a call on his CoFone. "Are we ready?" The reply: "*Ja*. Bring them out."

"Wait!" Corina Tritten called out. "My children are at home with their nanny. I need to go to them."

"It's not safe for them to be at your home," the agent said. "We need to bring them to a safe house to be with you."

"Our children, too," Hans said. "They are at our home."

The agent gathered information from each set of parents and keyed his CoFone. In moments police dispatched transportation to pick up the children in Bern and Geneva.

Another team of police stood outside the vault door. "We will take you to a safe location. I need you to come with me," the agent said.

"Wait. I've got to check the quantum system before we leave," Kyle said. "Cary, would you help me?"

He sat at Rick's console and ran diagnostics. The Quantum O/S reported nearly three-quarters of the Internet backbone was down. Sigma interface units installed in optical amplifiers around the world could no longer operate.

"Our system is crippled," Kyle said quietly. "Attacks on the backbone companies put us out of business. We can't keep the universal services program running. That means no one can replicate L-Gens until we can get the system back on line."

Cary's face clenched into a deep frown. She stared at him with a look of horror in her eyes. "Oh my God! L-Gens won't work anymore?"

Kyle gazed at the screen for a moment. "Yes, they're still working, but they won't replicate. They still work though." He tapped a few keys. "Cary, help me lock everything down." They worked for a few minutes, shutting down the Quantum O/S servers. They secured access to the system and powered down the API console. The sound of cooling fans died away and a death-like silence filled the vault. Activity indicators on the servers went dark as each rack of computers blinked off.

Kyle sat, staring blindly at the dark console. It was the command center of everything he and Rick had built. Now it was dark. Empty. Dead. He shuddered, shook his head and leaned back in Rick's chair, turning his closed eyes toward the ceiling.

Finally, Kyle let loose a deep sigh. "It's done. Let's get out of here."

Paul took Cary's hand and led her to the police escort standing outside the vault. Hans, Jörg and their wives followed. Karla stood behind Kyle, who still sat in Rick's chair staring at a blank screen. She put her hands on his shoulders and felt his body shuddering. "Come on, sweetheart. Let's go where it's safe."

The eZo team followed the police escort through the building, locking the vault and each office as they went. Along the way they picked up as many L-Gens as they could carry. The NDB agent led them out of the building and into waiting vehicles. Thirty minutes later they drove into a small town south of the Center. Roses grew everywhere: along streets, in yards and bordering the dense forests.

"Kyle, this is Rapperswill-Jona. It's the town I chose for our wedding." Karla said dejectedly.

CHAPTER 49

Man Who Keeps Away from Sin

The eZo team settled into the office building that had been converted into a safe house. Hans' children arrived safely, followed by Jörg's a few hours later. The NDB agent called the adults together while the nannies watched over the children.

"My name is Peter Schultz. I am with the NDB. We are the Swiss intelligence agency. Our government wants to protect you from further attack. We don't know when it may be safe for you to resume your normal lives. Until then, we ask that you remain here under our protection.

"However, I am afraid I have terrible news. I am sorry to tell you...your associate, Dr. Huggins, died on the way to the hospital earlier today. A gunshot pierced an artery and the medics were not able to save his life despite their best efforts."

A spasm of shock jolted Kyle's body. He jerked back in his chair. His face contorted, his mouth shaped itself into an "O" and he mouthed, "No! Not Rick." His eyes became shiny. Karla and Cary began sobbing. Hans, who had worked hand in hand with Rick for months, fell into a chair and cried openly.

"I'll leave you alone with your thoughts," agent Schultz said. He slipped quietly from the room and closed the door behind him.

Tears flooded from Kyle's eyes and his body seized with giant sobs that took his breath away. Memories of Rick raced through his mind. *Oh God! Rick's dead. I love you, Rick. Love you, man. Love you.* He buried his face in his hands. Karla sat next to him and wrapped her arms around him. Her body rattled with loss. Tears surged down her face. Kyle's rasping moans shook her as he blindly put his arms around her. Rick: his best friend since age twelve. They'd survived tumultuous childhood years. They'd gone to school and college together. Rick. A brilliant man who gave up his little paradise and gave everything he had to build out the quantum system. The man who discovered the solution for clean drinking water. For protein folding, and, most of all, for the replicator he named "L-Gen." The man who dubbed their project a "black hole in the Internet." Rick: The Chief of Quantum. Dead. *For what?*

Kyle awoke the next morning with a shudder as he realized again that Rick was gone. He looked at Karla, still asleep. Kyle relaxed into stillness and sought guidance from his Teacher. Knowing that bodies are only part of the illusion that allows people to feel separate from one another didn't quench his sense of loss. *Oh God. Poor Rick. I love you man. How can you be gone?*

In a moment, an answer formed in his mind. *What seems to be loss is illusion. The one you loved and who seemed to die lives eternally. There is no death. Only the laying aside of a body no longer needed. What is Real cannot be lost or destroyed. Each mind creates and loves and lives apart from time and from bodies and from everything that is unreal.*

Kyle thought on those ideas and knew them to be true, but they didn't ease his sense of loss or sadness. *I know it's all illusion, but it hurts anyway...oh God, it hurts!*

Karla awoke and put her hand on his. Kyle rolled over to face her. "Sweetheart, there's something I'd like to do for Rick," he said. "The world needs to know him as I did. We need to find a hectare or two of land and build a memorial for Rick so he'll be remembered. I'm thinking of a museum. People need to know about everything he's done. I'm going to call Meg Winters. She'll know a producer who can make a memorial video about Rick.

"I want that museum to have a replica of the vault with its computer screens and Rick's chair and his big console. That's where he worked and made so many discoveries. I think he'd like people to see that he called himself 'Chief of Quantum.' We can even put his pop-up camper in the yard. That's a fitting memorial for him and it will be a way to show people what kind of man he was. I love him. So much. I want the world to love him too."

Kyle got up, dressed and went to the main room where he found agent Schultz talking in low voices with Hans and Jörg and their wives.

"Good morning, Dr. Williams," Schultz said.

"Do you have anything new on the attacks yesterday?" Kyle asked.

"I didn't want to burden you with this yesterday, but yes. The group we all know as ZX is responsible. It's run by a man who wants to impose his beliefs on the world. He's a renegade theocrat, an extremist. He doesn't claim to represent any religion. No, he disavows them all and believes he is God in the flesh, as do his followers. His network of 'soldiers' who carried out yesterday's attacks want to destroy your quantum system. They believe by destroying it, the L-Gens will stop working. He sees that as a necessary step to winning his war against those who don't believe as he does."

"He's wrong. We can't *replicate* more L-Gens without the quantum system. But the L-Gens will continue to work without it. He's done a lot of damage, but has only caused pain and death and misery."

"Extremists rarely accomplish anything lasting," Schultz said.

"I spoke to the backbone companies last night and this morning," Jörg said. "Most of them have severe damage. None of them gave me a firm date when they can be up and running again. Until they do, most of the backbone is compromised. There are already huge jams of Internet data that can't get through. People everywhere are staring at blank screens. With all the demand for bandwidth, they'll be working day and night to restore service. I think they'll be back up in a matter of days, not weeks or months."

"Good." Kyle turned to Schultz. "What the status of our Center in Zürich?"

"There's some exterior damage but nothing that can't be restored. A window was blown out and has been boarded up. The police cordoned off the building. No one has been allowed entry. Your Center is secure," Schultz replied.

"What about those people who killed Rick?"

"We have them in custody."

"Where?"

"In Zürich."

"At Herr Langendanch's prison?"

"Yes, how did you know?"

"Just a guess."

Kyle dialed Langendanch. "You have the people who attacked us yesterday?" he asked.

"*Ja.* They are locked down," Langendanch answered.

"I want to speak to them. How many are there?"

"Two, but the NDB is in charge. You'll have to get their permission to see them." Langendanch paused. "I am sorry, my friend. I'm sorry for your loss. For Dr. Huggins' death. My heart goes out to you and your friends, Dr. Williams."

"Thank you. I'll see about making arrangements to talk with your prisoners."

Agent Schultz assigned an officer to drive Kyle to the prison. He was escorted to a cell block that held a man and a woman in separate cells. The man was named Aasim, which means "the man who keeps away from sin." The woman, whose name translates as "right guidance," was named Hudah.

Kyle sat with them while prison guards looked on. "You fired into our Center and killed my friend. The man who discovered how to bring Love into the world. Why?"

The two simply glared at Kyle. Aasim spat on the floor.

"Whatever you hoped to accomplish...you have failed. Our quantum system and L-Gens are alive and well. The world has become a place where Love prevails. What you did was driven by fear. There is nothing to fear from us. You and your leader bow down to fear. You make it your reason for being."

Hudah spoke. "What you do is wrong. An abomination."

"You may believe that, but Love can never be wrong. Furthermore, attack is never justified. It solves nothing. I hope you will both learn that simple lesson."

Kyle stood up and left the cellblock. "Herr Langendanch, please be sure to turn on an L-Gen for those two. They'll see the mistakes they made and how to look past them. How to get on with a better way of living."

Back at the safe house, Kyle sat down with agent Schultz. "Most people in Switzerland have L-Gens. I'm surprised to find your NDB is still in operation."

"*Ja. Ich auch.* Me too. The government is changing and the NDB is coming apart, becoming an anachronism. Same with the police force. In another year or two, I don't know if any of us will be needed. What you have done with your computer and your L-Gens has changed everyone. When my wife and I sit at home with our L-Gen running, we talk. We both see there will soon be no need for an NDB. For a CIA. The world is changed. My wife and I...we wonder what will happen next. People still go to work, but they no longer work for money. They work because they choose to. Because they want to do what they can to help others." Schultz stood up before Kyle with his arms hanging at his sides. "Dr. Williams, where is this all leading?"

"I think it's leading to the end."

"Of what?"

"The end of what has been since men began walking the earth. The end of the ego. The end of people believing they're all separate individuals. The end of projecting beliefs on others. The end of fear; that 'god' we made when we came to live here. The end of judging everything. The end of believing in separation. A new beginning. Life powered by Love where fear has no place."

CHAPTER 50

End of Dreams

Rick joined with Aimer and Marci. "Hey! Marci. Aimer. Good to see you guys." He looked around, puzzled. "Where am I?" he asked.

"Where you've always been," Marci answered.

"This is what you've been telling us about? This 'place' we can't imagine?"

"Yes," Aimer said. "It's yours. It's Real. It's Eternal, as you are. It's your home. Welcome."

Rick looked out into Eternity. He saw the webwork of kaleidoscopic colors folding in and out upon itself, filling Everything with beauty. He noticed new colors he'd never before seen—a blend of something that was neither pink nor chartreuse, but that might have been both. A gentle undertone of music filled the webwork, always drifting and shifting into new strains in a glorious symphony that mixed with the colors. He saw that Knowledge filled Everything. It was permanent and fixed, with no possibility of anything existing that was not Knowledge. For it was eternal, unbounded, permanent and complete, beyond all concepts of time and space.

"I remember this, and now I *see*," Rick said.

"Yes. You now see with true Vision," Marci said.

Rick shimmered with excitement. "Love created this, Marci! You told us that once..."

Marci laughed a tiny laugh that reverberated in the music and made the iridescent colors glow brighter. "Yes. As you see, there's nothing dark about this. It is the Light."

Aimer spoke to him. "Now, my dear friend, please take a deeper look." Rick turned, then noticed he had no body. Only Mind.

Even without form, he scintillated. "I *see*," he said. Then, with the deepest possible comprehension, Rick joined into All That Is. He reveled in the Oneness, the Ultimate Intelligence, the webwork that was Knowledge. He saw that learning was no longer needed because Knowledge gave him *certainty* beyond anything learning ever had. Likewise, he saw that hoping, faith, believing, forgiveness and wanting were no longer, for Knowledge and Love left them all behind in the illusory world he would still remember, for a little while, until that entire dream faded from his memory, just as his nighttime dreams had always vanished into nothingness.

He reached out to Marci and Aimer with unbounded Love filling him. He thought of his dearest friend. Rick turned his awareness to Marci.

"Would you help Kyle? Would you show him this? This Knowledge? This Love?"

"Yes, Rick. Of course."

Kyle and Karla sat in the safe house at the breakfast table, dabbling at their food. Hans and Jörg and their wives and children joined them. Paul and Cary sipped their morning coffee. Three L-Gens cast clouds of Love from corners of the room.

Jörg took a moment between bites. "I found some property here in Rapperswill-Jona for the memorial to Rick. We can begin building it whenever you're ready."

"What's it like?"

"A park. Trees. Roses. It's beautiful. I know an architect who can design a memorial to match the beauty of the land."

Jörg's son dropped his fork on the floor with a clatter. He pointed out the window and his little eyes went wide. *Vas ist das, Papa?*

Jörg glanced out the window, then exclaimed *Leiber Gott!* A symphony of brilliance swelled forth from the sky, changing the white clouds and blue sky to a serene blanket of rainbow colors that reached to and caressed the trees, the grass, the flowers, the soil. Kyle got up from the table and went to the window. He watched the colors swirl through the sky toward the safe house, like a gentle wave rolling onto the shore as if it belonged there.

Kyle heard a sweet song reverberate through the room, an ancient song dimly remembered. Dim, perhaps, and yet not unfamiliar, like a song whose name is long forgotten, and the circumstances in which he had heard it completely unremembered. A little wisp of melody, attached not to a person or a place or anything particular. But he remembered from just the little part how lovely the song was, how wonderful the setting where he had heard it, and how he loved those who were there and listened with him.*

Beyond his body, beyond the sun and stars, past everything he could see, and yet somehow familiar, an arc of golden light stretched into a great and shining circle filled with an all-encompassing light. The edges of the circle disappeared, and what was inside it was no longer contained or bounded in any way at all, for the light expanded and covered Everything, extending beyond infinity, forever shining with no break or limit anywhere. He could not imagine that anything could be outside the light, for he saw there was nowhere the light was not. *

Karla went to the window and threw her arms around Kyle. "Oh my! How beautiful! What *is* that?" she called out, pulling him close. The rest of the group rushed to join them, Jörg carrying his son while Corina held tight to her daughter.

The tsunami of colors and music drifted ever closer to the building. All three L-Gens in the room picked up the song. The colors they broadcast gleamed brighter in synchrony with the music.

Kyle stood serenely at the window, his arms around Karla, watching the wave of colors and music make its leisurely advance. He closed his eyes and took a deep breath, holding it for a moment, his mind instantly silent.

The wave reached the safe house and joined with everything, permeating walls, floor, furniture, people and the very air in the room. Kyle turned to the group and saw each of his friends transfixed by the beauty. "This is Love," Kyle said. "God is holding us in His hand."

A brilliant light burst forth. Marci and Aimer emerged from the radiance and stood before them. Their Love beamed from their entire beings as they both glowed and scintillated. They seemed to merge into the colors, flickering alternately between their human forms and bodies of light.

"Good morning," Marci said. "Rick asked us to join you. He wants you to know all is well." As Marci spoke, her words danced joyously in the sublime beauty that filled the room.

* ACIM OE T-21.II.8,10

"Rick?" Kyle whispered in astonishment. "You've seen Rick?"

"Yes. He asked us to show you Love's final lesson." Marci's glimmering grew brighter. "He wants you to know death is nothing more than ego's cunning last trick. It is the grand finale ego uses to keep you in fear. Death is an illusion. It isn't Real. Rick wants you to know that."

She approached the group and spent a moment speaking quietly to Karla, then touched the top of her head. She pulled Cary into a deep and loving embrace, whispering into her ear. She took both of Kyle's hands in hers and gazed into his eyes before drawing him close to her body. Marci gracefully loved and touched each person, then became a body of light and rejoined Aimer. The group stood without words, but tears ran down faces filled with expressions of awe and joy.

"The world you made is a symbol, like the rest of what perception made," Aimer said. "Mankind has perceived this world through fearful eyes that bear witness to the terror that lives in ego minds.*

"Eternity stands for what is opposite to the world. You see Eternity through the eyes forgiveness blesses, where terror and fear are impossible. Today, you have brought the world to this new Vision where all barriers to knowing Love have fallen away and Eternity is opened to your awakening."

The symphony of color and beauty and music extended and grew even more profound until Love encompassed all of it. "Rick loves you," Marci said. "He wants you to Know Eternity." She turned her face toward the sky, then looked again at the group. "Rick asked us… to show you…*THIS!*"

Marci touched her hands to her chest, then opened her arms slowly, ever so slowly. As her arms drew apart, the Love in the room grew richer. The walls of the room and the entire building faded from view as if they had never been, replaced by the eternal webwork Kyle had seen on his trip into the Oneness. Love wove itself through each person.

Marci blessed the group with her words. "Many have hoped to find peace on Earth. You have led the world to that peace, dear ones.

---

* ACIM OE W-ST291:1

The entire Sonship now sees with true Vision and basks in endless, unbounded Knowledge for all Eternity. Humanity now forgives its fears, themselves and one another. They *Know* the Love they Are with the certainty only Knowledge delivers.

"You've led them on a path that removed every block that kept Love hidden. One where your brothers and sisters now *Know* that giving and receiving are the same. You have shown them that all are One, that we are One with our Creator."

Marci extended the Love that she was to each person. As she did, each person began to glimmer and shine and merge into the beauty that was unspeakable Love beyond all comprehension. Finally, she brought her arms together until the palm of each hand touched the other. She raised her face to where the sky had been only a moment ago, but where Love now filled Everything.

"Join with us, my friends. The time for faith… and learning…and forgiving…and choosing again—those are all done. Knowledge Is. Love Is. God Is. And Time is no more. The dream…it is ended.

Join us in Eternity, which is your birthright, your home.

Epilogue

The World-o-Meters website continued to run, for a few minutes. It showed the birthrate and world population drop to zero.

The entire Earth glowed with Love, which then reached out from the planet to fill the solar system and the galaxy.

Miracles effervesced through the universe as the sun and Earth, stars and galaxies blinked out and disappeared.

The place that had only seemed to be a home to what called itself "humanity"—that place filled only with illusion the sleeping mind of the Sonship dreamed and imagined it had made—merged into All That Is, into Eternity, and was no more.

In Reality, it had never been.

• • •

Afterword

Acknowledgments

I am grateful for the efforts of many outstanding people whose help made this book possible, beginning with Ms. Pat Dobie for her deep thought and editorial expertise. To Dr. Bob Rutter, a friend for many years, who survived the reading of an early draft and provided invaluable feedback. I thank Sue Quate for her careful reading and meticulous line editing; and, my wife, Becky (herself a writer and artist), for painstakingly poring over the manuscript several times. As well, I thank fellow authors Barbara Samuels and David Tienter and ACIM student Maureen Lynch Yarbrough for beta reading, as well as members of the Treasure Coast Writers Group and the Port St. Lucie Florida Writers Association for their helpful input. Finally, my thanks to everyone who participated in the Indiegogo campaign that supported this book.

A Course in Miracles

I am also thankful for the greatest teaching device I've yet discovered—the *curriculum* alluded to in Part I and elsewhere throughout this book. That curriculum began its unexpected formation during the 1960s. Since then it has been translated into more than twenty languages, and is known around the world as *A Course in Miracles* (ACIM).

It teaches that we each, at every moment, can make a choice to change our mind about life rather than trying to change and fight against life itself. Among its many powerful, but at first seemingly strange ideas, it teaches that ...

Our earthly lives and everything we perceive are illusion. That what we project upon the world makes our perception. That we can learn true forgiveness by not judging and "looking past" what only seems to be. That our bodies are only an illusory "proof" we are separate from one another and from our Creator. That ego is the devious master planner blocking us from knowing What we truly Are. That sin, guilt and fear need not rule our lives. That our Right Mind is the patient, mostly silent gift our Creator left within each of us to discover, even while we dream we are separate from Him. That we each can choose in every moment to think with our Creator from our Right Mind rather than our ego mind.

Assimilating these unusual ideas into one's thinking takes time while we live on Earth. Gradually though, one begins to realize our lives exist in a world ruled by duality where everything we perceive seems to come in two forms. Hot and cold. Happy and sad. Pleasure and pain. Love and hate. Life and death. *A Course in Miracles* teaches we can choose to begin seeing the world differently. Over time, its lessons can lead us to a new understanding of our place in this seeming universe.

Kyle and his friends discovered they could help every person release the blocks their egos had erected that kept love hidden. I would like to believe, as ACIM's teachings continue reaching ever-greater audiences, that its timeless principles and message will continue to transform our minds and speed our return from the insanity we see in the news each day to lives of peace and joy and Love.

The Introduction to the ACIM book summarizes the purposes of the Course nicely.

"This is a course in miracles. It is a required course. Only the time you take it is voluntary. Free will does not mean that you can establish the curriculum. It means only that you can elect what you want to take at a given time. The course does not aim at teaching the meaning of love, for that is beyond what can be taught. It does aim, however, at removing the blocks to the awareness of love's presence, which is your natural inheritance. The opposite of love is fear, but what is all-encompassing can have no opposite.

"This course can therefore be summed up very simply in this way:

Nothing real can be threatened.
Nothing unreal exists.
Herein lies the Peace of God."*

For Further Reading

The 1972 edition of the writing known as *A Course in Miracles Original Edition* is available at www.jcim.net. Many ideas expressed in *Computing Love* have their origins in the *Original Edition.*

You can find further information on *A Course in Miracles* at www.acim.org. This site, known as the Foundation for Inner Peace, provides detailed history and facts about the *Course* as well as various free services.

The *Foundation for A Course in Miracles,* www.facim.org, serves as its teaching arm and intends to "help you decide whether the spiritual path of A Course in Miracles is for you."

Finally, the *Miracle Distribution Center,* www.miraclecenter.org, helps ACIM students connect with one other and integrate Course principles into their daily lives

Research for *Computing Love* turned up many fascinating websites. Visit www.Computing.Love to find links to...

- Klein bottles, the strange fourth-dimensional objects that have no inside and no outside.
- World-renowned scientist and TED presenter, Dr. Clifford Stoll, where you can buy your own personal Klein Bottle.
- The GuruGanesha Band performing its beautiful song, "1000 Suns."
- ...and much more at www.Computing.Love.

* ACIM OE Introduction

Contributions

A portion of the proceeds from the sale of this book support *The Course in Miracles Society, The Foundation for Inner Peace* and the *Miracle Distribution Center.* Please take a moment to post a review of *Computing Love* at Amazon.com or at Goodreads.com. Your reviews will help promote the book, which will bring invaluable help to this charitable effort. Thank you.